The CASEBOOK of
SIDNEY ZOOM

ERLE STANLEY GARDNER

Erle Stanley Gardner was not only the creator of classic courtroom dramas about Perry Mason; he was also one of the finest writers of novelettes and short stories for the fiction magazines of the 1920's through the 1940s.

Working with the agents for the Erle Stanley Gardner Trust, Bill Pronzini and Crippen & Landru will publish in its Lost Classics Series the following books featuring Gardner's pulp characters:

NOW AVAILABLE

The Danger Zone and Other Stories
The Casebook of Sidney Zoom

FORTHCOMING

The Adventures of Señor Lobo
The Exploits of the Patent Leather Kid
The Investigations of Small, Weston & Burke
The Feats of the Man in the Silver Mask
The Return of Ed Jenkins, Phantom Crook
The Return of Lester Leith

THE LOST CLASSICS SERIES

The CASEBOOK of SIDNEY ZOOM

ERLE STANLEY GARDNER

edited by Bill Pronzini

Crippen & Landru Publishers
Norfolk, VA
2006

Cover artwork by Juha Lindroos

Lost Classics series design by Deborah Miller

Crippen & Landru logo by Eric D. Greene
Lost Classics logo by Eric D. Greene, adapted from a drawing by Ike Morgan, ca. 1895

ISBN: 1-932009-46-9 (cloth edition)
ISBN: 1-932009-47-7 (trade softcover edition)

FIRST EDITION

Printed in the United States of America on acid-free paper

Crippen & Landru Publishers
P.O. Box 9315
Norfolk, VA 23505
USA

e-mail: info@crippenlandru.com
web: www.crippenlandru.com

CONTENTS

INTRODUCTION

by Bill Pronzini

AMONG THE two-score series characters created by Erle Stanley Gardner for the pulp magazines of the 20s and 30s were such colorful and colorfully named individuals as Ed Migrane, the Headache Detective, Speed Dash, the Human Fly, Señor Lobo (whose exploits will appear in the next volume in this series), The Man in the Silver Mask, Go Get 'Em Garver, and Fish Mouth McGinnis. None, however were more unique, well-developed, or eccentric in name and nature than Sidney Zoom, the Master of Disguises.

Zoom is a strange, complex man, a true rugged individualist. Tall, slender, purposeful, cultured, independently wealthy, possessed of fierce hawklike eyes and a dominant, aggressive personality, he lives on an expensive yacht, the *Alberta F.*, with a tawny police dog named Rip and a devoted young secretary, Vera Thurmond. He is a loner by nature, adopting a hardboiled manner with women that borders on the rude—a pose, Vera Thurmond suspects, because he is secretly afraid of the female sex. He "hates civilization and all it stands for," believing instead in the sanctity of the individual; "scoffs at laws which sought to curb crime and safeguard property rights" and has his own ideas of how to balance the scales of justice. His mission is to right wrongs, to "live for good" by rescuing would-be suicides and other downtrodden individuals and providing them with new leases on life. He refers to himself, in all seriousness, as a Doctor of Despair, a Collector of Lost Souls.

Disguises of one sort or another figure prominently in all of his adventures. He maintains a large closet filled with wigs, mustaches, spectacles, hats, coats, beards, grease paint, stains, and other methods of altering his identity. His reputation as a carefree man about town is another masquerade, carefully established and nurtured to conceal his mission and the fact that he once served in the intelligence departments of three nations.

The Zoom series, a total of sixteen short stories and novelettes, ran in *Detective Fiction Weekly* between March 1930 and May 1934. The ten collected here, all reprinted for the first time, represent the best of these tales. Each demonstrates Gardner's remarkable skill at finding new twists on staple pulp storylines involving stolen jewelry and artworks, confidence swindles, hidden fortunes, missing wills, disappearing bodies, murder frames, and the like. The stories also make clever use of disguises as integral plot devices, and contain plenty of swift action as the pulp markets of the day required.

Eccentric though he may be, Sidney Zoom ranks as one of the most interesting early characters to come from Gardner's fertile imagination. It's a pleasure to introduce him to modern readers after three-quarters of a century of dusty and undeserved obscurity.

Petaluma, California
June 2005

ACKNOWLEDGMENTS

The editor and the publisher are grateful to Lawrence Hughes of Hughes and Hobson LLC, agents for the Erle Stanley Gardner literary rights, for permission to publish this book; and to Monte Herridge for copies of several of the Sidney Zoom stories that follow.

WILLIE THE WEEPER

IT HAD been known as "Lovers' Lane" until a dejected sweetheart, jilted by his lady, had chosen to blow out his brains on the very bench where caresses had been exchanged.

He was rather artistic about it, too. He waited until the big clock at City Hall chimed the hour of midnight. The cough of the revolver merged with the last booming note of the clock.

The newspapers featured the story. The girl in the case cried and had her picture taken with a handkerchief at her eyes. She had pretty knees, so the newspapers put her on page one.

It was a good idea. Another rejected swain, lacking originality, but appreciating the publicity, committed suicide in the same place a week later. The hour was after midnight. Evidently he had almost lost his nerve and had battled the decision for some thirty minutes.

A newspaper made the mistake of calling the spot "Suicide Park."

Now the psychology of suicide is subtle and but little understood. Police know that suicides run in epidemics. An account of one suicide inspires others to take the step.

And this relates to places. Let a certain locality once become known as a spot for suicides and it can never live down the name. Morose persons with a suicide complex will see that the reputation is kept alive. Niagara Falls found this out. And there are other spots.

Hence the casual remark of a newspaper writer changed Lovers' Lane overnight. Lovers no longer resorted to the place. The benches were grim, the shadows filled with stalking specters. Lone men came to the spot to brood over their troubles. Occasionally one of these men failed to leave the place. He would be found sprawled on a bench in the shadows, the cheap revolver at his side.

Then the newspapers would build up more hypnotic complexes.

An extra policeman was assigned to the park. The city government decided to erect a municipal building there and eliminate the shadow-filled stretches of midnight menace.

But all of these things take time, and, in the meantime, while architects labored over plans and specifications, while voters waited the issuance of bonds, the park continued to beckon the unfortunate. There was in its very silence a hint of rest. Its shadows became psychic vortexes in which a weak soul might spin down into oblivion.

9

For the most part men did not come to the park twice. They came to it at night, as though drawn by an invisible cord, sat upon the benches in silence, watching the patrolling forms of the special police officers. Then they departed in slinking, cringing silence.

One man alone came there regularly, night after night.

Tall, slender, purposeful, grimly silent, a tawny police dog trailing his steps, this man strode through the night shadows as though upon some gruesome sentry duty.

The police sought to find out more about him.

The man was courteous, but reserved. He gave them such information as they could have found out by other means. Beyond that he was as a clam.

His name was Sidney Zoom. He lived upon a small, expensively equipped yacht, which lay anchored in the harbor just beyond the park. The police dog was named Rip, and needed exercise.

The park was a convenient place to stroll. It was a lovely evening, and good night to you, officer.

And the grim, silent figure, walking, walking, always walking, became a midnight fixture of the park. At times the dog trailed behind, at times ran ahead. Sometimes the dog would revert to wolf habits, and come skulking through the shrubbery, a tawny shadow against the midnight black of the grass. Twice he had given one of the officers such a start that the minion of the law had tugged at his holstered weapon.

They had suggested to Sidney Zoom that dogs must be leashed and muzzled. And Sidney Zoom had shown them a clause in the old deed by which the park had been dedicated. That clause had made it a condition of the dedication that pets could run free within the confines of the park.

The officers yielded the point, but in such a manner that boded no good for the police dog, should he give the patrol any legitimate excuse to send a bullet crashing into his tawny body.

But Sidney Zoom and his dog seemed entirely oblivious of any danger. They continued their midnight pacings through the park.

The officers noticed that, at times, some unfortunate attracted the attention of Sidney Zoom. At such times there would be long conversations, then the unfortunate would leave the park, arm in arm with the well-dressed figure of Sidney Zoom, the police dog bringing up the rear.

That unfortunate never returned to the park.

II

IT WAS approaching midnight.

Suicide Park lay a blotch of shadow. The lighted boulevard terminated in a sweeping circle. The street lights caught the tower of City Hall, showed the hands of the big clock. Then the shade trees and grass patches of the park contrasted their blackness with the white illumination.

Beyond lay the lapping waters of the bay, black, mysterious broken occasionally by the drifting lights of some cruising craft.

Sidney Zoom walked the graveled walks with the mechanical step of one who knows his way through the constant repetition of thousands of similar steps. The police dog darted ahead, paused, slipped beneath a bit of shrubbery, and stood motionless as a statue.

The man on the bench held his right hand beneath his coat. He was listening, not to the lap of the water along the shore of the bay, not to the gentle whisper of faint wind in the trees, but listening for some sound which was not, yet which would be.

The clock on City Hall tower gave a preliminary click. Then the first stroke of midnight boomed forth upon the air.

The man upon the bench sighed.

Behind him, the trained police dog crouched, tense, eyes two glittering points of phosphorescent scrutiny.

—nine—ten—eleven—twel—

The man whipped his right hand out from beneath his coat. The trained police dog became a streak of blurred motion.

The light, reflected from the white tower of City Hall, glittered upon some metallic object. The right hand was elevated. The right arm became rigid.

A streak of hurtling motion terminated at the arm.

White fangs caught in the sleeve of the coat. A body that was as firmly muscled as the body of a timber wolf flung itself to one side and down.

The revolver clattered as it slid along the gravel.

The man uttered a single sharp exclamation.

The dog barked, a swift, yapping, purposeful bark, then was quiet, haunched on the gravel the coat sleeve still in his teeth, gleaming eyes fastened upon the white face above them, in motionless appraisal.

Sidney Zoom came at once.

"That's good, Rip. Down and quiet."

The dog released his grip upon the sleeve of the coat, flattened his body upon the gravel.

Sidney Zoom kicked the revolver out of sight, sat down upon the bench, and turned to the astonished man at his side.

"Good evening," he said.

The man sought to mutter something, but his voice refused to function. The white blur that was his face continued to point toward the form of the dog.

"You have nothing to fear from the dog," said Sidney Zoom, "as long as you offer no resistance and come quietly."

Emotional reaction had gripped the man on the bench.

His hands jerked and quivered. The corners of his mouth twitched. When he spoke his voice was husky.

"I—I'm under arrest?"

"No. Let us not use that term. You are being restrained for the present. You will come quietly?"

"Yes. I'll come—I don't know what possessed me—yet it's the only way—Good God! Let me end it all! What's the use of just prolonging the agony!"

Sidney Zoom linked his arm through the quivering elbow of the unfortunate.

"Walk quietly," he said.

Together they strode from the park. The dog brought up the rear, alert and watchful.

It took them ten minutes to board the palatial yacht which Sidney Zoom kept in the sheltered anchorage. Another five minutes sufficed to find glasses, whisky, bring a tinge of color to the face of the shivering man.

Then they confronted each other in appraisal.

The man who had trembled upon the brink of eternity saw a tall man, lean, muscular, head thrust slightly forward. There was a suggestion of taut springs, steel wired muscles, panther energy. And the eyes dominated that face as though the other features had been nonexistent.

Hawk eyes they were, fierce, keen, but, more than that, they were untamed.

And Sidney Zoom saw a quivering huddle of humanity that was hardly more than a boy. The eyes were dazed. The flesh still quivered as though shrinking from the caress of the icy hands of death.

"Tell me about it," said Zoom.

The young man opened his pale lips, closed them again, lowered his eyes, shook his head.

Sidney Zoom fell to pacing the carpeted floor of the cabin.

"Come on. Don't hesitate. No need for fear. No matter what it is I'm your friend. I hate civilization and all it stands for. Civilization is a vast machine. Men are mere cogs in the machine they have created. They spin frantically, are worn out and cast aside. There's no longer room for an individual. Society wants cogs, parts that are uniform, interchangeable!"

He spat out the words with an intensity of feeling that tinged his tone, made his tongue whip out the words with the rattle of machine gun fire.

The dazed eyes of the young man followed him. The lips were half parted.

Swiftly, almost fiercely, Sidney Zoom turned to him.

"You won't confide in me. I frighten you. Bah! Cowards, all of you! You would plunge headlong into death, yet you fear me! But wait, I have my secretary coming. You'll talk to her. They all do."

As though the words had been an announcement, there sounded light steps on the half ladder that ran from the deck. The door swung noiselessly open. The dog wagged his tail in a series of violent thumpings.

Upon the threshold stood a young woman, a radiant vision of youthful beauty, sparkling with the sheer joy of life, yet maternally tender with it all. She had been dancing if one could judge by the filmy beauty of her evening clothes. Her cheeks were slightly flushed, red lips half parted, eyes starry.

"I saw your emergency light and came as quickly as I could," she said, starry eyes fastened upon the hawk-like orbs of Sidney Zoom.

"My secretary, Vera Thurmond," snapped Sidney Zoom. "You'll talk to her. They all do."

And, with that, he strode to a connecting door, jerked it open, motioned to the dog. For a moment they stood motionless, then man and dog blended into rippling motion. Noiselessly they slipped through the door into the adjoining cabin, wolf-dog and hawkman, savages both, beneath the veneer of civilization.

III

THE GIRL crossed the room, sank to the floor by the side of the pallid, dazed mortal who had so recently gazed into the black mystery of death.

Her hands slid along an arm, possessed five cold fingers in a warm clasp, then she raised her eyes and spoke.

"You mustn't fear him, ever. He lives for good. Less than two months ago I was like you. The world seemed hopeless. I jumped from a wharf. He saved me. And I told him my story.

"He started to right the wrongs that had been done me. I can't tell you all about it, but you'll find out for yourself. You must tell me your story."

The young man nodded. It had needed but that touch of feminine tenderness to restore him to the psychology of living. The last touch of death's fingers slipped from him, and he encircled the girl's shoulders with an arm that was clinging, yet impersonal.

There were tears in his eyes as he talked. His voice choked at times, but he talked freely. His words did not seem words alone, but his speech was more the outpouring of a soul, a lonely, terrified soul that had found life too stern for it, yet had recoiled from the black abyss of mystery which comes after life.

"There's no way out. It will kill the folks. The officers are looking for me now. But I didn't do it. I couldn't have done it—oh, why won't they listen?

"It's so foolish. Why should I go to all that trouble to steal a diamond necklace? I'd have simply skipped out, not returned with that miserable imitation."

He halted for a moment, and the girl nodded, squeezed his hand.

"Of course," she said.

The calm faith of her tone heartened him, and he went on. His tale was more coherent now.

"I'm at Cremlin's, you know, the jewelry house. They used me as messenger to take gems out for inspection. There was a Franklin T. Vane at the Westmoreland Hotel who wanted a diamond necklace. I took him two yesterday. Neither satisfied him. Today he telephoned and wanted the same two brought back for a second inspection.

"I took them. He had two men in his room. One was an expert appraiser. The appraiser examined the necklaces, advised against a purchase, and I had to take them both back.

"I'd swear they put the same necklaces back in the bag. I know they did. And then—well, then I did the thing that damns me. I didn't go directly back to the store.

"There's a girl. She wanted to see me about something awfully important—we were going to be married—and she'd telephoned. I though it'd be all right to run a little out of the way to see her.

"I wasn't there over ten minutes, and only she and I were there. She didn't even know what I had in the bag. But when I got back to the store—well, the genuine necklaces weren't in the bag. There were two paste imitations, fairly good imitations, but not perfect.

"They telephoned for an officer, and they gave me two hours to restore the originals. I told them the whole story, but they wouldn't believe it.

"Franklin Vane was awfully bitter. He said I looked nervous when I was in his room at the hotel. And, of course, the others back him up in his statements about returning the originals to me. There was Cohen, the expert appraiser, and there was Purdy, from the bank. The word of those men can't be doubted."

The young man gave a dry, choking sob.

"*She* won't believe me. She won't even see me again. And the officers are looking for me. I got in a panic, knocked down the chap who was guarding me and bolted through the back door.

"Think of my folks. My mother's sick—I can't go on with it. I've got to end it all. Kindness is wasted. Oh, why didn't he let me go through with it. It'd have all been over by this time."

The girl stroked his cold hand.

"This girl, how long had you known her?"

"A week, but it was—gee, it was love at first sight."

Vera Thurmond nodded, then got to her feet with the easy grace of a trained dancer, walked to the inner door, flung it open.

"Come in," she said to Sidney Zoom.

Sidney Zoom entered the room, the dog at his heels. The hawklike eyes fastened themselves upon the shamed face of the young man, then turned to the girl.

"Well?"

In short, simple words she formed crisp sentences that told him the story of the young man. During the recital, the visitor nodded from time to time, watched the expressionless face of Sidney Zoom anxiously.

When Vera had finished her recital, Sidney Zoom regarded the young man.

"Your name?"

"Otto Shaffer."

"What sort of a bag did you carry the diamonds in?"

"A black hand bag."

"Locked?"

"No, but I held it in my hand all the time."

"The girl's name?"

"Lois Manly."

"What does she do?"

"Works—I don't know just where."

"Vane? What do you know about him?"

"Nothing. He gave credit references at the store. He was just a customer."

Sidney Zoom made a swift turn or two about the room, then his eyes caught those of his secretary, made a suggestive flicker toward an alcohol lamp upon which sat a teapot.

The girl sighed, set about brewing tea. Sidney Zoom walked the floor in purposeful concentration.

At length the tea was made. The girl set out three cups. As she poured the tea into the cup that was placed nearest the hand of Otto Shaffer, she gave a slight flickering motion of her left wrist. A small portion of white powder drifted unnoticed to the cup, was instantly dissolved in the tea.

They drank, talked for a few minutes. Then, as the eyes of the young man filmed under the influence of the drug, Sidney Zoom walked to a closet, flung it open.

Within the closet were numerous disguises, wigs, mustaches, spectacles, hats, coats, beards, grease paint, mirror, stains. In the hands of a novice they would have been ludicrous. But Sidney Zoom had been known as the Master of the Disguise when he had served the intelligence departments of three nations.

The young man tried to say something. His head nodded forward, then his eyes closed in surrender, and he slept.

"You gave him a strong dose?"

"Yes. He'll sleep for twenty-four hours."

"He'll need to. This may prove a difficult case. I think I know what happened, but I can't tell until I've looked up the girl."

As he spoke his deft fingers fitted a small mustache to his upper lip. A stick of grease paint slid rapidly over his features, left little lines which suddenly blended into a composite whole. The man had apparently aged twenty years in as many seconds.

"You'll be back, when?"

"Some time before morning. I'll put that young man to bed."

And he stooped, picked up the sleeping form, carried it with effortless ease to a bunk, covered it with a blanket, loosened the clothes.

"It seems horrible to drug them this way."

Sidney Zoom snorted.

"Getting squeamish? Quit if you are. We're snatching souls back from black despair. It takes rest. And we can't soothe their nerves until we've relieved their troubles. We can't do that by a wave of the hand."

Her eyes were starry now as she regarded him.

"But you seem to do it by magic."

"Well, it's hard work."

His tone was gruff, the eyes busy surveying a mirrored reflection of his face.

"It's a wonderful work!"

He either did not notice the admiration in her tone, or else chose to disregard it.

His hands busied themselves over a selection of garments, finally removed a rather shabby suit of brown worsted, shiny, baggy, frayed.

"We deal," he said, "in lost souls, and our methods must be more or less irregular … I'll be back by ten o'clock in the morning."

IV

BUT IT was noon before the deck planks thudded to the returning steps of Sidney Zoom.

The girl rushed to meet him. The dog flung himself wearily in the sunshine. Sidney Zoom's skin showed some trace of graying fatigue, but his eyes were as bright as ever.

"You've found out something?"

The Master of the Disguise nodded. His voice was sharp, his words rapid.

"As I suspected. There were altogether too many witnesses to what happened in that room at the Westmoreland Hotel. It was too much of a coincidence that two men who were gem experts and of unimpeachable veracity should have seen those gems returned to the bag, the bag given to Shaffer.

"That would lead one to believe Franklin T. Vane knew of the impending robbery. So I started with Vane. I've traced his record, but it's been a job. He's really a fence from Chicago.

"And the girl, Lois Manly, was an accomplice, of course. Thus it's not difficult to reconstruct what happened.

"The girl had the messenger in love with her. Vane had a credit at the jewelry store. He ordered gems for inspection. While he had them in his hands he observed sufficient details to enable copies to be made. And he had a copy of the black bag made up.

"Then he surrounded himself with reputable witnesses, telephoned for the same gems to be sent up again. And Lois Manly, relying on the young man's love for her, gave him a pleading call for help. He *must* stop on the way back to the store.

"The boy called on her, his bag contained two necklaces that had been determined in advance by the real criminal. It only remained for the girl to switch the imitation bag with the duplicate necklaces. No one thought of bag and everything being changed. And, of course, the fact that Shaffer had strayed from the direct route to the store was all that was needed to clinch the case against him."

Vera Thurmond nodded brightly.

"So you've notified the police of the real facts?"

Sidney Zoom flashed her a single glance of cold scorn.

"Certainly not. Your sex is impulsive, and you seem to share the common fault. The police, indeed! What would they do? What could they do? They'd bungle the case, of course. They wouldn't move until they'd looked Vane up, and by that time he'd have completely covered up the crime.

"No, Miss Thurmond, I shall resort to my usual methods. I returned for another disguise. Did you, by any chance, ever hear of Willie the Weeper?"

"Willie the Weeper? What an odd name!"

"A rather unfortunate creature of the underworld, Miss Thurmond, who has been famed in song and fable. He is, of course, not a real character, and yet it is a character that has always appealed to me. I rather fancy I shall become Willie the Weeper."

She knew him too well to ask for further explanations.

"I've switched on the electric coffee-pot and toaster. Our patient is still sleeping."

Sidney Zoom nodded, absently, strode across the deck, entered a cabin and began throwing garments in a suitcase.

Then he bathed, shaved, and came to coffee and toast as Sidney Zoom, an eccentric, millionaire yacht owner, cruising about for pleasure.

"Keep the boy asleep until midnight. By that time I hope to have a solution."

"Will I hear from you before then?"

"No."

"Will you tell me your plans?"

"No. Certainly not."

She propped her elbows on the table, regarded Sidney Zoom with level eyes, eyes which contained a glint of maternal tenderness, and also a hint of an emotion that was warmer.

"What a strange creature, what a wonderful man you are!"

"The coffee," said Sidney Zoom in measured tones, "is excellent."

And the girl's throaty laughter pealed through the cabin.

"Thank you *so* much."

And again she laughed.

"Your amusement comes from …"

"From your evident fear that I'm going to bite you," said the girl, arising from the table. "Do you know, I believe your hard-boiled manner with women, amounting at times to rudeness, is caused by … well, guess."

Sidney Zoom gulped half a cup of coffee in a single scalding swallow, and scraped back his chair.

"Is caused by fear," laughed the girl. "And some day I'm likely to puncture your pose just to hear you go 'boom.' "

But Sidney Zoom might not have heard the words. In cold dignity that had something of hostility in it, he picked up his suitcase, crossed to the companionway, flung back a single comment over his shoulder.

"Midnight," he snapped. "Rip, you'll stay here and guard the girl."

The dog paused, mid-stride, cocked his ears, lowered his tail. For a long moment he gazed after his departing master, hoping against hope for some change in orders.

There was none. A door banged. Rapid feet crossed the deck. The dog stood, listening, head on one side. And Vera Thurmond, swooping her supple body down and around, caught his head in her hands and implanted a swift kiss upon the shaggy forehead.

In the after cabin, Otto Shaffer, his nerves relaxed by a sleeping potion that brought a deep, natural sleep, slumbered as peacefully as a child.

V

SIDNEY ZOOM strode to the desk at the Madison House and fastened his glittering eyes on the clerk.

"A suite. The best in the house."

The clerk spun the register, glanced at the signature, at the single suitcase.

"The best in the house will run a hundred and forty dollars a day."

Sidney Zoom flipped a roll of currency from his pocket. The outside bill contained a five followed by two ciphers.

"The rest of my baggage will follow. This will establish my credit."

"Yes, Mr. Zoom. Yes, indeed," purred the deferential clerk.

"And I wish to purchase some rather expensive diamonds—oh, say around a hundred thousand dollars," continued Mr. Zoom. "Can you refer me to a good store. I'm somewhat of a stranger here."

The clerk's eyes widened, caught those of the house detective who was loitering near the desk.

"Cremlin's is right across the street. They're rated as the most exclusive in the city. I can ring them up and make an appointment, Mr. Zoom."

Sidney Zoom nodded his acquiescence.

"My sister will join me later. It's her birthday, and I want to get something appropriate. Diamonds are her birthstone. Please tell Cremlin's that I will be over there within half an hour."

And then Sidney Zoom strolled to the elevator, was shown to his suite, and gave the bell boy a ten-dollar bill in token of appreciation for having a suitcase carried a hundred feet.

Thirty minutes later he beamed upon the clerk, shook hands with the house detective, strolled across the street and purchased one fifteen-thousand-dollar diamond necklace, one ten-thousand-dollar diamond brooch. And he paid for these articles in cash, upon the distinct understanding, however, that they could be returned at any time within twenty-four hours and the cash refunded.

Then Sidney Zoom strolled back to his room in the hotel, telephoned for the house detective, opened an excellent bottle of Scotch, and had some ginger ale sent up by a bell boy.

"Think she'll like 'em?" asked Sidney Zoom, flipping his hand toward the dresser.

Harry Colman, the house detective, stared with wide eyes and a mouth that tried to appear sophisticated, yet showed a tendency to sag in a gape.

"Some ice!"

"She should like them. She'll be in during the next two or three hours. I've left instructions with the clerk to give her the duplicate key. My sister, you know, the one I'm buying the diamonds for. It's her birthday."

"Yeah," remarked Harry Colman, pouring himself another drink. "You'll leave the stones in the safe?"

"No, I think not. They'll be safe in the room. No one knows they're here, and I'd like to have Alberta find them on the dresser when she comes in."

Harry Colman sat the whisky bottle back upon the table with such violence that the resulting thump sounded like the stroke of a hammer.

"You're going to ... leave ... those ... stones ... here!"

"Certainly."

"But there's a fortune there. The hotel won't be responsible for them. Why, there's half a dozen pass-keys out for the rooms on this floor. Good heavens ..."

The cold, passively hostile eyes of Sidney Zoom impaled the startled orbs of the house detectives.

"And, of course, there being no responsibility on the part of the hotel, it is no concern of yours what I do with them."

Harry Colman sighed, averted his gaze.

"Except as a matter of friendly advice. And, of course, the hotel doesn't get any benefit from having a burglary pulled in one of the rooms."

Sidney Zoom abstracted a cigarette from a gold case, took two deep drags at it, then flipped it into a porcelain cuspidor with casual fingers.

"Have some more of that Scotch," he remarked, as though the matter had been closed.

Harry Colman poured himself a stiff drink.

"When'll your sister be in?"

"Inside of a couple of hours."

"How'll we know the jane's your sister?"

"My sister," said Sidney Zoom, with that dignified stupidity which can only be safely assumed by millionaires who casually purchase twenty-five thousand dollars in gems and leave them hanging around a hotel bedroom, "wouldn't lie about it. When she states that she is my sister you may accept her word."

Harry Colman drained his second drink and reached for his third.

"And," resumed Sidney Zoom, "*you're* about the only person who knows the gems are here."

"Case of a robbery that'd make it interesting for me," commented the house detective.

Zoom waved his hand toward the bottle.

"Take it with you. If you'll excuse me, I wish to bathe and change my clothes."

The house detective accepted the dismissal, left the bottle on the table.

"And if you think this room ain't in for some special watching during the next two hours you got another think coming," he promised grimly as the door slammed.

Sidney Zoom rasped the key in the lock, then set to work.

He dragged the clothes from the bed, even slit the mattress with a sharp knife. He cut the pillows, scattered the feathers about the room. He took the bottle of excellent Scotch, emptied it down the drain, pulled the drawers from the bureau, ripped up a section of the carpet. He opened his suitcase, scattered his things about the feather-strewn floor.

Then he took the jewels from their ornate caskets, slipped them in the pocket of his coat, tore the paper wrappings into fine bits and threw them in the waste basket.

When he had completed this work of destruction he took from an inner pocket a grimed, soiled card. Upon this card was scrawled in pencil the number of a room, the name of a hotel and the cryptic words, "Stuff that's too hot to handle."

Then Sidney Zoom emerged from the room, carefully locked the door behind him, slipped the key in his pocket, and left the hotel.

A taxicab took him to the Union Depot. Here he redeemed a suitcase which had been checked over the parcel counter, and sought a cheaper hotel, where he engaged a very modest room.

Within this room he set about making over his entire character.

Shabby clothes, glaringly cheap, yet pressed with some attempt to simulate well-being, shoes that had been battered out of shape, a celluloid collar and gaudy tie, a shirt that shrieked to high heaven, and a derby hat, all came from the suitcase and were carefully donned.

A shock of graying hair was properly adjusted. A few strokes of a bit of grease paint weakened the mouth. The hawklike glitter of the untamed eyes was concealed behind a pair of colored spectacles.

When these preparations had been made, carefully checked, skillfully executed, the personality of Sidney Zoom, adventurer extraordinary, collector of lost souls, doctor of destinies, became merged in a personality that could only be fittingly placed by reference to that well known song of the underworld which features the adventures of Willie the Weeper.

When the transformation was complete Willie the Weeper left the confines of the cheap hotel and presented himself cringingly at the house telephones of the Westmoreland Hotel.

The hearty, confident voice of Franklin T. Vane boomed in his ear.

"Yes, what is it?"

"A friend of yours."

"Name?"

"Never mind the name."

"I'm afraid you've got the wrong party."

"You're Franklin T. Vane, ain't you?"

"Yes. Who are you?"

"You wouldn't know the name."

"What do you want?"

"To make you a proposition."

"Well, I'm not open to any proposition. I don't know you and I don't care to. Good night."

"From Chicago," whined Willie the Weeper.

There was a biting silence. It almost seemed that the telephone wire transmitted a squeak made by a tightened grip on the receiver at the other end of the wire.

"I know no one in Chicago."

"But I do."

"Where are you?"

"Downstairs. I'm coming up."

And Sidney Zoom, completely merged in the personality of Willie the Weeper, slipped the receiver back on the hook, surreptitiously took something from his pocket, and rubbed it just beneath the lids of his eyes.

The effect was almost instantaneous. The eyes reddened, began to ooze water.

Then Willie the Weeper went toward the elevators and was shot upward to the seventh floor. From there he groped about, found seven forty-nine, and scratched on the door.

The door flung open. A portly, heavy-voiced man let glittering eyes sweep over the cringing figure.

"What the hell?" he exploded.

"From Chicago," said Willie the Weeper, and oozed against the half-open door.

The big figure drew back, let the unwelcome visitor in, and then thrust out an inquisitive head. After a swift glance up and down the deserted corridor, Franklin T. Vane slammed the door, locked it, turned toward the man who stood in the center of the room.

"Who in hell are you?"

"Willie. Folks call me Willie the Weeper."

"Willie the Weeper! Hell, there ain't no such animal. That's just a song hit that Nell—"

The dejected figure shook its head.

"That's where you make a mistake. The song was first all right. Then I started panhandling, and the boys called me Willie the Weeper, 'cause I got something wrong with my eyes. I made a fortune outa panhandling the boulevard in Chi, but I found I had talents better suited for other things."

"Yes?"

The voice of Franklin T. Vane was cold in its guarded note of inquiry.

"Yes, I got to collecting hot ice."

Vane's figure stiffened.

"What brought you here?"

"I don't know the local ropes very well. A strange fence tried to cross me, an' I seen you come out of the hotel this morning."

Franklin T. Vane shook his head.

"You're crazy," he said, "as crazy as a bedbug."

Willie the Weeper nodded, and reached a hand in the side pocket of his coat. When it came out the fingers seemed to catch the late afternoon sunlight, magnify it, send it sparkling in corruscating fire about the hotel room.

"What's that?" snapped Franklin T. Vane, and his glittering eyes contained the fire of avarice.

Willie the Weeper passed over the necklace. It was the same necklace which had been purchased from Cremlin's for fifteen thousand dollars. And Sidney Zoom had selected it because, among other things, a certain odd cutting of the stones, a certain distinctiveness of the clasp, made the necklace one which could be readily identified.

"Hot ice," he said, in the whining voice which characterized him.

"Not interested!" snapped Vane, but his eyes belied his tongue.

"Too hot to handle here," pursued Willie the Weeper. "It might be handled in Chi. If I had a stake I'd go back there. If you don't wanta handle it, how about a stake for get-by money?"

Vane shook his head. His massive neck gave a suggestion of dominant power to the gesture. But his feverish eyes and eager fingers gave evidence of continued interest.

"Got any more?"

Willie the Weeper rubbed beneath his eyes with a dirty handkerchief. The streaks of moisture still remained upon his sallow skin. His hand slipped furtively into his other pocket, brought out a diamond brooch.

"I got this."

The cupidity which glittered so avariciously in the eyes of the fence crystalized into sudden determination.

"Sit down," he said, and there was a cooing softness in the voice which gave the words an oily suggestion of smooth hypocrisy. "I'm going to give you a square deal, one hell of a square deal."

Willie the Weeper sat down, raised red rimmed eyes which peered through the darkened lenses of spectacles.

"Yes?"

"Yes. I'm going to give you some get-by money for a get-away, and I'm going to give you a trade. This stuff is hot, too hot to handle. But I've got some stuff that's nearly cold. You can take it to Chi, and it'll be a cinch."

Willie the Weeper hesitated, shifted his eyes doubtfully.

"I want cash."

"But you'll get cash, and a hell of a good trade to boot. Those diamonds of yours are worth perhaps eight grand. I've got some that would be worth twenty thousand if they weren't hot."

"Eight grand!" expostulated Willie the Weeper. "Why, those rocks would retail for a cool twenty-five thousand!"

Franklin T. Vane threw back his head and laughed. The laugh was more forceful than mirthful.

"What a boob *you* are! Somebody's been kidding you. If you think those things would retail for twenty-five thousand you'd think mine would sell for a hundred. Tell you what I'll do. I'll give you three thousand in cash and trade you one of the finest strings of rocks you ever saw. Or I've got two strings I'll trade you even."

"I want cash."

"Well, take this trade I'm offering. Three grand and a swell string."

Willie the Weeper looked at the diamonds in necklace and brooch.

"Le'me see the string."

The string which Vane offered was made up of rather small stones. There was not the perfect fire, not the matching which makes necklaces run into real money. Yet it was a good necklace, well worth lifting.

Sidney Zoom, sitting there with his dominant, aggressive personality completely dissolved into that of Willie the Weeper, had no difficulty whatever in recognizing that string as one of the necklaces which had been taken from Cremlin's, and the theft of which had been laid to the door of young Otto Shaffer.

"Four thousand and I might consider it."

"Three's the price."

"Make it three fifty."

"Three's the limit. That's really too much. I should make it two fifty."

Willie the Weeper sniffled. A streak of moisture slimed his cheek, drifted uncertainly past his quivering lips and dropped to the carpet.

"It's robbery," he whined.

Franklin T. Vane sat in sneering contemplation of the weeping man. Willie the Weeper lived up to his nickname. He whined with voice and eyes, sniffled, cried. The tears dropped from his reddened eyes to the carpet.

At length he gave sniffling acquiescence.

Franklin T. Vane stripped three one thousand dollar bills from a roll and handed them over.

"That's a swell string I'm giving you. You can hock it in Chi for more than both of your pieces were worth."

Willie the Weeper sniffled over the consummation of the deal. He whined, cried, hung around until Vane had dropped the necklace and brooch into a secret compartment of the wardrobe trunk. Then he sniveled himself out of the door.

Franklin T. Vane snorted, slammed the door shut and locked it.

VI

WILLIE THE WEEPER became a very busy man. He took a cab to the cheap hotel where he had placed his suitcase. Within a matter of minutes he transformed himself into his true character. Eye wash stopped the watering eyes, leaving them red.

Attired in a tailored suit which proclaimed itself as having cost much money, Sidney Zoom returned to the Madison House.

"Evening, Colman," he saluted the house detective. "Wonder how my sister liked the diamonds."

"She hasn't shown up," announced the detective.

"Hasn't shown up! Good Heavens, there must be some foul play. I sent her a message—I wonder if that message could have miscarried."

The house detective shrugged his shoulders.

"I wish you'd left those diamonds in the safe."

"Nonsense! The diamonds are all right, but how about my sister. Come on up and we'll put through a call."

The house detective, mindful of the excellent Scotch, nodded assent. Together they approached the door of the room. Sidney Zoom fitted a key, flung the door open, gave a slight, hospitable push upon the shoulder of his guest, and switched on the light.

Harry Colman's muscles became rigid beneath Zoom's hand which rested on his shoulder. He jumped back.

"Burglars! Great Heavens! Look at that room!"

Sidney Zoom sprang forward.

"The diamonds!" yelled Colman.

"Gone!" screamed Zoom.

There followed a period of seething activity. The police were notified. Colman started searching for clews, muttering to himself as he looked about.

"Funny they'd make all this commotion when the diamonds were in plain sight. Wonder what the idea was?"

"Looking for my money, perhaps," volunteered Sidney Zoom, moving slightly so that one foot rested almost upon the crumpled bit of cardboard bearing the mysterious address and the significantly scrawled words.

"Well," muttered Colman, "they sure made a—What's that?"

"What?"

"By your foot?"

"Looks like a card."

Colman pounced upon it.

"Stuff that's too hot to handle!" he read. "Gee, what a break."

"Too hot to handle?" muttered Sidney Zoom in an apologetic undertone.

"Yeah," explained Colman, "a yegg term. It means stolen goods that are wanted badly by the police and for which a description's gone out. I'll bet you fifty dollars that's the address of the fence that was going to handle this job."

"I'm afraid I shouldn't bet," retorted Sidney Zoom, "but if you recover those gems there'll be a little reward of two thousand dollars, cash."

And the face of Sidney Zoom set in such grim lines of righteous indignation at the criminal act which had deprived him of his property that Colman found it necessary to place a restraining hand upon the taut arm.

"There, there, don't worry. Here are the police now. They'll have authority to make a search of this room in the Westmorland Hotel."

"You think we have enough evidence upon which to predicate a search?"

"Say, baby, when there's two thousands bucks reward I'd search George Washington's tomb for a stolen dollar. Come on."

The police listened.

A whispered conversation took place between the sergeant in charge of the detail and the house detective. Then the red police automobile sirened its way through the crowded thorough-fares.

Once more Sidney Zoom found himself at the door of Franklin T. Vane's suite. But this time he was not in the disguise of a whining crook. He stood erect, indignant, a picture of righteous indignation, such as any honest citizen might feel toward a crook, particularly if that crook had just lifted twenty-five thousand dollars in diamonds from the aforesaid honest citizen.

Franklin T. Vane saw the bluecoats, the glittering eyes, the firm lips, and his heavy face blanched.

"What is the meaning of this outrage?" he stormed, before the police had even stated their errand.

The words placed him definitely in an attitude of antagonism.

"It means," bellowed Sidney Zoom, "that you're a fence, a receiver of stolen property. You've got my diamonds here, taken from some crook with whom you connived the robbery."

Franklin T. Vane recoiled before the very violence of those words, the blast of righteous wrath which accompanied them.

"Really, gentlemen—"

But it was too late. Sidney Zoom had shouldered the door, marched resolutely into the room. The officers followed.

Ten minutes later they found the secret compartment in the wardrobe trunk.

"The diamonds!" yelled Sidney Zoom. "Colman, you're a wonder! Sergeant, you'll get a promotion for this! I never saw such prompt work!"

The police sergeant was gazing at another diamond necklace with a puzzled frown.

"And here's another one. By George, that's one of the necklaces from that Cremlin job yesterday. We thought the kid pulled that one. Maybe he used this guy as a fence. But—wait a minute! My God, yes! This is the very room! I see it all now. Why, you're the man who had the messenger bring up the stones. Aha! so that's your game, eh?"

And Franklin T. Vane, taken unawares at the start, showing a positive genius for doing the wrong thing, made the fatal mistake of trying to rush for the door.

There was the thud of a well placed fist, the flop of a huge body, the adjustment of handcuffs.

"Colman, your reward!"

Sidney Zoom peeled two one thousand dollar bills from his pocket, handed them to Harry Colman.

Colman flashed the sergeant a meaning glance, pocketed the bills. Both men were grinning.

On the floor, Franklin T. Vane raised a bruised eye, saw the denomination of the bills, gave a violent start, muttered an oath, and gazed with wide eyes at the form of Sidney Zoom.

"I get my diamonds?" asked Zoom.

"Certainly," purred the sergeant. "The identification's beyond any doubt."

"Then, Colman, you can take them back to Cremlin's to-morrow I don't think sister would like any stones that have such unpleasant associations. I'll ask for a cash refund, as was arranged between us when I purchased the stones.

"In the meantime, you gentlemen have no further use for me?"

"Go right along, Mr. Zoom," boomed the sergeant. "I understand Colman knows where to get you if we want you."

"Aboard the yacht *Alberta F.*," smiled Zoom, "and now, gentlemen, good night."

Franklin T. Vane groaned, stifled a curse, then clamped his mouth tightly shut.

Aboard the yacht, Sidney Zoom gazed at the curious face of his secretary. There was a quizzical gleam in his eyes.

"The second necklace was mailed back to Cremlin's before I boarded the boat. I'll secure a return of my twenty-five thousand dollars from the jeweler to-morrow. In the meantime, after deducting the reward, there's a thousand dollar note that remains a clear profit. I think that should go to Shaffer. He might want to pay his folks a visit."

The girl sighed.

"How perfectly wonderful!"

"Nonsense!" snapped Sidney Zoom. "There's a tendency on the part of your sex, Miss Thurmond, to exaggerate any small mental effort that shows successful results. I certainly trust you will not fall into that habit."

And Sidney Zoom turned abruptly to the closet where he kept his various disguises, and began putting them in order, making ready for the next case.

The girl stared at him, and her eyes showed a light of admiration that was far from being impersonal.

But Sidney Zoom, keeping his back turned, kept busy with his disguises. It was only the police dog that turned yellow eyes upward and surprised the expression of tenderness in the eyes of the young woman.

The dog wagged his tail, softly thumping it against the carpeted floor, signifying his entire approval.

A faint wind ruffled the dark waters of the bay and the boat creaked gently as it swung about, the water lapping its sides.

In the inner cabin Otto Shaffer, just awakening from a peaceful sleep of drugged tranquillity, rubbed his eyes with his fists, and smiled dreamily.

"MY NAME IS ZOOM!"

SIDNEY ZOOM stood in the main cabin of his palatial yacht, scissors in one hand, paste in the other. On the table before him was a photograph.

The picture was of a thin man with eyes that seemed almost white. The cheeks were hollow, the mouth a mere razor-thin line of wire lips. A synthetic smile, twitching the corners of that mouth, yet failed to soften it. The picture gave forth an aura of cold cruelty. But the forehead showed keen intellectuality.

Back of Sidney Zoom, her eyes wide with interest, her shapely figure poised gracefully, Vera Thurmond, the newly employed secretary, gazed at the photograph.

"Another one for your rogues' gallery?"

Zoom nodded, a terse nod that was but a single bob of the head.

"Who is he?"

"Albert Pratt, a banker."

"Why put him in the rogues' gallery?"

"For a variety of reasons. The principal one is the Citizens' Rediscount Company."

"And that is?"

"A little subterfuge by which Albert Pratt gets usurious interest. He turns down loans at his bank whenever he thinks the applicant is in desperate need of funds, but mentions that the Citizen's Rediscount Company might be interested in the loan, at a high rate of interest, of course.

"And there are other reasons. Of late he made an unwise investment in some mining stock. But he didn't have to stand the loss. Certain inexperienced depositors were tipped off that the stock was a good buy. They came to Pratt for advice. Pratt shrugged his shoulders, opened his safe and showed them that he had invested his own money in the company.

"The poor depositor invariably closed with the broker, and the broker supplied the stock, not from the capital stock of the company, but from a reissue of Pratt's holdings."

The girl's eyes were dark with emotion.

"You're sure of these things?"

Sidney Zoom turned to her, and his fierce, hawklike eyes fairly bored into her soul.

"Sure? Of course, I'm sure! I've heard the story from a dozen different men, from a dozen different angles. What do you think I do when I walk the streets of the city at night, prowling into the free parks, chatting with those in the bread lines? It is my hobby, finding those who are making their money through legalized fraud. I have here a list of half a dozen men who have lost money through their dealings with this man Pratt."

She sighed.

"And you intend to do something? You'll get a lawyer to handle the cases?"

Sidney Zoom laughed—a harsh, metallic laugh.

"Law! Lawyers! Bah! This man is above the law. The law is crude at best, a mere composite of rules passed by legislatures that are usually incompetent. A smart man can find thousands of legalized frauds which can be perpetrated. And this man, Pratt, is smart. He keeps within the law."

There was silence for a moment.

The two figures in the cabin were each occupied with thoughts that could not be well clothed in words. Outside, the water of the bay lap-lapped against the smooth sides of the craft. Occasionally there was a gentle bump when the trim boat rubbed against the side of the float to which it was moored.

Sidney Zoom opened a little cabinet. There appeared a sheet of cardboard. Upon this sheet were pasted some half dozen photographs. These were men who made a habit of fleecing the unfortunate, who knew the game of legalized crime and waxed fat from their knowledge. Sly criminals who yet were not criminals, but slipped furtively through loopholes in the law, dodged from statute to statute, and emerged smugly complacent with ill-got gains, stared forth from this sheet of cardboard, photographed, numbered, indexed.

Such was the record kept by Sidney Zoom, that strange individual who rebelled against the vast machine of civilization and scoffed at the thousands of laws which sought to curb crime and safeguard property rights.

A scratching against a panel of the outer door caused the girl to turn the knob.

A tawny police dog, heavy of shoulder, yellow of eye, came into the room. A dignified wag of the tip of his tail by way of greeting, and the dog crouched down on the floor, tense as a coiled spring.

"What's the matter, Rip?" asked Sidney Zoom, over his shoulder.

The dog gave a single thump of his tail, then lowered his muzzle to his paws, cocked his ears forward.

"He thinks you're going out."

"I am."

"Soon?"

"Yes."

"You want me to remain here?"

"No. Go to your apartment. I'll telephone if I have anything for you to do."

"Did you intend to call upon Mr. Pratt?"

"No. It would do no good. He prides himself on being able to find a legal excuse for everything he wants to do. He's smart. A word of warning would be wasted."

"You intend to make him pay over some of his ill-got gains?"

Sidney Zoom whirled and faced her.

Tall, well muscled, though slender, there was about him something of the untamed tension of the crouching police dog.

"Yes!" he snapped, and the word was full of menace.

"Some day you'll get into serious trouble with your ideas of justice," she said.

He shrugged his shoulders.

"At any rate, my method is better than the courts. They have so many laws they stumble blindly through a maze of procedure, lose sight of the primary purpose of all courts—to do justice. However, there's no use going into that now. I'm going out. Come, Rip."

And Sidney Zoom, whirling an arm, slammed the door of the cabinet, picked up a hat and coat, flung open the door. The dog at his heels, he ascended the companionway, pounded across the deck and leaped to the float.

Behind him the girl, her eyes suddenly tender, looked at the little cabinet, then at the door.

"He's like that," she murmured to herself. "Whenever I get at all personal he runs away. Heavens, I'm not going to bite the man."

Then she laughed, but there was a throaty catch in the laugh.

II

SIDNEY ZOOM had dinner at an exclusive club, placed his dog on leash, and strolled through the lighted shopping district. But his keen eyes did not so much as glance at the window displays. He looked at faces, darting his hawk's gaze into the features of passing pedestrians.

How much he saw, only Sidney Zoom knew, but it was said of him that a single, swift glance could tell him all about the character of any person, man or woman.

For more than an hour he walked, the dog tugging at the leash, attracting attention. Then they swung from the shopping district, picked up Zoom's expensive sedan and cruised about the city. By ten o'clock Sidney Zoom parked his car near the entrance to one of the city parks, and resumed his walk.

This time his feet crunched over smooth gravel, and there were few pedestrians. For the most part, the occupants of the park were clustered in shadow; couples, sitting on benches. Occasionally the soft murmur of a subdued voice was heard, but this was exceptional. The park was shrouded in silence.

The dog flung his nose to the wind, caught the odor of every one he passed. It has been said that a dog can smell emotion. Certain it is that he can smell fear, and he can smell rage. There is more reason to suppose that a dog can smell the other emotions than to presume that he cannot. But a dog's keen nose can smell one thing remarkably well, and that is the odor of burned powder in the barrel of a revolver.

Hence, when the dog suddenly stopped, flung himself around and strained at the leash, Sidney Zoom turned his eyes to the figure at which the dog's nose pointed.

A single dejected figure sprawled on the bench, head supported on a crooked arm, one leg crossed over the other.

The dog barked once, a short, imperative bark.

Sidney Zoom moved forward.

"Pardon me, my friend, but you have a loaded revolver in that coat pocket."

The man gave a single convulsive leap and was on his feet, his eyes wide with panic.

"A holdup man, perhaps?" The voice of Sidney Zoom was kindly.

The man shook his head, would have run, but a throaty growl from the dog stopped him.

"I wouldn't try to escape. You see, my dog's been trained for police work. And he can detect the odor of a fouled barrel on a gun. I would say the gun had been discharged and not well cleaned. Of course, you know it's a crime to carry one of those weapons."

The man tried to say something, failed.

Sidney Zoom placed a firm hand on the elbow.

"Come with me."

"Am—am—I arrested? Good God, not that! I meant no harm to any one except myself—"

Sidney Zoom shook his head. "Come," he repeated.

When he had placed his unwilling guest in the sedan and started the motor the man broke into swift speech.

"Say, what are you doing? Are you an officer or not? You've got no right to—"

Sidney Zoom turned cold eyes upon him.

"You want me to call an officer?"

"No, no!"

"Why did you have the gun?"

"I can't tell. It's none of your damned business."

Sidney Zoom nodded, the nod of one who merely confirms an earlier opinion.

"People don't often confide in me," he said, and swung the car in to the curb.

"You'll stay here with the gentleman, Rip," he said to the dog, and slipped the leash.

The dog half bared his fangs and growled.

Sidney Zoom telephoned his secretary.

"Come to the yacht at once," he said, hung up the telephone, returned to the car.

The drive was completed in sullen silence.

"I might use that gun on you, you know!" rasped the captive, as Sidney Zoom escorted him across the float to the deck of the yacht.

It was the dog that made answer. Something in the man's tone carried to the canine's brain an understanding of the threat. He growled and bared his fangs again.

"Come," said Sidney Zoom, and led the way to the cabin.

Vera Thurmond had preceded them. Her eyes were dark with emotion, her lips half parted.

"Another?" she asked.

"Another," intoned Sidney Zoom. Then he turned to the man.

"You'll talk with her. People never talk with me."

And he strode to a connecting door, walked into an adjoining room, and slammed the door shut.

The man turned to the girl.

"If I'm not out of here in ten seconds," he snapped, "somebody's going to get hurt. I can shoot that damned dog before he can get to me."

But his only answer was a smile from the girl, a smile of tender understanding.

She crossed to him.

"Sit down," she said. "A few weeks ago I was like you. I, too, thought life too stern to tackle. I tried to end it. He saved me."

And she inclined her head toward the closed door.

"I don't want to be saved. I know what I'm doing."

She motioned toward a chair.

"It's his hobby—righting wrongs. He calls himself a Doctor of Despair, a Collector of Lost Souls; and he makes things come right."

"Bah! I don't want charity."

"It isn't charity. He's a fighter, and he teaches others to stand up and fight. Suppose you tell me?"

The man dropped in the chair. The girl drew up a stool, looked at him and smiled.

"You're married?" she asked.

The man's jaw clamped.

"Yes."

"I wonder if your wife—knows—"

That remark crashed down the barriers of sullen antagonism. He averted his head that she might not see the swift rush of tears that filmed his eyes.

"Clara," he said, and the name was breathed with the reverence of one who prays, "and Effie! They'll know afterward, but it's the only way. You see there's a life insurance policy for two thousand dollars, and it's good, even in the event of suicide."

She nodded.

"And you'd break their hearts for two thousand dollars?"

"It isn't that. They've got to have the money, and—and I'm no good. We had some money laid aside for a rainy day. That's gone. I—well, I had some money that was a trust fund. That's gone.

"They persuaded me to borrow money and then they wiped me out. I was a boob. Clara didn't know. She must never know—until afterward."

"Two thousand would save them?"

"Yes. It would pay off the trust fund and leave a little. Clara can work. She's done it before, but there mustn't be any disgrace."

The girl was on her feet.

"You coward!" she blazed. "We help poor, unfortunate souls here. But you're just a boob. I don't believe you even love your wife. You're selfish. You haven't got nerve enough to face the situation. That's all. You don't care how much you hurt—"

The door of the adjoining room flung open, and Sidney Zoom strode into the room.

"Shut up, Vera. You don't understand. You see things only from a woman's viewpoint. This is one case I can handle better." He turned to the man, whose face was now the color of a boiled beet. "You see, there's a secret telephone between these cabins. I heard every word you said. Will two thousand dollars square you and take you out of your difficulties?"

The red face nodded.

"Very well. I'll get you two thousand dollars. But I'll expect a certain service in return."

"I don't want charity."

"You won't get it. I want you to do something risky. You won't be committing any crime. You won't be in danger of jail. But you'll have to do exactly as I say."

III

"WHAT DO you want me to do?"

"There's a private banker here who owns the entire interest in a bank; it's one of the few private banking institutions in the city. He's been defrauding people who couldn't afford to be defrauded. I want to make a little collection. Will you help?"

The man tugged a nickel plated revolver from his side pocket.

"Would I need that?"

Sidney Zoom reached out a hand, took the weapon, walked to the open port hole, tossed it into the outer darkness. There sounded a sudden splash.

"No," he said, with a half smile twisting the grim mouth, "you won't need that."

"What do I do?"

Sidney Zoom spun the combination of a wall safe.

"Your name?"

"Robert Dundley."

Sidney Zoom abstracted a packet of letters. They were frayed, dog-eared envelopes, addressed to Miss Myrtle Ramsay, and the street number was that of a cheap theater. The packet was tied with a pink ribbon.

Sidney Zoom gazed at it with eyes that had softened.

"One of life's little tragedies," he said. "Miss Ramsay was a chorus girl in a burlesque. She died leaving a little girl, penniless. The public administrator auctioned off the personal property—a few clothes, a cheap suitcase, and these letters. I bought the letters."

There was silence in the room for a few moments.

"Why did you buy them?" asked Vera Thurmond.

Sidney Zoom shrugged his shoulders.

"A human document. People pay fabulous prices for old manuscripts of fiction. Here is a manuscript of fact. One George Stapleton was in love with Miss Ramsay. His letters are filled with expressions of affection for her and uncomplimentary references to his wife. Yes, Stapleton was married. It's an interesting subject for speculation, whether the chorus girl saved the letters because she intended to use them for blackmail, or whether because she loved Stapleton."

Vera Thurmond leaned forward.

"Did Mr. Stapleton bid for the letters when they were sold by the administrator?"

"Stapleton was dead. He shot himself the day after Miss Ramsay died."

There was a silence for a few minutes.

Sidney Zoom handed the packet of letters to Robert Dundley.

"To-morrow morning at precisely ten minutes past eleven you will go to the Pratt State Bank and ask for Mr. Albert Pratt. You will then give him this package of letters. He will give you ten thousand dollars in cash. You will keep three thousand dollars for your trouble. The remaining seven thousand you will distribute to these people in the amounts set opposite their names."

Sidney Zoom tore a list from a page of his notebook.

"It happens that those persons are ones who have been defrauded of various small amounts by Albert Pratt. You will refrain, however, from mentioning the reason the money is paid, or the source of that money. Simply hand to each one of those people the amount indicated."

The man's mouth sagged.

"But—what—how—"

"You will pay no attention to details. You have my assurance that you are not violating the law in any way. And you will agree that it is better to secure three thousand dollars for your wife in this manner than to have the insurance company pay her two thousand."

He took the packet of letters. Tears blinded his eyes. He held forth a groping hand, then suddenly stiffened.

"If this is another fake—" he began.

Sidney Zoom's face suddenly became hard as flint. His hawklike eyes stared into the other's face with an expression of such untamed ferocity as to make the other recoil.

"You will do exactly as I said," snapped Sidney Zoom, "and you will receive the exact amount indicated. You will answer no questions and you will ask none. You will state that you have a packet of letters to be delivered upon receipt of ten thousand dollars. Beyond that you know nothing. And now I will take you to your home."

Sidney Zoom, locking a firm hand upon the other's arm, escorted him to the float, marched him to the sedan, drove him to a taxicab stand. There he handed a driver a ten-dollar bill.

"Take this gentleman home—wherever it is," he said, and turned with no word of farewell.

Back at the boat he found Vera Thurmond regarding him with questioning eyes.

"Do you know what you are doing in this case?" she asked.

"I always know exactly what I am doing."

"You're dealing with a shrewd banker, one who knows the law. Are you certain you won't slip up upon some technicality and be guilty of crime?"

His voice remained cold, formal.

"I, too, know the law. I have specialized in legalized fraud. The law—bah! What a crude system it is! Every year they pass thousands on thousands of new laws, and still the system is deficient. The very number of laws, the very complexity of our civilization makes it easy for one who knows his way about to perpetrate frauds that are perfectly legal."

She sighed. "Do you know, I know very little about your real activities. You have never allowed me to really share in your life."

"This time you will have the chance," he assured her. "You have had some stage experience. Can you make-up like a loud-mouthed burlesque actress who is an expert on blackmail? Can you play the part of a flashy woman to whom profanity comes naturally?"

She laughed lightly.

"I would love to—if it would help *you!*"

But Sidney Zoom seemed to notice neither the softness of the tone nor the gleam of her eyes. He had whirled to his cabinet, where he kept his disguises. His fingers were busy checking over clothes and equipment.

"Take the sedan to your apartment," he said gruffly. "I'll sleep on the boat. Be back here at nine o'clock in the morning, and have some loud clothes. Better invest in some cheap perfume, too."

"But," she protested, "chorus girls aren't all like that."

"The one you're going to take the part of is," he assured her. "And, good night."

She paused, opened her mouth as though to speak, then clamped it shut.

"Good night!" she said, and whirled on her heel.

At the door she paused again. But Sidney Zoom was apparently entirely lost to his surroundings. His long, artistic fingers were busily engaged with the disguises, and his touch contained a delicacy of handling that was almost a caress.

Swiftly the girl took two steps back into the room, stooped, pulled the dog's shaggy head to her cheek, then opened the door.

"Good night," she called again.

But Sidney Zoom apparently failed to hear the words. He was adjusting a false mustache to his upper lip, trying on a pair of horn-rimmed spectacles, contemplating the result in the mirror.

IV

ALBERT PRATT rested his bony knuckles upon the mahogany desk and frowned.

"You insisted upon seeing me personally, Mr. Stapleton?"

Sidney Zoom, so perfectly disguised that his personality seemed to have entirely melted into another individual, nodded a cringing assent.

"I'm sorry to disturb you. It's most important."

And there was in his appearance just the right touch of servility to match the part he was to play. To all appearances he was a man about town who liked to pose as a lion under the white lights, who expanded his chest and boomed a welcome to prosperity, but who cringed when luck ceased to smile, whined when he was hurt.

His hair was parted in the middle, slicked down almost to his cheek bones with some oily preparation which emanated a sickly sweet odor. His eyes blinked behind a pair of massive spectacles, obviously chosen to give him an appearance of owlish wisdom. His upper lip sported a trick mustache which looked like an elongated smudge. His tie was loud, flashy; his clothes, though well tailored, were cut in the style affected by extreme youth.

Albert Pratt was familiar with the type. Ordinarily there was no money to be made from them. He cast his pale eyes over the figure in haughty disapproval.

"If it's a loan," he said in his most icy manner, "you'll have to make an application—"

He broke off as his visitor reached a well manicured hand toward an inner pocket and began pulling out money. The money was in crisp, new bills; the denominations were five hundred dollars each, and the stack which began to grow on the mahogany desk indicated that there was a small fortune in immediate cash being placed before the greedy pale eyes of Albert Pratt.

"There is a man bringing in some letters," whined Zoom in his disguise of George Stapleton. "You see, he wouldn't take any chances with them. He insisted that he'd deliver them to you in person and you could deliver him the money."

"Ah, yes," purred Albert Pratt. "Letters, letters, eh?"

"Yes. Letters."

"Ah, yes, yes, indeed, letters. Oh, yes. And you're to pay how much for them?"

"Ten thousand dollars."

Albert Pratt extended his bony hands. The avaricious fingers curled about the sheaf of currency.

"Five, ten, fifteen, twenty—Why, there's an even fifty thousand dollars here, Mr. Stapleton!"

The man leaned forward, lowered his voice.

"I know it. The man who has those letters doesn't know how absolutely vital they are. My wife is ready to sue me for divorce, and I have over a million and a half involved. And this girl is threatening a suit for breach of promise, and she could collect a hundred thousand at the least.

"I've made a very advantageous bargain over the telephone. The letters are to be returned to me for ten thousand dollars. But, if anything should go wrong, I've simply got to have those letters. That's why I want to leave the extra forty thousand. Then, if there's any hitch, I can instruct you over the telephone to go higher and you'll have the money available."

Albert Pratt lowered calculating lids over his pale eyes. His tongue licked his wire-thin lips.

"Ah, yes," he murmured, and his tone showed keen mental concentration.

"I'll make a deposit of the money. Then I'll leave you a check payable to cash for ten thousand dollars. If there should be any hitch I'll send down another check for the balance, or so much of it as may be necessary."

Pratt nodded.

"But how about the letters? Shouldn't you identify them in some way before I pay over the check?"

Stapleton shook his head.

"Myrtle Ramsay is a hard baby to deal with when she's sore, but she's square as a cornerstone. When she says she'll deliver those letters, she'll deliver 'em. And she won't jump the price, either, but—well, if anything *should* go wrong, I'd like to have the money right here where we can deal with it."

"Those letters are worth more than ten thousand, eh?"

"I'll say so. I'm willing to give fifty if necessary, and I guess I'd give a hundred if I had to."

Pratt nodded.

"And the—er—collector, wouldn't do business at your bank, eh?"

"No. He insisted upon the deal being made through this private bank."

"I take it Miss Ramsay will not make the collection in person?"

"No. It'll probably be Robert Dundley who makes the deal."

Albert Pratt placed the tips of his fingers together.

"It's really blackmail. You know, we could have a detective in here, and save that money—"

Stapleton shuddered, placed his hands before his face.

"No, no! Good heavens, no! Nothing like that! That would mean publicity. I can't stand publicity."

"Where can I reach you, Mr. Stapleton—just in case things shouldn't go right?"

The visitor handed over a card with a telephone number.

"I'll be waiting right there at that telephone. I can get over here in three minutes from the time you ring me, if it's necessary."

Albert Pratt sighed, the sigh of perfect contentment which comes to a cat that has just found a pitcher of rich cream.

"I think it can be attended to. It's rather irregular, Mr. Stapleton, but we'll handle it—for a consideration, of course. Come this way, and we'll open an account and you can give me your check."

The details disposed of, George Stapleton extended a flabby hand.

"You won't forget the telephone number?" he inquired, anxiously.

"Most certainly *not*," assured Albert Pratt, the pale-eyed banker, and there was a wealth of sincerity in his booming tone for the first time during the interview.

Stapleton nodded.

"I didn't think you would," he muttered cryptically, bowed, and walked rapidly through the front door of the bank.

The clock on the wall showed exactly ten minutes to eleven.

Albert Pratt walked back into his private office, chuckling to himself, rubbing his bony hands together.

"Forget the telephone number, indeed!" muttered Albert Pratt to himself, then banged the private door which closed him in his palatially furnished office.

V

THE CLOCK shifted to ten minutes past eleven.

Robert Dundley entered the bank, his face pale, his mouth taut with determination. In his hand was a package of letters tied with a pink ribbon. From the package there came the faint odor of perfume.

"Mr. Pratt?" he asked of a clerk.

"Right this way," soothed the deferential clerk, and led the way to Albert Pratt's private office.

"I've got some letters to be delivered. I get ten thousand dollars for 'em," said Dundley, using the toneless voice of one who recites a well rehearsed speech.

"Let me see them."

Pratt extended his greedy hands, scrutinized the letters, the addresses, looked at the postmarks, cancelled stamps, stretched his razor-edged mouth into a smile.

"Ah, yes," he said, summoned a clerk.

"Cash this check and get the gentleman ten thousand dollars," he said.

The clerk brought in the money, handed it to Dundley.

That individual tried to count it, but nervousness made his hands tremble until they refused to function.

"I guess it's right," he said, thrust the money into his coat pocket, arose from the chair, made a short bow and dived for the door.

Ten thousand dollars! It had not all been some dream then; the words of the mysterious yachtsman had been true. He was to get three thousand, and the balance was to be distributed as instructed. But three thousand went for himself, his wife and daughter.

As the realization gripped him, he sprinted for the outer door.

Behind him, Mr. Albert Pratt sucked his lips into his mouth as he gave a dry chuckle. Then he proceeded to untie the pink ribbon and read the letters.

They were warm letters, letters that would make a jury lean forward on chair edges. They were the sort of letters that sound damning in a court room, look foolish in print, only seem natural when tied with scented pink ribbon.

Carefully, giving close attention to contents, Albert Pratt picked out two of the most lurid of the letters and dropped them into a desk drawer. Those two letters contained, in essence, all that the rest of the packet contained.

Then Mr. Pratt retied the package with the scented pink ribbon and reached for the telephone.

"Ah, Mr. Stapleton," he purred, when the connection had been made. "It gives me pleasure to report that your little matter has been entirely closed in accordance with your instructions, and I didn't have to go above the ten thousand dollars, either."

"I'll be there in three minutes!" yelled Mr. George Stapleton, his voice a crescendo of joy, and slammed up the telephone.

In fact, he beat his estimated time by thirty seconds.

Puffing, breathless, his face beaming, eyes blinking rapidly behind his owlish glasses, he reached for the letters, clasped them in eager hands.

Albert Pratt watched him with cold, pale eyes.

Stapleton untied the ribbon, glanced through the letters, nodded eagerly.

"Yes, yes—these are the ones. What a fool I was to write them! But ... Good God! No! ... It can't be ... Why ..."

Albert Pratt leaned forward, suave, courteous.

"Something wrong?" he inquired with just the right trace of impersonal concern.

"Two—two letters missing," stuttered George Stapleton.

The banker tilted back in his swivel chair, nodded gently as though his judgment had been confirmed in a matter that was of no moment to him.

"I thought you might find something like that. You'll remember I suggested the letters should be identified in some way before I handed over the money. But you were positive that this Miss Ramsay would be a square shooter! 'As square as a cornerstone' was the expression you used, I believe."

Stapleton sighed, then flung his head forward on his arms.

"Good heavens! What will that mean? Those two letters are as damning as the other eight."

Pratt nodded.

"Probably more so. When you start dealing with blackmailers, you must be on your guard."

"What shall I do? What shall I do? What shall I do?" asked Stapleton, his voice rising to a note that was almost hysterical.

Albert Pratt sighed.

"Return to your office. You'll probably hear from the blackmailers soon. It will cost you money. But you can rest assured that's all it will cost you. You're too good a thing to lose. They'll shake you down for another thousand or two. Probably they'll let you off for a thousand dollars a letter."

Stapleton got to his feet in a daze.

"I'd pay fifty thousand if I had to," he muttered. "I still have forty thousand on deposit here, and I can get more."

"Tut, tut," warned Mr. Pratt, "you're talking foolishness. If they gave you the letters for ten thousand and only held out two, it's likely they'll fix an outside price of an additional three thousand dollars. You're all wrought up. Go back to your office. I have your telephone number. If anything happens I'll let you know. A Mr. Dundley brought in the letters. I believe you said it was Mr. Dundley who would bring them. Perhaps he was the one who took out the two letters?" Pratt's tone was politely inquiring.

"No," said Stapleton, reluctantly. "It must have been Myrtle herself. Dundley hasn't sense enough."

"You can't ever tell," said Pratt.

Stapleton shook his head.

"No. It was Myrtle. I'll get her on the telephone if I can."

The banker's shake of the head was more crisply positive than any gesture he had made.

"I'm quite sure it was Dundley. I can read character, and that young man had something he was concealing. You should have followed my advice and left me a list of the letters. As it is, return to your office. I'll telephone if I hear anything. Be sure you don't leave your telephone for a moment. This is important."

"Of course," promised Stapleton, and went out, the packet of letters clutched in a moist palm.

VI

ALBERT PRATT watched him go with that peculiar synthetic smile twisting the corners of his lips yet not changing for a moment the calculating expression of the pale eyes.

Ten minutes later he clapped on his hat and left the building.

He took a cab for half a mile, walked into a public pay station, called the number which Stapleton had given him.

"Hello," he said, when he heard Stapleton's answer, and disguising his own voice as much as possible. "You know who this is?"

"No," said Stapleton's anxious voice. "Who is it?"

"Never mind who. It's a man who has two letters of yours, addressed to Miss Myrtle Ramsay, all in your writing, signed by you. Those letters are for sale."

"Who are you?" yelled Stapleton.

"Never mind. Do you want to buy the letters?"

"I'll give two thousand for them," said Stapleton.

A hollow laugh was his answer.

"Come again. Just because Myrtle's a fool is no sign I am. Those letters will cost you forty thousand dollars—cash!"

"No, no!" groaned Stapleton.

"All right. I'll offer them to your wife's lawyer then. I could get more money from him, anyway. I was just being a good sport and letting you off easy."

There was a period of tense silence. The wire vibrated and buzzed. At length it transmitted a sigh which came from the Stapleton end of the line.

"How would I get the letters?"

"Same way you got the others. They were left at some bank, weren't they?"

"Yes."

"What bank was it?"

"As though you didn't know!"

"No, I don't know. I'm an independent operator who horned in on the deal. You'll

have to tell me the name of the bank. I'm willing to take a chance on you shooting
square. You did this morning with Myrtle. You should this afternoon with me."

"It's the Pratt Bank, and you'll ask for Mr. Albert Pratt," said Stapleton.

"Wait a minute," muttered Pratt. "I'll have to write that down. Pratt Bank, eh?
How do you spell it? ... P-R-A-T-T, eh? All right, I've got it. I'll take the letters over.
This guy Pratt honest?"

"Yes," answered Stapleton. "If I'd taken his advice I wouldn't have been in this
pickle. He's protecting my interests, but you can trust him to do what he says he will."

"All right," grinned Pratt. "When will you get over there?"

"I've got a conference with my wife's lawyer in ten minutes. It'll be two thirty
before I can make it. But you be sure and take the letters over there right away. I'll get
down just as soon as I can."

"All right. Forty thousand bucks, cash, and no funny stuff!" warned Pratt, and
hung up the telephone.

Then he called the bank of which he was the head, talked with the girl at the
telephone desk.

"Listen, Sadie, a fellow's going to call up for me right away. Don't tell him I'm out.
Tell him I'm busy talking on the other telephone, but that you'll have me call as soon
as I'm at liberty. Get that? G'-by."

And Albert Pratt sprinted from the booth, climbed in a cab and made time back to
his bank.

The telephone girl greeted him with a wise smile.

"That fellow called you twice. I told him you were still talking. Want him?"

"Yeah. That's a good kid. You rate a box of candy on that, Sadie."

Whereupon Albert Pratt passed into his private office, picked up the telephone
and heard Stapleton's voice.

"I've been trying to get you for ten minutes, but you were talking."

"Yes, a very important call from a stockbroker. You've heard something from
your people?"

"Yes. They've stuck me for forty thousand dollars!"

"What? You're crazy!"

"No, no. This chap who called knew his business. He threatened to take the letters
to my wife's attorney, and I couldn't have that. It would have nicked me for half a
million."

"I see," remarked Albert Pratt. "Well, of course, you know your own business
best. Personally, I'd have told 'em to go to the devil. But you're fully decided to pay
the forty thousand dollars?"

"Yes, yes! Now this fellow's going to bring the letters in to you and leave 'em with
you. I can't get down right away. He's a new party, some one I don't know. I don't
even know how he got the letters; but I'm playing a little foxy with him. He's going to
leave them with you. I told him he could trust you. Now I want you to be sure they
are the missing two letters. Look at the handwriting and everything, will you?"

"Certainly, Mr. Stapleton, but you'll understand I'll have to protect the interests of both parties. Much as I despise all forms of blackmail, if this chap leaves any letters with me to be held until you pay forty thousand dollars, I'll have to demand the forty thousand before I turn them over. You appreciate my position in that, don't you?"

"Of course. Hang it, man, I *want* to pay forty thousand for those letters. When I get them I'll be the most relieved man in the world. Don't worry about that, but get the letters."

"Very well," said Mr. Pratt with a cold smile. "I'll keep you advised." And he hung up the telephone.

"Going to lunch," he informed the chief clerk.

Mr. Albert Pratt treated himself to a very good lunch, and returned to the bank at one o'clock. Ten minutes later he called Mr. George Stapleton on the telephone.

"The chap has just left those letters," he said. "And they're the letters all right. I tried to beat him down a few thousand, but he wouldn't come down a penny. He seemed a mighty tough customer, and I guess you did the wise thing. I'm holding them until you can check out the forty thousand; and then he's left positive, but confidential, instructions as to what I'm to do with the forty thousand."

"I'll be there inside of half an hour!" yelled Stapleton. "I'm sorry you even tried to beat him down. Almost anything might have happened, and I must have those letters, simply *must* have them. My wife's attorney would wring the last cent out of me if he even knew of them."

And Sidney Zoom hung up the telephone, nodded to the girl who waited at his side.

"Go down and strut your stuff, Miss Thurmond. You look great. Now see if you can act the part."

And Vera Thurmond, attired in the garb of a flashy burlesque actress, one of the type who stops at nothing, nodded eagerly and made for the door.

VII

ALBERT PRATT looked up as the brass doorknob turned.

The mahogany door of his private office swung inward, and there came to his nostrils the assault of cheap perfume copiously applied.

"This is a private office!" rasped Albert Pratt.

"Go sit on a tack!" retorted the short-skirted female who strode into the office, slammed the door behind her, and dropped into a chair.

One leg crossed over the other, disclosing the top of a meshwork stocking, a liberal expanse of bare flesh. The reddened lips were fairly dripping paint. The cheeks were crimson, and the eyes flashed. The heaving bosom could be seen beneath the filmy waist.

"What a hell of a guy you turned out to be," she snorted.

Albert Pratt reached a bony finger for a button.

"Don't do that," snorted the woman. "Wait till you hear the stuff I gotta spill and you won't let your finger get within a million miles of that button. Press it an' you're goin' to jail!"

Albert Pratt hesitated.

"Who are you?" he asked.

"Myrtle Ramsay!"

The banker's face paled slightly. He stiffened in his seat.

"And you want?"

"Those two letters you snitched on me this morning."

Albert Pratt pressed the tips of his fingers firmly together. His lips clamped into a line of grim determination.

"Those two letters were taken by some person whom I do not know. They have been placed with me in an escrow for the payment of money."

The girl elevated one knee as she scraped a match across the sole of her foot, applied the flame to a cigarette which was placed between her vivid lips.

"Horse radish!" she said. "Bob Dundley brought in the whole ten letters. He'll swear to it and I'll swear to it. I was outside waiting in the car. I seen him come in, an' I seen him come out. Don't think Mrs. Ramsay raised no foolish children by the name of Myrtle who would trust any Bob Dundley with ten thousand berries of her money."

Pratt shook his head.

"There's a mistake somewhere."

"You're damn tootin' there's a mistake. You made it when you lifted those two letters. They call that by an ugly name down at the district attorney's office. You fork over those two letters an' be damned speedy about it, too."

Pratt shook his head, not quite so emphatically as he had before, but, nevertheless, in a strong negative.

"No. They are held in trust."

The woman blew out a cloud of smoke, reached for the telephone.

"All right. I'll just call your bluff, you bat-eared, white-eyed bum. I'll just call up Papa Stapleton and tell him not to worry, that I'll swear the letters are forgeries if anybody tries to use 'em. If you're holding 'em for some one else, you just turn 'em back to that bozo, an' tell him he's goin' to be arrested for blackmail if he even tries to use those letters.

"Old Stapleton was a luke-warm daddy, but he used me square when he decorated the mahogany with the ten grand. That's the price I made, an' that's the price I stick to. I'm a woman of my word. Maybe I could have got more with a breach of promise suit, but juries don't figure much heart balm for a poor jane that has to work the chorus of a burlesque—"

And the woman lifted the receiver from the hook.

Albert Pratt's hand crushed down upon the hook, stopped the connection. There were beads of perspiration on his forehead.

"Listen," he soothed. "You want money. Here's your chance. Take five thousand dollars and walk out of town for an afternoon."

Her eyes narrowed.

"Applesauce. It's worth twice that. Gimme the telephone, or have I gotta call a cop?"

"All right," hastily agreed the agonized banker, with a swift glance at the clock. "I'll give you the ten thousand. But get out of here and lay low."

She got to her feet, nodded.

"It's a rotten trick, but a workin' girl has gotta take the breaks as she gets 'em. Fork over the ten grand."

It took exactly one minute and thirty-eight seconds for Albert Pratt to produce the money and bow his unwelcome visitor to the door.

There followed an interval of fifteen minutes, and then Sidney Zoom, still disguised as the fictitious Mr. George Stapleton, entered the bank.

Albert Pratt welcomed him with a cordial handshake, ushered him into the inner office, produced a check made out to "cash" in the sum of forty thousand dollars, flipped the two letters from his desk drawer.

"Just sign there, and I'll turn over the letters," he said. "After all, I guess you were right. These letters are pretty purple. They'd wreck you if they ever got out."

George Stapleton beamed at him.

"Would you believe it? I made a settlement with the wife. Her attorney relented just after you telephoned. I settled with her for forty thousand dollars. And that means I don't care a hoot about the letters."

VIII

ALBERT PRATT clutched the edge of the desk.

"But Myrtle Ramsay! How about her breach of promise suit?"

"Nonsense!" said his visitor. "Myrtle Ramsay is a gold digger, but she's square as a cornerstone. When she sets her price she'll abide by it. She said ten thousand dollars, and she got the ten thousand dollars. Congratulate me, Pratt. I feel like a new man. Hang it, you don't seem pleased!"

And Stapleton extended his hand, a frown of puzzled perplexity on his features.

Albert Pratt took a deep breath, extended a moist, limp lump of flesh.

"But the letters, those damning, purple, passionate, foolish letters! What'll I do with them?"

"They're left with you as an escrow holder?"

"Yes, for forty thousand. Of course, the man might take less, perhaps twenty thousand, possibly even fifteen."

Stapleton gave a glad laugh.

"Forget it. Hand him back the letters on a silver platter. Tell him to frame 'em and hang 'em in the city hall if he wants to. What the devil do I care. I've made a settlement with the wife. I gave her a check on my account here. That cleans it up. We're all quits."

Albert Pratt's trained mind, skilled in chicanery, suddenly clicked the parts of the puzzle into a perfect picture. He lunged forward. His clutching fingers caught the horn-rimmed glasses, jerked them off. His other hand clutched the trick mustache, tore it loose from the upper lip.

"Framed!" he yelled. "Defrauded. I can have you arrested for criminal conspiracy. You're not George Stapleton at all, and that woman was a confederate!"

And Sidney Zoom, straightened to his full height, letting his cold hawk-like eyes bore into the pale orbs of the banker, nodded.

"I didn't care much for this disguise, anyway," he said, "but I had to look the part of a sucker."

And his hands, going to his head, slipped off the oily, perfumed wig he wore.

"My name is Zoom! Sidney Zoom, at your service. A specialist in legalized fraud, a subject, by the way, to which I understand you have devoted much of your life, Mr. Pratt."

The banker stared at him with eyes that were as palely inexpressive as twin clam shells fished from a chowder.

"Specialist in what?"

"Legalized frauds, those little chicaneries by which a man can take advantage of his fellow mortal, yet be well within the law."

"Legalized fiddlesticks! If I can't convict you of criminal conspiracy in this case I'll go out of the banking business."

Sidney Zoom perched his tall frame upon a corner of the desk, reached for a cigarette. His eyes were now as hard as those of a swooping hawk.

"Yes? Well, think again. You'll have to admit the theft of two letters before you can make out any case. And that will convict you of larceny to start with. In the second place, there was no wrongful act on my part. I merely deposited money with which to redeem certain letters that were being delivered by a confederate. In other words I was merely buying letters from myself.

"You were the one that committed the crime, and you were the one that did the conspiring. You paid the young lady ten thousand dollars to keep quiet about your theft of the letters. Try that on your thinking apparatus and see if you can get the answer without turning to the back of the book."

And get the answer Albert Pratt undoubtedly did, for his mouth sagged open. He swallowed painfully a couple of times, then raised his eyes to confront the rigid forefinger of Sidney Zoom, jabbing into his necktie.

"And this is just a warning. As I mentioned, I specialize in legalized fraud. I know a hundred ways by which I can take money from you, yet never violate the letter of the law. I specialize in lost souls, and you've contributed your share. You with your damned rediscount company and your bum stocks. Sit still! Move and I'll alter your features so the directors won't know you when you try to preside at the next meeting!

"I've had my eye on you for some time. This little visit is long overdue. I'm taking ten thousand dollars as a warning. That money is being given, three thousand to a deserving applicant, seven thousand toward making partial restitution to some of the fellows you've charged illegal interest, wiped out their little savings with bum stock deals. You've got a chance to turn over a new leaf right now. If you don't, I shall call again. And the next time your fine will be twenty thousand dollars!"

Albert Pratt rubbed a bony forefinger around the inside of his collar. Then he laughed, a hollow, mirthless laugh.

"Well, if you're counting on getting any of the ten thousand dollars from the woman who got it from me, you've got another guess coming. I happen to know something of her type of woman. She may be a confederate, but she'll skip out with the ten grand."

Sidney Zoom thrust his face close to that of the banker.

"That young woman," he snapped, "is just like I told you—as square as a cornerstone. Think that over, and keep this to remember me by."

And Sidney Zoom swung his open hand from the vicinity of his hip, hard, forward.

The open palm struck the banker's cheek with such force that it sounded like the crack of a miniature pistol.

Albert Pratt staggered back, got to his feet, his pale eyes flabby with fear.

"I shall call an officer!" he threatened.

Sidney Zoom laughed in his face.

"Call out the reserves, you cheap crook," he said, and then slammed the door, leaving the private banker alone with his thoughts and his smarting face; leaving him with the knowledge that he had no redress, either civil or criminal. He had been outsmarted by a past master in the art of legalized fraud.

BORROWED BULLETS

CHAPTER I

A Fight on the Wharf

SIDNEY ZOOM turned the wheel of the *Alberta F.* hard to star-board.

The yacht swung in a sweeping curve through the dark water of the bay. The lighted ferry slips, backed by blinking electric signs advertising half a dozen national products, were blotted out by a projecting wharf.

In their place loomed the black hulks of towering freighters, massive wharves against which the little wavelets slapped invisible fingers.

Here and there, one of the big boats was preparing for sea. Half-naked men toiled like white beetles in the glare of incandescents. Donkey engines rattled, cables clanked against metal spars. But for the most part the black hulls of the boats towered in dark silence.

Sidney Zoom turned to the figure at his side—a young woman, well formed, alert, vital.

"Looking for someone?" she asked.

Sidney Zoom thrust forward his grim features. The hawklike eyes peered into the darkness.

"The Willmoto," he said. "I want to see Captain McGahan. You'll get a kick out of him, Vera. Most efficient captain in the coastal service. Gets more cargo aboard in less time, moves more freight faster with less crew—"

He broke off.

Over the chug of the engines, through the damp darkness of the waterfront, there sounded a scream. It was the scream of a woman in terror.

Sidney Zoom slammed the throttle shut, kicked out the clutch.

In the comparative silence the scream sounded the second time, knifing the darkness of the yacht's pilot house. It was followed by the sound of a masculine laugh, and that laugh contained many emotions other than humor.

"There!"

The girl's arm pointed and Sidney Zoom's gaze followed the direction of the outstretched finger.

46

A little knot of struggling forms cast grotesque black shadows out on the end of one of the piers. Back of them showed a freighter, getting ready for sea. All the hatches were loaded except number four, and the donkey engines were busily clattering supplies into that hold. The lights were concentrated upon the section of the freighter that was being loaded. For the rest, the boat was dark and silent.

Sidney Zoom twisted the spokes of the wheel. In his eyes showed a sudden lust of conflict. At his side, in the darkness, came the sound of a low growl, and a tawny police dog, a bulking shadow of ominous strength, got to his feet and stood braced, shoulders low and forward.

"Steady, Rip," warned Sidney Zoom. "I'll handle this. Hold her against that pier head. Vera. There's a rope ladder there. No, no, not so far over. There it is, right on the end. Throw her into reverse as you make the swing. Then stand by."

And Sidney Zoom was out of the pilot house, on to the deck of the yacht in four swift strides that sounded merely as rapid thumps upon the planking. He went to the rail, paused, leaped out into the darkness.

His long arms swung his weight into the night as his hands clenched the rungs of the rope ladder. The yacht swung around, then bumped into the pilings of the wharf and flung clear.

Sidney Zoom went up the ladder, all angles, like a huge jumping-jack, yet with the swift efficiency of a climbing monkey.

The struggle was over when he reached the pier. Three men were carrying some limp object which might have been a sack of meal, but was not.

Sidney Zoom padded purposefully through the half darkness.

A masculine voice, coming in irregular spasms of sound, after the manner of a man who is talking after a struggle, reached his ears. "... so damned anxious ... to travel ... let her travel."

"We can't help it if she stows away," said another.

And then there was another laugh, coarse, primitive.

"Gentlemen," said Sidney Zoom.

They whirled at the sound.

"Just a moment," said Sidney Zoom.

The men set their burden to the wharf.

"Well?" rasped one of the group.

"I heard a woman scream," Zoom said.

"You're a liar," said one of the men, and rushed.

The other two followed, spread out a bit, one on either side. They came in, crouching low, men who had learned the advantage of being close to the ground in a rough-and-tumble.

These were no amateur fighters, but men who had learned the art of conflict in various ports of the world. The science of the padded gloves was not for them; rather, had they mastered the little tricks of the trade that were dirty, but effective. A trick with the knee, a bit of shoulder stuff, a butting with the head, and all combined with a swift aggression of purposeful silence that had been the result of long and bitter experience.

The leader reckoned without the terrific length of arm which had fooled more than one antagonist. His head snapped back as Zoom's fist crashed out. Then the other two closed and the planks of the pier thudded to the rapid tattoo of swift conflict.

The struggling knot of figures milled into a circle.

There was the sound of a terrific impact and one of the men staggered backward and out of the circle. For what seemed a long breath he paused teetering on the edge of the pier, then he vanished into the night. An appreciable interval later, there sounded the noise of a terrific splash.

The other two drew back, hesitated, then charged again.

The inert figure that had been lowered to the wharf by the three men at the challenge of Sidney Zoom, stirred, got to its feet, ran blindly toward the struggling figures, veered off.

Sidney Zoom's voice sounded from the midst of the mêlée.

"There's a rope ladder at the end. Go down it to the yacht."

But the running figure seemed in a daze. It dashed to the end of the pier, flung itself outward, and again came the noise of a splash.

The three figures separated for a split second. Zoom's fist thudded home. A man staggered backward, wobbled, charged blindly once more.

In the interval, however, there had sounded twin thuds. The third combatant had reeled away, and Sidney Zoom, running lightly, made for the end of the pier.

He went out into the darkness in a long arc of graceful motion. Down, down, down ... a vast sea of black before him, a splash, the cold waters of the bay hissing past him, then a few swift strokes as he fought his way to the surface.

The *Alberta F.* was almost on top of him as he came up into the dark night. He could see her white sides, the knife-like overhang of her bow. He swung to his side, kicked out, made a long, powerful stroke, and shot to the side.

"He's right over there behind you, sir," said the voice of one of the crew, standing in white watchfulness against the rail of the yacht.

Sidney Zoom caught the ripple of water, the sound of hands beating frantically, and went to the place from which those sounds emanated, in a racing flurry of overhand strokes.

His questing fingers caught a woolen garment just as a rope snaked through the darkness and splashed to the water within an arm's length.

"Okay," said Sidney Zoom, clutching the garment with one hand and the rope with the other, "pull away."

The rope tightened. The yacht loomed again. Strong hands clutched and heaved, and they had her on the deck, a bedraggled figure clad in men's rough clothes. But the clothes had been torn almost to shreds. It did not need the revealing clutch of the moist garments to show that here was no man at all, but a young woman whose right eye was swollen nearly shut and growing very, very black.

She sat up and spat out salt water, loked at Sidney Zoom with her single good eye, and grinned.

"Thanks," she said, "for the buggy ride."

Sidney Zoom smiled, and there was approval in that smile.

"If you'll go into that cabin," he said, "Miss Vera Thurmond, my secretory, will see that you have dry clothes."

She got to her feet, clutched at the hand rail on the top of the cabin for support, turned back to Sidney Zoom.

"Okay," she said, and entered the cabin.

Sidney Zoom walked to the pilot house.

"Clothes, sir?" asked one of the men.

"Can wait, Johnson. I'm taking her into the mooring float. Get the lines ready. Make her fast when I come up alongside. The tide's running fast, so I'll come in with it on the port bow. Get the bow line first. The tide will swing in the stern."

"Aye, aye, sir."

The door of the pilot house slammed. The deep throated motors purred into coughing life and the yacht slipped through the dark waters in a long circle of increasing speed. The lights of the ferry slips showed once more. The blinking electric signs threw varicolored reflections upon the waters. A ferry boomed a hoarse warning.

The yacht crossed the ferry lanes, swung into the more gloomy channel, and nosed its way past the small craft moorings to bump against the mooring float maintained by Sidney Zoom.

Lines thudded. The motors idled. Feet ran along the booming planks, and a voice from the darkness shouted, "All fast, sir."

CHAPTER II

An Ungrateful Rescue

SIDNEY ZOOM cut off the motor, the lights, turned on the cabin lights, and started for the locker where he kept dry clothes. His feet squashed water with every step, and the pilot house was steeped with that peculiar smell which comes from woolen wet with salt water.

Feet on the deck. The door was flung open, and Sidney Zoom found himself gazing at the business end of a squat automatic. Over the blued steel gleamed the almost shut right eye of the girl he had rescued. It was, by this time, turning a livid bruise color.

"All right, all right," rasped the girl. "D'you think I've got all night. Get 'em up— and be quick about it."

Sidney Zoom's hawklike eyes challenged the glittering eye that bored into his over the barrel of the automatic.

"That," he said, indicating the weapon with a toss of his head, "is not at all necessary— here."

"*Will* you get 'em up," asked the girl, "or have I got to spatter you all over the cabin?"

Sidney Zoom smiled.

"If you put it that way, I'll get 'em up," he said, and did so.

"All right," rasped the voice of his visitor, "now get away from that locker and let me get some man's clothes. Make any hostile moves and you'll get drilled."

Sidney Zoom moved away from the locker. There was in his eyes a glint of appreciation.

"If you want anything I can give you, you don't need—"

"Shut up!" she snapped, and threw open the locker.

"My own clothes are far too big," said Sidney Zoom, from the opposite end of the pilot house, "but there's an assortment of yachting flannels over there on the left. Some of them will fit you."

She reached gropingly in the closet with her left hand, her right holding the gun. She pulled out an assortment of garments and dumped them on the floor. Still covering the owner of the yacht, she pushed the garments with a bare foot until she found trousers, coat and shirt that suited her.

"Don't move," she warned, and started to strip off the soaked rags which covered her.

Zoom noticed that, beneath the outer garments of the male, she had the finest of sheer silks, lingerie that had been tailored to order from the finest materials.

"I can go out," he ventured.

"You can stand right there, and keep 'em up!"

She kicked aside the soggy outer garments, gazed ruefully at the wet undersilks. And Sidney Zoom saw that there was a money belt circling her slender waist.

She fumbled with the pockets of that belt, took out a packet of gold backed currency. She unfolded it, and Sidney Zoom's eyes widened as he glimpsed the figure on the corner of the outer bill.

"That didn't get so wet," she remarked. "Any underwear in that place?"

"In the drawer below," said Zoom.

"All right. I've got to take a chance on you. Turn your back, keep your hands up. Don't look and—"

She never finished the sentence.

The door of the pilot house shook to the impact of a great weight. The girl turned the weapon toward it. There was a fumbling with the catch, the knob turned, then a moment's silence.

"I'll shoot!" warned the girl.

The door crashed open. The girl fired, breast high, the ruddy flame spurting in a stabbing streak of vicious death, straight toward where the heart of a man would have been.

But it was no man that shot through that door, rather low to the ground, fangs bared; but a tawny police dog. The bullet thudded over his head as he rushed. A low, throaty growl came from his great jaws.

Sidney Zoom sprang forward.

"Down, Rip!" he roared, and grabbed for the dog.

But the animal was already in the air, red lips twisted back from gleaming white fangs as he shot like a released arrow, straight for the girl's throat.

But, at the command, he turned his head slightly. The girl flung up an arm. Then Zoom, the dog and the girl all collided at the same time in one confused impact of thudding motion that hit the floor and churned about in a heap.

From that heap came the form of Sidney Zoom, pulling and tugging. Next emerged the tawny police dog, his claws scraping along the floor of the pilot house. The girl sat up, looked at the dog, then at Sidney Zoom, and grinned.

"You win," she remarked, and fainted.

Sidney Zoom frowned at the dog.

"Back, Rip, and stay there. Now watch! Guard! Careful."

And then Sidney Zoom went through the door with swift strides, down the dark deck and into the cabin where he had left his secretary.

She was neatly bound and gagged, lying on the bed, her face red with rage and humiliation, her eyes glittering over the silken scarf that had been used as a gag.

Zoom slit the bonds, untied the scarf.

"The little devil!" exclaimed Vera Thurmond, sitting up on the bed.

Sidney Zoom grinned.

"I'm commencing to like her. I'm sick of these namby pamby women that are quitters. This girl looks like one that'd give a man a run for his money."

"Go to her then!" snapped his secretary, and there was in her voice more than impatience, more than rage. There was a trace of jealousy. But if Sidney Zoom noticed it he gave no sign.

"You all right?" he asked.

"Of course."

"Atta girl!" he remarked, and started toward the pilot house. At the door he paused.

"How did she do it—cover you with a gun?"

"Cover me with nothing!" snapped his secretary. "The little spitfire hit me over the head with something when I wasn't looking!"

Still grinning, Zoom gently closed the door and went into the pilot house.

The girl was conscious now, sitting up staring at the dog. And the dog, muzzle on paws, yellow eyes slitted to a savage glare of wolf-like menace, was growling throatily.

"Sorry if you were frightened," said Sidney Zoom. "He'll only guard you. He won't hurt you unless you try to escape."

"Yes," she said, "I found that out. I experimented. Give me a chance to put on some clothes and then you can ring the police."

The door opened and Vera Thurmond came in, looking rather dishevelled.

"Sorry," grinned the girl. "I was gambling for big things and I didn't want to take any chances. I guess I did crack you a little hard."

Vera Thurmond's eyes were unsmiling.

"I've got a beastly headache," she said.

The girl on the floor stretched forth a shapely limb.

"Headache's nothing. Look at those bruises. And you aren't seeing 'em all, not by a long ways."

Vera Thurmond glanced at the livid skin, and swift sympathy flooded her warm eyes.

She turned on Sidney Zoom.

"Get out," she said. "Let the girl dress, and take the dog with you!"

The girl reached for some white duck trousers.

"Oh, that's all right," she said. "He's a good scout, and the dog's all right, too. He just did his duty."

She slid her limbs into the white trousers, reached for a shirt.

"You're all wet underneath!" exclaimed Vera Thurmond.

"They'll dry out. Go ahead. Get the police and let's get it over with."

Vera Thurmond shook her head.

"We don't call the police—not from this yacht."

"What?"

Sidney Zoom replied to the girl's startled question.

"I'm tired of civilization. I hate the routine, the whole damned money-grubbing machine of treadmill existence! The police be damned! I sympathize with the unfortunate. I avoid the prosperous. Some day, I hope, there'll be a change. In the meantime I spend much of my life on the water. There, at least, I'm comparatively free—on the high seas."

The girl's left eye had widened in wonder. The swelling on the right had gone down sufficiently so there showed a little glittering slit beneath a circle of livid black.

"You mean—I'm not arrested?"

Zoom waved his hand toward the dark windows of the pilot house.

"Take dry clothes and go—out into the night. Or stay, and tell me your troubles. Perhaps I can help."

She sat, white, shaken, startled.

Sidney Zoom motioned with his hand.

"Go to her, Rip, old boy. She's afraid of you."

The dog arose from his crouching position, stalked toward the girl, sank to the floor and thrust his muzzle against the cold fingers.

She patted his head, stroked his ears, and the dog, moved by some intuitive understanding which is the heritage of well bred dogs, thrust his head upon her lap, snuggled down and thumped the floor with his tail.

She grasped the shaggy neck and began to cry, suddenly straightened and stared at the others with moist eyes.

CHAPTER III

Wanted—For Murder

"I'M NOT a cry-baby. I'll take my medicine. I've been through hell the last twenty-four hours. I'm Eve Bendley."

Vera Thurmond gasped.

"Not *the* Eve Bendley?"

The moist eyes regarded Sidney Zoom's secretary with smoldering hostility.

"Yes, *the* Eve Bendley. I'm the one that the police want for murder. You should have guessed it sooner."

Sidney Zoom nodded.

"Would you care," he asked, "to tell us the details?"

She shrugged her shoulders, hugged the dog's head to her breast.

"Why not? They'll be all over the newspapers. You wouldn't dare to protect me—not one wanted for murder. And I'm tired of hiding.

"I guess you know all the preliminaries. I was confidential secretary to Ralph C. Ames for five years. I believe I'm related to him by marriage. He was an old man, lovable when you understood him, but a bit of a tyrant at times.

"He didn't have any natural heirs, and he left a will that was to have given me rather a large sum of money. I don't know how much. The bulk of his fortune was left to charity; but I understood there was more than two hundred thousand left me under the will.

"Then this adventuress came along. The old man fell head over heels in love with her. That is, he fell for her line of talk. You know the one I mean, Nettie Pease.

"I tried to warn him against her. She was nothing but a peroxide adventuress. That made a scene. He threatened to discharge me, leave me without a cent and all that. And then he went out in a rage, came back and announced he had married the woman.

"She was with him, leering at me. He left the room and she told me where we stood—quick. She said I was out of sympathy with her, and that I could get out and stay out. You see Mr. Ames had his office in his house, and I was treated as one of the family, living under the same roof, handling his mail, helping the housekeeper run the house.

"When Mr. Ames came back he explained to me I was discharged, that I could take two weeks' salary and leave."

The young woman made these recitals in a flat, expressionless tone of voice, her fingers digging into the dog's fur, her arms straining the head to her.

"There was to be a bonus?" prompted Sidney Zoom.

She nodded.

"Yes. There was a bonus paid me every year. My year was up and I'd figured the bonus. It amounted to over three thousand dollars. I asked Mr. Ames about it. He said he'd changed his mind. That adventuress had him entirely under her thumb. She simpered at him, leered at me. Damn her, I wish I'd killed her!"

Vera Thurmond winced at the savagery of the girl's tone. Sidney Zoom's eyes glowed with a sudden sympathy, an admiration of a kindred spirit.

"Go ahead," he said, quietly.

She sighed and resumed her story.

"Gravy, he's the butler, was my only friend. He knew I'd been treated shamefully, and he suggested that I should take what was due me—the bonus.

"I had the combination to the safe, but Mr. Ames didn't know it. Gravy had found a paper that had it written on some weeks before and had brought it to me. When I saw it I knew it was some sort of a safe combination, and tried it out on the safe in the library. It worked.

"Then Gravy was afraid Mr. Ames would fire us both if he knew what we'd done, so he swore me to secrecy. You see, Mr. Ames was a most peculiar character, and that safe was sort of sacred with him. He loved to pop things in there and put them under lock.

"So Gravy got me to dress in some of his clothes and furnished me with a mask, just in case anything should happen. And it happened all right.

"Ames and the woman had been to some sort of a reception. They were to stay until midnight, but they came popping in, with a couple of people who were strangers to me, just as I was getting the money out of the safe. There I was, caught red-handed, as they say in the newspapers, the safe open, the money in my hands. But I was wearing men's clothes and a mask. I thought that would keep 'em from recognizing me.

"Of course, I started to run toward the servants' quarters. And Mr. Ames let out a bellow and started after me. I heard a shot and thought some one was firing at me. But there were a lot of screams and something fell to the floor.

"When I got to where I'd left my own clothes, I saw Gravy running after me. He was all excited. He said some one had shot Mr. Ames while I was running. He thought it was the woman who had fired the shot, but couldn't be sure. He said I'd better keep right on going because the woman had sworn she'd recognized my figure, even in the man's clothes, and was insisting that my room be thoroughly searched.

"So I just kept on going. I had the money in a money belt I'd purchased especially for that purpose. I went to a rooming house and went to sleep. Next morning I read of the murder. It seems the two people with him swear that Mr. Ames was running after a masked figure, that the masked man turned and shot him down, then made his escape.

"Personally, I'm satisfied it was the woman who fired the shot. She'll get all his estate now. That was what she wanted. Believe me, she was a fast worker. Married and kills her husband within forty-eight hours!"

Sidney Zoom studied the girl through narrowed eyes.

"The two people with Mr. Ames and his newly made bride were people of unquestioned integrity," he said. "They swear they saw the masked figure run toward a passage, suddenly turn and fire the fatal shot."

She shrugged her shoulders.

"I don't suppose my word or that of Gravy will amount to anything, but Gravy swears he heard the woman say, 'Let him have it,' just before the shot was fired. He thinks that it was the adventuress herself who fired the shot, but he wasn't where he could see. But he swears the shot sounded from behind Ames rather than in front."

Zoom gravely shook his head.

"I'm sorry, Miss Bendley, but the post mortem shows absolutely that the shot was fired from the direction in which Mr. Ames was facing, and the two witnesses, who are positive in their testimony, are men who are absolutely reliable."

"Oh, well," she sighed, "what's the difference? It's all up now. I knew when I read the account in the paper that I was in bad. I was disguised as a man, and I tried to stow away on a freighter. Some sailors found me, started to beat me up, found I was a woman—then you came along."

She gave her undivided attention to the dog.

There was silence in the cabin for several seconds.

"The new wife had a second will made?" asked Sidney Zoom.

"No. She didn't need to. In this State a marriage made subsequent to the execution of a will makes it void. Therefore the will is no good and the wife takes all the estate as the only heir. She was shrewd, that woman."

Sidney Zoom clipped the end from a cigar, smoked it meditatively. From time to time he stared at the girl with thought-slitted eyes. The girl, still sitting on the floor, caressed the dog's head. From time to time the heavy tail of the animal thumped lazy appreciation.

"There's something strange about this case," said Sidney Zoom. "From all the physical evidences, young lady, you're lying."

Her eyes showed no resentment. "All right," she said, "let it go at that."

Sidney Zoom glanced at his secretary.

Vera Thurmond avoided the questioning eyes.

Zoom gave his attention to the cigar. "My faith in human nature has given me some queer hunches in my time," he observed.

"If you fall for this case," snapped Vera Thurmond, "you'll be getting into trouble."

"Go ahead," murmured the girl, "don't mind me. Say it."

Zoom took the cigar from his mouth.

"The fighter," he said, "rarely gets sympathy. That is particularly true with women. Men like women who are beautifully helpless. I'm different. I like the fighter. I'm going to stand back of you, Miss Bendley."

"Meaning?" she asked.

"That we're putting out to sea. That is, you are. I'm going to get you outside of civil jurisdiction on the high seas. I'm staying behind to work on the case. I'll be in radio communication with the yacht.

"Tell me just one thing. This man, Gravy—who is he? Can I trust him?"

"Sure you can trust him. His name is Graves. He's the butler out there, been with us for two years, and he's a square shooter. He's stuck up for me through thick and thin."

Sidney Zoom stroked his chin.

"The return of Mr. Ames was rather unexpected?"

"You mean when he came back from the reception?"

"Yes."

"Sure it was. His wife got sick—damn her, I wish she'd croaked!"

"Nothing serious?"

"No. She even forgot all about it, whatever it was, after she'd seen that the bullet had made her a fortune."

"And you think she was glad the shooting took place?"

"Glad! I'm telling you she shot him. I don't care how reputable your witnesses are. That woman did the murder."

Sidney Zoom whistled to his dog, pressed his finger on an electric button. A white clad shape came softly and swiftly along the deck of the yacht.

"Put out to sea at once, Malcom. Stay beyond the twelve mile limit until you receive other orders via wireless. Understand?"

"Aye, aye, sir."

"Come, Rip!"

And Zoom's feet thudded to the planking of the float, followed by the padding of the dog's feet as the tawny shape arched through the night.

Almost at once a line hit the deck of the boat, the running lights switched on, and the motor started its rhythmic chugging.

On the rail of the boat, just aft of the pilot house, the figure of Vera Thurmond showed, her eyes straining into the night, her arm upflung in a gesture of farewell.

Beside her was the indistinct shape of the girl who had boarded the yacht under such exceptional circumstances. She was motionless, silent.

The yacht swung out on the tide, the motor speeded up and a churning of cheesy water just under the stern, marked the pulsation of the screw as the craft gracefully melted into the darkness.

CHAPTER IV

The Adventuress

MRS. NETTIE PEASE AMES regarded Sidney Zoom through tear reddened eyes.

"B-but you s-s-said you w-w-wanted to give me some information. N-n-now you're asking questions. I w-w-would not have seen you at all so soon after the tragedy."

Sidney Zoom nodded.

"I am very sorry, madame, to intrude upon your grief; but I must get certain matters clear in my mind before I can give you the information. Then I believe I can clear up the shooting mystery and have the culprit in your hands."

Her eyes narrowed.

"Come up to my sitting room," she said. "There are too many servants around here."

And the sobbing stammers had entirely disappeared from her voice.

Sidney Zoom followed her up a flight of stairs, into a room, tastefully furnished. The woman indicated a chair, facing the window, and sat opposite.

"Now spill it," she said.

Sidney Zoom chose his words cautiously.

"I know the police feel Eve Bendley is guilty of the murder. Yet there are certain facts which haven't as yet been satisfactorily explained."

The woman's eyes narrowed.

"Such as?"

"Several things. I will come to them later. In the meantime, may I ask another question? There's no possibility that the marriage didn't annul the will, I take it? In other words, you are the sole heir?"

The eyes widened.

"Of course, I hadn't thought of it. I'd been so prostrated with grief. But I guess that's right. In fact, an attorney so advised me this morning."

Sidney Zoom smiled, a close-clipped smile of frosty humor. "Your great grief didn't prevent you from consulting him, I take it?"

The woman crossed her legs, leaned back in her chair and grinned.

"All right. There's no use beating around the bush. I'm a gold digger. But I married him. I'm damned glad he's gone. I wouldn't have helped him along any, but I knew he wouldn't live forever when I married him. He was in the late seventies. I'm twenty-nine. You've suspected all this, and I might as well own up to it—privately. You ever repeat a word of this conversation and I'll call you a liar.

"But that's all I have been keeping under cover. As for the rest, it's right out in the open. The girl killed Ralph Ames. I don't know whether she did it deliberately or whether she lost her head. She was getting money out of the safe when we came in. I'd recognize her figure anywhere, man's clothes or woman's. I know the way she carries head, the little swing she has to her shoulders."

Sidney Zoom smiled.

"Thanks for being frank. You know, of course, that the girl only took the money from the safe that was due her under the bonus agreement with Mr. 'Ames."

"I know nothing of the sort!" snapped the woman. "I know that the books she kept had been doctored, and I have an idea there was a lot more money in the safe than she admitted or acknowledged in her books.

"And I know something else. I know that she has been traced to the waterfront, that she was dressed in men's clothes and tried to stow away on a freighter. I know that she was in a brawl with a bunch of sailors, and that some man who was about your build rescued her.

"Now you haven't told me what your interest is in this case and I don't know as you need to. But I'll tell you something. You either get that girl into the hands of the police, or I'll charge you with being an accessory!"

Sidney Zoom lit his cigarette, regarded the blazing eyes of the woman, and smiled, his frosty smile of cold humor.

"Very well, Mrs. Ames. Now we understand each other perfectly. If you'll dismiss the charge you made against the girl of theft and embezzlement, I'll have her come back here to answer the murder charge."

The laugh which greeted this comment was coarse and mocking.

"Go jump in a lake! The jury might acquit her on the murder charge. Juries have been known to do fool things. But I've got her dead to rights on the theft. I'm going to see she has plenty to occupy her mind for a while."

Sidney Zoom crossed his long legs, and sighed.

"Yes, of course," he said, "after—"

"After what?"

"After you catch her, of course."

The woman's face mottled with dull rage.

"Go ahead and wise crack," she said. "See what it gets you."

She reached for the telephone.

"Police headquarters?" asked Sidney Zoom, courteously.

"No," she snapped. "I've no confidence in the police. I have a private agency at work on this, and they'll pick you up from the time you leave here and tell me where you go and what you do."

Sidney Zoom arose and bowed.

"I enjoyed the chat, anyway. I suppose you'll be the heart-broken widow with the red eyes the next time I see you."

"Don't be a damned fool," sneered the woman. "Of course I will."

And, holding the telephone ready for her call with her right hand, she reached for a small bottle with her left, and drew it under her nose. Almost instantly tears welled into her eyes and trickled slowly down her cheeks. The eyes themselves reddened and the lids became swollen.

Sidney Zoom turned the knob of the door.

"Good day," he said.

The woman made no answer. She was giving a number to the telephone, a number which was, doubtless, the telephone number of the private detective agency, just as she had threatened.

Sidney Zoom closed the door, paused in the hallway.

A shadowy figure flitted from an adjoining door on noiseless feet. A long, bony finger was pressed crosswise upon thin lips. Gray eyes that set like jewels in a fine network of smile wrinkles, regarded Sidney Zoom with stern speculation. Then the bony finger left the lips, crooked in a gesture of beckoning, and the man led the way down the corridor.

Sidney Zoom followed.

Within a small bedroom on the ground floor, back of the kitchen, the figure once more confronted Sidney Zoom.

"You saw her?" husked a hoarse whisper.

Sidney Zoom laughed.

"You're Graves, I take it."

The man nodded, slowly, solemnly.

"*She* always called me Gravy," he remarked.

"You mean the girl?"

The nod was quick and eager this time.

"You're *her* friend?" asked the butler.

Sidney Zoom smiled. "Right at present I'm an investigator, getting certain facts together."

The butler's face twisted into a smile.

"Beg pardon, sir, but I was listening, sir, at the doorway, you know. It's a prerogative of servants, sir. I heard—and, if you'll pardon my saying so, sir, I *know* you're a friend of the girl."

And the gray eyes twinkled from their network of radiating wrinkles.

Sidney Zoom answered the smile.

The butler lowered his voice to a mere whisper.

"If they catch her, sir, I'm going to swear that the shot came from the other direction. I know she didn't fire that shot. Why, she wasn't the kind. She's so tender hearted she wouldn't hurt a fly, sir."

Sidney Zoom smiled again.

"She didn't impress me as being particularly soft," he remarked.

The affirmation of the butler was eager.

"Yes, sir. That's right, sir. She isn't, sir. But with those she likes she's always thinking of anybody but herself. I had to urge her to get the money in the way she did. And yet it was hers, sir. By every right and every justice it was hers!"

The gray eyes were blazing with earnestness now, and an anxious hand groped for the lapel of Sidney Zoom's coat.

CHAPTER V

Clews in the Yard

"OF COURSE, sir, you know that I was the one that gave her the idea in the first place. Probably I shouldn't say so, sir. But I don't want her to take all the blame. I guess I'm an accessory or something in the eyes of the law; but it was a mistake of the head and not of the heart, sir.

"I tell you what I'm afraid of, sir. I'm afraid that our conversation was overheard, and some one was lying in wait to grab the money from her. Or perhaps, it was that blond adventuress, after all, sir. Miss Eve swears that the shot came from the other side of the room, and it sounded so to me, sir."

Sidney Zoom let his eyes bore into the gray eyes with their puckered wrinkles radiating from the corners.

"Very well, Graves, could you swear to that?"

"Swear to it, sir! I'll tell the world, I'll swear to it. I'd even swear to anything that wasn't the truth to help the young lady out. And this *is* the truth, sir. That shot sounded from the back of the room, sir."

"But the bullet," said Sidney Zoom, speaking with the finality of a judge pronouncing sentence, "entered Mr. Ames's chest and came out at his back. Every one agrees that he was running after the masked figure."

The butler twisted his mouth in a grimace. For several long seconds he seemed lost in thought.

"Do you know, sir, I believe it was some one standing just outside the house, sir, in the yard. That would account for the peculiar sound of the explosion. The window in the south-east corner of the room was open. A man could have fired through that window, and—"

"Show me," snapped Sidney Zoom, his voice clipping off the words with machine gun precision.

The butler went to the door, opened it, peered cautiously up and down the corridor.

"Come," he said.

Sidney Zoom followed him to a wider corridor that went past the kitchen, through a door, and walked down a carpeted passageway. A long room opened before him.

"This was where it was done," whispered the butler.

Sidney Zoom surveyed the room, the safe in one corner, the entrance hall from the outer door, then, after he had given these things a close inspection, followed the direction of the butler's pointing finger.

He saw a window in an alcove, open.

"It's nearly always left open, sir."

Zoom regarded the window, the interior of the room again.

"The body fell here?" he asked.

"Just about, sir."

"The shot might have come through the window, all right. If the old man had been partially turned it could very readily have come from the window."

The butler nodded eager acquiescence.

"What I thought, sir, was that perhaps some one standing outside the window might have made a motion, and the old man half turned and caught it square in the chest."

Zoom pursed his lips.

"Have you looked outside the window?"

"No, sir, I haven't, sir. Fact of the matter is, I'm mixed up in this too much as it is."

Zoom strode toward the window.

"Have a care, sir. She's a devil, that adventuress. If she finds you—"

"Bosh!" snapped Sidney Zoom. "Look here, Graves. Here are foot-prints in the soil out here. Have they been made recently?"

"I couldn't say, sir. If you would not mind, sir, I'd like to leave the room—"

"Bosh again, Graves. Don't be so frightened of her. You want to help Miss Eve, don't you? Very well, then, you'd better stick by me for a little while. How can we get outside from here without using the front door?"

"Right this way, sir. Back of the curtain are French doors, sir."

Sidney Zoom walked to the curtains, pushed them apart, strode through the doors and began to examine the loamy soil which fringed the cement walk running around the house.

"Look here, Graves. This is serious. See where a box was planted in the soft loam there? And it looks as though some one had stood on it! And look here. Here's a perfect footprint!"

The butler bent down.

"Yes, sir. So it is, sir. But I'd rather not mix in it any further—"

Sidney Zoom grasped the man by the shoulder, whirled him back against the side of the house.

"Now, Graves, come clean. You're trying to duck out of this because you think you know who was standing out here. Tell me the truth and talk fast."

The butler gulped, stammered, swallowed with audible effort, then began to spill words with a rapidity that was almost hysterical.

"Amos Style, sir. He claims to be a cousin of the adventuress. But I think he's a son of hers by a former marriage. She's altogether too fond of him for a mere cousin, sir, and he's nothing but a callow lad. He comes to visit her and stays here in the house a large part of the time.

"If the woman wanted Mr. Ames out of the way quickly, she could have conspired with her son to do the trick—if he is her son. And the fact that Mr. Ames just happened to find Miss Eve at the safe, sir, was in the nature of a coincidence, and—"

Sidney Zoom regarded the imprint of the foot in the soft soil, the oblong indentation that had marked the place where the end of the wooden box was placed.

"Stays here in the house, eh?"

"Yes, sir."

"Here now?"

"Yes, sir."

"Could you get me his left shoe?"

The butler sighed.

"I don't know, sir, but I can try. I'd do anything for Miss Eve, sir."

And Graves melted away, as furtively silent as a shadow, as swift as a stalking cat.

Sidney Zoom leaned forward and searched the ground, inch by inch.

Between the cement walk and the side of the house there had been dwarf shrubbery planted. Between these shrubs there were stretches of bare ground, and it was in these bits of bare ground that the incriminating depressions were found.

But Sidney Zoom parted the little branches, looked with the intentness of a hawk searching good game cover.

And his search was rewarded.

A little glitter of metal struck his eyes, and he stooped. There was a brass cartridge of the type automatically ejected from a gun known as an automatic.

Sidney Zoom picked up the cartridge in his handkerchief, lest he should destroy some of the fingerprints on it. He renewed his search, and found the blued steel of a barrel sticking up from the base of one of the plants.

Once again he used his handkerchief, and dragged to light a small automatic, the same caliber as the shell, the same caliber as the bullet which had resulted in the death of Ralph C. Ames.

Sidney Zoom covered the evidence with the handkerchief, placed it in his pocket, straightened up from his search.

Almost at once he heard a door close, and then Graves came cat-treading down the cement.

"I've got it, sir!"

Sidney Zoom took the shoe from his hand, bent down and fitted the sole to the impression in the ground.

The fit was perfect.

"Good God!" exclaimed the butler. "You'll notify the police of this?"

"That," remarked Sidney Zoom, "depends upon a variety of things. Thanks, Graves, for your coöperation."

"You'll tell her I'm willing to do anything for her, sir?"

"If I see her?"

"Well, will you see her?"

"I'm afraid not," said Sidney Zoom. Then, as he saw the gray eyes film with disappointment, he flashed the man a reassuring smile. "Not right away, Graves, but later, perhaps. I'll tell her then."

And he strode down the cement walk, went to his roadster, where Rip was growling at a man with an undershot jaw and a cauliflower ear who stood on the sidewalk, studying the car. Slightly behind him, parked at the curb, was an automobile. At the wheel of this car sat a thin individual with a beak-like nose and a catfish mouth.

Sidney Zoom bowed to them both. He climbed in his roadster and pressed his foot on the starter. The car purred into motion, and the man with the cauliflower ear hopped into the other machine, which promptly swung out into traffic.

Three blocks down the street another machine, driven by a woman, casually cut in ahead of the car with the two private detectives. Thereafter, Sidney Zoom made certain highly intricate maneuvers. The car with the two men got lost in the shuffle.

The other machine, driven by a baby-faced brunette, somehow or other managed to show up after Zoom had finished his turns and twists from one street to another.

But Zoom paid no attention to that machine, which fact brought the faintest suggestion of a gleam of triumph to the baby-faced brunette.

CHAPTER VI

Past History

SIDNEY ZOOM lounged back in the chair at police headquarters. Captain Berkeley, seated across the desk, stared at a typewritten report which had been handed him by a messenger.

"Report of the finger-print expert?" asked Zoom, casually.

"Yes—and of the ordnance expert, too."

"Indeed," said Sidney Zoom, his eagerness showing in the crispness of his tone. "And what did they discover?"

Captain Berkeley drummed on the battered desk for a few seconds, the tips of his fingers beating a nervous tattoo.

"Zoom," he remarked, "you're in wrong."

"Yes?"

"Yes. You've allowed yourself to become prejudiced against Mrs. Ames. And you've pulled your usual big-hearted stunt of falling for the hard luck story of a girl in misfortune—"

Sidney Zoom's tone was hard as he interrupted.

"All of which is preliminary to stating what?"

"To stating," snapped Captain Berkeley, "that the fatal bullet was undoubtedly fired from this weapon. But every finger-print on it is the print of Miss Eve Bendley—the person, by the way, who did the shooting.

"Probably she tossed the gun out of the window after the shooting. We're tracing the numbers, but haven't had a complete report yet."

Sidney Zoom pursed his lips, a habit of his when thinking.

"You're right about one thing," said Captain Berkeley in a more gentle voice, "the so-called cousin is in reality the son of the widow. His real name is Amos Pease. She was a Nettie Pease. What's happened to the husband is shrouded in mystery.

"I've got her history here for the last ten years, however. She's been mixed up in all sorts of shady transactions. A man named Harry Garford was her partner for years. Finally, in Oregon, they were apprehended in connection with some minor crime. The authorities were determined to punish them, and made the bail pretty high.

"But they raised the bail, got out, and were formally married. Then, when the case came to trial, each refused to testify on the grounds that such testimony would be that of a husband against a wife, and a wife against a husband, which has always been considered a confidential relationship in they eyes of the law.

"The case was, of course, dropped, and they went to Idaho, then drifted into Nevada. Garford dropped from sight a couple of years ago. Nettie Pease, or Garford, to give her her right name, seems to have steadied down a bit.

"Garford had a criminal record. Nettie Pease Garford had none. She was arrested several times, but there was never enough evidence to make a case.

"Undoubtedly, she played her cards deliberately when she ran into Ralph Ames, claimed her son was her cousin, dropped about ten years from her official age, and managed to marry him. But how the devil she did it is more than I know. There must be some story in the background there.

"Anyhow, all of that doesn't change the facts. The girl did the killing. You haven't said so, but I have a hunch the girl is on that yacht of yours. Now then, do you want to surrender her, or have us go and get her?"

And Captain Berkeley's eyes glinted ominously.

"I don't think—" began Sidney Zoom.

"You never do," interrupted the police captain. "You cruise around the city at night, picking up flotsam and listening to the hard luck stories. Every one you befriend you think is as pure as the driven snow. I'll admit that your hunches have been pretty fair, and you seem to know human nature pretty well, but this is once you've made a mistake.

"The department would hate like the very devil to have to name you as an accessory, or get hard with you. But the department would hate a damned sight worse to have that girl slip through its fingers.

"So you've got until five o'clock tonight to produce that girl. If she isn't in custody by that time we'll go get her, and we'll put a charge against you.

"That's final."

Sidney Zoom smiled, looked at his watch.

"I have precisely five hours and thirty seven minutes."

"All right."

"Will you go to lunch with me, captain?"

The officer grinned and got to his feet.

"Okay. But you have that jane here by five o'clock, or you'll be having lunch with me at this time to-morrow."

Sidney Zoom smiled by way of reply, escorted the captain to his car, drove him to one of the most exclusive lunch places in the city, purchased a meal which made the officer stretch back in his chair and sigh contentedly.

"Captain," said Sidney Zoom, "I have a favor to ask."

"What is it?"

"I'll have my yacht in dock at five o'clock. The girl will be aboard. But I want you to come personally to make the arrest, without a word to the newspapers. And I want you to give me three hours after you come aboard to prove to you that there may be more to this case than you suspect."

A frown crossed the official forehead.

"That's the worst of you damned amateurs. You get sold on the innocence of some baby-face and then overlook all the proof in the world! I tell you, Zoom, you'll be the laughing stock of the department."

Sidney Zoom beckoned a very attractive lady who carried a tray supported by shoulder straps.

"A perfecto for the captain!" he said.

She came smilingly toward them, bent solicitously over the officer, struck a match when he had selected a cigar.

"Is that a promise?" asked Sidney Zoom.

Captain Berkeley glanced at the tip of the fifty cent cigar and smiled.

"Yes," he said.

And in a far corner of the room a baby-faced brunette with innocent eyes, made a surreptitious notation upon a leather covered notebook which she slipped adroitly from the top of her stocking.

CHAPTER VII

Ambushed

THE *ALBERTA F.* swung into the mooring float. The men tossed lines, jumped from yacht to float with frenzied rapidity, raced against the thrust of the tide. The white yacht was snubbed, warped gently into the float.

Captain Berkeley and Sidney Zoom stepped aboard.

Vera Thurmond met them.

"Oh, I hope you've solved it! She's the nicest girl, when you get to know her!"

Captain Berkeley twisted the cigar in his mouth, savagely.

"Yes," he said, shortly, "we've solved it. I'm sorry, Miss Thurmond, but you folks are in the wrong this time."

The officer stepped aboard, went to an inner cabin, where the formalities of completing the arrest were speedily complied with. Eve Bendley stared at the officer, then at Sidney Zoom, shrugged her shoulders.

"Fortunes of war," she said.

Sidney Zoom smiled reassuringly at his secretary.

"Now, Berkeley, I've given you a fair deal. Will you give me one?"

"Meaning?" asked the officer.

"Meaning that I've surrendered the girl on the dot as I promised. Now I want you to turn your official back on things for three hours."

"And what happens to the prisoner?"

"Lock her in a cabin, handcuff her to Vera Thurmond, call another officer to watch her, anything you want."

"And then?"

"Walk with me to the end of the wharf, don't register any surprise at anything I may say. Then come back to the boat, stay here for three hours, and then meet me at the end of the wharf again."

Captain Berkeley frowned, took a cigar from his pocket and meditatively regarded the end.

"Sounds simple," he commented.

The two young woman watched him with anxious eyes.

"All right," he said.

"Fine," commented Zoom. "Now we'll walk to the end of the wharf."

And it was then Captain Berkeley did that which cemented a firm friendship throughout the years to come with Sidney Zoom.

"Miss Thurmond," he said, "I'm paroling my prisoner in your charge," and, with the words, stepped to the mooring float and followed Sidney Zoom up the steep ladder stairs which led to the wharf above.

They strolled through the gathering dusk, Sidney Zoom, tall, almost gaunt, the police dog padding gravely at his side; Captain Berkeley, puzzled, saying nothing.

For a long seven hundred feet the big wharf stretched, an abandoned commercial dock on one side, Sidney Zoom's private mooring float on the other. A long warehouse partially covered the wharf. For the rest, it was littered with various piles of old lumber, odds and ends of various articles collected from years of service.

At the street side of the wharf Sidney Zoom turned to the officer and extended his hand.

"Very well, captain. It's now precisely five twenty-one. At exactly eight o'clock I shall meet you here again. And you'll have the pictures and complete police record of this Harry Garford."

Captain Berkeley tensed.

"Huh?" he said.

"Thanks," remarked Sidney Zoom. "I'm certain the matter will be cleared at that time. Good night."

And Sidney Zoom, followed by his tawny police dog, paced out into the gathering darkness. Captain Berkeley grunted and walked back to the yacht. From behind a pile of lumber, a baby-faced brunette with eyes that were utterly expressionless, oozed as a surreptitious shadow, sprinted for a roadster that had been parked behind the shadow of a warehouse.

The powerful roadster of Sidney Zoom snorted out into the twilight. The other roadster, keeping well behind, followed it as a hawk might trail a scurrying bevy of frightened quail.

Nor did Sidney Zoom glance back, or go to any trouble to disguise where he was going. He drove directly to police headquarters, and the baby-faced brunette trailed him every foot of the way.

He was closeted within the grim walls of stone and steel for nearly an hour. Then he emerged and reëntered his roadster. His shadow was nowhere in evidence. There were two men, clumsy, heavy-footed, beady-eyed, parked in a touring car. These men made an effort to follow him. But Sidney Zoom, more watchful than when the shadow had been the brunette, detected their presence and spun his car in a figure eight around a dozen blocks, swung into the boulevard traffic and then, disregarding all rules and regulations, made a complete turn about and rushed madly in the opposite direction, his throttle held near to the floor boards.

Thereafter he saw no more of the touring car with the two private detectives.

Precisely at eight o'clock, Sidney Zoom sent his car into the curb back of the warehouse, switched off the ignition, jumped out, and motioned to his dog.

That which followed was rather peculiar, for Sidney Zoom took the dog's head in his hands and talked to him, low-voiced, connected conversation which seemed more the type of conversation one would carry on with an intelligent child than with a dog.

The dog wagged his tail, glided off into the darkness.

Sidney Zoom looked at his watch.

Heavy feet, assured, authoritative, deliberate, sounded on the boards of the wharf.

"Hello," said Zoom. "Did you manage to get the pictures?"

Captain Berkeley grunted.

"Then," said Sidney Zoom in a low voice, "reach for your gun."

Captain Berkeley paused stock still to stare.

There was a blur of dark motion from behind a pile of empty gasoline drums. The darkness gave forth the sound of a low growl, ominous, menacing. The planks of the wharf reverberated to four feet thudding at a full gallop.

Fire streaked from the darkness, and answering fire stabbed from Sidney Zoom's hand. The dog barked once. A man screamed. A woman shouted some shrill command. More spurts of fire ripping the darkness. Bullets crashed through the night air, splintering the boards, glancing from metallic objects with long drawn snarls.

Captain Berkeley, veteran of years on the force, was down behind the nearest gasoline drum at the first sound of firing. By the time the third shot had been fired, his service revolver was out of its holster and barking an answer.

Once more there came the muffled thunder of padded four feet charging at a gallop. The scream of the woman knifed the night. There was a low, throaty growl.

"Steady, Rip!" called Sidney Zoom, and began to run, heedless of the danger which the night might hold. He ran directly toward the sound of that scream, the noise of that ominous growl.

Captain Berkeley lumbered into a flat-footed charge.

"I surrender!" shrilled a frightened voice from the darkness.

CHAPTER VIII

The Capture

THE ELECTRIC flash light of Captain Berkeley sent a white beam into the night, turning the black piles into dazzling brilliance.

Against the black background, a pair of white hands, stretched high above a barricade of empty boxes, caught the gleam of the light. There was a strained, drawn face below those upraised hands, a sagging mouth, eyes that bulged with terror.

"Take him, captain!" said Zoom, and continued in the direction from which the growl had sounded.

He found that which he sought, a woman shrinking from the bloody fangs of the growling animal. On the planking of the wharf was the glitter of a weapon. The right wrist of the woman bore red splotches where the teeth of the animal had locked and torn as he wrested the gun from her wrist.

Sidney Zoom grasped the dog by the collar, pulled him back, kicked the gun out of the way.

"Go find, Rip," he said.

And the dog rushed out in a great, questing half circle.

A revolver spat twice. A man's feet pounded the planks. They were the feet of a man who ran lightly, on his toes, running as a trained sprinter runs. But behind him came the tattoo of dog's feet, and those feet cut down the distance with a savage swiftness.

A growl, a tawny shadow in the air, the thud of an impact! The running form of the man skidded over the rough planks, rolled, twitched and lay still as the dog stood over him, fangs snarling at his throat, wolf eyes gleaming with blood lust.

Ten minutes later the three prisoners were on the yacht, getting wounds bandaged, a surly, shifty-eyed crowd of thwarted criminals.

"All right," said Captain Berkeley, turning to Sidney Zoom, "spill it!"

Zoom laughed.

"So absurdedly simple it seemed complicated," he replied. "So obvious that it almost escaped observation. The girl was advised to rob the safe and wear a mask by the butler. There was no need for her to wear a mask, really no pressing need for her to rob the safe.

"*But*, notice the significant fact that Ralph Ames returns with two responsible witnesses at the exact time that will surprise the young lady at the safe. That time, concededly, was controlled by Mrs. Ames, who became ill and insisted upon being taken home from the reception.

"Notice, also, the significant fact that Garford, the woman's accomplice, has vanished from police ken for approximately two years—almost exactly the length of time Graves, the butler, had been working for Ralph C. Ames.

"What more natural than that Garford alias Graves, knowing that the police were on his trail, and wishing to lay low for a while, should forge references and secure the position of butler to Ames? What more natural than that he should insinuate himself into the good graces of Ames and his secretary so that he could naturally bring about the entrance of his woman accomplice into the picture?

"Between them they worked the old man skillfully enough so that he actually married the woman. Then they wanted his fortune, wanted it quick before there should be any chance of Ames discovering how he had been duped.

"So, Garford, posing as Graves, the efficient butler, and the stanch friend of Miss Bendley, talked her into putting on men's clothes and robbing the safe, with a mask over her features. Then he arranged to have Ames, accompanied by unimpeachable witnesses, walk in on the affair. He knew Ames well enough, hot-headed, irascible, tight-fisted, he would naturally pursue a running figure.

"And Graves, wearing a mask, dressed as the girl was dressed, stepped into the doorway where he could be seen by the witnesses, shot the old man and then slipped off his mask and became once more the loyal butler.

"But he made the mistake of gilding the lily. He wanted the police to get the gun with which the killing was done. This gun doubtless belonged to Miss Bendley, and could be traced to her by the police. Also it had her finger-prints on it.

"So Graves, or Garford, planted the gun where I would find it, and turn it into the police. But he overlooked the fact that Miss Bendley couldn't have tossed the gun there after the killing, that she had rushed from the house immediately after the shooting. Finding the gun where it was, pointed conclusively to the fact that some one other than Miss Bendley had fired the fatal shot.

"But the butler was damnedly clever in letting me in on what he knew the police would soon discover, that the supposed cousin was, in reality, the woman's son.

"When he had his private detectives shadowing me, and learned I hadn't been fooled, but intended to get the pictures and record of Garford, he had two alternatives, flight, or to take the chance of killing and effectually silencing our lips.

"I had hoped they would resort to flight, but the bait of Ames's estate was too much. They decided to risk everything on silencing us until after the woman could collect at least a part of the estate.

"I felt certain they would either flee or be waiting for us—"

It was the woman who interrupted.

"Well, you've been damned smart. But you can't stop me from getting that money. Mr. Ames made a will. That was revoked by his marriage. The girl is no relation to him. I'm the only legal relative he has in the world. And even if a jury would believe your story, the money will, of course, go in *my* family!"

Sidney Zoom shook his head, mournfully, solemnly.

"Perhaps you've forgotten that you were forced to marry Garford, legally. That marriage has never been dissolved. Therefore your marriage to Ames was bigamous, merely an empty ceremony, and not legal. As a result the will was never revoked. It's just as good now as the day it was written."

The woman's eyes widened with a sudden realization of the full import of Sidney Zoom's words. She muttered an exclamation, sank back in her chair.

Captain Berkeley caught Zoom's eye.

"Just a minute now, Zoom. The girl's imprints were on the gun. We've traced the numbers and can show she picked it up in a pawnshop, and—"

"Of course," said Zoom. "The butler planned the thing well from the first. It was the girl's gun. She'd kept it in her room. Naturally her finger-prints would be on it. Garford simply took it, wearing gloves, of course, shot the man, tossed the gun to one side and later cast it out of the window.

"And he tried to throw me off the track by digging up clews that would seem at first to point to the girl's innocence, but later would serve to clinch the case against her. He simply borrowed the gun for the murder, knowing the bullet would be traced to the gun, the gun to the girl."

Captain Berkeley got to his feet.

"I think I hear the wagon," he said. "Zoom, I think we've got a case here a jury will act on, and do it damned quick. Help me escort the prisoners to the wagon, will you?"

HIGHER UP

CHAPTER I

The Girl with Diamonds

THE CITY was, for the most part, dark and silent. The theatrical district glowed with light. The narrow streets of Chinatown gave forth whisperings to the night as slithering feet slid along the pavement. The financial district was grim and gloomy, business houses were dark.

Between Chinatown and the theatrical district there was a street which glowed with lighted windows. This was the pawnshop district. Human misery, like human pain, becomes more acute at night, and the pawnbrokers in this district did much of their business around midnight.

Drab shadows flitted through this district on furtive feet, pausing now and again momentarily, then plunging into one of the lighted interiors, shortly to emerge and slink back into the realm of darkness which bordered the pawnshop lane.

Midnight boomed the hour.

The financial district, which was to the east, gave forth the sound of foot-steps. These steps contained nothing of the furtive. They echoed from the cold pavements with the rhythmic regularity of some metronome of fate. The footsteps were audible some seconds before the figure became visible. Then he strode into the half illumination of pawnshop lane, six feet odd of whipcorded strength, grim, gaunt, uncompromising. At his side padded a police dog.

That strange personality, known as Sidney Zoom, pacing the midnight streets, police dog at his side, hawk eyes utterly untamed, paused to scan the furtive figures which glided through the district where human misery might secure temporary relief, for sufficient collateral.

For some half minute he stood, surveying, appraising. Then he strode through the length of the narrow thoroughfare and was about to vanish into the darkness once more, when a figure arrested his attention.

She was young, attractive, well formed. A shabby coat was hugged about her figure with something of an air, as though it had been a coat of sable instead of cheap shoddy. The face was held rigidly, impersonally to the front, as becomes a young lady who must walk the night streets unescorted, yet wishes to convey no false impression.

Outwardly she was calm, cool, poised. Yet there was something about her which spoke of anxiety. Perhaps it was in the swiftly nervous beat of her tiny feet upon the pavement; perhaps it was in the way she hugged the coat about her figure, as though it had been a shield.

Sidney Zoom's eyes, as colorless as those of a hawk, and as keen, fastened upon her. At his side, the dog whined. Sidney Zoom turned, followed.

For two blocks they walked. The girl's feet patting the pavement with short, nervous steps, as rapid and sharp as the beating of an excited heart. Behind her, Sidney Zoom's feet banged upon the pavement at explosive intervals as his long legs swung through the night.

The girl paused at a door above which hung the conventional gilded balls. It was as though she waited to muster courage. Then her hand pushed the door open.

Sidney Zoom entered behind her. The dog crouched upon the pavement, tawny muzzle dropped to his paws, yellow eyes watchfully alert.

A thin figure with stooped shoulders and a bald head, upon the back of which was a black skull cap, came shuffling to the counter from a back room.

His eyes were watery, showing a great fatigue with life, yet there was uncanny wisdom in their watery depths. They were eyes that could flicker to a face and appraise character.

A cigarette drooped from the thin lips. Yet the air of the place was thick with heavy cigar smoke.

Sidney Zoom sniffed that cigar smoke, let his eyes fasten upon the cigarette, and then his lips clamped together. He knew the meaning of that cigar smoke. The detectives were waiting for something "hot."

The girl half turned, shot an anguished glance at Sidney Zoom. It was evident that she would have preferred to transact her business without an audience.

"Wait on him first," she said.

The thin man with the slithering feet and the drooping cigarette started to shuffle toward Sidney Zoom. That individual waved his hand.

"I shall be some little time," he said. "I want to see about purchasing a watch," and he bent over the counter upon which the watches were displayed under glass, giving every outward indication of being so utterly absorbed in his inspection as to be oblivious of what was going on in the place.

The thin man raised his watery eyes to the girl's face.

"Well?" he asked.

The girl's hand darted from beneath the folds of her shabby coat. She held it over the glass of the show case, then made a little flinging gesture.

Hard pellets of frozen fire rattled over the glass, sent coruscating beams of glittering light flaming about the place. There were half a dozen diamonds, and they were of sufficient size to make a respectable showing.

"How much," said the girl in a voice that quavered, "for the lot?"

The thin man swooped out a swift hand, scooping the pellets into a little group, as though his cautious soul rebelled at the liberal gesture with which the girl's hand had flipped them away.

"They are unset," he said.

The girl made no comment. None was necessary. The fact was self evident.

The pawnbroker fastened a jeweler's glass to his right spectacle, picked up the stones, examined them.

"But," he said slowly, "they have been set, and have been pried from their settings."

Leaning over the watch counter, Sidney Zoom noticed that the man had raised his voice, knew that this was for the benefit of the man who remained in the back room, smoking heavy cigars.

The girl asked her question again, in a monotone.

"How much for the lot?"

The pawnbroker's voice was quite loud now.

"You are the same girl who has been in here before, yes? And these stones are of peculiar sizes. They weren't stones from a necklace. They were taken from rings and stickpins, and they have been pried …"

CHAPTER II

Hot Ice

THE SMOKY entrance to the back room framed a hulking figure. A hat was back on one side of his head. From beneath the hat showed a shock of black hair. Insolent eyes surveyed the world in scornful appraisal. Thick lips held a half-smoked cigar clamped rigidly. Broad shoulders swung half sideways to clear the narrow doorway.

"All right, sister," he said; "where did you get 'em?"

And he flipped back a casual hand to his coat lapel, let her eyes catch the gleam of a silvered badge.

"Oh!" she said, and the exclamation was almost a scream.

Her hand darted for the diamonds.

They moved with quickness, those two. The pawnbroker swooped his clawlike fingers upon the diamonds. The detective did not reach for the stones. He slammed his great paw down upon the lean wrist, held it in the grip of a vise.

"Say-y-y-y!" he said, the word having a snarling emphasis, "none o' that! I asked you where you got 'em."

The girl's face showed conflicting emotions.

"I—I can't tell."

"She the one that's been in here before, Moe?"

"Yeah."

"All right, sister, you're goin' by-by in a wagon with wire over it. Better kick through right now. If you come clean we might give you a break."

"I—No, no—I won't!"

The detective laughed. The laugh was a sneer, coarse, grating.

"Th' hell you won't," he said.

And he pulled glittering bracelets of steel from the vicinity of his left hip. His right hand still held the girl's wrist.

"Take a look at these," he invited.

The girl shook her head.

"I won't tell. I don't care what you do to me."

The detective grunted.

"S'pose *I* tell then, if you won't?"

His eyes were scornful, sneering. The girl's face showed panic.

"You know?" she asked.

"Sure, I know. You're a friend of Sally Barker, an' Sally Barker's the housekeeper out at Jake Goldfinch's place. And Goldfinch got bumped off about five thirty this evening and there is a hell of a lot of diamonds missing. Now are you goin' to talk?"

The effect of his words was magical. The girl began to talk, swiftly, almost hysterically.

"Yes, yes, now I'll talk. I wasn't going to get Sally into trouble. I wasn't going to mention her name. But if you know of her it's all right. Only I don't want her to think that *I* was the one that told. You must explain that to her.

"It was yesterday that Mr. Goldfinch called Sally into his room. He told her that he was getting to be an old man. He said he hadn't made any provision for her in his will. He said that he was leaving these diamonds in a vase over his desk, that if anything happened to him Sally was to take these diamonds at once and pawn them.

"He made her promise that she wouldn't wait a minute, that she'd take the stones and sell them for the best price she could get. He said he wanted her to have them instead of taking anything from his estate. She'd been with him for years, you know."

The detective grunted.

"Yeah," he said, "I know." And he winked at the pawnbroker, then moved toward the telephone, picked up the receiver.

"Gimme police headquarters," he said.

There was a moment of silence, then the detective's voice rumbled through a formula.

"Let me talk with Sergeant Gilfillan ... Hello, sergeant. This is Renfoe talking. I've got the frail in the Goldfinch case and she was loaded with the hot ice. Came into the pawnshop. Yeah, I'm bringin' her down ... Okay ... Okay, g'by."

He hung up the telephone.

The thin man with the stooped shoulders and the bald head moved shufflingly over to where Sidney Zoom leaned against the counter.

"Watches?" he asked.

"I want," said Sidney Zoom, "a watch that is of a particular make, and you do not seem to have one."

The thin man lost interest in the detective and the girl in order to make a sale.

"I have here," he proclaimed, "the best watches in the country. Don't you want a good watch?"

Sidney Zoom raised his voice.

"I want a square deal, and I want to see that every one else gets a square deal."

The girl started at the timbre of that voice, as solemnly resonant as the tone of a rich violin.

The pawnbroker looked puzzled.

"Don't you believe my watches are the best in the country?" he asked.

Sidney Zoom's voice retained its solemn timbre.

"I disbelieve in nothing," he remarked, "not even in a divine justice which works through strange channels to see that wrongs are righted."

And he strode calmly to the outer door, pushed it open, and walked into the night, leaving behind him a startled, sagging jawed pawnbroker, a very puzzled young woman, and a scowling detective.

CHAPTER III

The Murder Room

SERGEANT HUNTINGTON regarded Sidney Zoom speculatively. Little puckers appeared at the corners of the keen eyes.

"I don't know too much about it. Sergeant Gilfillan's been handling most of the case. It broke around supper time to-night. Understand the old man was murdered, stabbed with a knife, I believe. We've got one of the brightest detectives on the force working on it. Think he came in a little while ago."

He jabbed a button with his forefinger. A head bobbed in through a doorway.

"Tell Jack Hargrave to come in here," rumbled the sergeant.

The head was withdrawn, the door closed. Seconds lengthened into minutes. Neither Zoom nor Huntington made any further comment.

The door abruptly opened. A young man with keen eyes, a whimsical smile at the corners of his mouth, walking lightly, easily upon the balls of his feet, stepped into the room.

"Hargrave, shake hands with Sidney Zoom. Hargrave's the brightest young detective on the force. Zoom's a man who butts into a case once in a while, makes everybody sore, and usually turns out to be one hundred per cent right."

The two men shook hands.

"Want to show Zoom around on the Goldfinch case?" asked Sergeant Huntington.

Jack Hargrave turned on the balls of his feet, his every motion as swiftly efficient as a prize fighter going into action.

"Let's go," he said.

It was the first word he had said since entering the room.

Sidney Zoom reached for his hat, grinned, strode his long length of gaunt strength toward the door. Jack Hargrave moved at his side, as smoothly and easily as water running along a flume.

They went down a flight of stairs, stale with the stench of poor ventilation, out into the crisp air of the night. Hargrave indicated a roadster with red spotlight and police siren.

Sidney Zoom got into the car.

"My dog," he said.

The tawny police dog was watching his master with expectant eyes. He had been waiting just outside the door of police headquarters.

The detective flipped back a rumble seat.

The dog gathered his feet, crouched, sailed through the air, lit neatly and accurately upon the rumble seat. Hargrave crawled in behind the wheel, slammed the door, stepped on the starter.

The car ripped into speed, skidded at the corner. The siren was wailing by the time it hit the center of the car tracks and tore through the almost deserted street. Hargrave handled the wheel with the easy precision of one who is utterly certain of his muscular coördination.

Fifteen minutes and they drew up before a dark, forbidding mansion which sat back from the road, surrounded by a gloomy iron fence. A policeman was strolling at the gate of this fence on patrol. A police car was in the driveway, back of the swinging gates which had provided a carriage entrance in earlier days.

Hargrave switched off the ignition, stepped to the curb.

"Hello, Haggerty."

The uniformed policeman stepped to one side.

"Evening, sir."

They went up the walk, Jack Hargrave first, stepping with the latent power of a coiled spring; Zoom second, striding grimly, purposefully; the dog third, padding behind his master with that cautious strength which a wolf might display in stalking a deer.

They went up the wooden steps of the porch, through the door into a corridor which smelled musty. The atmosphere of the house reeked of death and decay.

A man with broad shoulders and a bull neck stepped out of a room, looked at Hargrave.

"Hello, Jack."

"Hello, Phil. Are you working on this case?"

"Yeah. They asked me to take it over."

Hargrave nodded. His manner showed something of a chill of formality.

"I'm working on it," he said.

The bull-necked one grinned.

"You was," he stated. "I am."

Hargrave turned to Sidney Zoom.

"Mr. Zoom, meet Mr. Brazer."

The bull-necked one did not offer to shake hands. Sidney Zoom bowed. The bow was uncordial. Brazer didn't bother to bow.

"Whatcha want?" he asked.

"We're taking a look around," said Hargrave. "This way, Zoom."

Sidney Zoom placed his dog in a convenient corner of the hallway. Brazer, the bull-necked individual, glowered at the dog.

"He can't stay here!"

Sidney Zoom's smile was close clipped in its cool insolence.

"I wouldn't advise you to try to put him out," he remarked, and followed Hargrave up a flight of stairs, around a turn, through a short corridor and into a room.

"This," said Hargrave, "is the murder room."

It was a room which peculiarly adapted itself to scenes of violence and death. A gable formed an "A" at one end. A big window showed black and bleak. The furniture was old-fashioned, rickety.

Hargrave talked, and the words rattled like bullets.

"Goldfinch was a millionaire, many times over. Bought diamonds. He was a miser with diamonds just as some folks are misers with money. Every gem dealer in the country knew Goldfinch. He'd buy any sort of gems, smuggled or not. One thing he drew the line at. He wouldn't buy stolen gems, wouldn't deal with any one who might be even suspected of handling hot stuff.

"His housekeeper, Sally Barker, knew him better than any one. She told friends she thought he'd provided for her in his will. She wished he'd hurry up and die. The woman's one of those half cracked babies. She's got a friend who's class, Myrtle Crane. Myrtle's been visiting pawnshops some lately.

"Goldfinch is found, stabbed with a knife. No diamonds are found. We've searched the house from cellar to garret. Goldfinch was killed about four o'clock, not discovered for an hour or so. The housekeeper skipped out when she discovered the body. That is, she claims that was what startled her. We have our own ideas.

"Anyhow, the body was discovered by the butler and general utility man. He telephoned us. We made a round up, found the housekeeper gone, threw out a dragnet and picked her up as she was taking a train out of the city. We put a watch on the pawnshops, and they picked up her friend, Myrtle Crane, trying to hock some diamonds that were taken from the Goldfinch collection.

"She says the housekeeper told her she was afraid they'd try to pin the murder on her, so she was going to skip out, that the housekeeper asked Myrtle to hock the stones and send her the money.

"That's the lay. We've searched everywhere. No diamonds. No motive for the death except gain. Goldfinch was a funny crab. No one knew him. Had a manager to handle all his property affairs, chap by the name of Jed Slacker. He'll be in, maybe. He's been running around back and forth, all worked up. Seems he and Goldfinch had gone into some sort of a partnership deal on some stocks. Slacker put his own money up. Came out to get Goldfinch to check out his half and found him dead.

"Slacker's a lawyer. Says that under the law he can't testify to the transaction because death having sealed Goldfinch's lips the law won't let him testify.

"Guess he's right, at that. That means Goldfinch's estate gets the benefit of Slacker's money, and maybe Goldfinch didn't leave a will. We haven't found one."

Sidney Zoom grunted.

"Do you think the housekeeper did the stabbing?" he asked Hargrave.

The detective lowered his voice.

"No, I don't. That's why I'm getting switched off the case. It looks like an easy case to pin it on the woman and have the girl as an accomplice. It'll make a quick solution. That's what some of the department heads want—quick solutions and newspaper publicity. Understand, that's confidential."

Sidney Zoom nodded again.

"Taken any finger-prints?" he asked.

"Yes. You can see where I've brought out some latents and photographed them. The identification department is working on them. Haven't got the finger-prints of all the people in the place yet, though. We have the housekeeper and the dead man. We'll get the others later. The department has trouble some times getting folks to pose for their finger-prints. We don't do it unless they're pretty willing or else suspected of crime."

Sidney Zoom puckered his forehead in a frown.

"The prints of the butler, the dead man and the housekeeper would naturally be all over the place," he said.

"Sure," agreed the young detective. "What we'd be looking for, maybe, would be a strange finger-print that would tally with the prints of some fellow who might have pulled a diamond job.

"It's hard to identify from a latent, but where we've got the prints to check with we can check pretty fast. Maybe the inside end was just an accomplice. Maybe there's somebody higher up. We'll get the prints and check them against half a dozen big diamond men who are known to be in the city."

Zoom nodded thoughtfully. His eyes regarded an irregular dark stain upon the floor.

"What sort of a knife?" he asked.

"Big butcher knife. Came from the kitchen."

"Finger-prints on the knife?"

"Not a print."

CHAPTER IV

The Dodger

THERE CAME a nervous knock at the door of the death chamber. Almost at once the knob turned and a pasty-faced man thrust himself through the doorway.

He was fleshy in a flabby, unhealthy corpulency. Yet he moved with the nervous, jerking swiftness of a lighter man. His eyes were red-rimmed, his face haggard.

Hargrave looked up.

"Shake hands with Mr. Zoom, Mr. Slacker. Jed Slacker, Mr. Zoom. He's the manager I told you about."

The fleshy man thrust out a right hand with the explosive force of a man striking a blow. He spoke and the words came rushing out so fast that each word seemed to be treading on the heels of its predecessor.

"Howdy-do-Mister-Zoom-howdy-do-pleas'd-t'meetcha. Listen, Hargrave, there's gotta be a will here, simply gotta be. I can't sleep. My God, my money, all of it. I've looked up the law. I'm stuck. Checked out my own money. Goldfinch would have made it good in a minute. Came out here, find he's been murdered. Worst of it is that he was murdered after I'd put up the money. If he'd only been croaked an hour sooner I could have recovered. Furnished to the estate instead of to the dead man. See the point? But there's a will, and I know he'll remember me in the will. And—"

Hargrave interrupted:

"If you can think of any new place to search you're welcome. If there's a will there's likely to be diamonds in the same place."

The fleshy man fell to pacing the floor, quick jerky steps that made the flabby fat of his paunchy frame jiggle with the very violence of the motion. His hands were clasped behind his back, his head thrust forward. He seemed oblivious of every one in the room.

From time to time as he strode his feet passed over the irregular dark stain on the floor which marked the place where the life blood of a murdered man had oozed into the boards. But the fat man gave it no heed. He was utterly engrossed in his own problem.

Hargrave looked at Sidney Zoom, grinned, a wry twisting of the features.

Sidney Zoom fastened his eyes speculatively on the pacing form of the manager.

Of a sudden that form stopped with an abrupt cessation of motion, almost in mid stride.

"Got it," he said. "Remember Goldfinch said once that he had to have the floor fixed in his bedroom. He wanted a certain carpenter to come in for the job. I had to get that carpenter. He was an old man, a crab, but a friend of the old gent. I couldn't see anything wrong with the floor. Betcha he put something in there. Let's take a look."

He spun on his heel, worked his short legs like pumping pistons, and steamed through a doorway into an adjoining chamber. Zoom and the detective followed. The fat man dropped to his knees, started exploring the boards with his eyes and the tips of his fingers, keeping up a running fire of conversation meanwhile.

"Must be somewhere—bound to have a will—must have account books—funny old codger—but I can't afford to donate everything I've got to the estate—what a break!—what a break—ought to've known better—me, a lawyer, too!"

There were heavy steps. Phil Brazer stood in the doorway.

"Whatcha doin'?" he asked.

Hargrave jerked a thumb toward the figure of the fat man, crawling around on the floor.

"Thinks he can find something," he said, and fished a package of cigarettes from his pocket.

Jed Slacker crawled about the floor, making odd puffing noises as the fat pushed up against his lungs. He fumbled with his right hand.

"Here," he said.

Hargrave stepped forward. Brazer bent over the figure. Sidney Zoom stood aloof. The fat man pointed to a section of the boards.

"Feels funny. Put your fingers on it."

Hargrave bent forward. He pushed his hand against the place Slacker indicated. There was a slight click. A section of the floor lifted up on cunningly concealed hinges. There was disclosed an oblong opening in which appeared papers tied together with a pink ribbon.

The fat man sat back on his haunches, gasping for breath. A smile of serene satisfaction appeared on his features.

"That'll be the will," he said.

Hargrave reached for the papers.

"Just a minute," said Brazer, and his broad shoulders and bull neck pushed Hargrave aside as he reached a thick arm down into the cavity. "I'm in charge here now."

He pulled out the package of papers.

Slacker was wheezing, getting his breath back.

"Get the will—the will!" he said.

The detective thumbed through the papers.

"Lot of receipts, letters, cancelled checks," he said. "Here's some sort of a legal paper. Let's take a look at it."

He unfolded the oblong document, read it with corrugated brows, his lips moving soundlessly as they laboriously formed the words of the document. Jed Slacker peered over his shoulder, let out a whoop of delight.

"The will?" asked Hargrave.

Slacker answered the question.

"No. But it's a statement that we hold the stocks in trust as a joint venture and that I'm to be reimbursed for any expenditures I make. Dated only a couple of days ago, too. I don't care about any of his money, only I don't want him to take mine."

Brazer grunted.

"What," asked Sidney Zoom, "is this?"

Hargrave muttered an exclamation of surprise.

"By gosh it's a dodger," he said.

The fat man looked his relief, also his lack of comprehension.

"Dodger?"

"Yes. The sort that describes criminals, the type that's tacked up in post offices in the small towns and mailed to peace officers."

He unfolded the grayish sheet of printer's paper. It showed a front and profile view. Above it, in large letters appeared the words *Diamond Thief!* Below the photographs was a description. "Robert Reelen, alias Sid Whalen, alias Charles Gillen, super crook of the diamond industry. Age, forty-seven; height, five feet ten and one-half inches; weight, one hundred and ninety-four pounds. Scar on left hand running from base of thumb to wrist. Almost bald. Eyes gray, slight blemish scar on left cheek. This man steals rings and stickpins, also acts as fence for crooks dealing in such articles. He pries stones from settings and sells. Never been able to find his market, but he is able to handle stones for cash. When arrested will probably have diamonds concealed in lining of vest. I hold a warrant, detain and wire. I will extradite."

Below appeared the printed name and address of a sheriff.

"Humph," said Hargrave.

"Huh," snorted Brazer, "I don't remember no Reelan—but a guy can't remember every crook in the country. What else is in here?"

He finished going through the papers. Then he leaned over the opening in the floor, plunged his thick arm in to the shoulder, groped about. A slow smile wreathed his features.

He withdrew his hand.

Within the cupped palm were diamonds, half a dozen of them. They glittered in the light of the gloomy bedroom.

"More?" asked Hargrave.

"Yeah."

The bull-necked detective made another lunge down into the dark interior. Sidney Zoom watched him with narrowed eyes. Hargrave's expression was a mask. Slacker re-read the typewritten document and grinned.

"Let's me out," he breathed with that degree of satisfaction which is only seen in men who are fat.

CHAPTER V

Madison, the Butler

BRAZER STRAIGHTENED up after a few seconds. His face was very red from the strained position in which he had been lying. His huge hand cupped perhaps seven or eight diamonds. These were smaller than the others.

"That," he said, "is about all."

Slacker rotated his flabby head upon the thick neck.

"Can't be. There's a lot—somewhere."

"Not here," said Brazer.

Sidney Zoom lit a cigarette in silence.

"Let me feel," said Hargrave.

Zoom tapped him on the shoulder.

"I wouldn't," he remarked.

The detective regarded him in surprise.

"Wouldn't what?"

"Feel in there."

Brazer laughed.

"No traps in there. I've felt all around it. It's some sort of a metal box."

Sidney Zoom nodded.

"Quite certain there aren't any more, eh?"

Brazer grunted, got down on his knees again and groped around.

"Here's one," he said.

He brought out a stone smaller than any of the rest, a mere pebble of a diamond, looked at it, grinned.

"Wouldn't bend down for another one that size."

"Let's give headquarters a ring," suggested Hargrave.

Brazer grunted, walked to the corridor. "Telephone up here somewhere. Here it is."

He called headquarters, reported, listened while the receiver rasped forth metallic sounds, and then turned to Hargrave.

"That's a break," he said, slamming the receiver back on the hook.

"What is?"

"Some of those latents have been checked. They're the finger-prints of Shorty Relavan. Remember him? He's the gem man that got out of stir two years ago and vanished. We haven't been able to get him located. He hasn't pulled a job that we know of. Now he turns up on this thing. He must have been layin' low for a job that'd be big enough to make it worth his while.

"He's the guy higher up all right. He's the brains back of the thing. See the lay? He got the housekeeper planted, got her to spot where the sparklers was. Then he gets her to croak the old man and grab the rocks. Maybe he does the sticking himself … No, I guess the housekeeper did that, because we've got her. An' it's always better to have the guilty guy in jail than to have him outa jail. It makes a difference with the newspapers, see?" And Brazer winked one eye in a portentous and solemn manner.

There was a knock at the door.

"C'min," called Brazer.

A man entered, clad in a bathrobe.

"Pardon, sir, I heard voices and the conversation over the telephone. I thought perhaps, sir, you had found the diamonds."

Hargrave muttered an aside to Sidney Zoom.

"Madison, the butler."

Brazer fastened stern eyes upon the man.

"Madison, did you ever know there was a secret hiding place under the bedroom floor?" he asked.

The butler stared at the opened oblong of space and let his jaw sag.

"Good heavens, sir. No, indeed, sir!"

Sidney Zoom flung a question at the man.

"How long you been with Mr. Goldfinch?"

"About a year and a half, sir."

"Before that?" asked Sidney Zoom.

"I was in Australia, sir."

Sidney Zoom turned to Hargrave.

"Let me see the latents you developed, please."

The young detective swung on his heel, motioned toward the outer room.

"New knob on the door. I took latents from the knob that was on there. I took latents from the desk, from half a dozen other places where the man who had committed the murder might have searched for diamonds."

Sidney Zoom studied the spiral of smoke from the end of his cigarette.

"Madison, have you noticed any strangers about the place?"

Brazer snorted. Madison shifted uneasily.

"He's been asked that question at least a dozen times," said Hargrave.

Sidney Zoom remained unperturbed.

"This," he observed, "will make the thirteenth, then."

The butler squirmed inside his bathrobe.

"No, sir," he said. Then, suddenly, he started.

"The book peddler!" he exclaimed.

"Who?" asked Hargrave.

"I had forgotten when I told you before. He came here with a set of books. Mr. Goldfinch seemed much interested. The peddler came up here to the bedroom. And I remember he was talking with Mrs. Barker, the housekeeper, when I came into the corridor. They seemed to be quite well acquainted. They were whispering, sir.

"And I thought it was strange at the time, sir, and went so far as to mention the matter to the housekeeper, sir. She told me that they had a secret arrangement by which she was to share in the commission in the event a sale was made.

"The book agent was back here three times after that, sir. The last time was this afternoon. But I don't think he saw Mr. Goldfinch, sir, not this afternoon. I know he was talking with Mrs. Barker. Of course, sir, you will understand that us servants sometimes have our little commissions, sir, so I thought nothing of the matter."

Brazer grunted.

"This the first time you've told any one about that guy?"

"Yes, sir."

"Why," asked Jack Hargrave, "did you not say anything about it before?"

"Because it slipped my mind, sirs."

Brazer cleared his throat.

"What sort of a looking chap was this book agent?"

"Five feet nine, a hundred and eighty-five pounds, about forty-one or two years of age, dressed in a pin-striped suit. He had gray eyes, and a funny way of talking out of one side of his mouth, sir. He had a funny habit of reaching up with his right hand and rubbing the lobe of his right ear, I remember that well, sir."

Brazer whistled. "Whew," he said, "that's the description of Shorty Relavan. I remember now the dope that came out on him. He had that habit of tugging at his ear when he was excited. Gosh, what a break! We've got the higher up located right at the start. And we've got the housekeeper. This ties her in so tight she won't never get out. All the slick lawyers in the world won't never pry her loose."

Jack Hargrave glanced at Sidney Zoom. His eyes were glittering with concentration. Sidney Zoom's lips twisted, just a trifle.

"Where else," asked Sidney Zoom, "did you find the latents of this Relavan?"

"In the kitchen, on some of the knives. Not on the murder knife," said Hargrave. Brazer thrust out his chest.

"Well," he said, "I'm in charge of the case. I'm goin' to telephone headquarters and tell 'em of the new developments."

Jack Hargrave grinned at Brazer.

"How much credit do I get?" he asked.

Brazer grunted. "I'm in charge."

Hargrave nodded, wordlessly.

"I," remarked Sidney Zoom, "would like to check up on this dodger of Robert Reelen. Do you suppose, Mr. Hargrave, you could drive me to headquarters and go over the records? And it might be well to take Mr. Madison, the butler, with us, so that we can have him check over the photographs of Shorty Relavan."

The eyes of Sidney Zoom met with those of Jack Hargrave and locked there for one long moment.

Hargrave smiled. "Okay," he said.

Phil Brazer scratched his head meditatively.

"Yeah. I'm in charge here. You guys get out and let me think this thing out. It's red hot, all right."

The butler dressed, in company with Zoom and Hargrave they drove to police headquarters in utter silence. Hargrave led them to the presence of Sergeant Huntington.

"Understand Brazer's in charge of the Goldfinch case."

"Yes. Orders came through. Sergeant Gilfillan was working on it. You were under him. They switched it to the special duty department and ordered Gilfillan to lay off."

Hargrave nodded. "Is that notification official?"

Sergeant Huntington studied him long and earnestly.

"No," he said, "it's not official."

Hargrave turned to the man at his side.

"Shorty Relavan, alias Arthur Madison, I arrest you for the murder of Jacob Goldfinch, and warn you that anything you may say will be used against you."

Sidney Zoom heaved a sigh.

"I was hoping," he said, "that you would do that."

CHAPTER VI

The Butler's Confession

THE MAN who had acted as butler, his face the color of chalk, made two efforts to speak, but only succeeded in making weird throat noises.

Sergeant Huntington whistled softly, under his breath.

The butler cleared his throat.

"All right, you got me. I went after the sparklers. I got the job with Goldfinch hoping to find out where he kept 'em. I couldn't get the lay so I asked the housekeeper if she knew. She told me to get a market for the stones and she'd produce 'em.

"I told her the name of a fence. Then she crossed me. She went ahead on her own, pulled the thing without my knowing anything about it, and the old man caught her. They had a struggle. She had taken a butcher knife from the kitchen, and she croaked him. She admitted it to me right after the crime."

Sergeant Huntington looked at Jack Hargrave, a light of admiration in his eyes.

"Jack," he said softly, "where did you leave Phil Brazer?"

Hargrave grinned. "Out at the house, waiting for something to turn up."

"How did you know this was Relavan?"

"Simple. His finger-prints were all over the job. A man like Relavan wouldn't have left any prints unless he couldn't have helped himself. If he'd been going there once, or even twice or three times he'd have worn gloves.

"Then, again, when this man suddenly recollected how the book agent had pulled the lobe of his ear, I knew we had him. An old-timer like Relavan would have changed a habit like pulling at an ear as soon as he knew the police were using it as something to twig him by."

Relavan shrugged his shoulders.

"Right," he said, with a grimace. "Boy, they must have been gettin' a new class of dicks since I got out of stir!"

Hargrave turned on him. "What did you go to Goldfinch for, the diamonds?"

"No," said Relavan, "I didn't. I don't know that I was going straight, but I wanted to lay low. I applied for half a dozen jobs, all on forged references. This guy, Slacker, that runs things for Goldfinch, took a shine to me. He's a square shooter, too. He knew my references were forged, found that out before he hired me; but he hired me anyway. That is, he got Goldfinch to do it. Goldfinch'd do everything Slacker told him to."

Sergeant Huntington jabbed an accusing forefinger at Relavan.

"We're going to search your room out there at the house. You've got diamonds in it?"

Relavan shrugged. "Four or five small ones the housekeeper overlooked when she cleaned up the place."

The sergeant nodded. "Thought so. Book him, Jack."

The detective escorted his prisoner from the room. The first trickle of drab dawn percolated through the window. The sergeant grinned at Sidney Zoom.

That individual produced the dodger, describing Robert Reelen, alias Sid Whalen, alias Charles Gillen. "Can you find me his record?" he asked.

Sergeant Huntington took the dodger carelessly, jabbed his forefinger on a button. A man thrust his head into the room, caught the sergeant's beckoning finger and entered.

"Take this up to the Identification Bureau. Get me the dope on it right away."

The man vanished.

"Could we talk with the housekeeper?" asked Zoom.

Sergeant Huntington stared at him.

"What's the matter? Think this case isn't solved yet?"

Zoom took a cigarette from his pocket case, lit it deliberately.

"Your men arrested a girl in a pawnshop. I'm interested in her. I don't think she's guilty."

The grin on Sergeant Huntington's face was wide.

"Oh, her! Myrtle Crane her name was. Booked already, bail fixed at ten thousand cash, twenty thousand bond. Maybe she's telling the truth. I'll let you talk to the housekeeper."

He jabbed the button once more, gave orders that Sally Barker was to be awakened, brought in. There followed an interval of silence. After it had lasted for minutes Jack Hargrave came back. He was grinning.

"Notified Phil Brazer over the phone. You should have heard him."

Sergeant Huntington chuckled.

There was a knock at the door. A man walking swiftly upon rubber heels came to Sergeant Huntington's desk. He bent over, whispered. There was a rustle of paper, a grunt of wonder from Sergeant Huntington.

"Listen, you fellows," he said. "This dodger is a fake. It was printed on a hand press somewhere. The boys can't find anything on this guy or his record, nor did we get any such dodger."

Hargrave pulled his forehead into a frown.

"Well," he said, "what's the answer?"

Sergeant Huntington looked at Sidney Zoom.

At that moment there was another knock and the door swung open. A heavy set matron, clad in black, her face expressionless, led a slender woman with deep, lackluster black eyes into the room.

"Sit down, Mrs. Barker," said Sergeant Huntington.

The woman folded herself into angular compliance, arranged her skirts so that they were smooth across the knees, raised her black, lackluster eyes and spoke in a drab tone of utter listlessness.

"I can't tell you nothing more. You don't believe me, anyway."

Sergeant Huntington cleared his throat, leaned forward until the old swivel chair creaked under his shifting weight.

"All right. This'll jar you loose from some conversation. Arthur Madison, the butler, was Shortly Relavan, the noted gem thief and ex-convict. He's confessed. How do you feel about that?"

The woman's face remained a drab mask. The thin hand with the blue veins and raised tendons, showed just a trace of nervousness as it smoothed over the skirt once more. But the voice was the same as ever, a monotone of comment.

"Fancy me working with an ex-convict!"

Jack Hargrave slammed a remark at her.

"Ain't you interested in what he said?"

Her voice was in the same even, uninterested tone.

"What did he say?"

"He said you killed Goldfinch."

"I didn't."

"How did you get the diamonds?"

"I've told you. You won't believe me. Mr. Goldfinch told me he'd torn up his will. He gave me those stones in case anything should happen to him. I was to pawn them and get the money."

Sergeant Huntington squirmed forward to the very edge of his chair. His big fist banged on the desk. His expression showed that he was going to make one last determined effort to browbeat the truth from the woman.

Sidney Zoom stepped forward, his long arm picked up the dodger which had been left on the desk, the one containing the picture of Robert Reelen. He whirled, extended the paper toward the woman.

"Know him?" he asked.

The lackluster eyes flickered to the paper. For a swift instant there was an expression of surprise. Then it vanished.

"Yes," she said.

"Well?" asked Sidney Zoom.

"He used to come to the house. I think he sold diamonds. His name was Charles Gillen. He hadn't come for a while. I thought he was a smuggler, maybe."

Sergeant Huntington brushed aside the matter of the dodger.

"I want," he said slowly and impressively, banging his fist upon the desk as he spoke each word, "to get the rest of those diamonds. Tell—me—where—they—are!"

The woman's hand, sliding over the smooth surface of her skirt, gave a convulsive clutch at the cloth. It was but a momentary tightening of the fingers. Then the hand relaxed and the lackluster eyes were raised to the glittering eyes of the sergeant.

"I've told you all I know."

Sidney Zoom got to his feet.

"If you'll excuse me," he said, "I've work to do."

His long legs gained the door in four strides.

The two men watched him with eyes that were wide with surprise. Sidney Zoom's hand tightened upon the knob of the door, spun it. He pulled it open and vanished into the corridor without so much as a backward glance.

The door slammed shut and the two men looked at each other. Then they looked at the slender figure in the chair. She raised her deep-set, unsparkling eyes, lowered them almost at once. The fingers of her right hand clutched at the cloth of her dress.

CHAPTER VII

Zoom Visits an Office

SIDNEY ZOOM paused before a door on the seventh floor of a down town office building. Rip, his police dog, stood at his side, tail waving softly to and fro.

Sidney Zoom tried the lock with a key, failed, tried again. The third key clicked back the catch and Sidney Zoom entered the office.

Dawn had tinged the skyline of the city with a ruddy glow. Already the streets were commencing to rumble with the first signs of traffic, yet it would be some time before the office workers would throng into the business district.

The office air was stale after the freshness of the dawn. It assailed the nostrils as some foul poison, and Sidney Zoom's lip curled with disgust as he inhaled. But he mastered his disgust and set to work.

The office was a single room affair, and it was a litter of odds and ends. Dusty papers were piled in confusion. A desk was grimed with dust, covered with old correspondence. A pile of newspapers was in one corner of the room. A closet offered storage space for some old coats, a dust covered hat, an umbrella and a box filled with an assortment of letters.

Sidney Zoom set to work.

He uncovered the typewriter which stood upon a little stand, took a sheet of paper and began to write. His words were purely specimen words. Then he struck off the letters of the alphabet, writing each one several times.

When he had finished with that sheet he took another and did the same thing. Then he left the typewriter uncovered, left the sheets beside it.

Next Sidney Zoom did a strange thing.

He took from a hand bag he had brought with him, a large package of cheesecloth and a can of floor polish. He stooped to the linoleum and began to scrub the liquid polish upon the linoleum, working slowly, painstakingly.

The dog watched him from a corner, head on paws, eyes alone moving.

It took Sidney Zoom three-quarters of an hour to finish his task. Then he motioned to the dog, indicated the closet.

Slowly, questioningly, the dog entered the closet.

"Stay there, Rip," commanded Sidney Zoom.

Then he stepped to the outer doorway.

The corridor of the office building was of a white marble effect. Upon it, in front of the door of the office, Sidney Zoom sprinkled some white powder. It was virtually invisible against the white of the corridor.

"Wait there, Rip," he called to the dog who had crawled back into the corner of the closet at the command of his master, and closed the closet door until it was open but a half an inch.

The dog whined, but remained where he had been placed.

Sidney Zoom left the office. The latch on the outer door clicked as he pulled it shut.

Then Sidney Zoom took up a vigil before the entrance of the office building. There was in his posture something of the grim efficiency of a lion waiting by a water hole.

The traffic of the street increased. Early office workers began to straggle into the building. Slowly, almost imperceptibly, the stream increased. Abruptly it reached its crest. Young women, expressionless of face, bright of eye, shouldered their way into elevators, thronged the corridors.

Then almost at once, the stream thinned. Late comers sprinted for elevators, glancing anxiously at the clock. Business men bustled into the corridors, portly, important.

Sidney Zoom surveyed the whole stream of civilization's flotsam as it slid past. His scornful eyes showed his hatred for the entire affair, but they missed no face.

It was nine twenty that a pasty face showed at the doorway of the lobby. A fat man walked with swift, jerky steps, so nervously rapid that they jiggled the pasty balls of flesh which clung to his flabby face.

"Ah," said Sidney Zoom, "Mr. Jed Slacker."

The man jerked himself to an abrupt stop.

"Huh? Who? What?"

The words were explosive.

Sidney Zoom smiled, a cold, frosty smile.

"It's a wonder you wouldn't come to your office in the morning! I've been waiting an hour."

The flabby face twisted into a sudden smile that pushed the balls of fat about into a strange distortion.

"Oh, yes, yes, yes, yes! Zoom! Mr. Sidney Zoom. Met you out at Goldfinch's place. Sure had me worried last night. Or was it this morning? Guess it was this morning. Slept late. Seemed good to get to sleep. First sleep I've had for a long time— seems like a long time. Tried to get to sleep but simply couldn't. Worrying ... What d'yuh want?"

"Just wanted to talk with you. Thought maybe Hargrave had seen you."

"Hargrave? Hargrave? Hargrave? Oh, yes, Jack Hargrave. Detective. Young fellow. Nice chap that. Why should he see me? Looking for me?"

"I suppose so. He had the key to your office, I noticed."

The flabby face seemed for an instant to become more pallid. The skin took on a waxy luster of dead white.

"Key? Key? Key? Key to my office? Must be mistaken, Zoom. Nobody has a key to my office, only me."

Zoom's smile was patronizing.

"Well," he said, "you must have shut that detective up in the office all night then. When I went up to your office to see if you were in I met him coming out. He had a sheet of typewriting in his hand, and some sort of a legal looking document.

"I spoke to him and he didn't seem glad to see me in particular. Don't think he knew who I was. He figured I was some other tenant of an office on the same floor, I guess. But, even so, he wasn't at all cordial. Didn't seem to want to be seen. Hope I have not said anything I shouldn't."

The fat man suddenly broke into an explosive laugh.

"Say anything you shouldn't! Hell, no! Remember now. Hargrave asked me if I had a duplicate key. Said he wanted to try out my typewriter. Seemed like he wanted to trace the writing on that declaration of trust I found. Don't know why he wanted to do that, though.

"I'd forgotten about the key. Matter slipped my mind. That what he had with him, the declaration of trust?"

"The one you found last night?" asked Sidney Zoom.

"Yeah. That's the one."

Sidney Zoom puckered his forehead.

"Well now, I couldn't say for certain, but it looked like it."

Jed Slacker jerked a watch from his pocket.

"Gosh, late. Got to go meet some friends on a train. What was it you wanted, Zoom?"

"I wanted to see you for five minutes."

The man fingered the watch.

"Tell, you what you do, give me five minutes to open my mail. Then come up. Five minutes is all I want. Don't be longer. Five minutes. Remember."

Sidney Zoom inclined his head.

"Five minutes," he agreed.

But it was a scant three minutes between the time he said it and the time his hand twisted the knob on the door of Jed Slacker's office.

The fat man was seated at the desk, his hands holding the two typewritten sheets Zoom had written on his machine.

He glanced up as Zoom pushed the door open.

"Huh!" he said, dropped the sheets.

Sidney Zoom walked forward and took a chair.

He smiled, a cold, frosty smile.

"I've discovered about the dodger," he said.

"What dodger?"

"The one you had printed that had the picture of Charles Gillen on it. Rather clever, too. Gillen is listed in the city directory, by the way. Probably you knew that."

The fat man licked his lips with the tip of his tongue.

"Gillen, Gillen, Gillen?" he said. "Dodger, city directory?"

Zoom nodded affably, but coldly.

"Yes, the dodger you had printed describing Mr. Goldfinch's dealer as a thief."

The man rotated his head upon his massive neck in a gesture of oily negation.

"No. He never sold Goldfinch many diamonds. Just a few—comparatively."

CHAPTER VIII

The White Steps—

SIDNEY ZOOM leaned back in the chair, crossed his long legs, smiled, lit a cigarette.

"Now," he said, after the manner of one discussing a chess problem, "it's interesting to see how your mind worked. You could influence Goldfinch. You didn't dare to steal his diamonds, murder him, and at the same time have him leave a will in your favor. That would make it appear you were the beneficiary of his demise.

"You wanted to have suspicion point elsewhere. So you fixed things so the housekeeper would be placed in a position where she'd be convicted even before she came to trial. You fixed things so Goldfinch would actually tell her something that would sound so bizarre when it was repeated that it would make a jury laugh.

"And, in case anything went wrong, you wanted a second string to your bow. You were given applications for the position of butler by Mr. Goldfinch. In running down some of the references you found those of Arthur Madison were false. So you checked them a little more carefully, found Madison was an ex-convict who was trying to find a place where he could lie low for a while. That suited your purpose splendidly, so you hired him.

"Now let's see how things worked out."

Sidney Zoom uncrossed his legs.

Jed Slacker was listening with a face that had been drained of color. His right hand was lowered, resting upon one of the drawers in the desk. His eyes were huge, the flesh seemed to sag away from them, leave them round and gleaming.

"Crazy!" he exploded. "Crazy as a clam!"

Sidney Zoom nodded.

"Yes, only clams aren't crazy … However, as I was saying, let's see how it worked. You waited until Goldfinch had made a small purchase from Charles Gillen. You waited until you felt certain the butler convict had been able to steal and conceal some of the diamonds."

"Then you flashed your fake circular on Goldfinch. He had always had a horror of buying stolen gems. Not that he cared particularly about the ethics of the situation, but because he was afraid of paying good money for stones and then finding he had no title to them.

"So Goldfinch decided to get rid of the stones he'd purchased from Gillen, after you had convinced him those stones were stolen. Then was when you pulled a master stroke. You explained to Goldfinch that he'd left his housekeeper a sum under his will that would just about equal what he'd pay for the stones. Why not take those stones and give them to her, tear up the will and let the accounts balance?

"Goldfinch fell for the idea. It would save his face all around. He didn't dare to sell the stones, knowing they were stolen and might be traced. Nor did he want to keep them. He gave them to his housekeeper and told her exactly what she said he had. But it sounded so utterly improbable under the questioning of the officers that it was ludicrous.

"And you knew that sooner or later Shorty Relavan would enter the picture. And he could be counted on to do just what he did do. There was a murder and there was a robbery. If he said he was innocent no one would believe him, not with diamonds in his room.

"So it was up to him to make up a story that would admit theft, or the receipt of stolen property, but pin the murder more securely on to the shoulders of the housekeeper, where the police had already fastened it."

Sidney Zoom stopped talking.

Jed Slacker began to laugh, a nervous, almost silent laugh.

"Then what?" he asked.

"You wanted to get Goldfinch's fortune. You wanted to steal the diamonds. But you didn't dare to trust to a will. So you had Goldfinch give you a large block of stock and gave him a receipt and acknowledgment of trust. You knew where he kept those sort of papers.

"Then you killed him, and you planted a fake declaration of a half interest in some of your own stuff that hadn't turned out to be other than an expense, and you destroyed your own declaration of trust.

"The police were slow in finding the place where the papers were stored, so you led them to it. You'd taken out the bulk of the diamonds. But you left a few so it wouldn't look as though the place had been looted."

Of a sudden the man's tactics changed.

"Proof!" he bellowed, reaching for the telephone with his left hand. "Try to find any proof. I'm ringing the police right now. I'm going to have you arrested for defamation of character. I'm going to ..."

Sidney Zoom pointed to the floor.

"Clever, what? The police came in here and took the writing of your machine so they could show the declaration of trust they found was written by you on this machine, and I arranged things so your first tracks when you entered the room would be visible.

"Naturally, you were worried whether the police had found where you'd hidden the diamonds. Your steps show that you rushed at once to the framed picture over the radiator. I presume there's a hollow in the frame or something ..."

The basilisk eyes stared with the fascination of utter horror at the white blotches on the smoothly polished linoleum. As Sidney Zoom had said, they went directly from door to picture, picture to typewriter, typewriter to desk.

Jed Slacker sighed.

"Then," he said, with a cunning leer, "the police weren't here at all. You were the one who wrote off the things from the typewriter. Did it so I'd be nervous when I came in. If you polished the floor, the police weren't here."

Zoom nodded after the manner of one who concedes a trick in a bridge game.

"Well reasoned," he said.

The hand of the pudgy man whipped up from underneath the desk.

"Then you're the only one that knows," he half whispered, and Sidney Zoom found himself staring into the dark hollow of a gun muzzle.

Sidney Zoom was careful not to move his hands.

"All right, Rip," he said.

"And you die!" sneered the fat man, half rising from his chair, his lips curled back from his tooth tips. "I'd sooner take chances ..."

A tawny streak burst open the closet door, went across the waxed linoleum with a great scratching of claws as the police dog tried for traction.

Jed Slacker saw him coming, whirled the gun.

The police dog leaped. His teeth closed on the flabby wrist, just above the gun hand. The dog flung himself to one side so that his weight crashed against the arm, twisted the wrist.

Jed Slacker dropped the gun. The dog instantly released his hold and dropped to the floor, growling, the gun within a few inches of his curled lips and glistening fangs.

"I wanted, of course," said Sidney Zoom, speaking in casual tones, "something like that, a declaration of guilt. There's the typewriter. You'd better write a confession."

The fat man stared at him in utter incredulity.

"It was to be the perfect crime," he said. "I fixed it so it could never be pinned on me, and now ..."

Sidney Zoom shrugged his shoulders, a gesture of utter finality.

"Don't bother. I can't get any sympathy for men who commit murder and try to pin it onto an innocent woman."

"But ..."

"Get busy with that confession, or I shall have to turn the dog loose on you. He likes to save murderers from the chair. After all it's not so bad—having your throat ripped out."

The man shuddered, sighed, seemed to collapse. The spirit left him. He put paper into the typewriter.

Sidney Zoom sat and smoked.

CHAPTER IX

—of Death!

THE FAT man grew more enthusiastic as he typed. The pudgy fingers struck the keys, rattling off the letters. The face took on some semblance of color. Once or twice he smiled.

Sidney Zoom arose, looked over the man's shoulder.

The confession was written as one might gloat over a victory. Slacker reveled in the details, telling of how he had fooled the police, of how he had left some two dozen diamonds in with the papers, of his feelings when Phil Brazer had palmed many of those diamonds while he was groping around in the receptacle.

Even the police were not immune to the greed lust which had actuated Slacker. But Slacker had got hundreds of diamonds, the crooked detective but a dozen or so.

Sidney Zoom watched the confession as the sheets rolled out of the typewriter. When Slacker had finished Zoom told him to sign each page, and the fat man dashed off his signatures with a flourish.

"You missed lots of my moves," he complained. "The press will get this. I want to stand before the public in the true light, a master criminal."

Sidney Zoom nodded casually. "Of course."

"How'd you know I had the diamonds hidden here? Why not in my room?"

"Because you asked for five minutes after I told you the thing that would make you realize the police suspected you. If you'd suddenly remembered something that made you want to go back to your room I'd have followed you and burst in just when you were at your hiding place."

Slacker nodded. "Well," he said, "it's over."

Zoom shook his head.

"No. It's not over. Not until they come into your cell and shave off a bit of your scalp, and slit your pants leg. Then they start the grim march, down the corridor, the last steps you'll take, the steps of death ..."

"Don't!" yelled Slacker. "Good God, don't sketch the picture like that—Ugh, the chair—the horror of having people take you out and make you die. It isn't that I'm afraid of death. I don't fear dying. I hate to be dragged out by a lot of jailers, pulled down a corridor, strapped in an iron chair ... I hate to think that they're waiting, watching, night and day, ticking off the time ..."

Sidney Zoom got to his feet.

"They say electrocution is painful," he said. "I'm going out and bring in the police. Don't try to escape while I'm gone. I shall leave the dog against the door on the outside."

He got to his feet, his long angular length showing fine and strong against the flabby softness of the other's panic.

"Come, Rip," he said, and marched to the door, slammed it shut. The lock clicked into place.

He paused, standing to one side in the corridor, listening.

That for which he had been waiting came within a matter of seconds.

"*Bang!*" the roar of a single shot.

Something thudded to the floor. There was silence.

Sidney Zoom motioned to the dog.

Together, they sought the stairs and went down to the street. The noise of the shot might have been taken for backfire by the occupants of other offices.

Sidney Zoom went to the yacht basin where his small, but well-appointed yacht, the *Alberta F.*, rode at her anchor.

Vera Thurmond, his secretary, greeted him.

"Anything new?"

"Not much." His tone was weary. "Take ten thousand dollars. Go up and bail a girl named Myrtle Crane out of jail. She was arrested for complicity in the robbery of Jacob Goldfinch. Wake me up if anything happens."

And Sidney Zoom sought his cabin, apparently unaware of the look of maternal tenderness which welled in the eyes of his secretary.

With the dog stretched on a rug near the foot of his bed, he dropped into dreamless slumber, lulled by the lap-lap-lap of the water against the sides of the yacht.

He was awakened by a knocking against the cabin door.

"Sergeant Huntington," called his secretary.

"Come in," said Zoom, sitting up.

Sergeant Huntington strode into the room. With him came Jack Hargrave.

Huntington's manner was crisp, official. Hargrave looked at Sidney Zoom in a manner of respect. There was something almost of reverence in his glance.

"Hargrave got the hunch Slacker had acted funny," said Sergeant Huntington. "He started looking for him. He found him at his office a little afternoon. Slacker had been dead some time. Suicide all right, his own gun and all that, and a confession, and the stolen diamonds in the hollowed picture frame. Here's the confession."

He passed over the typewritten sheets.

Sidney Zoom read them. A smile twisted his lips.

"Funny?" asked Sergeant Huntington with sarcasm.

"Thinking about Phil Brazer groping around for the diamonds. He was palming as many as he could, working them up his sleeve," said Zoom. "That was why it took him so long to fish out the stones."

Sergeant Huntington grunted.

Zoom finished the confession, handed it back.

"This is one case I'm surprised on," he said.

Sergeant Huntington glowered at him.

"You went bail for Myrtle Crane."

"Yes. I frequently do when I think people are innocent."

"And," went on Sergeant Huntington, "some one had scrubbed the office floor and sprinkled white powder at the entrance."

Sidney Zoom raised his eyebrows.

"Yes?"

"Yes. And a tall man and a dog were seen hanging around the lobby of the office building."

Zoom nodded.

"Oh, yes. That was I. Rip and I waited. Then, when we got tired we left."

"What were you waiting for?"

"I wanted to ask Mr. Slacker a question."

"What about?"

"Something about that fake dodger, you know, the one about the diamond thief ..."

"Yes," said Sergeant Huntington, "I know. I also know, Sidney Zoom, that whenever you start to solve a case you solve it. Of late I've been noticing that when you start in on a murder case and find the real culprit, that culprit never lives to get to jail."

Zoom reached for a cigarette.

"The State executes men for murder?" he asked.

"Yes," said Sergeant Huntington.

Zoom said nothing further.

After the silence had begun to be awkward, Sergeant Huntington rasped into speech.

"Will you admit you saw Slacker this morning?"

"No."

"Do you know that Slacker's steps show when he entered that room, that there are white blobs going to the picture frame, to the typewriter, back to his desk?"

"Were there?"

"Yes. There were."

"And that same white powder shows the tracks of another man who entered the room and sat down, talking with Slacker."

Zoom looked interested.

"Tracks of a dog, too?" he asked.

Sergeant Huntington frowned.

"No, that's what puzzles me."

"Well," remarked Zoom, "it lets me out. I had my dog with me this morning. Your own witnesses admit that."

He yawned, looked at the tip of his cigarette, glanced at Sergeant Huntington.

"Steps of death, eh?"

Sergeant Huntington suppressed an exclamation, stepped back.

"Well," he said, "it looks like hell, that's all. Looks as though some one had made it easy for this chap to shoot himself."

Zoom's voice was only mild in its interest.

"You were looking for some one higher up in this affair, weren't you?"

"Yes."

Zoom made a motion with his muscular, angular shoulders.

"Look for something higher up in this, then."

"Higher up?"

"Yes. You might try divine justice, for instance."

Sergeant Huntington snorted, turned on his heel.

Jack Hargrave stepped to the bed.

"Good day, sir. I just wanted to shake hands."

Silently, solemnly, the two men shook hands.

"Higher up," said Hargrave.

"Higher up," repeated Sidney Zoom and his tone had the timbre of a tolling bell.

THE FIRST STONE

CHAPTER I

The Man on the Sidewalk

RAIN SHEETED intermittently out of the midnight skies. Between showers fitful stars showed through drifting cloud rifts. Street lights, reflected from the wet pavements in shimmering ribbons, were haloed in moisture. Intermittent thunder boomed.

The feet of Sidney Zoom, pacing the wet pavements, splashed heedlessly through small surface puddles. Attired in raincoat and rubber hat, the gaunt form prowled through the rainy night, his police dog padding along at his side.

Sidney Zoom loved the night. He was particularly fond of rainy nights. Midnight streets held for him the lure of adventure. He prowled ceaselessly at night, searching for those oddities of human conduct which would arouse his interest.

The police dog growled, throatily.

Sidney Zoom paused, stared down at his four-footed companion.

"What is it, Rip?"

The dog's yellow eyes were staring straight ahead. His ears were pricked up. After a moment he flung his head in a questing half circle as his nose tested the air.

He growled again, and the hair along the top of his back ruffled into bristling life.

"Go find, Rip."

Like an arrow, the dog sped forward into the night, his claws rattling upon the wet pavement. He ran low to the ground, swift and sure. He leaned far in as he rounded a corner, then the night swallowed him.

Sidney Zoom walked as far as the corner where the dog had vanished, then stood, waiting. He heard footsteps, the rustle of a rubber raincoat and a dark figure bulked upon him.

A flash light stabbed its way through the darkness.

"What are you doin' here?" grumbled a deep voice.

The hawklike eyes of Sidney Zoom stared menacingly at the flash light.

"Who are you?—and put out that damned flash!"

The beam of the flash light shot up and down the long, lean, whipcorded strength of the man, and the grumbling voice rumbled again.

"I'm the officer on the beat. It's no time for a man to be standin' out on a street corner, all glistenin' with rain, an' lookin' into the night as though he was listenin' for something. So give an account of yourself, unless you want to spend a night in a cell."

Sidney Zoom turned his eyes away from the glare of the light, fished a leather wallet from an inside pocket, and let the officer see a certain card.

That card bore the signature of the chief of police.

The officer whistled.

"Sidney Zoom, eh?" he said in surprise. "I've heard of you an' of your police dog. Where's the dog?"

Sidney Zoom's head was cocked slightly to one side, listening.

"If you'll quit talking for a moment I think we can hear him."

The officer stopped stock-still, listening. Faintly through the night could be heard the barking of a dog.

"It's around the other corner," said Zoom.

The officer grunted.

"What's he barkin' at?"

Sidney Zoom's long legs started to pace along the wet pavement. A sudden shower came rattling down upon the hard surface of their shiny raincoats. Water streamed from the rims of rubber hats.

"The best way to find out," said Sidney Zoom, "is to go and see."

The officer was put to it to keep pace with the long legs.

"I've heard of some of your detective work," he said.

He gave the impression of one who wished to engage in conversation, but the pace was such that he needed all of his wind. Sidney Zoom said nothing.

"And of your dog," puffed the officer.

Sidney Zoom paused, motioned to the officer to halt, raised his head and whistled. Instantly there came an answering bark.

Zoom's ears caught the direction of that bark, and he lengthened his stride. The officer ceased all efforts to keep step and came blowing along, taking a step and a half to Zoom's one.

A street light showed a huddled shadow. The dog barked again, and Sidney Zoom pointed.

"Something on the sidewalk," he said.

The officer started to say something, but thought better of it. Such conversation as he might have could wait until he had more breath to spare for it.

Zoom's stride became a running walk. His lean form seemed fairly vibrant with excitement.

"Some one lying down," he said.

The dog barked once more, a shrill, yapping bark, as though he tried to convey some meaning. And Sidney Zoom interpreted the meaning of that bark.

"Dead," he said.

The officer grunted his incredulity.

But Zoom had been right. The man was quite dead. He lay sprawled out upon the pavement, on his face, his hands stretched out and clenched, as though he had clutched at something.

There was a dark hole in the back of the man's head, and a welling stream of red had oozed down until it mingled with the water on the sidewalk, staining it red. The hat was some ten feet away, lying flat upon the sidewalk.

The man had on a coat, trousers, heavy shoes. But there were pyjamas underneath. The bottoms of the pyjamas showed beneath the legs of the trousers, and the collar of the pyjama coat showed through a place where the coat lapel had been twisted backward.

The officer ran his hands to the wet wrists of the corpse.

"Dead," he said.

"That," remarked Sidney Zoom, dryly, "is what the dog told me. He'd have come running to me, urging haste, if the figure had still had life."

The officer looked up with glittering eyes.

"You kidding me?" he asked.

Sidney Zoom shrugged his shoulders. Experience had taught him the futility of seeking to explain canine intelligence, highly developed, to one who had had no experience with it.

The officer turned the figure over. Zoom's hand thrust out, caught the officer's arm.

"Wait," he said, "you're destroying the most valuable clew we have!"

The officer's eyes were wide.

"I'm just turnin' him over."

He had paused, the corpse precariously balanced upon one shoulder and hip, the head sagging downward.

Zoom nodded.

"Precisely," he said. "But you'll notice that the shoulders of the coat, on the upper part, around the neck, are quite wet. That shows that he's been out in the rain for some little time. But the back of the coat is almost dry.

"That means he was walking, facing the rain, that he hasn't been lying very long on his stomach here. Otherwise the back of the coat would have been quite wet. But if you turn him over before we check on these things, and the back of the coat lays on the wet pavement, we'll have no way of determining the comparative degree to which the garments are soaked."

The officer grunted.

"You're right about the shoulders," he said, feeling them with an awkward hand. "And the front of his coat is sopping wet. It looks as though he'd been walkin' toward the wind, all right."

Zoom ran his fingers over the garments. His eyes held that hawklike glitter of concentration which marked his arousing interest.

"Now the wind," said Zoom, "was blowing in the same direction the head is pointing. Which means that he was either turned around, after the shot, or that he had changed the direction of his walk. You'll notice that he has no socks on, that the shoes are incompletely laced, and the strings hastily tied about the ankles.

"Apparently the man had retired for the night, when something aroused him, sent him hurriedly out into the rain with just the very barely essential clothes on.

"He was shot in the back of the head. Probably the shot coincided with a clap of thunder, since no one seems to have heard it, and it's a district where there are apartment houses. He probably has been dead less than quarter of an hour.

"Let's have the flash on his face, officer."

The beam of light played obediently upon the cold face.

They disclosed features of a man somewhat past the middle fifties. His face was covered with gray stubble. His hair was thin at the temples. The high forehead was creased with scowl wrinkles. The mouth was a firm, thin line, almost lipless. Deep calipers showed that the corners of the mouth were habitually twisted downward.

"A man," said Sidney Zoom, "who seldom smiled."

The officer's hand went to the coat pocket.

"Lots of papers in this pocket. You go notify headquarters. I'll stay here and watch."

Zoom's eyes focused upon the wet pavement, some three feet beyond the corpse.

"Officer, raise your flash light a bit—higher—there!"

"What is it?"

CHAPTER II

The Scattered Beads

THE RAYS of the flash light were caught, reflected back by something that glowed an angry red. Zoom walked over to it, stooped, picked it up.

"A red bead, or a synthetic ruby, pierced for stringing on a necklace," he said, "and I think there's another one a little farther on. Let's see."

The officer obediently elevated the flash. Once more there was a dull gleam of angry red from the darkness.

"From the direction he was travelin'," said the officer.

Zoom picked up the second bead, stalked back to the corpse.

"Look in his hands," he ordered.

The officer pried open the left hand. It was empty. He pulled back the fingers of the right hand. Half a dozen red beads glittered in the reflection of the flash light, glowing red and angry, their color suggestive of drops of congealed blood.

Sidney Zoom scowled thoughtfully.

"Is that a bit of white thread there?" he asked.

The policeman bent forward.

"It is that. What do you make of it?"

Zoom stared in unwinking thought at the small cluster of red gems. "They may be genuine rubies. I doubt it. They look like synthetic rubies. Notice that they graduate slightly in size. Evidently they were strung on a necklace. There's a chance, just a chance, that the necklace was worn by the one who fired the fatal shot, that the man clutched at this person, caught the necklace in his hand and ripped out a section of it.

"Then, when that person fled from the shooting, there were more of the rubies that dropped ... but I doubt it."

The officer lurched to his feet, letting the body slump back upon the wet pavement.

"It's gettin' too many for me," he said. "I don't want to leave the body, even if I do know you're all right. You go in that apartment house and get a telephone, notify headquarters."

Zoom nodded.

"Stay there, Rip," he said. "I'll be right back."

The dog slowly waved his tail in a single swing of dignified acquiescence, to show that he understood. Zoom crossed the street to an apartment house.

The outer door was locked, the lobby dark.

Zoom's forefinger pressed against the call button below the apartment marked "Manager" until he had received a response. When a fat woman with sleep swollen eyes came protestingly to the door, Zoom explained the situation, was given a telephone, called headquarters and reported the finding of the body.

Then he returned to the officer. The dog was crouched down upon the wet pavement, his head resting upon his paws. He thumped his tail upon the pavement by way of greeting, remained otherwise immobile. The officer was going through the papers in the pocket.

"Seems to be a man named Harry Raine," he observed. "There's a bunch of letters and papers here. Looks like he tried to carry all his correspondence in his pocket. The address is here, too. It's out West Adams Street, 5685. And here's some legal papers, looks like he'd been in a lawsuit of some kind.

"The papers have been carried around for some time. You can see where pencil marks have rubbed off on 'em and polished up until they're slick."

Zoom nodded. He was studying the face of the dead man.

"Ain't you interested in these papers?" asked the officer.

Zoom's expression was one of dreamy abstraction.

"I'm more interested in the possible character of this dead man," he observed. "He looks to me like an old crank, a man who never smiled, who had no compassion, no kindness. Look at those hands! See the gnarled grasping fingers ... Do you believe in palmistry, officer?"

The policeman grunted scornfully.

"Baloney," he said.

Zoom said nothing for a matter of seconds.

"It's strange," he remarked, "how character impresses itself upon every portion of a person's body. Hands, feet, ears, shape of the nose, the mouth, the expression of the eyes ... everything is shaped by that intangible something we call a soul."

The officer, squatted on the wet pavement by the side of the corpse, lurched to his feet.

"You're talkin' stuff that don't make sense," he growled. "This here is a murder case, and the law has got to catch the person that did the murder. What's the character of the dead man got to do with the thing?"

Sidney Zoom's reply consisted of one word.

"Everything," he said, and then reached for the papers which had been in the pocket of the corpse.

The officer grunted his disbelief.

"Murders," he observed, "are everyday affairs. Handle 'em as routine an' you get somewhere. Identify the dead guy, see who wanted him bumped, round up the evidence and maybe give a little third degree at headquarters, an' you're ready for the next case."

Sidney Zoom said nothing. In the distance could be heard the wailing of sirens.

"There are powder marks on the back of the head," said Sidney Zoom, after the siren had wailed for the second time. "Let me see your flash light."

The officer handed him the flash light. Zoom circled the gutter with its rays, steadied his hand abruptly, pointed.

"There it is."

"There what is?"

"The empty shell. See it, there in the gutter? He was shot with an automatic. The ejector flipped the shell out into the street, the running water from that last burst of rain washed it down into the gutter."

The officer bent himself with an effort, picked up the shell.

"You're right. A forty-five automatic."

The siren wailed again. Lights glittered from the wet street, and the first of the police cars swung into the cross street, then hissed through the water to the curb.

Another machine followed close behind. Then there sounded the clanging gong of an ambulance. Thereafter, events moved swiftly.

CHAPTER III

The Girl in Apartment 342

DETECTIVE SERGEANT GROMLEY was in charge of the homicide detail, and he heard the officer's report, checked the facts from Sidney Zoom, and started the men gathering up the various clews.

They started tracing the trail of the blood-red beads, found that they led to an apartment house some fifty yards away. They were spaced almost at even intervals, and they glistened in the rays of the searching spotlights.

The district was largely given over to apartment houses, and the wailing sirens had brought watchers to the windows. The cloud rifts drifted into wider spaces and tranquil stars shone down upon the concrete cañon of the sleeping street.

Officers started checking details, trying to find if any one had heard the shot, if any one had noted the time, if there had been any sound of running feet.

Sergeant Gromley scanned the apartment house where the trail of red beads ended and uttered an exclamation of triumph as he pointed to the row of mail boxes in the vestibule, each faced with a printed name cut from a visiting card.

"Notice the apartment 342," he said. "The name's been torn out of there within the last half hour or so. See, there's a wet smear on the cardboard backing, and ... it's a little smear of blood. See it?"

He turned toward the lobby where a man in a bath robe was peering curiously.

"Where's the manager?"

"I own the place. My wife and I run it."

"Who's the tenant in apartment 342?"

The man scowled, ran his fingers through his tousled hair.

"I ain't sure. I think it's a woman. Rainey or some such name. That's it, Raine, Eva Raine. Ain't her name on the mail box?"

The officer laughed. "Come on," he said to the little cluster of broad shouldered assistants who had knotted around him in a compact group. "Let's go."

They went, crowding into the elevator. Sidney Zoom took the stairs, his dog at his heels.

"Here, you," grunted the man in the bath robe, "you can't bring the dog in here!"

But Sidney Zoom paid no attention. His long legs were working like pistons as he went up the stairs, two at a time.

But the officers were debouching from the elevator as Zoom reached the upper corridor. The stairs emerged at the end opposite from the elevator shaft, and the apartment they wanted was close to the elevator.

One of the men pounded upon the door.

It was opened almost immediately by a girl in a kimono. She stared at them in wide eyed silence.

"Oh!" she said, after a moment.

Sergeant Gromley pushed unceremoniously past her.

"We want to ask you some questions," he said.

The others crowded into the little room, which was used as a sitting room during the daytime, a bedroom at night. The wall bed had been let down, apparently slept in, but the sheets were folded neatly at the corners. The girl must be a quiet sleeper, or else had not been in bed long.

She was robed in a kimono of bright red which enhanced the gleam of her eyes, the red of her lips, the glitter of the lights upon her hair, glossy black as a raven's wing.

"You're Eva Raine?" asked Sergeant Gromley.

"Yes. Of course. Why?"

"Know Harry Raine who lives at 5685 West Adams?"

"Y-y-yes, of course."

"Why say 'of course'?"

"He's my father-in-law."

"You married his son?"

"Yes."

"What's the son's name?"

"Edward."

"Where is he?"

"Dead."

"When did you see Mr. Harry Raine last?"

She hesitated at that, made a little motion of nervousness.

"Why, I can't tell. Yesterday afternoon, I think. Yes. It was yesterday afternoon."

"Weren't very certain, were you?"

She lowered her eyes.

"I'm a little confused. What is the idea of all of you men, who seem to be officers, coming here and asking me these questions? I've taken nothing—done nothing."

Sergeant Gromley nodded, a swift, single shake of the head, belligerent, aggressive.

"No one accused you of it—yet."

"What do you want?"

"Information."

"About what?"

"About who might have had a motive for murdering Harry Raine."

The girl came to her full height. The face paled. The eyes widened until the whites showed upon all sides of the irises. The forehead wrinkled into a suggestion of horror.

"Murdered?" she asked.

Her voice was weak, quavering.

"Murdered!" snapped Sergeant Gromley.

"I—I don't know."

"Was there bad blood between you?"

She hesitated, then became regal in her bearing.

"Yes," she said, "and I'm glad he's dead—if he is dead. He was a brute, parsimonious, narrow-minded, bigoted, selfish."

Sergeant Gromley nodded casually. The character of the dead man was of no consequence to him. It mattered not how much the man might have deserved to die. It was the fact that the law requires vengeance which mattered to the officer.

"Who murdered him?"

"I—I don't know."

"Have you a necklace of strung rubies, or imitation rubies, or red glass beads? Think carefully. Your answer may mean a lot to you—and don't lie."

"What have red beads got to do with it?"

"Perhaps nothing, perhaps a lot. Have you such a necklace?"

Her lips clamped tightly.

"No!"

"Do you know any one who has such a necklace?"

"No!"

These single syllables of negation were explosive in their staccato emphasis.

Sergeant Gromley remained undisturbed. There was a lot of ground to cover yet, and the veteran investigator feared no lie. The only thing that caused him consternation was a suspect who would not talk. Given one who would answer questions, and he was always certain of ultimate triumph.

"Where have you been since nine o'clock?"

"In bed!"

The answer came as though it had been rehearsed.

Sergeant Gromley raised his eyebrows.

"In bed?"

"Yes."

"Since nine o'clock?"

"Yes."

The answer was surly this time, defiant, as though she had been trapped into some answer she had not anticipated and intended to stick by her guns.

"What time did you retire?"

"At the time I told you, nine o'clock."

The sergeant's smile was sarcastic.

"You went to bed at nine o'clock?"

"Yes."

He looked over the graceful lines of her figure, the striking beauty of the face.

"Rather early for a young and attractive widow to retire on a Saturday night, isn't it?"

She flushed. "No matter what you are investigating, that is none of your business. You asked me a question, and I answered!"

Sergeant Gromley's smile was irritating. His manner was that of a cat who has a mouse safely hooked in its claws, who is willing to play for a while to torture the animal.

"Rather a coincidence that I was the one who selected the hour of nine o'clock, and you answered so promptly. I am just wondering, Miss Raine, if you hadn't resolved to give the bed story as an alibi, and when I asked you where you had been since nine o'clock, rather than asked you where you had been during the last hour, you said 'in bed' because you had expected the question to be different. Then, having said it the first time, you decided to stick to your story."

She was cool, defiant, but her shoulders were commencing to rise and fall with more rapid breathing.

"Your reasoning is too complicated for my childlike brain. Just confine yourself to necessary questions, please."

The sergeant continued to press the point.

"It is rather a peculiar coincidence that I should have been the one who predicted the exact time of your retirement by asking you the question, isn't it?"

She shrugged her shoulders.

"That, also, is a matter upon which I cannot give you an answer."

She swept her eyes momentarily from the boring eyes of the sergeant to the ring of curious faces which watched her, faces which formed a background, semicircled about the door, just inside of the room.

And, as Sidney Zoom caught her glittering eyes, jet black, shiny with excitement, his long forefinger raised casually to his lips and pressed firmly against them.

Her eyes had left his face before the significance of the gesture impressed her. Then they darted back with a look of swift questioning in them.

But Sidney Zoom, taking no chances that his signal might be seen and interpreted by one of the officers, was scratching the side of his nose with slow deliberation.

The girl returned her eyes to the sergeant, but now there was a look of puzzled uncertainty in them.

"Do you know what the weather is like?" asked Sergeant Gromley.

"It's showering."

He smiled again.

"Really, Miss Raine, you are remarkable. It was quite clear at nine o'clock. The showers started about nine forty-five and continued quite steadily until just before midnight."

She bit her lip.

"And you were asleep?" pursued the sergeant.

Quick triumph gleamed in her eyes as she swooped down upon the opening he had left her with that eagerness which an amateur always shows in rushing into the trap left by a canny professional.

"I didn't say I was asleep."

"Oh, then, you weren't asleep?"

"No, not all the time."

"And that's the way you knew it was raining?"

"Yes. The rain beat against the window. I heard it, got up and looked out. There was some lightning, thunder, rain."

"And that's the only way you knew it was raining?"

"Yes."

"You're positive?"

"Yes. Of course!"

"And you weren't out of this room after nine o'clock to-night?"

"Would I be likely to leave it, attired as I am?"

"Answer the question. Were you out of the room after nine o'clock?"

This time she shifted her eyes, trying to escape the pinning down of the facts as though she could avoid them by moving her eyes from the steady stare of the inquisitor.

And her eyes instinctively sought those of Sidney Zoom.

This time there could be no mistaking the impressive significance of the gesture he made, the forceful pressing of a rigid forefinger against his closed lips.

"Answer the question," boomed Sergeant Gromley, suddenly stern, unsmiling.

"No," she said. "I didn't leave the room."

But her eyes were hesitant, helpless, and they looked pleadingly at Sidney Zoom.

The sergeant swooped, pushed aside a filmy bit of silk, reached a long arm under the edge of the bed, brought out a pair of shoes.

"These your shoes?"

And she knew then that she was trapped, for the shoes were soaked with rain water. The knowledge showed in the sudden panic of her eyes, the pallor of her lips.

She looked at Sidney Zoom, suddenly stiffened.

"I have answered quite enough of your questions, sir. I will not make any more statements until I have seen a lawyer."

He simulated surprise.

"Why ... Why, Miss Raine, what could you possibly want to see a lawyer about? Has any one made any accusations against you?"

"N-n-n-oooo, I don't know as ..."

"Then why should you want a lawyer? Do you expect accusations will be made?"

She sucked in a rapid lungful of breath preparatory to speaking, then raised her eyes once more to Zoom's face.

"I have nothing to say," she said.

The sergeant snapped out a rapid barrage of words.

"Is it your custom to put powder on your cheeks, lip stick on your lips, have your hair freshly done up at one o'clock in the morning? Or were you expecting a call from the police, and, womanlike, wanted to look your best?"

It was plainly a relief to her that she did not need to answer the question. She simply shook her head, but the panic of her eyes was more evident now.

Sergeant Gromley turned to the men.

"Frisk the place, boys."

CHAPTER IV

Jewels in the Mail Box

HE SPOKE quietly, but the effect of his order was instantaneous. The men scattered like a bevy of quail. Drawers were pulled open, skilled fingers explored the contents. They even went to the bed, felt in the mattress, probed in the pillowcase.

Sergeant Gromley kept his eyes upon the defiant, but panicky eyes of the young woman.

"It might be much better for you, later on, if you told the truth now," he said, gently, trying to make the fatherly tone of his admonition break through the wall of reserve that had sealed her lips.

He was almost successful. The touch of fatherly sympathy in his voice brought instant moisture to her eyes. Her lips parted, then clamped tightly closed again. She blinked back the tears.

"I have nothing to say."

One of the officers turned from the dresser.

"Look what's here," he said.

And he held up a fragment of necklace, made of fine red beads, either rubies or colorful imitations, dangling with red splendor in the light.

"Where was it?"

"Hidden. Fastened to the back of the mirror with a bit of chewing gum. You can see where the string was broken, then it was tied up at the ends, and fastened to the back of the mirror."

Sergeant Gromley grunted.

"Let's see the gum."

The officer handed him a wad of chewing gum. The outside was barely dry, had not commenced to harden. It was still soft and pliable.

Sergeant Gromley fastened his eyes upon the young woman once more.

"Yours?" he asked.

She glanced swiftly at Sidney Zoom, shook her head.

"I'll answer no more questions."

Sergeant Gromley sat with his back to Sidney Zoom. He spoke now, quietly, evenly, without raising his voice.

"Zoom, I've heard of you, heard of some of the help you've given the department. It's customary to exclude all civilians from questionings such as these. I let you remain because of your record. Unfortunately you seem to have taken advantage of my generosity."

Sidney Zoom's voice was vibrant.

"Meaning," he asked, "exactly what?"

Sergeant Gromley kept his back turned.

"Do you think," he asked, "that I am an utter fool?"

And Sidney Zoom, rasping out his counter question in a voice that showed he was not accustomed to take orders or criticism, snapped: "Do you want me to leave the room?"

"Yes," said Gromley, without turning his head.

Sidney Zoom gained the door in two strides.

"Come, Rip."

Their feet sounded in the corridor, the man's pounding along in great strides, the dog's pattering softly, a rattling of claws sounding upon the uncarpeted strip of floor at the sides of the hallway.

There was a sardonic smile upon the features of Sidney Zoom as he gained the ground floor of the apartment house.

Here were a few of the curious inmates who had been aroused by the commotion, asking questions, babbling comments which were vague surmises.

Sidney Zoom walked to the outer lobby, paused, surveyed the row of brass letter boxes, each fitted with a keyed lock by which the box could be opened.

Sidney Zoom paused to take from his pocket a pair of gloves. They were thin, flexible gloves, yet they insured against any casual finger-prints being left behind.

"Fools!" he muttered to himself under his breath.

Then he took from a pocket a bunch of keys. They were not many in number, but each had been fashioned with cunning care by a man who had made the study of locks the hobby of an adventurous lifetime.

The third key which he tried clicked back the bolt of the mail box which went with apartment 342.

Sidney Zoom reached a gloved hand inside the aperture, removed a wadded scarf of silk. Within the scarf were several hard objects which rattled crisply against each other.

They might have been pebbles, or bits of glassware, but Sidney Zoom wasted no time in looking to see what they were. He simply dropped the entire bundle, scarf and all, into one of the pockets of his spacious coat, and then went out into the night.

He paused at the nearest available telephone, a small garage where a night man regarded him with sleep swollen eyes, and telephoned to the best criminal attorney in the city.

"This is Zoom speaking. The police are trying to pin a murder charge on a young woman, a Mrs. Eva Raine, who lives in apartment 342 at the Matonia Apartments. They're there now. I'm retaining you to handle the case under the blanket arrangement I have with you. Get out there at once. Tell her to keep quiet. Just tell her to shut up, and see that she does. That's all."

And Sidney Zoom clicked the receiver back on its hook.

He knew that the attorney would be there in a matter of minutes. Sidney Zoom kept him supplied with various and sundry cases which attracted the interest of the strange individual who had for his hobby the prowling of midnight streets and the matching of wits with both criminals and detectives.

Then Sidney Zoom summoned a cab and was driven to the palatial yacht upon which he lived.

Only when he was safely ensconced within his stateroom, did he take out and open the package which he had taken from the mail box.

It was filled with jewels, strung, for the most part, into necklaces.

CHAPTER V

Zoom Gets in Bad

IT WAS ten o'clock in the morning.

The musty air of police headquarters was filled with that stale odor which comes to rooms which are in use twenty-four hours a day.

Captain Bill Mahoney, a small man in the early fifties, but equipped with a large mind, raised dark, speculative eyes and regarded Sidney Zoom thoughtfully.

"Sergeant Gromley," he said, "wants to place a charge against you for aiding and abetting a felon."

"The felon being whom?" asked Sidney Zoom.

"The Raine girl."

Sidney Zoom tapped a cigarette impatiently upon the table, rasped a match along the sole of his shoe, lit the cigarette, shot out the match with a single swift motion of his arm.

"Sergeant Gromley," he said, "is a dangerous man. He is dangerous to innocent and guilty alike."

Captain Mahoney's voice remained quiet.

"He's the best questioner in the department."

"Perhaps."

"And he tells me you interfered with him in the Raine case."

"He's right. I did."

"That's serious, Zoom. We've orders to allow you to coöperate because you've always had a passion for justice, and you've helped us clear up some mighty difficult cases, but you're going to lose your privileges."

Captain Mahoney was never more quiet than when enraged. Zoom had known him for years in a close friendship which was founded upon mutual respect. Yet Captain Mahoney would have been among the first to have admitted that, despite his long intimacy, he knew virtually nothing of that strange, sardonic creature who made a hobby of patrolling the midnight streets and interesting himself in odd crimes.

Sidney Zoom regarded the smoldering tip of his cigarette.

"I'm afraid, Zoom, I shall have to ask you to surrender your courtesy star and your commission as a special deputy. I'm sorry, but you knew the rules, and you infringed upon them."

Sidney Zoom took the articles from his pocket, passed them over, heaved a sigh.

"I'd anticipated that, and I'm glad. I can do more fighting the police than coöperating with them."

He jackknifed his huge form to its full height, strode toward the door. His hand was on the knob when Captain Mahoney's quiet voice stabbed the tense atmosphere of the room.

"That," he said, "disposes of my duty as an officer. Now, Zoom, would you mind telling me, as a friend, why you took advantage of the confidence which the department reposed in you?"

"Because," snapped Zoom, "Gromley was about to outwit an innocent woman and pin a murder upon her."

"He's done it anyway."

"No. That he hasn't."

Captain Mahoney fished a cigar from his pocket, slowly bit off the end. His dark, luminous eyes regarded Sidney Zoom with curious speculation.

"Do you know who murdered Harry Raine?" he asked.

"No. I know who didn't."

Captain Mahoney lit his cigar.

"I wish I'd been there last night."

"I wish you had, captain."

Captain Bill Mahoney's eyes flashed swiftly above the first puff of blue smoke which came from his cigar.

"Because if I had been, I'd have sensed that your interference was for the primary purpose of getting yourself kicked out. I'd have figured that you wanted most awfully to leave that room without exciting attention, and you took that way of doing it."

And Sidney Zoom whirled, strode back to his chair, sat down, and laughed.

"Bill," he said, "it's a good thing you weren't there. You're a little too clever."

Captain Mahoney had not moved. He twisted the cigar slowly, thoughtfully, flashed his black eyes at Sidney Zoom's hawk-like face once or twice.

"And I have an idea you wanted to be relieved of your courtesy commission on the force because you're figuring on a fast one, and don't want any sense of ethics to stand in your way."

Zoom said nothing. For a few moments they smoked in silence.

"Bill," said Sidney Zoom, at length, "you're human. Do you want to solve that Raine murder?"

Captain Bill Mahoney spoke cautiously when he answered.

"Gromley says it's a perfect case, but that you and your lawyer have interfered with his proof and he may not be able to turn over enough evidence to get a conviction."

Sidney Zoom leaned forward.

"If you'll put your cards on the table, Bill, I'll try and clear up the case for you."

"If I put my cards on the table," asked the police captain, "will you put yours on the table?"

Sidney Zoom's answer was explosively prompt.

"No!"

"Why not?"

Zoom laughed lightly.

"Because I'm going to play with a marked deck."

"You think the woman isn't the guilty party?"

"I'm almost certain of it."

"It would hurt the police a lot if we should go ahead and try to pin a murder rap on her and then have it turn out it was a mistake," said Bill Mahoney, slowly.

Sidney Zoom knew when he had won.

"Get your hat, Bill," he said.

Captain Mahoney reached for his hat.

"Where to?"

"To Harry Raine's place, out on West Adams. I'll drive slowly, and you can tell me what the police have found out while we're driving."

"Sergeant Gromley would die if he knew I was doing it," sighed the captain.

But Bill Mahoney had seen Sidney Zoom perform seeming wonders upon many other occasions, and beyond the sighed regret he showed no other signs of hesitancy.

As they purred along in Zoom's high powered, multi-cylindered car, his police dog crouched in the rumble seat, sniffing the air with curious nostrils, Captain Mahoney gave Zoom a brief summary of the facts the police had discovered.

"It's a family fight affair. Guess old Raine was a man who had at least one killing coming to him. He had a son, Edward. Edward fell in love with Eva, the girl. Raine kicked the boy out. The boy started in doing some gem business, buying and selling. He was making good. Then, one day, he was killed, suddenly.

"There wasn't any insurance. The girl found herself widowed, with a stock of gems that had to be sold. She started probating the estate to get good title to the gems, and old Raine sued the administrator.

"It developed that there was an illegality about the marriage. He'd known it all along, had been saving it as a weapon. Therefore, Eva wasn't the boy's widow. Harry Raine was the only surviving relative. There wasn't a will. Raine claimed the gems. The court gave them to him. He and his lawyer took possession of them yesterday afternoon.

"The girl didn't have any money to carry on a fight. She let him have them. But she had some of her husband's old effects. Among these was a key ring with a key to the house. Apparently, the girl sneaked out to the house after every one had gone to bed and stole the jewels.

"She'd have made a good job of it, too, because no one suspected she had the key. But she was just a little clumsy in the get-away and knocked over a chair. That woke old Raine up.

"He dashed after the burglar, but she eluded him and got out into the night. He chased her for a ways in his pyjamas, then came back, got into his clothes, and started to go after her.

"He told his attorney he'd caught a glimpse of her, running into the wind and rain, and had recognized her. He was furious, wanted to catch her red handed and all that."

Sidney Zoom shot Captain Mahoney a swift glance.

"Told his attorney? What was his attorney doing there at midnight?"

"He lives there. Raine is a funny old codger, or was. He goes in for collecting things, stamps, first editions and what not. And he's a litigious old cuss, always in court. He sues his neighbors, sues the dealers who sell him things, sues the paving contractors who do work on his street, sues everybody.

"He's got a white-haired old lawyer that he found somewhere, down and out, and took the lawyer to live with him in his house. And he always keeps the lawyer busy. Then he's got a butler who's a character, looks like an old pug; and there's a Chinese cook. That's the household."

Sidney Zoom nodded.

"That," he said, "is just about how I figured the case."

Captain Mahoney shot him a shrewd glance.

"How'd you figure any of that out?"

"There were legal papers in the pockets of the corpse," he said, "and the latest of them was a case where he'd sued the administrator to quit title to some of the jewelry his son had had at the time of his death. A copy of the judgment was in his coat pocket at the time. The cop on the beat found it."

Captain Mahoney squinted his eyes.

"Well," he said, "here's the way Gromley reconstructs the case. Old Man Raine started after the girl and didn't catch up with her until he was almost at her apartment.

He grabbed at her and clutched a string of synthetic rubies she was wearing, a present from her husband.

"She broke away, shot him, then turned and fled to her apartment. She was panic-stricken, and ditched the jewels and the gun. She probably was so excited she didn't know he'd broken the necklace when he grabbed at her."

"She was afraid they'd be coming for her, however, so she ripped her name off the mail box to balk them of that much of a clew, and went to her apartment to pack, then she heard the sirens and knew any woman who started to leave the apartment house while the police were there would be stopped and questioned.

"So she pretended she'd been in bed asleep, and waited to see if the police were coming. If they hadn't found her she'd have ducked out as soon as the police left. She figured that if they did find her she could stall them off. And she might have done it if it hadn't been for Gromley's being so damned shrewd with his questioning."

CHAPTER VI

The Dead Man's House

SIDNEY ZOOM shook his shoulders as though to relieve them of some weight.

"That's what I didn't like about Gromley. He's damned clever, and he used his cleverness, not to reason out what must have happened there at the time of the murder, but to trap the girl. It wasn't fair."

Captain Mahoney smiled mechanically.

"Things in this world aren't always fair. But they're fairly efficient. It's the result that counts."

Sidney Zoom gave a single expletive.

"Bah!" he said.

"Still believe in divine justice, eh?" asked the police captain.

"I've seen something closely akin to that save several innocent people from jail or the death penalty," said Sidney Zoom.

Captain Mahoney shook his head.

"You've been lucky, Zoom. But it wasn't divine justice. It was your own damned cleverness, plus the fact that you've got sufficient money to ride your hobby as far as you want to."

Sidney Zoom said nothing.

"That's the place," remarked Captain Mahoney. "The one on the other side of the street. The big house with the iron gate and the padlock."

Sidney Zoom made a single comment.

"Yes," he said. "It looks like the type of place he'd have lived in."

"Evidently you didn't take a shine to him?"

"No, I didn't. His character showed on his face, even in death."

"It takes all sorts of people to make a world, Sidney."

Sidney Zoom's answer was typical:

"All sorts of things come up in a garden. But one pulls out the noxious weeds."

Captain Mahoney sighed.

"Your philosophy's too advanced for this age, my friend."

Sidney Zoom abruptly reverted to the clews which had led the officers to the crime.

"Would you ever have found the girl if it hadn't been for the beads?"

"You mean the synthetic rubies broken from the string?"

"Yes."

"Eventually, but we'd have had to go to the house first. When we got there and talked with the servants who had heard the commotion we'd have gone after the girl."

"But the beads were the clew?"

"Naturally. They led from the corpse to the outer door of the apartment."

"Of the apartment *house*, you mean."

"Well, yes."

Sidney Zoom fastened his intense, hawk-like eyes upon the man who was staring at him with sudden curiosity.

"Did it ever strike you as being a bit strange, Bill, that the beads only went as far as the outer door of the apartment house, and that they were spaced most evenly? Why weren't there any beads between the door and the entrance to the girl's apartment?"

Bill Mahoney laughed.

"There you go, Zoom, with some of your wild theories. The beads were the girl's all right. We've identified those beyond any doubt. And the rest of the string was found behind the mirror in her room where she'd tried to conceal it. She'd put it there. There was the imprint of a finger in the soft surface of the chewing gum. It was her finger.

"What happened was that the man she'd shot broke the string of beads with his last death clutch. They were spilling all over the street, but the girl didn't know it until she got to the door of the apartment. Then she gathered up what was left, probably some that were on a thread that had dropped down the front of her dress.

"She knew she had to hide them. She wanted to put them where the police would never find them. By that time she knew they had been spilling, leaving a trail directly to the apartment house. That's why she pulled the card off of the mail box. She knew the officers would trail those beads and, if they found a card bearing the same name as the dead man, they'd come right up."

Sidney Zoom stretched, yawned, smiled.

"Did you notice, by any chance, if there was a cut on the fingers of Eva Raine?"

Captain Mahoney's glance was gimlet eyed.

"Yes. There was. What made you think there might be?"

"The edges of the card container on the letter box were pretty sharp, and she was in a hurry. I thought she might have cut herself."

"And that such cut accounted for the red stain on the mail box?"

"Yes."

"I think," said Captain Mahoney, very deliberately, "that we'll go on in. You've told me too much—and not enough."

Zoom uncoiled his lean length from behind the steering wheel, grinned at the officer. "Come on."

They walked up a cement walk, came to the porch of the house. An officer on duty saluted the captain, regarded Zoom curiously. The police dog, padding gravely at the side of his master, managed a dignity which was the more impressive in that it was entirely natural.

The door swung open. Two men stood in the hallway.

Captain Mahoney intoned their names to Sidney Zoom in a voice that was informative, but not social.

"Zoom, this is Sam Mokley, the butler; Laurence Gearhard, the lawyer."

Zoom nodded, stalked into the hallway, suddenly turned to transfix the two men with his hawk-like eyes.

"I want to see two things," he snapped. "First, the room from which the jewelry was taken; second, the bed where Harry Raine slept."

The lawyer, white-haired, cunning-eyed, shrewd judge of human nature, swept his pale eyes over Zoom's tall figure, vibrant with controlled energy.

"Show him, Mokley," he said to the butler.

The man nodded. "This way, sir."

He was all that Captain Mahoney had described, a ferocious looking figure, massive, heavy-handed, his ear cauliflowered.

"Here is the room, sir. The gems were in a concealed cabinet back of the bookcase. Only a very few people knew of that bookcase."

But Sidney Zoom did not even glance at the place of concealment. Instead he dropped to his hands and knees and started crawling painfully, laboriously, over the edges of the carpet, his fingers questing over every inch of the carpeted surface.

He remained in that position, searching patiently for some three or four minutes. If he found anything he gave no sign. As abruptly as he had assumed the position, he straightened to his full height, looked at the two men.

"The bedroom," he said.

"This way, sir," said the butler.

They trooped into the bedchamber. It was a dank, chilly place of slumber, suggestive of fitful sleep, disturbed by periods of worry, or restless thoughts, of selfish desires.

Zoom inspected the cheerless room.

"Where," he asked of the butler, "did Raine keep his gun?"

The lawyer cleared his throat.

Zoom shot him a glance.

"I asked the butler," he said.

The butler's face was wooden.

"I haven't seen him with a gun for some time, sir. He used to have one, a thirty-eight, Smith and Wesson, sir."

Zoom strode to the dresser, started yanking open the drawers.

There were suits of heavy underwear, coarse socks, cheap shirts, a few frayed-edged, starched collars. In an upper drawer was a pasteboard box with a green label on the top. The sides were copper colored. Zoom pulled out the box, ripped open the cover, turned it upside down.

Upon the dresser there cascaded a glittering shower of brass cartridges, cartridges for a forty-five automatic.

The lawyer cleared his throat again. Then he shrugged his shoulders, walked away. Zoom stared fixedly at Captain Mahoney.

"I want to see the Chinese cook," he said.

Captain Mahoney studied the level intensity of Zoom's eyes for a moment, then motioned to the butler.

"Come with me and let's find the cook."

They left the room. The lawyer cleared his throat, turned, regarded Sidney Zoom.

"Going to say something?" asked Zoom.

"Yes," said the attorney. "I was about to remark that it was a nice day."

The door opened again and Captain Mahoney escorted the butler and the Chinese cook into the room. The cook was nervous, plainly so.

"Ah Kim," said Captain Mahoney.

Zoom looked at the man. The slant eyes rotated slitheringly about in oily restlessness.

"Ah Kim," snapped Zoom, "do you know much about guns?"

Ah Kim shifted his weight.

"Heap savvy," he said.

Zoom indicated the pile of shells.

"What gun do these fit?"

"Alla samee fit Missa Raine gun. Him florty-five, automatic."

Zoom turned on his heel, faced the lawyer.

"You made Raine's will."

It was a statement rather than a question. The pale eyes of the lawyer regarded Zoom unwaveringly.

"Yes," he said "Of course I did."

"Who were the beneficiaries?"

The lawyer pursed his lips.

"I would rather answer that later, and in private."

Captain Mahoney glanced at Zoom, then fixed the attorney with his dark, thoughtful eyes.

"Answer it now," he said.

The lawyer bowed.

"Very well. The property, what there is, and it's considerable, is left share and share alike to the two servants, Ah Kim and Sam Mokley."

CHAPTER VII

The Hidden Gun

THE CHINESE heard the news with a bland countenance that was utterly devoid of expression. Sam Mokley gave a gasp of surprise.

"What!" he said.

The lawyer bowed.

"I wasn't going to tell you until the investigation was over, but Raine left his property to you two."

"Did you share in it?" asked Captain Mahoney.

"No."

"He didn't leave any to Eva Raine?" asked Zoom.

"Naturally not," said the lawyer. "One does not ordinarily bequeath property to one's murderer. And the girl was utterly unscrupulous. She testified falsely in the lawsuit over the gems. She broke into the house and committed burglary."

Sidney Zoom nodded careless acquiescence.

"Do you ever read the Bible, Mr. Gearhard?"

The white-haired man smiled.

"I have read it," he said, dryly.

"It is an excellent passage," commented Sidney Zoom, "which remarks that the one who is without sin may throw the first stone."

The lawyer's lips settled in a straight line.

"If you mean anything at all personal by that," he snapped, "you had better watch your tongue. There is a law in this State against libel. Your attitude ever since you entered this place has been hostile."

It was apparent that the grizzled veteran of many a court room battle was very much on the aggressive whenever his personal integrity was assailed.

Zoom bowed.

"You are mistaken," he said. "My attitude is that of an investigator."

He turned to Captain Mahoney.

"The murder," he said, "is solved."

Captain Mahoney stared at him.

"Who did it?"

Zoom smiled.

"Since there is a law against defamation of character, I will say nothing, but will refer you to absolute means of proof. A step at a time, we will uncover the matter.

"Rip, smell of the gentlemen."

And Sidney Zoom waved his hand in a gesture, a swift flip of the wrist.

An animal trainer would have known that it was the gesture, more than the words which made the police dog do that which he did. But the effect was uncanny. The dog walked deliberately to each of the three men, smelled their clothing with bristling hostility, ruffling the hair on his back.

"Come, captain," said Sidney Zoom.

And he turned, stalked from the room.

"We will leave the car parked here," said Zoom as they gained the porch, leaving behind them three very puzzled individuals, "and start walking by the shortest route toward the apartment which the girl maintained."

Captain Mahoney fell into step.

"Zoom," he said, quietly, "have you any idea of just what you're after?"

Zoom's answer was a single explosive monosyllable.

"Yes."

They strode forward, walking swiftly.

"Search," said Zoom, and waved his arm.

The dog barked once, a short, swift bark, then started to swing out in a series of questing semicircles, ranging ahead and to either side of the walking men.

They walked rapidly and in silence. Captain Mahoney was put to it to keep the pace. From time to time, his anxious, speculative eyes turned upward to Zoom's face. But the rigid profile was as though carved from solid rock.

It was not until they had approached the place where the body of the murdered man had been found that the dog suddenly barked three times, came running toward them, then back toward a vacant lot.

Here was a patch of brush, back of a signboard. The ground was littered with such odds and ends as invariably collect in vacant lots. There were two or three automobiles which would never run again, a few tin cans which had been surreptitiously deposited.

"I think," said Zoom, "the dog has found something important."

Captain Mahoney sprinted into speed, was the first to arrive at the patch of brush. He parted the leaves. The dog pawed excitedly, as though to help.

Captain Mahoney straightened and whistled.

"Call back the dog, Zoom. There's a forty-five automatic on the ground here. There may be finger-prints on it. I want to preserve them."

Zoom snapped a swift command.

The dog dropped flat on his belly, muzzle on forepaws.

Captain Mahoney took a bit of string from his pocket. He lowered it until he had it slung under the barrel of the automatic, then he tied a knot and raised the gun.

Zoom muttered his approval.

For there were finger-prints upon the weapon, prints that showed unmistakable ridges and whorls. Those finger-prints might have been developed by an expert, so plain were they.

"A man's fingers," said Captain Mahoney.

Zoom nodded.

"Now, captain, if you don't mind, we'll return to the house where Raine lived and see if we can identify the gun. As a favor to me, I wish you'd tell no one where this gun was found until I give you permission."

Captain Mahoney sighed.

"Zoom, I'm going to give you a free hand, for a little while."

"Come then," said Zoom.

And they returned to the house as rapidly as they had made the trip from it, presenting a strange pair, the tall man with the hawklike eyes, the shorter officer, carrying a gun dangling on a string, careful lest the finger-prints should be obliterated.

Sam Mokley, the butler, let them into the house.

Zoom ordered him to summon the lawyer and the cook.

They gathered in the living room, a restless group of men, very evidently under a great nervous strain.

"Ah Kim," snapped Zoom, "is that Mr. Raine's gun?"

The Chinese let his eyes slither to the gun, then to Zoom's face, then about the room.

"Same gun," he said.

"Beg your pardon, sir," interposed the butler, "but it's not the gun. Mr. Raine's gun had a little speck of rust on the barrel, just under the safety catch."

Zoom's grin was sardonic.

"Oh," he said, "I thought you described Raine's gun as being a thirty-eight revolver, not a forty-five automatic."

The butler's wooden face was as a mask.

"Yes, sir," he said.

Captain Mahoney regarded the man curiously.

"Anything further to say, Mokley?"

"No, sir."

Zoom nodded, slowly.

"No," he said, "he wouldn't."

Captain Mahoney's eyes were thoughtful.

"We've got to have proof, you know, Zoom. We may satisfy ourselves of something, but we've got to get enough evidence to satisfy a jury before we can do anything."

CHAPTER VIII

The Killer Shoots Again

ZOOM STARTED to talk. His voice was crisp, metallic.

"Let's look at the weak points in the case they've built up against the girl, look at the clews and see what must have happened.

"Raine had the gems here. He heard a noise, found the gems gone—stolen.

"Something made him sufficiently positive to start out after the girl. That something must have been some tangible evidence. Let's suppose, as a starting point, it was the finding of part of a broken necklace with some synthetic rubies strewn over the floor.

"Naturally, he scooped up some of those rubies, to be used in confronting the girl. He started after her. He was walking toward the wind. It was rainy. He got wet. That didn't deter him. As I see his character, Raine was a very determined man.

"But, before he reached the apartment where the girl lived something caused him to turn back. What was that something? We can be fairly sure he didn't get to the apartment. Otherwise he'd have raised a commotion. He was that sort. And he was facing in the other direction when he was shot from behind, with his own gun.

"Now what would have caused him to turn back? What would have caused him to surrender his gun? Certainly some one in whose advice he must have had implicit faith overtook him and convinced him that he was going off on a wrong track, that he should return and summon the police.

"Then, when that person had secured possession of the gun, he waited for a clap of thunder from the passing shower, shot Raine in the back of the head.

"That person had picked up more of the scattered rubies. He used them to leave a trail to the front door of the apartment house where the girl lived. Those rubies weren't spaced the way they would have been had they come off a necklace. They'd have hit the sidewalk in a bunch and scattered. They were spaced just as they would have been had some one dropped them with the deliberate intent of causing the police to go to that apartment house.

"Now the only person I can think of who would have been able to dissuade Mr. Raine, cause him to surrender his gun, turn him back, is …"

And Sidney Zoom stared at the lawyer.

That individual laughed.

"Very cleverly done, Zoom, but not worth a damn. Your theory is very pretty, but how are you going to prove the necklace was broken here in this room? You got down on your hands and knees when you first came in here. You were looking for some of the rubies. You were disappointed. Your interest in the girl has led you to concoct a very pretty theory. It won't hold water—before a jury."

Zoom turned to the Chinese.

"Bring me the vacuum sweeper, Ah Kim," he said.

The servant glided from the room on noiseless feet.

The butler exchanged glances with the lawyer. The attorney cleared his throat, then was silent again.

The Chinese returned with the vacuum sweeper. Sidney Zoom opened it, took from the interior the bag where the sweepings reposed. He opened that bag, spilled the dust upon the floor.

Instantly it became apparent that that dust contained several of the rubies. They glowed redly in the light which came through the massive windows.

"Yes," said Zoom, "I looked for the rubies here. When I couldn't find them I knew I was dealing with an intelligent criminal. But I did find that a vacuum sweeper had been run over the floor very recently."

The butler looked at the lawyer, wet his lips. The lawyer frowned meditatively.

"That, of course," he said, "is rather strong evidence you've uncovered there, Zoom. Ah Kim would have profited by the death. He has acted suspiciously several times. There's a chance you may be right."

Zoom's smile was frosty.

"Ah Kim couldn't have dissuaded Harry Raine from going on to the girl's apartment," he said, slowly, impressively. "And I don't think it will be Ah Kim's fingers that'll fit the prints on that gun."

The attorney regarded the gun more intently than ever.

"Ah, yes," he said, "the finger-prints on the gun. Well, it's certain they're not mine, and I wouldn't have profited by the death of my client. I have lost by it. He kept me in a law practice."

The butler squirmed.

"Meaning that you're directing suspicion at me?" he asked.

The attorney shrugged his shoulders.

"The finger-prints," he said, "will speak for themselves."

Sam Mokley regarded the attorney speculatively.

"Well," said Captain Mahoney, "we'll take the finger-prints of the men here, and—"

"Perhaps," suggested Zoom, "we can also look over the clothes closets of the men. We might find evidence that one of them was out in the rain last night. And it's peculiar that the bed of Harry Raine shows no evidence of having been slept in. Every one agrees he jumped out of bed to pursue the burglar.

"I wouldn't doubt if there were clean sheets put on the bed, and the bed made up fresh because the old sheets and pillowcase might have shown that he kept a gun under his pillow."

The attorney spoke, slowly, in measured tones.

"The finger-prints on the gun are the most important evidence. A jury will act on those. The other things are mere surmise."

Captain Mahoney stared at the lawyer.

"Humph," he said.

"As a matter of fact," pursued the attorney, "the butler *was* out for a little while last night. I tried to locate him just after Mr. Raine went out, and—"

The butler's motion was so bafflingly swift that the eye could hardly follow. He had edged near the gun which lay on the table. With a sweep of his hand he scooped it up, fired, all in one motion.

The attorney's stomach took the bullet. A look of surprised incredulity spread over his countenance; before that look was wiped out by the crashing impact of two more bullets.

Sam Mokley jumped back, waving the gun at Zoom and Captain Mahoney.

"Get your hands up," he said.

But he had forgotten something—the police dog.

The animal made a swift spring, a tawny streak of motion. Teeth clamped about the wrist that held the gun. Seventy-five pounds of hurtling weight, amplified by the momentum of the rush, crashed downward upon that extended arm. The dog twisted his powerful neck, flung himself in a wrenching turn.

The weapon dropped from nerveless fingers.

Captain Mahoney stepped forward, handcuffs glistened.

"Let go, Rip, and lie down," said Sidney Zoom.

The police dog relaxed his hold.

Sam Mokley extended his wrists for the handcuffs, the right wrist dripping blood from the fangs of the dog.

"Put 'em on," he said, his voice calm, his face utterly without emotion. "I got that lying, cheating, murdering double crossing lawyer. You're right in everything, only both Gearhard and I went after Raine.

"The lawyer put up the plan to me on the way. I had a criminal record. He knew it. He got me the job here. He proposed that we had a chance to kill off old Raine, blame the murder on the girl. He'd stick by me, and I'd split my inheritance with him.

"He made me do the shooting so I'd be in his power. But I don't know how in hell you ever found the gun. We took it down to the bay and dumped it in the water."

Captain Mahoney turned to Sidney Zoom.

That individual was smiling, a cold, efficient smile.

"Certainly, captain. I had to victimize you a little to set the stage just the way I wanted it. Rip's well trained and intelligent, but even he couldn't have done what he appeared to do. The finger-prints on the gun are my own. I knew that the murder had been committed with a single shot from a forty-five automatic. Therefore I bought a similar gun, put very evident finger-prints on it, buried it where Rip could see it.

"When I told him to search for the gun, he naturally thought we were playing a game. He went to the place where I had placed the weapon—after I'd led him to the general vicinity. I thought it might help us in a third degree."

Captain Mahoney stared angrily at Zoom.

"And you left it loaded, ready to shoot because you thought that—"

Zoom shrugged his shoulders.

"As you said, you need evidence to convict."

Captain Mahoney sighed.

"Zoom, you're the most ruthless devil I ever saw work on a case … And how about the girl? Even if you have the right hunch about her, she must have come here and stolen the gems. She broke the necklace, didn't realize it until she got to her room. Then she found a part of the string, and, of course, tried to conceal it … and she tore the name off the mail box. I wonder if she didn't conceal those gems in the mail box. Do you know?"

Sidney Zoom met his gaze.

"Do you know, captain, you're rather clever—at times. But I don't think even you are clever enough to ever find out what became of those gems—or to get a case that you can make out against the girl for their theft. You know it takes evidence to convict.

"Personally, I have an idea those gems will eventually be sold to a collector who will be glad to pay a top price with no questions asked—and that the girl will receive the present of a sum of money."

Captain Mahoney licked his lips.

"Zoom, your ideas of justice are, perhaps, all right at times. But you're sworn to enforce the law. You've got to do your duty."

Zoom grinned.

"You forget you made me turn in my star and commission. Come, come, captain, you're going to get lots of credit for having solved a murder case swiftly and efficiently. You'd better let it go at that.

"And while you're talking about law, remember that there's always a higher law than man-made laws. Personally, I rather like that biblical admonition about the man who is without sin being the one to throw the first stone."

Captain Mahoney took a deep breath.

"Zoom, what a strange mixture you are! Big-hearted about some things to the point of taking risks, ruthless about others!"

Zoom shrugged.

"I live life as I see it."

It was Mokley who interrupted.

"Come on, cap, let's get this thing over with ... to think that damned crook Gearhard fell for that third degree stuff! And him a lawyer! He was the one who was going to see that I had a cinch ... stand back of me in a crisis, and all that! Then the dirty snake tried to squirm out from under and let me take the rap!

"Well, if there's anything in this divine justice business, this guy talks about, he certainly got his—the crook!"

Captain Mahoney went to the telephone.

"Send the homicide squad, the coroner and the wagon," he said, when he had contacted headquarters, "and tell Sergeant Gromley to lay off that Raine woman. He's got a wrong hunch."

THE GREEN DOOR

CHAPTER I

The Fleeing Girl

SIDNEY ZOOM swung the big sedan at the corner, crawled in close to the curb. He drove after the manner of cruising cab drivers who prowl the midnight streets looking for belated fares.

But the big sedan was no cab, nor would it readily be mistaken for one. It was low to the ground, long, slim, built for speed. The engine purred in powerful pulsations under the glistening sweep of the long hood. The body was streamlined for speed.

Beside the driver sat a police dog, yellow eyes glinting with a hard gleam of intense interest as he scanned the sidewalks, swept his gaze down the dark side streets.

The night was calm, and Sidney Zoom did not like the tranquillity of calm nights. He preferred, instead, the howl of the wind, the whip of rain, the lash of savage seas.

Upon such nights of storm Sidney Zoom could usually have been found out beyond the heads, aboard his yacht the *Alberta F.*, fighting the crashing seas, the light of joy in his eyes.

Zoom enjoyed the thrill of conflict, whether with man or with nature. And this night, being too calm to offer adventure in his yacht, sent him patrolling the midnight streets, searching for some adventure which would offer excitement.

The car crossed an intersection. The dog gave a throaty growl, flattened forward on his forefeet, muzzle pressing close to the windshield.

Sidney Zoom's foot touched the brake.

A running figure was coming down that side street, and the figure was that of a woman. Once she shot a glance over her shoulder, and then increased her speed.

She was running, not as most women run, trying to maintain some semblance of grace, careful lest their modesty shall be sacrificed to speed; but she was running as people run who are in a blind panic, heedless of appearances.

Her skirt impeded the action of her legs, and the left hand grasped at the folds, pulled it well above the knees. The feet spurned the pavement with a force and vigor which would have done credit to a trained sprinter.

Sidney Zoom brought the car to a dead stop. He reached back and flung open the rear door on the side next to the curb. The running figure made one final spurt, a leap, a grasping clutch of frantic hands. The car lurched with the weight of her body, the tug of her arms. Then she was on the rear seat, panting, gasping inarticulate words.

Sidney Zoom slammed the door.

A man's figure rounded the far corner, paused. The man took in the situation, raised his arm. There was the spat of a bullet against the side of the car, the sound of a revolver.

Another man joined the first figure. Then a third.

Sidney Zoom's hand flashed beneath the lapel of his coat.

The girl managed to get out words.

"Please, please don't. For my sake. I'll die. Please take me away!"

Sidney Zoom flashed her a glance, and knew the answer he must make. He disregarded the men who were running toward him, shooting as they ran, disregarded the snarling dog, fangs pressed against the glass of the door, begging with whimpered pleadings to be allowed to get out and launch an attack of his own.

Sidney Zoom snapped in the clutch, pressed on the throttle and the multi-cylinder power of the car produced instant results. The wheels gripped the pavement. The headlights swung, the car roared into speed.

It was not until they had gone some twenty blocks, straight down the road, shooting like an arrow from a bow, that she made explanation.

"They're gangsters," she said. "I run a little millinery business. These men were organizing a racket. I blocked them. I refused to pay tribute for myself, and also organized the other shops in a resistance. They—they were taking me for a ride. Can you imagine that?"

"How," asked Sidney Zoom, "did you escape?"

"The car got a puncture," she said. "They had to get tools from out of the back seat. They kept me guarded, but the car slid backwards on the grade, off the jack. It pinned one of the men by the foot. The others forgot about me for a moment and rushed to his help. I sneaked away, quietly at first, then running as fast as I could.

"That's why they didn't follow in a car. Their own car is disabled. They had to run. Thank goodness you were there!"

Sidney Zoom bowed.

"Perhaps it was chance," he said, and his tone indicated that he might have other thoughts. But he kept those thoughts to himself. "If you'll give me your address, the address of your shop, and tell me the names of those men, I'll take great pleasure in seeing that no further demands are made upon you, and that you're not taken for any more rides."

She shook her head.

"No. They're dangerous. I can't let you do that. My name is Muriel Drake, and I live at the Continental Hotel. I have a millinery shop, but I won't tell you the name. You'd just run into danger, and you've done enough for me already. I certainly hope they didn't get your license number, or they'd make trouble. They're dangerous men."

Sidney Zoom swung the wheel.

"You wish to go to the Continental now?"

"Yes. Please."

"You'll communicate with the police?"

"Yes."

"And you won't tell me who the men are, nor where you have your shop?"

"No."

Sidney Zoom smiled.

"Very well," he said. "Naturally, I won't press the matter. However, I shall take certain steps looking toward your protection."

"No, no, don't do that! I'll telephone the police!"

Zoom bowed, wordlessly.

The electric sign of the Continental Hotel flashed on and off in red brilliance, a few blocks down the street.

Sidney Zoom stepped on the throttle.

"Call the police at once. They may try to follow you."

"Oh, no," she said. "They don't know about the Continental."

Zoom piloted the car to the curb, alighted, opened the rear door. The young woman gave him her hand, her eyes and a smile.

"It was good of you."

"Don't mention it," said Sidney Zoom.

"Come and see me. Drop in tomorrow afternoon."

"Thank you," said Sidney Zoom, and bowed.

She swept into the hotel. Sidney Zoom could see her through the plate glass windows of the lobby. She walked directly to the desk, engaged the night clerk in conversation, smiled sweetly at him, and walked toward the elevators.

Sidney Zoom parked his car, opened the door, nodded to his police dog.

"Out, Rip, and stay by my side."

Then he rounded the corner, found a shaded doorway where the night shadows clung, and sat down to wait.

He waited ten minutes. Then a figure emerged cautiously, scanned the street, looking up and down it with furtive caution. Reassured at what she saw, the figure of the girl who had given her name as Muriel Drake started walking swiftly along the cement sidewalk.

Sidney Zoom spoke to the dog, held him by the hair on the neck, talking to him.

Not until the figure had been gone for a good ten minutes did Sidney Zoom loose the dog.

If she had taken a cab, Zoom knew the pursuit would be useless. But she had seemed so certain of herself and of the Continental Hotel, that Zoom felt her real residence might be close by.

He turned the dog free.

"Find," he said, "then come back here."

The dog barked once, a short, swift bark of excitement, and then started running along the sidewalk, snuffing, nose held close to the cold cement, tail wagging in a slow circle as he rounded the corner of the block and vanished in the cool night shadows.

CHAPTER II

Surrounded

ZOOM WALKED back to the car, climbed into the front seat, lit a cigarette, turned to survey the back of the car.

Something that glittered on the floor of the car caught his eye. It was a red glitter, much like the reflection of a frozen drop of pigeon's blood.

Zoom switched on the dome light, leaned over the back of the front seat, and picked up the object.

Sidney Zoom knew something about stones. That was a very fine ruby. The depth of color, the fire, the flawless perfection of the stone told of its value.

Zoom held it cupped in his hand, examined it closely. Then he crawled into the back of the sedan and began a systematic search.

He found where the rich robe had been folded over and jammed so as to form a pocket of cloth. It had been hastily done. Zoom straightened the cloth.

Instantly a showering cascade of glittering light shot into view, rained to the floor of the sedan, sparkled in brilliant reflections.

Zoom started picking them up.

They were unset stones of rare brilliance, and they included rubies, diamonds, emeralds.

Zoom pocketed them, switched out the light in the dome of the car. He heard running feet, a short, excited bark. The police dog, Rip, had returned, was wagging his tail; his mouth, the lips twisted back in a canine smile, telling of the success of his mission. For the dog had been well trained in police work, and knew the art of trailing, as well as the reason for it. When his quarry took to rubber-tired transportation and eluded the keen nose of the dog, Rip felt the disgrace of failure as keenly as though it had been caused by some lack of skill on his part.

Sidney Zoom left the car, locked the ignition and transmission, accompanied the dog.

The dog paced at the side of his master, tail held erect, waving slightly at the tip, tongue lolling out, panting slightly from his run.

Together they went through the deserted streets of the city, the dog's feet padding along, rattling claws making more noise than the sound of his cushioned feet.

Sidney Zoom made no effort to muffle the noise of his steps. He strode forward with a vigorous, purposeful gait. It was as though he were going into a battle and was eager to taste the first thrill of conflict.

The dog took the lead from time to time, then, as his master kept on the trail, dropped back to his side. That trail led to an apartment house, some seven blocks from where Zoom had left the car. The apartment house was simple, unpretentious. The name was scrolled in gilt on the glass of the door.

"Bratten Arms Apartments."

Sidney Zoom tried the door. It was locked. The lobby was dark.

Zoom pursed his lips, looked at the directory. There was no person listed under the name of Drake; nor did the first name of any of the tenants seem to be Muriel.

Sidney Zoom walked across the street, paused in the shadows, looking up at the front of the building, seeking to ascertain if there was a light in any of the front apartments.

While he stared, the front door of the apartment opened. A man emerged. He had on a gray-checked overcoat, a gray, wide-brimmed hat, carried a stick, wore gray gloves, and pounded the steps leading down to the sidewalk with feet that seemed to be very much in a hurry to get somewhere.

Zoom started to call to this man, then thought better of it.

He walked back across the street, tried the door once more, found that it was still locked. There had been, in his mind, the possibility that perhaps the catch hadn't clicked as the door had swung slowly shut after the exit of the man in the gray overcoat.

Zoom muttered a word to the dog, turned, walked swiftly back toward the place where he had left his car. The man in the gray overcoat, hearing those steps, suddenly whirled, stared at Sidney Zoom.

Zoom caught a glimpse of the face. It was white, drawn. The cheeks were high and bony. The skin was drawn tightly over the forehead. There was a little, close-clipped mustache, and the eyes were dark, bright as with a fever.

For a long moment the light of the street corner shone on the features. Then the gloved hand jerked the wide brim of the hat down. The right hand dropped into the side pocket of the overcoat.

Sidney Zoom walked past, apparently giving no heed to the man who waited, watchful, poised.

Zoom turned to the right. The man in gray turned to the left, abruptly.

Zoom returned to his car. He made no effort to follow the man who had emerged from the apartment house. Zoom had absolutely nothing to connect him with the girl. Nor did he have any reason to regard the man with suspicion. It is not unusual for the belated wayfarer to scrutinize carefully those who come purposefully from behind. And this is particularly true of those who materialize suddenly from streets that are apparently deserted.

Zoom walked back to his car. He had a nebulous idea of cruising the streets and picking up the man in gray, offering him a ride.

He unlocked the transmission and ignition in his car, stepped on the starter.

The police dog growled.

Sidney Zoom paused, his hand creeping slowly toward the lapel of his coat. A dim shadow lurched from an adjacent doorway. Another man came walking diagonally across the street. A car which had been parked without lights, came drifting silently down the street, shortening the distance between it and Zoom's car.

Zoom's lips set in a grim line. The hawklike eyes snapped cold fires. Then a red spotlight flooded the scene. One of the approaching men jerked back his coat and disclosed a police star.

He walked to the running board of the machine.

"Okay, buddy. Don't make any sudden moves. Nothing's going to happen to you unless you've got it coming."

The police dog, hearing the antagonistic tone of the man's voice, stared at his master appealingly, waiting for the command which would enable him to forget restraint and tear into these men. But that command did not come. Zoom sat quiet, calm, scornful.

A man's voice drifted in through the open window to the left of the driver. The man was examining the back of the car.

"This is the car!" said the voice. "I can tell by the way it's shaped in back ... And here's a bullet hole. That's where my shell hit!"

The plainclothes officer nodded his head, called in a low voice to the men who were in the police car with the red spotlight: "This looks like the guy. Watch him!"

Sidney Zoom, his lip twisted in something of a sneer, made no move, said nothing.

"Where were you about twenty minutes ago, buddy?"

Sidney Zoom regarded the questioner with cold eyes.

"I was cruising the streets."

"What for?"

"Pleasure."

"Yeah. Well, you seen a broad making a getaway, and you acted as the getaway guy. You had the car planted ready for her to make a break ..."

Sidney Zoom interrupted.

"I did nothing of the sort. I was cruising the streets. I saw a young woman, running from a group of men who seemed to be filling her with fear. Those men opened fire upon me without warning."

The man who stood at Zoom's side pushed a little closer. The police dog gave a low, throaty growl. Two men from the back of the car moved up.

"Yeah?" said the man at the window. And his tone conveyed utter disbelief.

"Exactly!" snapped Sidney Zoom. "I am telling you exactly what occurred. This woman was running, evidently in fear. I opened the door. She jumped in. Three men showed up and started shooting. The woman told me later that they were gangsters and racketeers who were trying to take her for a ride."

The plainclothes man grunted.

"Well, buddy, you got yourself in a tough spot. That woman was being taken to Headquarters for questioning in connection with a robbery an' murder. Then you horned in and gave her a getaway ... Where'd you take her?"

"Continental Hotel," said Zoom unhesitatingly. "She walked in, talked with the night clerk and then went up."

"What's your name?" asked the officer.

"Zoom, Sidney Zoom."

The officer was plainly surprised.

"The hell it is!" he said.

"Exactly," said Zoom. "And if those men who pursued the girl were police, why the devil didn't they blow a police whistle or give me some sort of a sign instead of just opening fire? Furthermore, if they were police, taking a lone, unarmed woman to Headquarters, why didn't they take her there instead of letting her get a seventy-five yard headstart on them?"

The plainclothes man was a little less belligerent.

"They were private dicks, from the company that was engaged by the store that got robbed. They'd pinned something on the woman. On the way to Headquarters they had a blowout. When they jacked the car something happened and it slid off the jack and down on the leg of one of the boys. It broke the leg, and the other three had to lift the car to get him out.

"The broad was giving them a good song. She's a clever little liar. They didn't think she was particularly hot. Then she dusted out. When they found her making a getaway they knew she was mixed up in it bad. Pete, go over to the Continental and check that information about her going in there. If she's there, get the place surrounded. She's slippery."

"So you're Zoom, eh? The guy that prowls around at night looking for adventure, eh? Well, buddy, you've got plenty of adventure now. You're an accessory after the fact, an' you'll go up on the carpet!"

Sidney Zoom's level, hawk-like eyes bored in scornful appraisal into those of the officer.

"Since when," he asked, coldly, "has it become a crime for a citizen to offer a young woman a lift? And since when has it become a crime to drive away from three men who open fire without a word of explanation?"

The plainclothes man's face darkened.

"None of your brass!" he growled.

"That," snapped Sidney Zoom, "is not brass. It's steel!"

The plainclothes man moved away, over to the police car.

"Sidney Zoom," he growled. "I've heard he's got some sort of a special commission, and he's in solid with the mayor. Better let Headquarters know and see what they say."

CHAPTER III

Murder

THE DRIVER of the car nodded. He turned a microphone into action, spoke in a harsh, mechanical voice.

"Police car sixty-two. We've located the car in which Muriel Drake made her escape. It's driven by a man named Sidney Zoom who claims he saw the woman running down the street, gave her a ride, and didn't stop when he saw the private dicks, because they just opened fire, and the girl said they were gangsters. There's a lead that the girl went to the Continental Hotel. We're checking that lead. Shall we bring Zoom in?"

He switched off the microphone, grinned at the other.

"We'll pass the buck to somebody higher up."

There was a period of brief silence. Then a man came running across the street.

"A dodge," he said. "She went in to the night clerk all right, told him she might like a room for a week, asked him to let her take a look at it. She got a key, and the elevator boy showed her the room. She stalled around for five minutes, gave him back the key and a dollar, let the boy take the key to the desk while she ducked out the side door."

The plainclothes officer who seemed to be in charge of the investigation, puckered his forehead.

"That checks with this guy's story. She pulled that to throw him off the trail."

He turned back to Zoom.

"Just what'd she say to you?" he asked.

"Said she had a millinery store, that some men were organizing a racket and she'd been fighting them, that these men were taking her for a ride when the car had a puncture. That the car slipped off the jack, and that one of the men was caught under it. When the others were lifting the car she beat it."

The men exchanged glances.

"Pretty slick!" said one of the men.

"It's a damned lie. He was in on it. He was the getaway car!" stormed the man who claimed to have been the one who fired the shot that had taken effect in the side of the car. "I could tell from the way she ran into the car without hesitating or anything, that it was a plant ..."

"Shut up, Joe," said the plainclothes man. "She couldn't have told when the car you guys was in was going to have a blowout, nor that the jack was going to bust. She got a break, that's all, and she took it. I've heard of this guy. He drives around the streets all the time. He's helped the department on a case or two."

He turned to Zoom.

"Now, then, did you see this broad leaving the hotel? She ducked out of the joint to give you the slip and there's a chance you might have seen her."

The man paused, stared at Sidney Zoom.

A harsh, metallic voice rasped into raucous sound from the automobile.

"Police car sixty-two! There's been a murder at the Bratten Arms Apartments. A young woman was killed in the elevator. She answers the description of Muriel Drake. The body was found wedged in the elevator by a man named Hackett who was coming in from a party.

"Better chase around there, look at the corpse, interview Hackett and make sure he's on the square. The corpse was searched thoroughly by the man who did the job. Clothes were ripped and torn. Looks like Muriel."

There followed a startled silence which contrasted strangely with the mechanical voice, magnified by a loud speaker, coming in over the police radio; a voice that mentioned murder in so matter-of-fact a manner.

The man who had been standing near Zoom's car jerked his head at Zoom.

"Get your dog in back and make him behave. I'm coming in."

Sidney Zoom nodded, made a motion to the dog, a waving motion of the right wrist. "Back and down, Rip."

The dog cleared the back of the front seat in a graceful leap, stretched out on the back seat. The plainclothes man walked around the car, flung open the door.

"No rough stuff," he said. "Follow that police car."

The siren wailed. The exhaust of the police car roared. The two cars shot out into the middle of the street, gathered speed, flashed past intersections.

It was but a matter of seconds until the lights of the lead car showed the knot of curious spectators which had gathered, even at that hour of the night, impelled by a morbid curiosity to gaze upon the features of the dead.

There was an ambulance backed up to the curb, a pair of uniformed policemen, keeping the crowd back. Lights blazed in the windows of the apartment house, as well as in the windows of adjoining houses. Oblongs of light framed the black silhouettes of the curious.

The cars swung to the curb, lurched to a stop. The plainclothes man touched Zoom on the arm.

"We go in," he said.

Zoom turned to the dog.

"Stay here, Rip, and watch."

The dog pricked up his ears then drooped them.

The pair left the car. A knot of police and detectives pushed their way into the lobby of the apartment house. It was now a blaze of light. A middle-aged woman with sagging flesh drooping from the bones of her face, a triple chin and puffs under her eyes, rushed toward them. She was clad in a kimono and slippers with a glimpse of silk showing at the neck of the kimono.

"I'm the manager. She wasn't registered here. She didn't have an apartment. It ain't fair to pin a black eye on the place just because ..."

The men pushed her to one side. An officer led the way.

"We parked her in a vacant apartment," he said, "soon as we knew she might be connected with the stick-up."

They pushed their way through white-faced, half clothed inmates of the apartment house, who had huddled together in the hallways as chickens huddle when the dark shadow of a hawk skims along the ground.

The officer opened a door. The men walked in. Zoom felt a hand on his arm, felt himself pushed forward. Then he was in a semicircle of men who stared silently down upon a still form.

"Choked," said one of the officers.

"And how!" agreed another.

"Clothes just the way they were when she was found?" asked the man who was in charge.

"Just the same," said the officer. "She was wedged in the elevator when we got there."

"You put the elevator out of business?"

"Yeah. Sure. The boys are looking it over for finger-prints."

The plainclothes man nodded.

"Well," he said, "somebody sure as hell wanted something this broad had, and he wanted it bad. Lookit those clothes!"

Sidney Zoom stared at the distorted features.

"The girl you gave the ride to?" asked the plainclothes man.

"The same," agreed Sidney Zoom.

"Got her identified?" asked the officer who had been at the apartment when the others arrived.

"Yeah. Name's Muriel Drake. She works at Harmiston's Wholesale & Retail Jewelry. She was there when the stick-up took place this afternoon. You know, the one where they gunned out the guard and looted the box.

"There was plenty of evidence it was an inside job and the boys were getting ready to give her a shake-down. She got a break and made a getaway. Went to the Continental and ducked. She lives at the Wentmore Apartments over on Ninety-sixth. But she was too foxy to head for there. She's probably got a friend in this joint.

"The door's locked at night, and she couldn't get in unless she had a key or unless somebody answered the ring and gave the door a buzz. Better start checking 'em over ..."

He was interrupted by a commotion at the door.

"Here's the baby she called on," said one of the officers, and pushed a girl into the room.

CHAPTER IV

In the Clear

THE GIRL was clothed in a kimono over pajamas and slippers. Her hair was uncombed. Her face was white, eyes staring. She drew back from the gaze of the men, purposeful, appraising, hostile as that gaze was.

The officer behind her pushed her forward.

Then the girl saw that which was on the bed.

She screamed.

Her right hand, clenched into a fist, sought her mouth. The white teeth sank into the knuckles, and she screamed again.

She turned, tried to run. A man grabbed her around the waist, whirled her back so that she faced the bed.

"Take it easy, sister," he said.

The girl stood rigid, staring, quivering. Then she started to cry and the sobs twisted her frame, shook her shoulders, sent tears coursing down her cheeks. The circle of men stared at her, nor offered her their slightest sympathy.

"Okay," said the man who had brought her in. "She's Stella Denny in 639. I knocked on all the doors and asked 'em if they knew a Muriel Drake. This jane gave me a tumble. I found she was holding something out and that she knew the broad, so I brought her down."

The plainclothes man who had questioned Sidney Zoom moved so that he was between the sobbing girl and the bed.

"Okay, sister," he repeated, "take it easy. That's Muriel?"

The sobbing girl nodded.

"How long you known her?"

She tried to speak twice before the words came.

"T-t-two years."

"Pretty friendly?"

"Yes."

"You knew she was working for Harmiston's Jewelry?"

"Yes."

"Where do you work?"

"In a law office, Mr. Stringer's office."

"I see. And you were out some place tonight?"

"No. I was here. I came to my apartment right after I quit work. I cooked supper and didn't go out."

"Okay. You read the evening paper?"

"Yes."

"Then you knew about the stick-up at Harmiston's?"

The girl hesitated for a second before she answered.

"I d-d-don't know. I guess so!"

"Guess so, hell!" roared the plainclothes officer. "You know so, don't you?"

The girl nodded.

"That's better. Now, you may be all right, sister, or you may be in a tough spot. So you kick through and don't hold anything back and we'll give you the breaks.

"Now, you tried to get Muriel on the telephone to see if she was all right and ask her about the stick-up, didn't you?"

The girl nodded.

"And Muriel said she'd come over a little later and talk things over, didn't she?"

Another nod.

"And you kept waiting for Muriel to come, and she didn't come, and you rang her apartment and a man's voice answered, and you got frightened and slid the receiver back on the hook, didn't you?"

Her answer was a gasp.

"How ... how did you know?"

"We had men planted in that apartment, waiting for Muriel to come back. And you called and they took the call.

"So you sat up and waited for Muriel and got tired, and went to bed. And then what happened?"

There was a moment or two of silence. Stella Denny had ceased to sob now. The necessity for answering questions had served to distract her attention somewhat from that which was on the bed.

"The telephone rang," said the girl.

"Yes, who was it?"

"Muriel."

"What'd she want?"

"She said she was in a jam and that I was to be all ready to let her in as soon as she rang the bell, and she didn't know just when she'd get here, and then she hung up."

"Well, what happened after that?"

"Nothing. Not for a long time. I moved the chair over by the button which opened the front door, and waited. I waited so long I fell asleep. I woke up when someone was pressing the button of the front door bell. I immediately pressed my button, the one that opened the door.

"Then I waited for Muriel to come up, and I waited and waited, and nothing happened. So I thought maybe someone had rung my bell by mistake. That sometimes happens. Or sometimes someone wants to get in, and he'll press all the buttons at once to make sure someone will give him a tumble.

"So I waited, and then I heard the siren, and I knew the police were coming, and I remembered what Muriel had said about being in a jam, and I thought the best thing I could do was to sit tight.

"So I just sat there, and the door-bell rang, the one that's on the apartment door, and I opened it, and it was this man who asked me if I knew Muriel.

"I thought it was a message from her, so I told him I knew her, and then he showed me his badge and told me to come with him. And that's every single thing I know."

The officers exchanged glances.

One of them flung the girl around so she faced the body on the bed once more.

"You're the one that killed her. She had something you wanted. She had some of the stones that were stolen, and ..."

"No, no, no!" screamed Stella Denny. "Don't make me look. For God's sake, don't make me ..."

She slumped in a faint, her lips bloodless, her face the color of death.

The plainclothes man picked her in his arms, dumped her unceremoniously into a chair.

"It wasn't a woman's job," he said wearily. "It was a man that did it. Let's go up to this frail's apartment and give it a good frisking. Then we'll check up on her boy friends and give them a shake-down. And we'll check up on Muriel's boy friends, and see what they know."

He turned, regarded Sidney Zoom.

"I guess you're in the clear," he said. "You seem to have given us the straight dope.

She ducked through the hotel to give you the slip. We can locate you whenever we want you, eh?"

Sidney Zoom nodded.

"Aboard the yacht, *Alberta F.*," he said uncordially.

"Guy," the officer said, "you're gettin' all the breaks, an' you ain't got sense enough to know it."

Sidney Zoom said nothing. He strode from the room, tall, gaunt, unsmiling, pushed his way out of the apartment house, to his car, and stepped on the starter.

As he drove away, his left hand dropped to the side pocket of his coat. The gems which he had found in the robe in his machine rattled like pebbles.

He smiled, an enigmatical smile.

Nor did he return to his yacht. He went, instead, to a hotel where he registered as Loring Grigsby of Chicago. He went to his room, left the dog in the car at the garage near by, and slept until morning.

CHAPTER V

Edgar Carver

IN THE morning he read the newspaper accounts of the murder of Muriel Drake and a rehash of the account of the hold-up at Harmiston's.

The bandits, two in number, had moved with perfect efficiency, and with a knowledge of the exact location of what they wanted which led the police to believe that there was an accomplice employed within the stores. There had been a guard who had refused to surrender when he saw a gun poking at his stomach. He had made a motion toward his hip and had been shot down in his tracks.

The crime had been singularly businesslike, utterly merciless, and had netted gems worth almost a hundred and fifty thousand dollars wholesale. There had been a big shipment received but a few hours earlier in the day, and the bandits seemed fully aware of this shipment, its nature and extent, and exactly where it could be found.

Sidney Zoom digested the newspaper accounts.

With the finding of Muriel Drake's murdered body, the police and newspapers alike had concluded that the case was virtually closed, so far as the inside accomplice was concerned.

It seemed that a private detective agency, taking the employees in turn for grilling, had interrogated Muriel Drake. Her answers to questions had not been entirely convincing. She seemed unduly nervous. The private detectives had bundled her into their car, started for Headquarters, had an accident which had distracted their attention, and the girl had escaped, gone to the apartment house where her friend lived.

The police theory was that one of the men concerned in the hold-up had been afraid Muriel would confess if she were taken to the station, or that some independent criminal had sensed that Muriel was an accomplice. In any event, the man, knowing in advance that she planned to spend the night with Stella Denny, had secreted himself within the apartment house and waited for the girl to show up.

He had overpowered her, choked her, made a search of her garments, found, perhaps, that for which he searched, and made his escape. No one had seen him come, and no one had seen him go. He had waited, accomplished his sinister purpose and then faded into the night.

Police were conducting a systematic round-up of the men friends of both Muriel Drake and Stella Denny. Those men were being questioned, asked to prove where they had been when the murder was committed.

Sidney Zoom strolled to a barber shop, was shaved; went to the garage where he had stored his car, took his dog for a brief walk, and then went to Harmiston's Jewelry Company.

He entered the store and noticed that there were quite a number of people present. They were the curious who desired to see the safe which had been rifled, the exact spot where the man had fallen.

Mechanics were busy repolishing the floor, removing certain sinister dark stains. The place where a bullet had entered the wood work was being repaired so that the dark hole in the polished mahogany was no longer visible.

Sidney Zoom strolled the length of the store, peering into the show cases, studying the display of gems, flashing glances at intervals at the watchful clerks who stood at courteous attention.

As he started back toward the door, on the other side of the store, he saw the man he had expected to find. He was standing behind a counter displaying diamond rings, looking quite expressionless of feature, wary of eye.

It was the man who had worn the gray suit and overcoat, the man Sidney Zoom had last seen leaving the Bratten Arms Apartments shortly after Muriel Drake had entered the place, and but a short time before her body had been discovered.

Sidney Zoom let his attention focus upon the diamonds.

The man moved forward.

"Was there something?" he asked in the tone of voice one uses when striving to be courteous, but expecting nothing reassuring in the way of a reply.

"Yes," said Sidney Zoom. "That diamond pendant interests me. What is the price?"

Harmiston's was the sort of a place where the commercial side of the transaction is kept purposely subordinate to the merit of the merchandise, the artistic beauty of the design. The man in gray looked slightly shocked.

"You had better examine it, sir," he said, and took out the pendant.

Sidney Zoom stared at it, did not touch it.

"The price?" he demanded.

"Twelve hundred dollars!" snapped the clerk.

"Wrap it up," said Zoom.

The man in gray gave an exclamation of surprise.

"What was that? Er ... what did you say?"

"I said wrap it up," said Sidney Zoom, and reached in his inside pocket, opened his wallet, examined the contents.

He raised his eyes to the man's face.

"You sometimes take jewelry out for inspection?"

"Yes, when a deposit is made."

"I shall make a deposit then, have you go with me to determine whether or not it meets with the approval of the person for whom the gift is intended."

"Yes, sir. A deposit of, let us say, two hundred dollars?"

Sidney Zoom flipped two one-hundred-dollar bills upon the glass show case.

"I am in a hurry," he said.

"Yes, sir," said the man behind the counter. "I'll be with you at once. Let me get my hat and coat, and get this pendant wrapped. Then I'll give you a receipt."

"Very well," said Sidney Zoom. "We'll take a cab to the garage where I have my car stored. Then I'll drive you to consult the young lady."

"I'll take along another design as an alternate," the man in gray called over his shoulder, and bustled away. Within five minutes he was back, ready for the street. Zoom called a cab, drove to the garage, indicated the sedan, and opened the door.

Rip, the police dog, stretched his tawny length, turned a questioning nose toward the newcomer.

"Your name?" asked Sidney Zoom.

"Edgar Carver," said the man.

Zoom nodded.

"I want to present you formally to the dog. Rip, this is Edgar Carver."

The dog extended his paw. Carver took it with a nervous laugh.

His eyes turned to Sidney Zoom, and there was a peculiar expression in them, an expression of bewildered wonder with just the faint glint of panic.

"You keep him with you all the time, that dog?" he asked.

"Yes," said Sidney Zoom. He meshed the gears, and swept out of the garage at a rapid rate of speed.

Carver showed that he was uneasy.

"I ... er ... wonder if I didn't see you last night. I saw a man of about your build, walking with a dog."

Zoom shook his head.

"I'm sure I don't know," he said, "whether you saw me or not."

And he yawned.

The man in gray showed visible relief.

"After all," he said, laughing a short nervous laugh, "there are lots of police dogs who walk around with their masters at night."

"Lots," agreed Sidney Zoom.

The car was flashing into speed.

"Where do we go?" asked Carver, as the better class of apartments dropped behind and they turned toward the water front.

"To my yacht," said Sidney Zoom.

Carver settled back, lit a cigarette.

"This is the life," he observed.

Zoom garaged the car at the wharf, motioned to Carver to accompany him, walked down the planks of the big wharf, then down a flight of steep stairs to a mooring float against which was his trim white yacht.

Carver walked aboard.

"This way," said Zoom.

He led the man down the deck, into a cabin, down a short, steep flight of stairs. There was a door at the side of the little passageway at the foot of those stairs, and that door was painted green.

CHAPTER VI

Caught!

CARVER DID not notice the color of the door, nor did he notice that the door was so low that he had to stoop to enter. That stooping prevented him from seeing the interior of the room until after he had entered it.

Then he straightened, grinning, started to say something, and stopped. The smile faded from his face. His eyes grew large and glassy with horror. He screamed, whirled, tried to run from the room.

There was a deep-throated growl at his heels.

Rip, the police dog, barred the way with bared fangs.

Carver's hand raced to his hip, came out with a weapon that glinted an ominous blue in the half light of the horror chamber.

The dog moved with incredible speed. His fangs caught the wrist, clamped down. The dog flung his weight in a sideways lunge, wrenching the wrist.

The gun thudded to the floor.

Sidney Zoom indicated the room.

"Go in," he said, "and sit down."

Edgar Carver seemed about to faint. His knees wobbled. His eyes stared at the gruesome interior of the room. That room was barely furnished. The chief object in it was a chair. Wires ran from the floor into that chair. It was straight-backed, businesslike, horrid.

"What does this mean?" yelled Carver.

"Go in," said Sidney Zoom, "and sit down."

The man whirled in a fear and fury. He lashed out with his fists, bit, struck, clawed and kicked.

The dog rushed forward, but was sent to the floor at a single sharp command from Sidney Zoom. Zoom's long arms wrapped around the panic-stricken, struggling figure, bore him from the floor, carried him to the chair, flung him down.

A strap circled the body, held it. The arms and legs frantically kicked. Sidney

Zoom secured one of the arms with a strap which was fastened to the arm of the chair. Then he secured the other arm. Next he strapped the legs.

He made his motions with a swift efficiency which showed skill and practice. And he pinioned the flying arms and legs with a speed of motion that indicated the great strength which was in those long, sinewy muscles.

Zoom stared down at the man and nodded.

"How does it feel?" he asked.

"Good God, are you mad!" screamed the man, struggling against the straps.

Zoom shook his head.

"Very sane, thank you. I thought you might like a little taste of that which is to come. The chamber with the green door, the iron chair, the electrodes. Presently, I shall turn on a little current. Not too much. Just enough to let you know how you'll feel when the state gives you the big jolt. They say that prisoners rise against the straps, that the chair shivers with their agony.

"It's all for the best, the performance of justice. You have killed, and you shall be killed. You have lived by the sword and you shall die by the sword.

"I'll go out for a while and you can sit and see how you look. Let your mind think ahead to the thing that is in store for you."

And Sidney Zoom, stooping, backed through the green door, closed it after him.

There was a mirror in the other side of that green door. It was so adjusted that the occupant of the chair stared at his reflection every time he raised his eyes.

There was also a little peek-hole in the door, just to one side of the mirror. Through this hole, Sidney Zoom, unobserved, could study the features of the man who occupied the chair. It was a subtle bit of third degree which Zoom had perfected.

He pressed his eye to the opening, watched Edgar Carver.

Carver stared, fascinated, at the reflection of himself in the chair. His complexion was a sickly yellow. His eyes were wide and there was sweat dripping from his forehead.

The man tore his eyes away, strove to look elsewhere and failed. The eyes, fascinated, always came back to that reflection.

After a few minutes Sidney Zoom opened the green door.

"Why," he asked, "did you kill Muriel?"

"I didn't kill her," said Carver.

Zoom leveled a finger.

"My friend, you have one chance, and one chance alone to escape the torture of that chair. I want a confession. If you confess to me you stand some slight chance of escaping the embrace of the electric chair. If you fail to confess, then nothing can save you."

"I have nothing to confess," insisted Carver, the sweat dropping from his forehead.

"Very well," said Sidney Zoom, "I shall summon the police. They will take you to jail. You will be convicted, sentenced, and the fate that is in store for you will weigh on your mind day after day, sleepless night after sleepless night!"

And he stepped outside, closed the green door.

He heard the man's scream as the eyes once more sought the grim reflection.

"No, no! Come back! Come back!"

Sidney Zoom opened the door.

"Almost too late, my friend," he said, and his voice held the timbre of a solemnly tolling bell.

Edgar Carver burst into speech.

"I'll tell it all! I didn't mean to kill her. I swear I didn't. I didn't know what to do, I was between the devil and the deep sea. I had to do it! You won't understand. You don't, you can't understand! It's horrible.

"I got drawn into it, a little at the time. It started when I got to taking a few stones on my own. Then I felt I was likely to be caught. I knew they were going to take an inventory. The shortage would be discovered. I had to do something.

"I knew this gang of gem thieves, I arranged to get in touch with one of the men in that gang. I wanted them to rob the place so that my own shortage would never be known.

"I didn't tell him I was short. He was a fence, I guess. He didn't do the work himself. He said he could arrange to have it done for me. But, he said I'd have to tip the gang of when there was a heavy shipment of valuable stones coming in, and that I'd have to see that the vaults were on open so they could make a clean-up and a quick getaway.

"I never met the real gangsters. I carried on everything through the fence. The girl, Muriel, knew something was going on. Maybe she'd been dipping in some, herself. I don't know.

"I only know that the gang staged the stick-up. But things didn't go right. The watchman was a fool. They killed him. That was the first time I realized what I was up against. There had been a murder, and I was in on the job!

"It meant the chair! Think of it—the chair! The chair!"

His voice rose to a crescendo of hysterical fear, then trailed into silence as he sat and shuddered.

Sidney Zoom regarded him with unsympathetic eyes.

"But the girl's death," he said, "What of that?"

The man went on with his story.

"The girl was wise, too wise. She knew what was in the wind, and she started to hi-jack the proposition. Just before the gang came in, she made a sweep of the cream of the stock. She got a bunch of the stones that were the best values and could be the most easily sold.

"Then the stick-up, and the gang found, when they went to fence the stuff that they had the inferior merchandise, and not as much of that as they should have. Naturally, they thought I was the one that had pulled the fast one on 'em, and the fence sent for me and gave me something to think about.

"That started me using my wits. The fence gave me twenty-four hours to produce the missing stones. If I didn't produce them within that time I was to be put on the spot.

"I hunted up the girl and found that she had left her apartment. I figured she'd go to spend the night with Stella Denny, so I hot-footed over there and stuck around. The girl came in to the apartment house. I caught her in the elevator.

"She denied it at first, and then admitted what she'd done, but claimed she'd ditched the stones. Then when I got to pressing her, she told me I could either like it or lump it, and that if I said anything more she'd tell the detectives what she knew and I'd fry for murder.

"That was what set me crazy. The idea of being in the power of Muriel Drake, having her threaten to spill what she knew, and send me to the chair. I knew right then that it was my life or hers. I figured she had the stones on her somewhere.

"And if I didn't get those stones I was going to be croaked. If the girl talked, I was due to be killed. So I grabbed her and choked her. I guess I was crazy at the time.

"And then the damned broad didn't have the stones on her at all. It was a pickle. I chucked her body against the corner of the elevator and beat it. No one knew I had been waiting in the corridor for her, and there wasn't any one moving at that hour of the night. I'd run the elevator way up to the loft before I started in working on her, and there wasn't any one who had heard a thing.

"So I just pressed the button which took the elevator to the third floor, got out, closed the door. When the door closed that made the contact, and the elevator went down. I ducked out by the stairs and came out the front."

The man was rattling out the words with no regard for the effect they might have. He gave the impression of telling the truth.

Sidney Zoom stared at him.

"When was your twenty-four hours to be up?" he asked.

"At nine o'clock tonight."

"Who was the fence you dealt with?"

"Sol Asher. He's got a pawnshop on Harrison Avenue."

"Ever seen anybody besides Asher—any of the gang?"

"No. Not a one."

"You contacted them through Asher, made all the arrangements through him?"

"Yes."

"How did you happen to meet Asher?"

"I used him to pawn my stuff through. Remember I'd been taking a stone or two on my own hook when I needed the money. I figured it was safe for a while. Then, when they were going to take inventory, I had to do something. I asked Asher for advice. Maybe Asher knew I had been dabbling, but he didn't pass on the information to the gang."

Sidney Zoom let his eyes narrow.

"Then at nine o'clock tonight, or before, you were to be at Asher's place with the missing stones?"

"Yes."

Zoom nodded.

"Okay. Where do you live?"

"At a little apartment in the Monadnock Apartments. That's off Central Avenue."

"Asher know where you live?"

"Yes. I think so."

"What's the number of your apartment?"

"Three hundred and ten."

CHAPTER VII

In Apartment 310

SIDNEY ZOOM nodded his head, went to the chair, released the straps. He had to give Edgar Carver a hand to assist him from the chair. The erstwhile dapper clerk was as weak as a half drowned kitten. He could hardly stand when he had got to his feet.

"I will have to take steps to see that you are quiet," said Sidney Zoom, "while I make an investigation."

And he led Carver into a small cabin, stretched him out on a couch, mixed a glass of whiskey and ginger ale, shook in a white powder.

"Drink this," he said. "It will soothe your nerves."

The man drained the glass.

He was nervous, weak. From time to time, he shivered, as with cold, moaned.

"What a mess! There's no way out. I'd better kill myself. And I thought I was so smart. I'm in the power of the gang, in your power, in the power of a crooked fence. They can all kill—kill *me*, and they're going to kill me, too. There's no escape! I don't mind dying so much as that cursed electric chair. Good God! I nearly died when you opened that door and sent me into that room. I'd thought of the chair before, but I never dreamt it was so hideous, so sinister!"

Sidney Zoom stared at him sternly.

"You knew that crime doesn't pay. You knew that sooner or later all criminals come to grief. It's just a question of time. Yet you went blindly rushing into the crime web, floundering deeper and deeper. And, even now, you're not sorry for what you've done. You're only sorry you got caught. And you've got sympathy for yourself—none for that unfortunate girl you strangled with your greedy fingers."

Carver tried to sneer, but the sneer was a failure.

"You talk like one of those damned reformers," he said. "Lots of crooks make a good living, and they don't get caught. I just didn't get the breaks, that's all. I had bad luck. I ... shouldn't be ... shouldn't be ... blamed ..."

And his head dropped on the pillow and he slept.

Sidney Zoom knew exactly the strength of the sleeping powder he had given the man. He knew almost to the hour when the man would awaken.

He walked to the front part of the yacht, rapped on the door of a cabin.

"Yes?" called the deep, rich voice of his secretary, Vera Thurmond.

"I have a man asleep in the guest cabin," said Sidney Zoom. "He will probably not waken before midnight. But he is not to be allowed to escape. See to that. I will be back some time tonight."

The young woman opened the door, giving the finishing touches to her complexion. She looked at Sidney Zoom with tender eyes in which there was a hint of the maternal.

"You're going into danger?" she asked.

"I hope so," rasped Sidney Zoom. "Going into danger adds zest to life."

She made a little grimace.

"I do wish you'd get over that everlasting love of conflict, of danger, of struggle." Zoom's voice was solemn.

"That is the way that nature brings about evolution. We grow from conflict. Our periods of pleasure are but the mental bromides which enable us to recuperate. We get our growth from adversity."

Vera Thurmond shook her head.

"You're hopeless … Tell me, what's behind that green door? You've had a new lock put on it, and carpenters and electricians working …"

He smiled at her and shook his head.

"No. That is one of my secrets. Perhaps I am a bluebeard, and keep the bodies of my victims hidden behind the door of that room. Never open it. Don't worry about me, and don't waste sympathy on the man who occupies the guest cabin. Have the captain make everything ready for sea. I may want to get away as soon as I come aboard."

And Sidney Zoom turned on his heel, strode down the narrow passageway to the stairs which led to the dock. The police dog padded at his side.

There was, in the manner of Sidney Zoom, that subtle something which characterizes a man who is going into a welcome danger. And the dog sensed this attitude, whether it came from some extra force with which the heels of the master pounded the planks of the boat, or from something more subtle, some auric emanation of tension.

Sidney Zoom walked to his car, drove to the Monadnock Apartments, went boldly to the door of apartment 310, paused over the lock long enough to insert the key he had taken from Edgar Carver when that individual had dropped into his drugged sleep.

Zoom entered the apartment, looked around him.

It was a typical small apartment, furnished with conventional, uncomfortable overstuffed furniture. The apartment was used as a single, but there was a door which led to another single apartment, enabling the suite to be let as a double furnished apartment if desired.

Sidney Zoom knocked upon that connecting door.

There was no answer. He went out to the hall, approached the hall door of the adjoining apartment. He knocked, received no answer, and picked the lock of the door. The apartment was vacant.

Zoom opened the connecting door between the two apartments, saw to it that his gun worked easily in his shoulder holster, pulled a sheet from the bed, tore it into strips, placed his police dog just within the door of the apartment which adjoined that rented by Edgar Carver. He ascertained that any one entering apartment 310 could not see the dog, crouched in the adjoining apartment.

Then Sidney Zoom opened the collar of his shirt, loosed his necktie, sprawled in a chair, and gave the impression of being very much at home. He found a book which interested him, alternately read and dozed, while the dog slept.

It was rather late in the afternoon when there sounded a knock at his door.

"Come in," called Sidney Zoom.

The handle of the knob turned. A well tailored man walked into the apartment, stood near the door.

"I'm looking for Edgar Carver," he said.

Zoom got to his feet.

"Yes, sir, what can I do for you?"

"You're Carver?"

"Of course."

The well tailored man took a step inside the door.

"I'm from Sol Asher," he said.

Zoom let his manner become cold.

"Yeah?" he asked.

The man nodded.

"You been actin' funny, and we read about what happened to the broad. You ducked out of the store today, and didn't leave word where you was goin', or when you was comin' back, and that's not so hot. There's talk going around."

"Yeah?" said Zoom.

"Yeah!" snarled his visitor. "Now did you get those stones or not?"

Zoom's right hand dropped to the side pocket of his coat. The hand of his well tailored visitor darted to the lapel of his own coat.

"Bring that hand out clean!" he said.

Zoom brought out his hand. In the cupped palm were stones of a quality and fire to arouse the greed of either a crook or a collector.

"These," he said.

A gun snapped out of his visitor's shoulder holster. He advanced menacingly.

"Okay. I'll take those."

"You will like hell," snarled Zoom, adopting the manner which his visitor would evidently have anticipated had Zoom actually been Carver. "Those are mine. I'll make a division—with the proper parties. That's all."

"Bah!" sneered the other. "You, with a murder rap hanging over you, start to tell us what you will and what you won't do!"

He pushed the gun toward Sidney Zoom.

"Fork 'em over!"

Zoom smiled.

"All right, Rip," he said.

The gangster whirled to face the tawny streak which charged out from the adjoining apartment. He had expected some man, either an accomplice of the tenant of the apartment, or, perhaps, an officer. His eyes were raised about the height of a man's chest, and he was swinging the gun, holding it at about that level.

Not until too late was he able to get his eyes down sufficiently to see the charging dog. He tried to lower the gun and fire, but he was far too late.

The dog's jaws clamped about the wrist. The gangster gave a low cry of pain, tried to brace himself, and was swept to his knees.

"That's all, Rip," said Zoom, speaking in a low, conversational voice.

The dog let go his hold, backed away, eyes watchful and hard, lips curled back from fangs.

CHAPTER VIII

The Sleeping Powder

ZOOM WAS apologetic.

"Trust you haven't been inconvenienced," he said. "The dog is really dangerous, you know. He's been trained for exactly that sort of thing. If you do exactly as I say, you won't have any more trouble."

"Go in to that adjoining room, lie down on the bed, stretching out flat on your stomach."

The gangster took a deep breath, let his eyes sweep the room appraisingly. Zoom motioned to Rip. The dog took a swift step forward, eyes glaring, lips curled back, hot breath coming on the gangster's nostrils. The gangster moved at once, obediently, toward the door of the adjoining apartment, stretched himself on the bed, and let his wrists be bound with the strips of cloth. His ankles were also fastened.

Zoom gloated over him.

"Hang a murder rap on *me*, will you? I'll show you a trick worth two of that. You can't pull that stuff on me and get away with it!"

Then he strode from the room, leaving the dog on guard behind him.

He walked to the telephone and took down the receiver, holding his right forefinger, however, over the catch so that the hook did not rise up and complete the connection. He called a number, and that number was the number of Charles Stanhope, the well known criminal attorney.

After an interval, Sidney Zoom carried on a one-sided conversation, speaking into the transmitter of the dead telephone.

"Hello. Let me speak with Mr. Stanhope at once. He's expecting me to call ... Yes, the name's Carver ...

"Hello, Mr. Stanhope. This is Carver talking. Say, listen, that idea of yours worked like a charm. The dog was a wonder. I tied the man up just like you told me to. Yes, I've got the gems ... Now what do I do next?"

And Sidney Zoom waited a minute as though receiving telephoned instructions.

"Not until tomorrow, eh?" he said, at length, injecting a note of disappointment into his voice. "Gee, that's sort of long to wait, ain't it? I know the district attorney don't come into his office until ten o'clock. But we should be able to get a deputy ... I see ... Can't grant immunity, eh? Only the D. A. himself. Okay.

"Now, listen. I can tie this bird up so he'll stay, and I'll gag him. I can keep him here. What the hell do I care if he does choke on the gag? Yeah!

"Well, I'm going down to a guy's yacht tonight. A man named Zoom. He's got a yacht, the *Alberta F.*, moored down near the commercial docks. Yeah, it's easy to find. Just remember the name, *Alberta F.* I'll be there a little after midnight. Then I'll duck out some place and hide until nine o'clock. Then I'll come direct to your office.

"I won't come back to this place. It's too hot. And if you want me you can send a messenger to that yacht. Yeah, the *Alberta F.* But if you send a messenger see to it that he's got that secret password I gave you. Otherwise I won't pay no attention to the message.

"Yeah, that's right. Okay. I'll be there until midnight. Yeah, sure I got the stones. That's right, you get half of them as your fee. Yeah, sure. First thing tomorrow morning. Okay. G'bye."

He slammed the receiver back on the hook, making considerable racket with the instrument in doing so. Then he walked into the adjoining apartment, stared down at the bound gangster.

"I don't think you're the kind to let out a bellow," he said, "but my lawyer says I gotta slip a rag in your mouth. You got a long wait, buddy. You'll have to stick around until tomorrow morning. So take it easy. You're getting the bum breaks. When you leave here it'll be to take a nice ride in a black wagon. After that you'll have some more bad luck. I don't even dare to tell you what it is. G'bye."

"I won't talk," mumbled the gangster, speaking through the gag Zoom was thrusting into his mouth.

"You're right about that," grinned Zoom, and pushed the gag deeper into the mouth, tied it in place.

Then Sidney Zoom called to his dog, left the apartment occupied by the tied and gagged gangster, paused long enough in the Carver apartment to adjust his collar and tie, and then left the house.

He had seen to it that there was a loose knot in the strip of cloth which tied the gangster's wrists. He estimated that less than fifteen minutes would suffice to bring about the man's release.

SIDNEY ZOOM went to a pay station, called police headquarters.

"Detective Sergeant Staples, please," he said when the connection had been completed.

Sergeant Staples was a man who had one code. "Never compromise with crooks," was his slogan. He had waged a bitter war against gangsters, and the gangs hated and respected him. Sergeant Staples was about due either to find a bomb fastened to the starter of his car some morning, or to learn that he had been demoted and transferred to some quiet spot where he could do no harm.

In the meantime, he had become friendly with Zoom, was interested in the savage philosophy of the yacht owner, and came to dinner once in a while.

"Hello," said Detective Sergeant Staples, speaking with that gruff accent which creeps into the voices of those who have the courage of their own convictions, yet know that the world is against them.

"Sidney Zoom talking, Sergeant. Can you come down to the yacht for a midnight supper tonight? Yeah, come around eleven o'clock. I've got something to show you, and I've got some rye bread and cheese, some mighty fine claret, and ..."

There was no need to say more.

"At eleven on the dot," growled the sergeant's voice.

"And better come in plain clothes with a coat that has a collar turned well up," went on Zoom. "I may have a couple of chaps watching the boat, and I'd rather they didn't think that I was getting too chummy with the police ... That's right. Okay, Sergeant, eleven o'clock. G'bye."

And Zoom hung up the receiver, got in his car, went to his yacht with the expression of a man who has done a good day's work.

He summoned his Chinese cook, explained just what he wanted for a midnight supper, reassured his secretary, looked in on the sleeping form of Carver.

Then Sidney Zoom stretched out in his own cabin and slept peacefully. There was about him nothing to suggest that gaunt savagery, that uncanny ingenuity, and that grim skill as a fighter which puzzled the police and had caused so many criminals to come to a luckless end.

Sidney Zoom was awakened promptly at ten thirty as he had ordered; shaved, showered, dressed, and received Detective Sergeant Staples as that individual thudded to the deck of the yacht.

Sergeant Staples was a quiet, unassuming man who felt that society was at war with organized crime, and wasn't so certain that the outcome would be favorable to society.

He had twinkling, rather kindly eyes, broad shoulders that showed no inclination to stoop, and a jaw that was like a jutting chunk of granite.

He enjoyed the food which was served, enjoyed the companionship of Sidney Zoom and his secretary.

The table was spread in the dining salon. The food was excellent, and the conversation dear to the heart of a sergeant of detectives who goes about his work with a religious zeal.

In the guest cabin the Chinese cabin boy squatted on his heels against the wall, stared with beady, glittering eyes at the form of Edgar Carver, the man who had been directly guilty of one murder, indirectly guilty of another.

Through the door which opened to the dining salon, came the hum of voices, the occasional sound of feminine laughter. The conversation was dealing, among other things, with the very crime which the unconscious sleeper had committed.

The figure on the bed stirred, moaned. The mouth made little tasting noises.

The Chinese cabin boy arose, slipped as noiselessly as a shadow through the side door of the guest cabin, entered the dining salon, caught the eye of Sidney Zoom.

Sidney Zoom arose, affably expansive, glowingly cordial, the perfect host, entertaining guests who were enjoying themselves.

"Excuse me for a moment," he said. "A small matter which requires personal attention. The cabin boy had orders to summon me."

And he bowed, smiled, left the salon, entered the guest cabin through the side door.

Edgar Carver was struggling to a sitting position.

Sidney Zoom smiled at him.

"I'm afraid I owe you a very abject apology, young man," he said. "I certainly didn't know that my secretary had put a sleeping powder in the bottle of whiskey which was on the buffet. You'll remember you had a drink from it, and lost consciousness almost at once.

"But that's not the worst. I understand that the drug is used as a heart remedy and is inclined to give horrible nightmares. I hope you haven't had any bad dreams."

Slow incredulity upon Carver's face gave way to an expression of horror.

"Good God! You! The green door! The chair ..."

He broke off, wildly staring.

Sidney Zoom soothed him with his voice.

"I'm afraid you *did* have some dreams after all. Really, I don't care for the pendant, but I'd appreciate it if you'd keep the two hundred dollars I paid as a deposit. That will be for your personal account, and will compensate you to some extent for the annoyance."

Carver blinked his eyes, started to say something, then checked himself.

"You see," explained Zoom, "you came aboard the yacht. We sat down and I asked you if you'd have a drink. You took whiskey, and I took brandy. You dropped over like a log as soon as you'd had the drink, and then I realized what had happened.

"Sometimes the drug plays thunder with your memory, makes you forget things that have happened, and think other things happened. Now I trust that your own memory is all right. You're Edgar Carver, you know, and you're employed at Harmiston's Jewelry Company. I came into the store this morning to purchase a diamond pendant, and you showed me one that I liked. I asked you to take it to let the prospective wearer see it, and made a two-hundred-dollar deposit on it.

"You came here with me. We stepped aboard, and I offered you a drink. You immediately showed signs of being drugged, and then I knew that I had given you a drink from the whiskey bottle which contained the opiate."

Edgar Carver made a swallowing motion with his throat.

"That's all?" he asked.

"Why, yes," said Sidney Zoom, "that's all."

He sighed, lowered his eyes.

"Was there ... was ... was there a room ... with a green door?"

Sidney Zoom's eyes widened.

"Room with a green door? My dear chap, you've been dreaming. I feel guilty. You most certainly *have* been dreaming! I hope it was nothing very alarming?"

Edgar Carver reached a surreptitious hand down along his leg, pinched the muscle, then smiled.

"Shucks, no!" he said. "It wasn't anything alarming at all. I had a perfect system worked out, and I dreamt it didn't work, that's all. Of course it was a dream!"

Zoom nodded.

"That's fine. Just wait here for a moment until I excuse myself to some dinner guests and I'll see that you're driven to your apartment."

Sidney Zoom bowed, withdrew, leaving behind him a very bewildered, but greatly relieved young man.

CHAPTER IX

Lusting for Conflict

HE RETURNED to the dining salon, smiled at Sergeant Staples, crossed to a sideboard, opened a drawer.

"Sergeant, I have a little present I want to make you, something that will show my regard for you, and something that you can always keep with you."

He opened a handsome wooden box, disclosed a pair of revolvers. These were the newest type of gun designed for police work, throwing a shell with a terrific muzzle velocity, guaranteed to pierce the body of an automobile, and be able to account for itself when it had gone through the metal.

There was a leather belt, two holsters dangling from it, and the belt was filled with shells.

"The guns," explained Sidney Zoom, "are loaded. I purchased four of them. I have a pair that are exactly like yours. You'll find them quite satisfactory, I'm certain."

Sergeant Staples gave a deep inhalation.

"Gosh," he said, "I've been wanting one of these ever since I saw them advertised! Gee, Zoom, I can't thank you enough. I'll keep 'em with me all the time, one of 'em at any rate. Two guns are all right for the cowpunchers, but that's a little too much hardware for a plain cop."

He grinned, fingered the guns.

"Buckle them on, man, let's see how they look."

Sergeant Staples buckled on the guns.

Sidney Zoom took out a similar box, extracted from it similar equipment and buckled them on himself. There was a gleam in his eye.

Vera Thurmond looked at that expression on his face, and then inhaled with a sharp catching of her breath.

"You're not ... not ..."

Zoom silenced her with a glance, and the remark passed unnoticed by the officer who was busy admiring the balance of his weapons, throwing them down upon imaginary criminals, fingering the triggers.

"Sure a bunch of guns!" he exclaimed in admiration. "Only thing is I'll never get a chance to use them. Other chaps have had the breaks lately. They've been in on the fights. Gosh, Zoom, there's nothing that gives a fellow the advertisement a good gun fight does. You know what I mean, not one of these kind of shootings where you have to cut down on somebody that's running away, but a pitched battle with thugs where you stand up and swap lead, and the police come out on top of the heap.

"That's the sort of stuff the public like to read about when they sit down to their toast and coffee in the morning. It makes 'em feel the cops are on the job. And that's the sort of stuff that puts us in solid with the chief. He likes to feel that we're getting the confidence of the public. You know this thing of public confidence is a pretty big factor with us.

"Now that crooks are getting organized, it's a pretty vital thing to have the public feeling the police are a part of their side of the game. Now that we've got such a split in sentiment over prohibition, there's a tendency on the part of lots of people to sneer at the police."

Zoom nodded his sympathy.

"I know, Sergeant. I know how you feel. And I know something of your skill with six shooters. I've heard of your wonderful target scores. Well, I'm wishing you luck with these guns. I have a hunch they'll see use before long."

Sergeant Staples grinned.

"Think so? Well, I bet the babies can sure talk!"

Vera Thurmond's face was drained of color. She watched Sidney Zoom with eager, apprehensive eyes. Full well she knew the significance of that glitter that was in his eyes, that slight expansion of the aquiline nostrils, that tightening of the corners of the mouth.

"Please," she said to him, "won't you remember ..."

And she said no more.

There was the crack of a revolver, sounding very close, the smashing impact of a bullet against the deck of the yacht. A man screamed a curse. There sounded the patter of running feet, then a fusillade of shots.

The police dog was on his feet, hairs along his back bristling, eyes gleaming. Sidney Zoom gained the door in three swift strides. Sergeant Staples was at his heels.

They raced down the corridor, up the companionway to the deck.

The darkness of the wharf loomed like a vast mass of ink against the sky. There were boxes and barrels, odds and ends of piled timbers. The deck of the yacht was also dark save where the after companionway opening caught the rays of light that streamed down from a drop light.

A man lay on the deck of the yacht, hardly twenty feet from that opening. He was gasping. Red stains streaked the white deck of the yacht. One leg was doubled under him. His white face was twitching, but he was holding a revolver, shooting slowly, regularly. Three shots he fired, and then the hammer clicked.

And the darkness of the wharf was spurting little tongues of flame.

Bullets flicked down upon the deck. Long furrows appeared in the white wood as by magic. The body of the stricken man twitched under the impact of a bullet, straightened, gave a convulsive quiver. Two furrows appeared in the deck within inches of his body, then another bullet thudded into the inert flesh.

Sergeant Staples fired one of the new guns.

A man leapt up from behind a pile of timber, screamed, flung himself half around and pitched forward. The flickering tongues of flame from the wharf were directed toward the two men who had debouched from the forward companionway. Bullets hummed and sang.

Sidney Zoom, his face showing a keen zest for conflict, looking like the face of some savage eagle as it is about to swoop, shot twice from the hip.

Sergeant Staples fired once more.

The police dog gained the landing float in a single long leap, tore through the night, his paws beating a tattoo upon the heavy timbers of the wharf.

A man yelled and jumped up. A tawny figure was springing through the air. The man swung his gun.

He was dead before he fired, dead before even the dog's fangs sank in his throat. Staples had fired one of his deadly accurate shots, and the bullet, hitting its mark with that terrific smashing impact which is the distinguishing mark of the new weapon and ammunition, hurled the man as though he had been blasted by some unseen thunderbolt.

Sidney Zoom, grinning with savage joy, was running after the dog. Sergeant Staples, feet flat on the boards to give him a steady support, lips compressed in a thin line, twinkling eyes gleaming in cold calculation, studied the black outlines of the wharf.

Suddenly there was a hissing noise, a blinding glare of light.

A switch on the yacht had been turned, and searchlights rigged on the masts, directed toward the wharf, turned the night into day.

A man screamed, jumped to his feet, fired almost point blank at Zoom. Zoom returned the fire. The man crumpled as though a pile driver had smashed him in the stomach.

"They're running, Sergeant!" yelled Zoom.

Sergeant Staples nodded grimly.

Tongues of fire were still flickering toward him from the far corner of the wharf. He ran for cover. A bullet ticked his shoulder, striking with enough impact to falter him in his stride.

"Get him, Rip!" yelled Zoom.

The dog charged. The gangster, realizing the import of that charge, jumped to his feet to fire, and was blasted back by two bullets which thudded into his body with simultaneous impact.

A car exhaust roared. Then a siren sounded. Police whistles were blowing.

The wharf was now silent.

The roar of the fleeing car mingled with the wail of a siren. There sounded the spiteful clatter of a machine gun. Then a battery of sawed-off shotguns belched forth noise. The sound of tires screaming in a death skid on pavement was swallowed in a terrific crash, then silence.

Zoom and Sergeant Staples ran the length of the wharf. A red spotlight flooded them.

"It's Sergeant Staples," roared that individual. "Don't let them get away. They've done murder."

The voice of an excited officer sounded from the darkness back of the red light.

"They're not gettin' away, Sergeant. Sol Asher and Bill the Biff were in that car. There was one other one. We don't know him. They ain't gettin' away."

Sidney Zoom sighed and holstered his weapons.

"Come, Rip," he called.

TWO hours later, Sidney Zoom sat in the hospital beside Sergeant Staples. The sergeant was grinning, smoking a cigar. The room was temporarily cleared of reporters, but the haze of flashlight smoke still clung to the ceiling.

Sergeant Staples gazed at Zoom.

"Well," he said, "it was a great fight. I always figured that if I got in a fight with gangsters I could shoot as well as I do on the targets. I've always held that thought in mind, it's subconscious. I've trained myself to think it every time I pull down on a target in the police revolver range."

Zoom nodded.

"You sure cleaned up on 'em tonight, Sergeant. The gang was the toughest bunch of birds that's ever been rounded up. Sol Asher confessed the whole business. They pulled a couple of frying jobs before this one. Those that aren't killed will be meat for the chair.

"And it cleans up that Harmiston job."

Sergeant Staples let his smile fade. A pucker appeared between his eyebrows.

"What gets me, Zoom, is how this chap happened to be on your boat."

Zoom grinned, a frank and open grin.

"I went into the store to get a pendant for my secretary," he said. "I wanted her to see it. This man came out to bring the pendant, also one other. They were found in his pocket, you'll remember.

"I paid a deposit of two hundred dollars on the pendant. Fortunately, I have the receipt, which fully accounts for his presence on the yacht. You see, he had a drink or two, and became a little befuddled. He was sleeping it off in the adjoining cabin. I guess he woke up, heard some of your conversation when I gave you the guns, and realized you were an officer.

"That bothered him, and he tried to make a sneak. He couldn't take the forward companionway without having to pass the open door of the dining salon. So he took the back exit, and the lights were blazing down on the deck there.

"He came out, was recognized by Sol Asher and the gang, who felt he had turned state's evidence, and were waiting to bump him off. Then you know what happened."

Sergeant Staples sighed.

"Yes," he said. "I know what happened. But I'd sure like to know what was back of it all. It was a funny coincidence that you happened to shove two loaded guns into my hands just before the fireworks started!"

Zoom grinned.

"It was that! Well, I'll toddle along and let you get some sleep. They tell me you're slated for a captaincy, and you'll want to get your beauty sleep so you can look pretty for the pictures."

Sergeant Staples sighed again.

His sigh was one of perfect contentment. It was the sigh of an epicure who has dined well, of the artist who has completed a first class canvas.

"Zoom," he murmured contentedly, "I don't know how you did it, and I don't give a damn, but it was a pretty fight, and if anybody asks you embarrassing questions, refuse to answer and refer 'em to me!"

And Sidney Zoom, smiling, tiptoed from the hospital room.

But there was to be no sleep for him that night.

The wind had come up. The seas would be crashing out beyond the heads, and Sidney Zoom, the lust for conflict aroused within him, would be unable to sleep until after he had sent his yacht out to fight with those giant combers, letting the huge seas sweep over the frail craft.

For Sidney Zoom, grim, uncompromising, believer in dealing with criminals as they deserved, detested ways of peace and the humdrum routine of life. He wanted conflict and adventure. His soul craved combat as the soul of many men craves strong drink.

The girl's death had been avenged. A desperate gang had been routed in fair fight. A good sergeant had been given the opportunity to go far on the force. A crooked employee and murderer had been given the chance to cheat the chair.

But Sidney Zoom craved still more action, demanded more conflict before sleep could come to his taut nerves.

And so he headed for his yacht, anxious to gain the open sea.

CHEATING THE CHAIR

SIDNEY ZOOM, tall, gaunt, his profile suggestive of that of a hawk, sat in the spacious cabin of his trim yacht, surrounded by a litter of newspapers. His secretary Vera Thurmond, watched him with eyes that were luminous with solicitude.

Sidney Zoom was entirely oblivious of her scrutiny. He was concentrating his attention upon the contents of the newspapers. At his feet, muzzle on paws, stretched his tawny police dog, Rip.

"The rich," said Sidney Zoom, "get the breaks."

His secretary made no answer to a remark which was so patently logical.

Sidney Zoom indicated a newspaper half column.

"Here," he observed, "is the account of a man who is being tried for the murder of a county attorney. The man was a convict. He claims he reformed. He had previously been convicted by this same county attorney.

"The murdered man was found in his office, an automatic on the table in front of him with one shell discharged. The ex-convict had written a threatening note.

"The newspapers give it a scant half column now that the case has come on for trial, and most of that half column contains the list of the victim's official activities during his lifetime. Bah!"

His secretary was frankly puzzled.

"But," she observed, "what would you expect? It's news from one of the outlying counties. There wasn't any element of love or greed in the crime, no particular mystery. I read that account myself and didn't notice anything out of place about it. The man was a criminal. The letter's in his handwriting. It had been received by the county attorney but a few hours before his death. The ex-convict threatened to kill him to get even for his conviction.

"The case is dead open and shut. The court appointed a lawyer to defend the convict ... what's his name? ... Oh, yes, I remember, Crandall. The man's receiving a fair trial. What more could you ask?"

Sidney Zoom crumpled the paper into a ball, dashed it to the floor.

"I could ask," he said, in a voice that was vibrant with irritation, yet deeply resonant, "that the newspaper would either offer some explanation of why a convict should write a letter to the man he intended to murder, telling him that he intended to kill him, or else that they wouldn't print that fact at all.

"Damn it, they arouse the curiosity of any sane man, and then they go off on some fool tangent. I wouldn't mind if this man had money; but he hasn't. He's a pauper. The court has appointed an attorney to defend him. That means this man gets representation in court, but there's no one to work out the hidden facts.

"A criminal case is like an iceberg. The biggest part of it is submerged from view … Where the devil is this place? Dellboro, eh? We could take the boat up there if we had to. There's a bay, and a river runs up to Dellboro. Probably isn't a decent hotel in the place. They wouldn't let dogs in …"

The young woman regarded him with eyes that twinkled.

"But why should you want to go there?"

"To find out about that damned letter," he rasped, irritably, "and to make certain this ex-convict, Crandall, gets a fair deal."

She spoke to him in a tone of patient reproach.

"You've got to get rid of this under-dog complex of yours, Mr. Zoom. You can't use up all your nerve force running around to protect the interests of every poor man who gets entangled in the meshes of the law. I know how you feel. You like to fight. You enjoy the conflict, and you've got a heart that's entirely too big. You can't use up all your time, though …"

He was on his feet, shaking his head impatiently.

Now that he stood up, he showed as a lithe man, tall yet graceful, long of arm, leg and neck, with a strange force of dignity about the expression of his features that made him seem like some gaunt spectre of doom.

"I'm going to find out about that letter," he said, "and I'm going to do it before Crandall gets sent to the chair … Oh, Captain, get her out in the stream. I'll take the wheel as soon as you get her free!"

And Sidney Zoom strode from the cabin, his long legs moving like stilts, the police dog padding at his side, never letting his master out of his sight.

Vera Thurmond sighed, stooped, gathered up the papers. She knew the habits of the man for whom she worked well enough to know that he would soon be calling upon her for every scrap of newspaper material dealing with the case of the State vs. Crandall.

For Sidney Zoom, once started on a case, would no more think of quitting than would a bloodhound, started on a warm trail, think of turning back. Sidney Zoom was not a detective, nor was he interested in crime detection as such. He was a fighter. He loved to battle the raging seas on a stormy night, out beyond the heads, his graceful yacht smashing into the waters or riding the roaring crests of booming waves.

Then, when calm seas offered no conflict with the elements, Sidney Zoom would bring his craft into port, and restlessly search through the midnight streets of the city, or ponder the newspaper accounts of crime, seeking for some case where the under-dog was being persecuted by reason of the fact that he was an under-dog.

When he had once sunk his teeth into such a case, he never let up.

CHAPTER II

The Letter

BILL DUNBAR, the attorney who had been appointed by the court to represent James Crandall, was plainly flattered that he had been invited to dinner aboard the yacht.

Sidney Zoom's craft was far too beautiful and trim not to have attracted much attention among the inhabitants of Dellboro when it swung into dock at the river bank. And Bill Dunbar was far too shrewd an attorney not to recognize the advertising value of being the first citizen of the town to set foot aboard.

With a good dinner under his belt, a glass of cordial at his elbow, a lighted cigarette between his fingers, Dunbar talked calmly and frankly about the case.

"Of course," he said, "there are some things that I can't tell you. My professional obligations, and my duty to my client require that I use discretion. Crandall was without funds. The court appointed me to defend him. I'll do it to the best of my ability. It's a part of the duties of my profession.

"The facts in the main are as reported. Three years ago Frank Strome, who was then the county attorney, tried a case in which James Crandall was the defendant. The charge was forgery. Crandall claimed he was innocent, but Strome secured a conviction. Crandall was very bitter.

"A year ago Crandall was released. He dropped out of sight. Where he was and what he was doing are mysteries that the police have never been able to solve. He simply keeps his mouth shut and won't say a word.

"On the eighteenth of April, at about three o'clock in the afternoon, Frank Strome was found dead in his private office. There were a lot of legal papers scattered over the floor, also some mail. It looked as though papers had been thrown broadcast.

"There was an automatic with one shell discharged. It lay on the desk. The door from the private office into the hallway was open. Strome always kept it locked. That showed that someone had left by that door, and, probably had entered by it.

"Carl Purcell, the present attorney for the county, was chief deputy at that time. He had been in to see his chief upon some matter of business, and found that some papers were required. He went out into the outer office and enlisted the aid of the stenographer in finding the files.

"Strome was alive at that time. He called to Purcell as the chief deputy left the inner office. The stenographer heard his voice plainly. It didn't sound excited in the least, nor did it sound as though there was anyone else in the room, for he was referring to some very confidential papers. They related, I understand, although it's being hushed up, to a charge that was being investigated against Sam Gilvert, a banker here.

"Anyway, the papers were gone. The deputy and the stenographer searched for them high and low. They were occupied for some half hour in the search. The papers were important. They dreaded to tell their boss about the loss.

"Finally, Purcell decided there was nothing else to do. Afterwards they wondered why Strome had been so patient. He had evidently expected the papers to be brought to him within a matter of minutes. But he sat in his office and said nothing.

"Purcell went in—and came running out. He yelled that Strome was dead. Subsequent events showed that he'd been dead for some fifteen or twenty minutes. In fact, there's one way the exact time the shot was fired can be told ..."

Sidney Zoom interrupted.

"You mean to tell me that the shot wasn't heard?"

The lawyer shrugged his shoulders.

"One of the peculiar facts of the case," he said. "Yet it's one of those things about which there can be no doubt. The shot was fired from that private office, and yet no one heard it. That leads up to what I was going to tell you about the time of the murder. There was only one moment when that shot could have been fired, yet not heard.

"That was when a machine was going past, setting off heavy bombs. It was a part of the drive that was being waged to find employment for some of the needy workers in the city. The car had a lot of publicity stuff pasted on the sides, and was setting off bombs at regular intervals.

"The sound of those bombs would have drowned the noise of the gun. The man must have managed to get Strome to let him into his private office, through the hall door, then shot him when the machine went past."

The lawyer sipped his cordial, stretched out his legs, puffed at his cigarette.

"That, of course, is a telling point in the case against us. It shows premeditation. Otherwise I'd try to claim that there was an argument, that the murder must have been committed in the heat of the argument ..."

Sidney Zoom's voice was impatient.

"The letter?" he said.

The attorney shrugged his shoulders.

"After all, that's a matter for the handwriting experts and for the jury. It was received through the mail. There can be no doubt about its receipt. The stenographer remembers when it came in, remembers when Strome opened it and took out the letter. He showed it to her. He remarked at the time that it was the second threat he'd received from the same party."

Sidney Zoom was scowling.

"And Crandall signed that letter?"

The lawyer was cautious.

"It purports to bear his signature," he said, "and handwriting experts employed by the state are prepared to swear that it's Crandall's handwriting."

"The gun?" asked Sidney Zoom.

"Same story," said the attorney. "The police claim they can show where the defendant purchased this gun, claim they can show his handwriting on the register that the retailer kept. He purchased it in another state several years ago."

"Any chance this evidence is faked?"

"That's something for the jury to decide. Personally, I wouldn't trust George Frink any farther than I could throw the courthouse by the cornerstone."

"Frink? Who's he?"

"He's the head of the county attorney's secret staff. He has all the drag around here, acts like a tin god."

"Anything else you know about the case?" Zoom inquired.

"Plenty," agreed the lawyer, "but I can't tell it."

"And no one knows where the defendant's been since he left the big house?"

"No. That's one thing he won't tell, even to me."

"If he doesn't tell on the witness stand he'll go to the chair," Zoom remarked.

The lawyer sighed.

"That's what I've told him. He says that he'll go to the chair, if that's the case. He won't open up about where he's been."

Sidney Zoom dropped one of his long arms. His strong, tapering fingers massaged the dog's ears as the animal sprawled at the side of his chair.

"Do you know," he remarked casually, "I'm glad I came down here, after all?"

"Why?" interrogated the attorney.

"Because," said Sidney Zoom, "that crime never happened the way you and the county attorney seem to think it happened—never in God's world."

The lawyer sipped his cordial, and said: "Well, I'm glad you feel that way. I wish you could inspire me with some of your confidence."

"When will the case go to the jury?" snapped Zoom.

"The latter part of the week, maybe sooner."

"Could you get a continuance if we uncovered something interesting?"

"Not a chance. I've tried twice for a continuance."

Sidney Zoom's lips clamped in a thin line.

"If the defendant had been wealthy, could you have secured a continuance?"

"Why ask?"

"Nothing. Do have some more cordial, and we'll quit talking shop and let you get a little relaxation."

CHAPTER III

The Girl in the Park

THE CITY of Dellboro quieted down early at night. After the second picture show there were a few stragglers who debouched upon the streets. But they dissolved almost at once. Cars roared into motion, pulling away from the curb, running with purposeful speed toward the residential section.

Sidney Zoom patrolled the sidewalks. The police dog padded along at his side. Zoom was thinking. And, as some people find it necessary to pace the floor when they are wrestling with some mental problem, so did Zoom find it conducive to clarity of thought to stalk through the night streets of a city, his heels pounding the pavements of the deserted sidewalks.

Sidney Zoom had found his adventures in various places and in various ways. But always he had specialized in ferreting out human misery. And the police dog had been with Zoom for years, long enough to know his system.

Which was why the dog gave a low throaty growl, turned his muzzle toward dark shadows of the little park which showed as a black blotch in the middle of the city. Here were little benches, miniature fountains, dark hedges and patches of grass, cool and green in the daytime, but showing dark and forbidding at night.

Sidney Zoom knew that the dog's keen ears had detected some sound which was inaudible to his own ears. He paused in his pacing, said softly to the dog:

"All right. Go find."

The dog at once took the lead. His noiseless feet padded toward the dark shadows. And then, when some few yards had been traversed, Sidney Zoom could hear those sounds which had caught the attention of the dog.

Somewhere within a patch of shadow, back of a hedge, a woman was sobbing. They were those dry sobs which indicate utter despair.

Sidney Zoom frowned.

He had been turning over in his mind the problem of the murder. It had happened in a manner that was impossible. Yet he knew that he could not convince anyone of its impossibility unless he secured more information.

Now he was confronted with a bit of human misery which could not be overlooked. Sidney Zoom would never rest until he had solved the mystery of those sobs. Fighter that he was, he chose to exert his fighting qualities in the helping of the weak and oppressed. And, in the course of years, he had come to know the sound of female sobs. There were the rapid sobs of heartache, sobs which came from emotion, and which no man could help. Then there were those dry, slow-paced, deadly sobs which told not of taut nerves seeking the relief of a good cry, but of the black hopelessness of utter despair. These sobs were like that.

Sidney Zoom moved forward, and, as he did so, the woman got to her feet. Zoom could see the top of her head and her shoulders as she stood up. The rest of her was concealed by the line of the ornamental hedge.

Zoom hesitated, then followed as the woman began to walk.

She was young, he saw, as the hurrying figure crossed a patch of light near a fountain, and she was going some place in a hurry. Nor was she sobbing any longer. Her shoulders were set with a grim purpose.

She left the park behind, turned to the left at the first corner, pounded the pavement with her determined little feet, heedless of the man and the dog who trailed along behind her.

Sidney Zoom kept his distance. There was no chance of losing the trail, not with the keen nose of the dog to help him. Once let that police dog get the idea that they were trailing some human, and he would thread the way through a labyrinth of streets if necessary.

It was when she came to the entrance to an office building that the girl paused. Sidney Zoom ducked into the shadows of a dark store entrance.

The young woman looked up and down the sidewalk. Then she vanished.

Cautiously, Sidney Zoom followed down the sidewalk, and came to the place where she had ascended a flight of stairs leading to a one-story office building.

Sidney Zoom's eyebrows raised a trifle.

The stairway led to the offices of the county attorney. Under the regulations in effect in that county, the county attorney was permitted to engage in civil practice, and to keep offices in the business district, rather than in the court-house.

Sidney Zoom spoke to the dog, quieting him. Then he walked up the stairs. The dog padded at his side.

Sidney Zoom paused at the head of the stairs.

He could hear keys rattling against the metal face of a lock a few doors down the corridor. The building was one which was typical of small towns. There were stores on the street level, a wide flight of stairs, a long corridor, and offices on the single upper story. In this building, the offices of the county attorney occupied the entire upper floor.

The girl had some trouble with the lock of the door. Finally, however, Zoom's keen ears heard the click of the bolt, and then the creak of a door on hinges.

Sidney Zoom whispered a command to the crouching dog. Together, they moved into the dark hallway, stepped cautiously toward the row of office doors which fronted on the corridor.

The girl had not switched on the lights. But she was using an electric flashlight with great caution, keeping the beam from striking against the windows. Zoom could see the intermittent flashes of the light on the frosted glass of the oblong panels in the corridor doors.

He frowned, moved closer, and listened.

The girl was opening filing cases. Zoom's ears could hear the sounds made by the steel drawers as they slid out on their well oiled rollers, could hear the noises made by the questing fingers as they riffled the pasteboard guides.

Then Sidney Zoom became aware of another sound.

Cautious feet were ascending the stairs leading from the street.

Rip, the police dog, growled, swung about, crouched, bracing himself for a rush, should his master order it. The feet on the stairs were coming up rapidly, with assurance, yet with an attempt at stealth.

Sidney Zoom placed a hand on the dog's collar, flattened himself against the lower part of one of the dark doors and crouched, holding the dog.

CHAPTER IV

A Fight in the Dark

THERE WAS enough light coming up from the street to enable Sidney Zoom to see the black hulk of the figure as it reached the top of the stairway. It did not hesitate. The shoes squeaked slightly as the big man, broad of shoulder, heavy of neck, tiptoed toward the door through which the girl had vanished.

For a second, during which the muscles of the police dog were as taut wires under the restraining fingers of Zoom's hand, the man paused, listening to the sounds of surreptitious activity from the inner office.

Then the man's shoulders lurched forward. He flung open the door. A flashlight was in his hand. The beam stabbed through the half darkness.

"Stick 'm up!" he growled.

The little scene was enacted not six feet away from the place where Zoom crouched with the dog. Zoom could see the silhouette of the big figure, hulking against the light reflected from the beam of the hand torch. He could hear the scream which the girl gave, and then could catch the note of gloating in the man's voice.

"Well, if we needed anything to strap Crandall to the chair we've got it now. Come out, you little—"

She hesitated.

Sidney Zoom pressed the police dog firmly to the floor. He gave one last final push between the blades of the shoulders where the muscles bunched into hard knots. That pressure had a definite significance. It meant that the dog would remain there, no matter what happened, until he was ordered by Sidney Zoom to leave that position.

Then Zoom made two long, cautious steps, moving with the lithe grace of a stalking panther, and making no more noise.

He found himself in a position from which he could peer over the broad shoulder of the man who blocked the doorway. He could see down the beam of the flashlight, could detect the expression of stark terror on the face of the girl.

She was masked, her forehead covered by a cloth.

The wide, terror-stricken eyes showed through the holes in that cloth mask. The mouth sagged open. The lips were white with terror. She was standing before an open filing case. The flashing beam of pitiless light had speared her in the very act of searching the files. She held one marked "State vs. Crandall."

"Come here, you little—, and let me rip that mask off," growled the man in the doorway. "I've had an idea all along there was a broad in that Crandall case."

She moved toward him, slowly, as one in a trance. She tried twice to speak, the white lips moving in a futile effort. The fear-constricted throat muscles could not function.

She was within three feet of the man.

"Take off the mask," he said.

She halted, motionless.

"Take off the mask!"

She still remained motionless.

The big arm of the man flashed out in a sweeping swing. The hand did not rip at the cloth, but swung, instead, in a swishing blow. It caught the young woman squarely on the side of the jaw. She was swept to one side, stumbled over a chair, fell. The beam of the flashlight pinned her in its glare.

"Take off that mask!" bellowed the man.

The girl's hands went to her face, not removing the mask, but in a gesture of instinctive terror, holding the cloth to her face.

The man moved forward.

"If you want to get beat up," he said, "I'm the guy that'll do it!"

As he spoke, he drew back his foot, preparatory to making a vicious kick.

It was at that instant that the long arm of Sidney Zoom flashed out in the darkness. The talon-like fingers, as rigid as though they had been fashioned from steel, clutched the cloth of the man's coat collar. The arm jerked.

The big man had been poised on one foot, swinging the other in a kick. The swift pull at his collar jerked him off balance. The twisting motion of the snapping arm sent him into a spin. Sidney Zoom's other hand swooped down, struck the thick wrist of the hand that held the flashlight. The flashlight was snapped from the man's grasp, thudded to the floor. All was darkness.

"Never," said Sidney Zoom, "strike a woman."

The man gave one inarticulate bellow of rage and rushed.

Even in the darkness, he showed an uncanny judgment of spacing, of timing, and of distance. His blows had all of the swift speed, all of the vicious follow-through which characterizes the performance of a professional fighter.

Sidney Zoom gave ground before that charging rush, before that avalanche of human weight. But he gave ground in a scientific manner, his left foot always advanced, his right foot tapping out the retreat, his left shoulder hunched forward, protecting his chin and the side of his face. His left hand was held in readiness, his right flung in such a position as to protect the solar plexus, leaving a protruding elbow as a menace to the flying fists of his assailant.

On the floor, the police dog whined his anxiety, chattered his teeth in an ecstasy of desire to tear this man limb from limb. Yet the iron discipline under which he had been schooled held him crouched to the floor, the saliva dripping from his quivering jaws.

As the men cleared the doorway, the girl, jumping forward, ran for the stairs. The big man was heedless of her escape. But Sidney Zoom, his ears waiting for those very sounds of flight, knew the girl had eluded her captor.

He suddenly ceased to be on the defensive.

The big man, irritated that his flailing blows should find no vital mark, his right hand tender from having flung into that protruding elbow upon two occasions, set himself for a crashing rush.

The left arm of Sidney Zoom suddenly ceased to be merely a wall of defense. It flicked out in swiftly stabbing blows, as smoothly and as rapidly as the tongue of a snake flickers in and out.

One, two, three blows found their mark upon the face of the big man, every blow having the effect of throwing him off balance, keeping him from getting set for his rushing offensive.

Then the fourth blow measured the distance, told Sidney Zoom exactly where the right should cross over. The right flashed in a swift hook, thudded to the jaw with a jar of impact that lifted the big man from his feet, sent him hurling back into the dark room where he had trapped the girl.

Sidney Zoom flung the door of that office shut. There was a skeleton key in the mortise lock. He twisted it, locking the door.

"Come, Rip," he whispered, and ran lightly to the stairs which went to the street. He looked up and down the sidewalk.

There was no sign of human life. The girl had vanished utterly and completely.

Sidney Zoom had no means of knowing who she was. Nor could he tell the identity of the man with whom he had fought. Nor, truth to tell, did he greatly care. Sidney Zoom was a born fighter. He longed for conflict, mental and physical. This man had been taking advantage of a woman. Sidney Zoom asked for no other cause to make war.

Man-made laws of property rights meant but little to this man who would have been a pirate leader in another age. Zoom recognized certain basic principles of right and wrong, and no other. He longed for conflict, and asked not too many questions concerning the technical laws governing the merits of such conflict. All that he required was to find the weak being oppressed by the strong. Then he hurled himself into the fight with a whole-hearted ferocity which swept all opposition before it.

He had not the slightest doubt that the man he had locked in the office on that upper floor represented the law enforcement agencies of the city of Dellboro. And he did not care a hoot. Sidney Zoom's concern had to do entirely with the identity of the young woman who had been sobbing her heart away on a park bench under the quiet stars of a midnight sky. He wanted to find her, to relieve her sufferings, if that were possible.

He turned to the dog.

"Find," he said.

CHAPTER V

Della Rangar

THE DOG, glad of an opportunity for action, placed his muzzle to the cold cement, sniffed, ran a few steps toward the west, then turned to the east, ran, sniffed, wagged his tail, started following the scent, his tail wagging vehemently.

Sidney Zoom's long legs moved in great strides.

The dog led the way to the mouth of an alley, up that alley, to the back entrance of a rooming house, up a flight of stairs, through a back door, along a corridor, paused before a dark door, and looked up at his master.

Sidney Zoom knocked on the door.

There was no sound from the room.

Sidney Zoom knocked again, tried the knob.

"Open up," he said, "and do it quickly."

There came the sound of bed springs creaking, a sleepy voice asked: "Who's there?"

"A friend," said Sidney Zoom.

"I'm in bed—asleep. Go away."

Sidney Zoom was impatient with such prevarication in the face of the infallible identification which the dog had given.

"I will give you ten seconds," he said, "to open the door."

There came the sound of bare feet thudding to the floor. Garments rustled. The feet came toward the door, a lock clicked, and Sidney Zoom stared into the eyes of a young woman who looked very much as though she had been asleep for some hours, save for one thing. That one thing was the red, swollen spot on the side of her face where the fist had crashed home.

"This," she said, "is an outrage."

Zoom moved into the room, locked the door behind him.

"Now the first question," he said, "is whether or not you left anything behind in that office by which you could be identified? A purse, perhaps? Perhaps a compact?"

"I don't know what you're talking about," she said with dignity.

She wrapped a kimono about her, first taking care to let it flap open for a sufficient length along the front to show Sidney Zoom that she was, indeed in night attire. There were feminine garments piled on the chair. Sidney Zoom walked to them, thrust his hand down among the filmy silks. They were still warm with the heat from the body of the young woman.

She stared at him.

Sidney Zoom regarded the red welt on the side of her face.

"Look at yourself in the mirror," he ordered.

The girl moved to the mirror. Her eyes fastened upon that tell-tale mark, and her lips clamped into a thin line.

"Who—who—who are you?" she stammered, her voice issuing from a mouth that was dry with terror.

Sidney Zoom grinned at her.

"I," he said, "am the man who slammed the big boob who struck you, after you'd had a chance to make good your escape. I knocked him off his pins and locked him in the office. Here's the skeleton key you left in the lock. Now tell me your story, and tell me whether there's anything you left behind that would bring the officers to this place."

She stared at him.

"Who are you?" she asked again.

"I am the man who heard you sobbing in the park. I followed you to the office of the county attorney. Then when the big hulk came in and started to bully you, I gave you a break. Now answer *my* questions."

Her hand, unconsciously seeking the contact of companionship, had descended to the head of the crouching dog. The animal had first stiffened, then his ears had relaxed. The tip of his tail waved gently. In that manner he communicated to his master that the touch of this young woman spoke of sincerity and of honesty. Sidney Zoom needed no further endorsement. An intelligent animal can tell more from the touch of a human's fingertips than most men can tell from a week of constant association.

The dog's head turned. His tongue shot out, gently caressing the girl's hand, and that sign of sympathy broke through the wall of suspicion and reserve, and words poured from her lips.

"I'm Della Rangar," she said. "No one knows me here, and no one knows I'm here. I recognized the picture of James Crandall which was published in the papers when his trial started. He—he's my sweetheart. I knew him under another name, in another city.

"He's been living there, and going straight. We were to be married. He won't tell where he was, or what he was doing because he knows that will mix me into the mess. He hoped I'd never hear of this. I thought—thought that he'd just run away and left me. You see, I haven't always been so straight myself. I've had my experiences with the seamy side of life, and I've even done time.

"Crandall knew that. And he knew that if the police found out about me they'd drag me in as an accomplice. He was going to take the rap, go to the chair in silence, just to protect me. When I saw his picture, I came on here. I thought I could break into the office of the county attorney and steal the file in the Crandall case. I've known of such things being done."

She paused, staring defiantly at Sidney Zoom, as though expecting to hear his denunciation.

Sidney Zoom, however, merely nodded his head approvingly.

"Good girl," he said. "Did you find anything?"

"No evidence. The file of the case was there. The letter wasn't in the file. It's that letter that will send Jim to the chair."

Sidney Zoom pursed his lips.

"You haven't answered one other question. Did you leave anything behind by which you can be identified?"

She shook her head. Then her head suddenly became motionless. The cheek blanched again.

"I made notations," she said, "on a sheet of paper that I took from this rooming house. It had the address on it. The files were indexed, you know, and I first looked up the index numbers, and then wrote the numbers ..."

Zoom interrupted.

"You left that paper behind?"

"I'm afraid I must have. I had it in my hand when—when he struck me."

Sidney Zoom strode toward the door.

"Get your things together," he said. "I'll watch the corridor. Make it snappy. Get 'em on quickly."

He jerked the door open, strode into the corridor, stood rigidly alert, the dog at his side. From the interior of the room came sounds of swift motion. Almost within a matter of seconds the door opened again and the girl, garbed for the street, stood at his side.

"Ready," she said.

There was in her tone the implicit confidence of one who trusts. It was an emotion which Sidney Zoom inspired, particularly in the helpless, as well as in dogs, horses and children.

Zoom led the way.

They left by the front door, walked across to the other side of the street.

And, as they rounded the corner, the night silence was disrupted by the noise of a speeding motor. A light car, filled with men, came swiftly down the street, skidded to a stop before the entrance to the rooming house. The men jumped from the car, ran across the strip of sidewalk, and vanished within the dark doorway.

Sidney Zoom turned to the girl at his side and smiled.

"We weren't any too soon," he said.

There was no longer any fear in her voice.

"Somehow, I don't feel afraid any more," she said. "I have a feeling that justice is going to be done—real justice."

Sidney Zoom took her elbow, assisted her down from the curb to the street, piloted her to the place where the shadows were the deepest. Keeping to those clinging shadows, he guided her to his yacht, slipped her aboard.

Vera Thurmond, the secretary, regarded the girl with eyes that were warm with sympathy. There was, in the secretary, a maternal affection for those strange outcasts of the night whom Sidney Zoom picked up from time to time and brought to safe sanctuary aboard the yacht.

"Keep her safe, and keep her out of sight," said Sidney Zoom.

Vera Thurmond flung a protecting arm around the waist of Della Rangar.

"Come, my poor dear, you need sleep," she said.

Taut nerves relaxed. The girl smiled.

"I'm commencing to believe that God's in his heaven after all," she said.

For Sidney Zoom's character was such that no one could come in contact with him without feeling the strange influence of the man. He influenced the lives of those about him as a lodestone influences the needle of a magnet. The weak and the helpless found in him a haven of refuge, a gigantic wall of strength. The oppressor found in him a grim enemy, tireless, uncompromising, letting no man-made law stand between him and his prey.

CHAPTER VI

Rip Smells a Banker

THE MORNING sun streamed through the long, narrow windows, reflected from the polished surface of the walnut desk, and made little splotches of uneven illumination upon the tinted wall.

Sam Gilvert sat in the swivel chair, a filing drawer of a card indexing system in front of him. Several of those cards represented past due obligations owing to the bank. These had red tabs on their margins. The tabs were a bright red, and the gnarled fingers of the banker went from red tab to red tab, pulling out the cards.

At his side, a secretary held an open notebook with a poised pencil. Occasionally the banker snapped an order and the secretary made a series of swift pothooks. Upon each such occasion the secretary would mutter a mechanical, "Yes, sir."

Sam Gilvert chuckled.

"Not entirely an unpleasant task, Miller."

"Yes, sir," said the secretary, mechanically.

"Three years ago," said the banker, "every one of these men used to look down on me. They were rich, gloatingly rich. Now we're closing them out ... Card number four thirty-five; Harrison, secured note for five hundred. Close out the security. Have our attorney get judgment for the deficiency. Attach his car."

"Yes, sir," said the secretary.

"Card number four fifty-three; secured note for fifteen hundred ..."

There was a knock at the door.

The banker frowned.

"Open it, Miller. I left orders I wasn't to be disturbed. See what ..."

The secretary opened the door.

The tall form of Sidney Zoom stood in the doorway. Behind him an apologetic clerk was endeavoring to explain.

"I'm busy," rasped the banker. "I left orders ..."

Sidney Zoom made a surreptitious motion with his wrist.

The police dog, keen eyes seeing that motion, trained as he was to take orders from his master by a mere flip of the fingers or a slight movement of the hand, walked deliberately into that room and sniffed at the banker, then sniffed at the secretary.

Sidney Zoom smiled sardonically.

"Pardon the intrusion," he said. "The dog is engaged in certain police work. I wanted him to get your odors. That is all. Come, Rip."

The dog trotted to him. Sidney Zoom turned away. The banker jumped to his feet instantly, his face flushed.

"Here, what's the meaning of this unwarranted intrusion? You can't get away with that. I shall call the police. You walked in back of the counters of this bank without permission. You ..."

The banker broke off, sputtering in rage.

"Exactly," said Sidney Zoom, pausing mid-stride to look back at the banker. "I assure you, Mr. Gilvert, that had the information not been most vital, I would not have resorted to this means to get it."

His voice was formal, well modulated, yet it had something in it akin to the tolling of a bell.

"I am investigating," he went on, "the murder of Frank Strome. You are probably aware that, coincident with that death, certain papers disappeared. You may or may not be aware of the contents of that file. Thank you for having given the dog the information."

And Sidney Zoom resumed his progress toward the street.

But, over his shoulder, he could see the banker. That individual was reaching for the telephone. And the color of his face was whiter by several shades than when he had been showing his rage at an unwarranted interruption.

Sidney Zoom strolled down the main street of Dellboro. He was conscious of eyes that turned to him in swift curiosity, of whispered comments that were made as he passed. News travels fast in a country community and word had passed about as to the identity of the owner of the strange craft that had slipped so quietly to a mooring.

Sidney Zoom walked directly to the stairway which led to the offices of the county attorney. Those offices had been taken over by Carl Purcell when he had succeeded to the office upon the death of his superior. They were the same offices into which Sidney Zoom had entered during the dark hours of the early morning, following the trail of the mysterious young woman.

Now Sidney Zoom surveyed those offices, looked about the street at the various store buildings, craned his neck upward at the cloudless blue of the sky.

Then he slowly walked out into the middle of the street, paused, stared about him.

A motorist paused to hurl some sarcastic comment. Another driver applied the brakes with sufficient force to skid the tires. But Sidney Zoom seemed entirely oblivious of them. He was engaged in looking up and down the street, carefully scanning the buildings upon either side.

At length he crossed to the opposite side, walked down the sidewalk for some fifty yards, and turned into an entranceway which led to a flight of stairs, stairs which were musty and dark with the grime of years. They showed no sign of paint or care. Cobwebs were in the corners. They led up to a dark and gloomy hallway.

Sidney Zoom, the police dog at his side, ascended those stairs with an unhurried gait. His entrance to the building was not unnoticed.

The building had once contained offices of the cheaper sort. Some of the doors still bore signs which indicated the occupations of the previous tenants. One and all they were the sort of occupations which required plenty of space at a very low rental.

The offices were now vacant. Some of the doors stood open, disclosing rooms which were littered with refuse. Some of the doors were closed. One was locked.

Sidney Zoom gave some attention to that locked door. He produced a skeleton key from his pocket and opened the door. He went into the room.

The litter in this room was not as bad as the litter in the other rooms. There was even a chair in the room. It was rather a run-down chair, to be sure, but a chair, nevertheless, and it was faced in such a position that a person sitting in it would be facing the window of the room on an angle.

The window of that room was grimy with dust, dirt and cobwebs. The sash had once been varnished, but the varnish had deteriorated into dirty lumps which showed only a faint trace of gloss. Dust had settled upon sash and sill.

Sidney Zoom left the door open behind him. He deposited himself in the rickety chair, took a cigarette from a pocket case, lit it, sat smoking, apparently without a single thing to do other than to enter the deserted offices of vacant buildings and while away the morning hours.

The police dog, sniffing around him at the litter of the room, regarded his master with curious, attentive eyes, then flung himself upon the bare floor, and settled his head upon his paws.

For several minutes they remained in this position, the man on the chair, smoking, the dog on the floor sleeping.

Then the keen ears of the dog caught some sound. He raised his head and cocked his ears. He glanced at his master with yellow eyes that were suddenly hard and alert. Then he gave a low growl.

Sidney Zoom heard that warning signal. He got to his feet.

"Steady, Rip," he said. "Don't move. Keep quiet. It's all right."

Sidney Zoom went to the dust-covered sash of the window. He took his fingers and pressed them into the dust of the sash, put the tips down on the sill. The fingers left very plain prints in the dust. He pressed a finger against the glass of the window. Then he took a small box from his pocket, opened the lid, and disclosed a yellow powder, a chrome which is particularly efficacious in bringing out the distinguishing marks of latent finger-prints.

The police dog growled once more, ominously.

Steps sounded in the outer corridor of the vacant office building. The steps were audible, yet cautious, the sort of steps a man would make who was of heavy build, yet was trying to walk cautiously.

Sidney Zoom quieted the dog once more, ordered him to stay where he was, no matter what happened. Then he turned his attention to the finger-print on the window. He opened a little book, and started sketching.

A figure bulked in the doorway.

A booming voice suddenly cut the silence.

"If that dog attacks me I'll shoot him!"

CHAPTER VII

The Vanishing Shell

SIDNEY ZOOM gave a convulsive start, the start of a man who is absorbed in work and fancies that he is alone, yet who is suddenly surprised by the sound of a human voice.

He turned and stared at the big man in the doorway.

The man had a gun in his right hand, a wide-brimmed black hat on his head, a gold shield on his vest, and a left eye which was almost closed, and which had turned a very deep shade of black. The gun he held was a heavy automatic.

"The dog," said Sidney Zoom, "will not bother you unless you bother him. And may I ask what you're doing here with a drawn gun?"

The man held Zoom with his eyes, the one steady, granite hard and baleful, the other bloodshot, rimmed by flesh of greenish black.

"I'm here," growled the man, "to find out what the devil you're doing here. This building has been condemned. You've no business here. What's more, this door was locked. You've evidently picked that lock. That's breaking and entering, and that's a penal offense."

Sidney Zoom raised his eyebrows.

"But there was nothing in here, and I haven't any felonious intent."

The heavy-set man rumbled his answer.

"That's got nothing to do with it. Technically, you're guilty. You broke and entered."

Zoom pursed his lips, thinking over the man's words.

"You're an officer?" he asked.

"Yes. Frink, head of the county attorney's investigation squad. Now you tell me what you're doing here."

Sidney Zoom spoke rapidly.

"I was figuring on renting an office here."

"What's your business?"

"I haven't any. But I was contemplating opening up an office as a private investigator."

Frink scowled, moved purposefully forward.

"All right. Now we'll get down to brass tacks. You ain't going to open up any office here. You ain't going to do any private investigating here. You ain't even going to stay here. You're going right back to that nice little boat of yours and cast off the mooring lines and get out of here and stay out of here."

Sidney Zoom stared about him in a bewildered manner.

"Why—why, I never was talked to like that in my life. Why can't I stay here?"

The head of the investigators was now sure of his ground. He moved forward in a bullying manner.

"Because you're a confounded nuisance. That's why. You busted in on Sam Gilvert an hour or so ago and insulted him by having your dog go over and smell him. You were prowling around the streets last night ... and somebody broke into the county attorney's office and tried to steal some papers. It was a woman. I cornered her, and somebody smashed me with a club and knocked me out. I don't *know* who it was."

Sidney Zoom raised his eyebrows.

"But what's that got to do with me? Why should I leave town? You don't suspect that I hit you with a club, do you?"

The eye of George Frink which was not discolored hardened into an icy stare.

"If I *did* think that you did it," he growled, "I'd ..."

He didn't finish his threat.

His eyes slithered away from Sidney Zoom's, came to rest on the finger-print, colored with the yellow stain.

"What you doing here?" he asked.

"Just looking out of the window," said Sidney Zoom.

And, as though to give some atmosphere of truth to his statement, he turned, and peered through the dusty, cobwebby glass of the window.

The main street showed below him, across the street, some forty yards up, were the entrances to the county attorney's office, the windows of the room in which Strome had been killed.

As Sidney Zoom watched, a compact group of men, carrying brief cases, emerged from the entrance to the office building. Carl Purcell, the new county attorney, and his assistants were about to go to the courthouse to carry on the trial of James Crandall, charged with the crime of murder in the first degree.

Frink's voice was sneering.

"Yeah, you was lookin' out of the window all right! And I suppose you smeared that yellow chrome over that finger-print to help you see out! What's a finger-print on a window down in this building got to do with the murder of Frank Strome?"

Sidney Zoom suddenly became confidential.

"If I should tell you, would you keep it a secret? And if it sounds plausible, could I continue to remain here and carry on my investigations?"

Frink poised the gun in his hand, stole a glance at the police dog.

"Go ahead," he said. "I'll listen to anything you've got to say, but I won't make any promises."

Sidney Zoom spoke rapidly, and in a low tone.

"Very well. The account of the shooting, as we have it, is impossible. No one heard the sound of the fatal shot. That's out of the question. The theory of the prosecution is that the noise made by the exploding bomb of the publicity car on the unemployment drive drowned out the noise of the shot.

"That's foolish. People who were in the next office would have heard that shot as being distinct from the explosion of the bomb. Moreover, there wasn't any exploded shell found in the office of the murdered man. Now the gun that was found in there was an automatic. The automatic mechanism would have ejected the empty shell as soon as the weapon was fired. Yet that shell wasn't found. Of course, the murderer might have crawled around on the floor, picking up the empty shell, but there was no reason for him to do so.

"On the other hand, had that murderer been intent upon removing evidence, he would have undoubtedly taken the automatic from the room with him. If Crandall killed that man, it would have been utterly incredible that he would have gone to the bother of taking the shell from the room, yet leaving the weapon which could have been traced to him."

Sidney Zoom regarded the investigator questioningly.

"What's your theory?" asked Frink.

Zoom lowered his tone, as though giving a sacred confidence.

"That the murderer didn't kill Strome in his office at all. That the murderer came down here, opened this window and waited. That the stage was set in Strome's office. That the publicity car came by here, setting off bombs. That the murderer rested an automatic on the sill of the window, and fired through the open window of Strome's office, killing Strome."

Frink scowled meditatively.

"Why this office?"

"Because the door was locked. The murderer had to lie in wait with a drawn gun. Naturally, he wouldn't want to be observed by some person who might chance to come up in the building. So he took pains to see that the door behind him was closed and locked. Then it would have been only natural for him to have locked the door behind him when he left."

Frink walked to the window, stared.

"Then this would be the finger-print of the murderer?"

"Yes."

"What makes you think the window in Strome's office was open?"

"Because the papers were scattered all over the floor. It has been the theory of the prosecution that the murderer, making a hasty search for some paper, threw the papers on the desk all over the floor. More natural, the window had been left open, a sudden wind blew the papers over the floor, and the window was subsequently closed before the arrival of the police."

"Then the window would have been closed ... Good Heavens, man! Do you know what your charges imply? They mean that Carl Purcell must have been an accessory!"

CHAPTER VIII

The Finger-print on the Window

SIDNEY ZOOM nodded, casually.

"Of course. That's self-evident, even if we can't prove who it was that did the actual killing. You'll remember that Strome mentioned the threatening letter he had received was the second threat he had received from Crandall. Yet, when they came to search for the first threat, it couldn't be found. What undoubtedly happened was that Purcell, seeing the original threat wasn't dated, simply took it from the files, put it in an envelope, and remailed it to the county attorney.

"The same thing's true of the gun. It was purchased before Crandall was sent to prison. He'd hardly have had that gun with him all the time he was in prison. It's natural to suppose, therefore, that the gun had been taken from him by the authorities at the time of his first arrest. Since his crime wasn't one of violence, the gun naturally wasn't introduced in evidence. The authorities probably even forgot that they had such a gun. But Purcell could have taken it, secreted it, and planted it for evidence.

"Purcell isn't a gunman. Therefore, he forgot that he should have planted an empty shell to make the murder appear convincing."

Frink whistled.

"Man alive, but you go after big game when you start. What possible motive would Purcell have had to kill Strome?"

Sidney Zoom smiled.

"The motive of greed and of gain. Charges were about to be placed against Sam Gilvert, the banker. The file in that case disappeared. Purcell was a deputy. Now he is the county attorney. He inherited the office, so to speak."

Frink shook his head.

"No. Your motive isn't strong enough to get you anywhere. You insinuate that Gilvert paid Purcell to sneak the papers out of the file, that Purcell got that money, and that he was afraid of discovery, so he wanted to cover up that theft. Then you insinuate that he wanted to get the job of his superior officer, and so he murdered him. That's far-fetched. It isn't a strong enough motive."

"There's logic in that," Zoom said. "Yet we know that the crime couldn't have been committed the way Purcell claims. We know that, if it wasn't committed in that manner, then Purcell must be trying to conceal the manner in which it actually was committed.

"But we can let Purcell go for the minute. We're on the trail of the real killer down here. I think this fingerprint will give us sufficient evidence. Somewhere around here, in the litter of rubbish around the room, may be the empty shell from the gun that really killed Strome.

"That must have been an automatic of the same calibre as the one in the office, the one that was found there. The distance isn't over thirty yards or so in a direct line. A good shot could have hit a mark the size of a man's body at that distance. In fact, he could have even picked the exact spot on the body that he intended to hit."

The chief investigator for the county attorney's office put the automatic he held back in its shoulder holster.

"Guy," he said, "you win. We'll find out more as we go along, but you sure have got the case doped out so it sounds reasonable to me. I'm going to coöperate with you and give you all the assistance I can.

"But this is a small county. We're messing around with some pretty big men when we start after Purcell and Sam Gilvert. We've got to be absolutely certain that we're going to make a case before we even breathe a word about it."

"Naturally," Zoom observed, "we will not go running into court and shooting off our faces. We'll collect the evidence. In time, if we can, to save Crandall from conviction, we'll announce that evidence. If we haven't built up a case, we'll let him be convicted, and then get a pardon from the governor."

Frink drummed upon the back of the chair with the fingers of his right hand. His eyes narrowed to slits.

"Listen," he said, "we've got to get those finger-prints photographed. That's the first thing. Then we'll have to pull the whole window out and take it down to the vault where we can keep it for the jury to look at."

Sidney Zoom nodded.

"You got a camera?" asked Frink, "one that'll take finger-prints?"

Zoom shook his head ruefully.

"I'm sorry. I certainly should have had one, but I was careless and neglected to include it with my things when I came down here."

"Okay," said Frink, "it doesn't make any difference. You go and get mine. I'll stay here and watch the prints so I can testify afterwards that nothing happened to 'em, see? My office is on the lower floor of the courthouse. You'll find a blond kid at the desk. She'll give you the camera. Tell her that I sent you, and that I said to keep quiet about it afterwards. I don't want a whole lot of talk around town about this thing before we crack it."

Zoom allowed himself to be dominated by the positive personality of the other. "Come, Rip," he said to the dog, and left the room.

But he did not descend the stairs. Instead, he waited in the corridor, motioning the dog to silence. For a good ten seconds he stood so, and then he returned to the door, gently turned the knob, and pushed the door open.

Frink was standing by the window, his face grave with concern. His right hand was extended. He was staring at the whorls of the fingertips with a magnifying glass. Then, from time to time, he would check these with the finger-print on the glass.

Sidney Zoom betrayed his presence by a low laugh. It was a mirthless laugh of hollow mockery, and there was challenge in it.

Frink whirled.

It took him one swift instant to take in the situation. Then his hand flicked to the holster where he kept his weapon.

Sidney Zoom spoke casually.

"Take him, Rip."

The dog had waited patiently for that moment. Twice when he would have defended his master against this man, he had been restrained by a command. Now the dog went across the room, belly to the floor, like a tawny streak. And then he was in the air.

Frink fired, once, and he might as well have taken a snapshot at a streak of lightning. The dog's teeth closed on the wrist of the gun arm. The dog's weight hurled itself in that peculiar twisting motion which is taught to police dogs, as a part of their training, on the continent. Frink screamed with pain. The gun thudded to the floor.

Sidney Zoom rushed in and grabbed the left arm.

"All right, Rip," he said.

The dog dropped to the floor. Sidney Zoom's right hand snatched the handcuffs from the investigator's hip pocket. With a swift dexterity, he flipped the handcuff over the left wrist.

"The other hand," he rasped.

The investigator flung his weight against Sidney Zoom in a lunging attack, halted as a deep-throated, ominous growl came from the dog on the floor.

"You can either give me that wrist, or the dog will get it for me," said Sidney Zoom.

The investigator's face was sallow. Perspiration beaded his forehead. He extended his wrist, with the prints of the dog's fangs still imbedded in the skin, through which red drops welled slowly.

Sidney Zoom clicked the handcuff.

"Of course," he said, "you were too shrewd in such matters to leave finger-prints. But I thought I could raise a sufficient doubt in your own mind to get you to betray yourself."

The handcuffed man muttered an exclamation.

"Slick, eh? All right, try and convict me. Try and get the evidence that'll show that I did anything. You can't prove a damned thing. A jury will acquit me within ten seconds of the time the case is put up to them."

Sidney Zoom's tone was ominous.

"Man-made law," he said, "is a thing of makeshifts, of injustices, of technicalities that make a mockery of justice. But there is a higher court. Laugh if you wish, but the time will come when you will realize that the way of the oppressor is hard. You have sought to blame murder upon the innocent. And I tell you that there is a price you will have to pay—a frightful price."

Frink laughed, yet the laugh was nervous. There had been something solemnly prophetic in the voice of Sidney Zoom, a something that was as the tolling of a bell.

"Bah!" he said, "you talk like some ranting reformer ..."

Sidney Zoom took handkerchiefs from the man's pocket and thrust them into his mouth, fashioned an effective gag. He took some fine, strong cord from his own pocket, and trussed Frink's legs. Then he motioned to the dog, and left the room, leaving behind him a man who could move neither hand nor foot, who could not even speak.

CHAPTER IX

A Confession

HE DESCENDED the stairs, went at once to a telephone, got Gilvert's bank on the wire, and demanded that Sam Gilvert be put on the telephone. He told the clerk who answered that he was the assistant of Bill Dunbar, the lawyer who was defending

James Crandall, and he told the banker the same thing, when he had that individual on the wire.

"Exactly where were you," asked Sidney Zoom, "when Frank Strome was murdered?"

"Why—why—what—er—isn't this a bit unusual and irregular and all of that?" asked the banker.

"Certainly," said Sidney Zoom, "but the answer to that question is very important to you."

"Well," said the banker, "when I heard of the death of Frank Strome, I was standing, talking to—"

"Not where you were when you *heard* of his death, but where you were when he actually died, at the time of the killing," interrupted Sidney Zoom.

"Oh, my goodness," exclaimed the banker, "you're asking for something entirely different now. I don't know. I haven't the slightest idea. I don't even know exactly what time it was they decided that he had died."

"Thank you," said Sidney Zoom. "Now Mr. Frink, Mr. Purcell and myself want you to come down to the row of vacant office buildings just across the street and down a half a block from the county attorney's office."

"I can't get away," snorted the banker.

"You'll have to get away. You wouldn't want to be subpœnaed as a witness would you, and have to wait around in the court?"

"What would I be a witness to?"

"Something you wouldn't want to testify to. But if you come down here right away you probably won't have to give your testimony in public."

The banker cleared his throat.

"I'll come," he said.

Sidney Zoom slipped out to the street and waited. It took the banker less than ten minutes to arrive. He looked perturbed, and his eyes darted about as though seeking out some tangible menace.

Reluctantly, he crossed the street to the stairs, and started up those stairs. Zoom emerged from his place of concealment, started up after the banker.

Gilvert had reached the upper landing when some subtle warning caused him to whirl. He saw the gaunt form of Sidney Zoom, the police dog at his side.

"You!" said the banker.

"Yes," remarked Sidney Zoom. "I came here to protect you."

"From what?" snarled the banker.

"From being made the goat and convicted of the murder of Frank Strome," said Sidney Zoom, speaking casually, as though being framed for murders might have been a mere matter of everyday occurence.

The banker stared, speechless.

"If you'll step this way," said Sidney Zoom, "I'll show you exactly what I mean."

He indicated the closed door, unlocked it, waved his hand in a gesture that indicated the bound, gagged body on the floor.

"George Frink," he said, "the murderer of Frank Strome."

The banker stared. He grasped his left hand with his right hand, twisted the fingers, then started cracking his bony knuckles. One by one, he cracked the knuckles of his right hand. His lips writhed as though he wanted to speak, but no sound emerged from the parched throat.

"You see," said Sidney Zoom, indicating the window with its finger-print treated with chrome, the two prints on the sill, outlined in the dust, "how simple it was. Frink came down here, waited. He's a good shot with an automatic. Purcell managed to raise Strome's window. The publicity car of the unemployment drive started shooting its bombs. Frink watched for his chance and shot.

"It wasn't at all necessary to wait for the explosion of a bomb. This building is deserted. A shot from here wouldn't be heard.

"As a matter of fact, it would have been hard for a murderer to have synchronized a shot with a bomb explosion. And, in any event, he'd have had to sit with gun ready, waiting. Which shows how absurd it was to think Crandall could have committed the crime. Strome would never have sat at his desk while Crandall stood there, gun ready, waiting for the bomb explosion to cover the sound of his shot."

The banker blinked his eyes.

"What does Frink say?" he asked.

Sidney Zoom bowed.

"That's where you come into the picture. Frink confesses, but he blames you for being the leading spirit. Of course, Frink had to confess, what with his finger-print on the window, and the exploded shell from his automatic found here on the floor."

Frink, bound and gagged, made little convulsive motions with his body and bound limbs. Inarticulate sounds gurgled in his throat.

"Blames me!" screamed the banker. "He blames me?"

Sidney Zoom nodded.

"He said that you suggested it to Purcell. You'd managed to steal those files, and were afraid of discovery—"

"Liar," yelled the banker, "a black-hearted, deliberate liar. That's what he is!"

Sidney Zoom raised his eyebrows.

"Indeed?" he muttered politely.

"Yes, damn it, indeed!" shrilled the banker. "They can't put that over, not on me. I got that file from Purcell, all right. I knew he was worried about Strome calling him on it. It seemed there'd been two or three other files that Purcell had taken from the office, and Strome was all worked up about that. He threatened an investigation.

"So Strome threatened to make a scandal over it. He'd given Purcell notice to quit. Purcell came to me the night before the murder. He wanted the papers back. I'd destroyed them. He was all worked up and afraid that he was going to be disbarred.

"I was worried myself. Then when I heard that some ex-convict had murdered Strome, I thought it had just been a break for Purcell. I never put the two together at all.

"I knew Purcell was very much afraid. If Strome had found out the papers in my file were missing, after the bootlegging files had been missing, he'd have had Purcell arrested. I'm sorry now that I didn't stand right up and face the music. The papers related to an irregularity. I could have squared it. Purcell sold me the file. I paid his price."

Zoom nodded.

"And they were going to frame the murder on you," he said.

The banker's face was the color of putty.

"My God! Murder!"

Zoom handed him his notebook and a fountain pen.

"Write out your statement and sign it," he said.

The banker seized the fountain pen, laid the notebook against the wall, started to write. Frink, on the floor, made significant motions, rolled his eyes, tried to attract attention.

Sidney Zoom spoke to his dog.

"Watch him, Rip. Make him stay quiet."

The dog walked stiffly to the prostrate form, stood over him, lips curling back, teeth glistening. Frink moved his head. The dog growled, snapped toward the man's throat. The teeth clicked as the jaws snapped together a scant half inch from the tender flesh, a canine warning which even the hardiest must have heeded.

Gilvert finished the confession, signed it with a flourish. "Now," he said, "I feel better. That cursed thing's been weighing on my mind for a long time."

CHAPTER X

Angel or Devil

SIDNEY ZOOM pocketed the notebook with its signed statement. He indicated the bound and gagged man on the floor.

"He can't blame you now. I'm going to get you in the clear. He'll try to shift the entire blame to Purcell next. These rats are always looking for some one to make the goat. When they get cornered, they squeal.

"You've got one more responsibility. I want you to go directly to Bill Dunbar, who's defending Crandall, and tell him what you told me."

The banker nodded.

"When will Purcell be arrested? I take it he's an accomplice."

Sidney Zoom's tone was like the tolling of some bell.

"I'll have to leave his arrest for the regular police."

"And you're leaving Frink here?"

"For the present, yes."

"He's confessed?"

"After a fashion. He blames the job on Purcell. He tried to put the blame on you, at first. Then he implicated Purcell as the originator of the murder plan. Let's go to the street. I want to telephone. You want to hunt up Dunbar, and explain things to him."

They left the room together. Only after they were in the echoing corridor, did Sidney Zoom give the command to the police dog which relieved the bound man of his guard.

Gilvert hailed a passing car, driven by a man he knew, and demanded that he be taken to the courthouse. Now that he had made a clean breast of his share of the matter, he seemed to carry his shoulders straighter, his head higher.

Sidney Zoom went to the telephone, called the office of the clerk of the court, and demanded that Bill Dunbar be called from the court immediately, upon a matter of life and death.

There was a small amount of argument, and then he heard Dunbar's voice on the wire.

"Yes; what is it?"

Sidney Zoom spoke rapidly.

"The prosecution have never introduced a test bullet fired from the automatic found in Strome's office, or compared it with the fatal bullet," he said. "Perhaps the significance of that fact has never dawned upon you."

Dunbar grunted.

"This is Mr. Zoom?" he asked.

"It is."

"Well, Mr. Zoom, there are certain matters in that connection which I dare not talk about over the telephone. In fact, we are willing to let sleeping dogs lie. If the prosecution doesn't introduce such evidence, we'll make a point of it in our argument to the jury. But we certainly won't—"

Zoom interrupted.

"Yes," he said, "you will. You will walk into the court room with a wise smile on your face, and demand that the court appoint an expert testing agency to make such a test. At about that time Sam Gilvert, the banker, will try to talk with you.

"Listen to what he has to say, and, if possible, let Carl Purcell overhear some of the remarks. Otherwise allow Purcell to get in touch with Gilvert, which he'll be only too anxious to do."

The lawyer's voice was aloof, dignified.

"I am quite capable of conducting this trial without outside interference," he said, "and am not particularly anxious to be drawn from court upon an urgent summons merely in order to hear suggestions as to how I should try my cases."

Sidney Zoom's voice changed its tone or timbre not at all. He spoke with the solemn dignity of a person intoning a ritual.

"You will return to the court room and do exactly as I said," he observed, "or you will be sorry. If you do as I have instructed, your defendant will be released before the afternoon session of court."

The very assurance of his voice carried conviction.

"What makes you think so?" asked the lawyer, interested.

"I don't think so. I know so," said Sidney Zoom, and slammed the receiver back on its hook.

THE yacht was ready for sea. The crew had cast off the main lines, were standing with ropes snubbed around piles, waiting for the last order.

On the deck of the trim yacht two people were locked in a close embrace. The girl's glad eyes were still incredulous. The man, so lately the defendant in a criminal action in which he had been headed straight for the chair, was dazed with joy.

Bill Dunbar, shrewd criminal attorney, eyed Sidney Zoom with an expression of puzzled contemplation.

"You knew," he said, "that Gilvert would tell everyone Frink had confessed and blamed Purcell. You knew Gilvert would let it be known that Frink was bound and gagged in the room from which the fatal shot had been fired."

Sidney Zoom's expression was inscrutable.

"One does not know the future," he said, "one merely makes a surmise."

The lawyer shook his head impatiently.

"Having planned so far in the future, having tipped off the police so that they came for Purcell at the exact moment when he was in that room with Frink ... Well, what I'm getting at is that you must have known Purcell would kill Frink and commit suicide!"

Sidney Zoom shrugged his shoulders.

"I anticipated that Purcell, like all his stamp, would try to cheat the chair. And I realized that he would be bitter against Frink. But it is no concern of mine if these sort of men eliminate themselves without expense to the state. In the meantime, you are detaining me. I want to get out to the open sea. Della Rangar and James Crandall are going with me. We are waiting only to get clear.

"I became interested in this case when I realized that it was impossible for the murder to have been committed in the way they claimed. I freed an innocent man. That the guilty ones had the chance to cheat the chair is incidental. I wish you good-by."

The lawyer shook the proffered hand.

"I guess there are some things I'll never know," he said. "But I'll say this much for you, you sure cracked the case—wide open."

Then as he gazed into the saturnine features of the gaunt man, he added: "And whether you're angel or devil is more than I know!"

For the first time during the interview, Sidney Zoom's face softened into a half smile.

"You might catalogue me as a little of both," he observed, "and, if you have to have me card-indexed, make a mental note that I believe in fighting the devil with fire."

And he waved his hand, signal for the men to let go of the lines, jump aboard.

The propellers of the yacht churned the water into a yeasty foam, and the trim craft moved away from the dock.

Bill Dunbar stared at the lines of the graceful craft, mirrored in the placid waters of the river. Then he looked at the two figures who were clasped together on the deck. He sighed, shrugged his shoulders, turned and walked away.

The boat curled a hissing wave under her bow as she set her course for the open sea. Sidney Zoom stood near the bow, like some huge, gaunt figurehead, arms folded, eyes staring straight ahead, out toward the vast tumbled mass of untamed water.

It was a face that was utterly devoid of softness or mercy. The lawyer looked back, saw it, and shuddered. But the two figures on the after deck, smiling into each other's eyes, shuddered only when they saw the buildings of Dellboro slipping astern—the huge white pile of the courthouse dominating the other buildings.

The sun gleamed from that structure of justice, and made it snow white, yet, withal cold and hostile, formal and distant. That same sun, touching the stern, sad face of Sidney Zoom, seemed to soften it and to make it more human.

INSIDE JOB

SIDNEY ZOOM piloted his powerful roadster over the wide stretch of boulevard, along which the night stream of after-theatre traffic was flowing.

Through a loud speaker, concealed under the dash of the car, came the steady sequence of police reports broadcast from headquarters.

These reports were preceded by a blast on a siren whistle which commanded attention. Some were for specified cars, some were general broadcasts.

Sidney Zoom passed a slow moving car in which a young man and a girl were huddled closely over the steering wheel. As he swung back to the right, there sounded the noise of the siren whistle.

"Car eighty-two attention! Attention eighty-two!"

There followed a short pause, then a voice that was mechanical as though reading from a typewritten report.

"Car eighty-two will go to the corner of Third and McAlpin for an investigation. There has been a report that a man is loitering about who is carrying a gun.

"A passing pedestrian witnessed the gun when a gust of wind blew the man's coat to one side.

"Car eighty-two, go to Third and McAlpin Streets for an investigation and report."

There was an interval of silence. Sidney Zoom knew that he was on the beat of car eighty-two. He was within a few blocks of Third and McAlpin, and he spun the wheel, turned down a side street that would give him a clear run to McAlpin.

Not that Sidney Zoom was a part of the police force. Far from it. Independently wealthy, owner of a palatial private yacht upon which he spent most of his time, he was tired of the ways of civilization. He demanded conflict, this gaunt, grim fighter. He had found that conflict in patrolling the midnight streets of the great city, listening to the reports which came over the short length radio from police headquarters, selecting such cases as sounded interesting, and speeding to them, gave him relief.

His activities were never quite illegal. That is, their illegality could never be proven. But those activities were very effective at times. There were occasions when he protected the weak, occasions when he fought the strong, and always, of late, he was in conflict with the police.

In the rumble seat of the roadster, crouched his companion of the night prowls, a tawny police dog, trained in the work of the police, trained, also, to obey the commands of Sidney Zoom. Master and dog worked together with unerring efficiency.

Sidney Zoom knew that car eighty-two had beat him to the call as he swung his roadster into McAlpin. He could see the red tail light, just above which was a tiny pinprick of blue light, signal of the police car. It was ahead of him and speeding along the boulevard.

Sidney Zoom did not care to tangle with the police unless he derived some pleasure or benefit from the contact. The mere routine of a casual investigation was not a sufficiently alluring bait. He swung his car to the right on Fourth Street and let the police car go on to the corner of Third.

Zoom drove in close to the curb and slowed down. He was listening for another call that would prove of interest. The siren whistle commanded attention while the mechanical voice of the police announcer reported a man chasing a woman, armed with a big knife. The chase was in a far corner of the city, however, and Zoom knew that car thirteen would be on the ground.

Another call reported a burglary on the beat of car twenty-nine. Then there was a period of silence, and Zoom saw the man who was walking rapidly and purposefully along the curb, his face turned back, as though looking for a cruising cab.

It was a section of the city where cabs rarely cruised, at that hour of the night. The business district was near, and this place was given over to wholesale offices, little retail stores that could not afford high rentals. Pedestrians were far from plentiful.

The lights of Zoom's car fell full upon the white, strained face of the man at the curb. He was dressed in a brown sack suit, wore a black felt hat, had on a red necktie and brown shoes. He was, perhaps, forty-three or four and was stocky in build.

Sidney Zoom's hawk-like eyes fastened upon the face of the waiting man, and something of tension in the strained, drawn expression of the mouth and eyes caused this connoisseur of adventure, to brake his car to an abrupt stop.

"Perhaps I can give you a lift," he said. "There won't be a cab along here for half an hour, perhaps."

He saw the instant relief which flooded the face of the pedestrian.

"Thanks," said the man and moved forward.

Sidney Zoom kicked a switch which shut off the radio from operation. The man climbed into the car and sat down.

"Nice dog you have there," he said.

"Yes," answered Sidney Zoom, shortly.

The police dog leaned forward, smelling of the newcomer, his paws placed upon the folded top of the roadster. He gave a deep sniff, then braced himself and growled throatily.

The man moved hastily.

"Won't bite, will he?" he asked.

"No," said Zoom. "That's all, Rip. Get back and lie down."

The dog stepped back to the cushion of the rumble seat, dropped down; but he gave another of those low, rumbling growls.

Sidney Zoom understood that growl as plainly as though the dog had spoken to him in words, and said: "I can smell a gun in this man's pocket. It's been shot somewhere recently. There's the odor of powder, burnt powder."

But Sidney Zoom gave no sign that he had learned that the man he had picked up on the dark side street was carrying a concealed weapon. His manner remained courteous, but aloof.

"I'm driving uptown," he said.

"I wonder if you're going past the Raleigh Arms Hotel on Madison Street," said his guest.

"I can," said Zoom, and spun the wheel.

The man he had picked up stared at him in surreptitious appraisal. Zoom kept his unwinking eyes on the road. He seemed to have no curiosity, no desire for social conversation. The car came to Madison Street. Zoom drove to the hotel, slowed the car.

"Thanks," said his passenger.

"Don't mention it," said Zoom.

He speeded the car away from the curb, turned to the right at the corner, turned to the right again at the next corner and swung once more into Madison Street when he came to the intersection. He parked the car, ordered the dog to crouch down behind the lines of the car body so that he would be invisible to passers-by. Then Zoom walked to the other side of the street, stood in a position where he could watch the hotel lobby, both the front and side exits.

He waited five minutes. The man he had carried in his car came out of the side door, looked about him, held up his hand for a cab. Zoom walked swiftly back, along the curb, climbed into his roadster and started the motor. By the time the cab had swung into the main street Zoom was on its tail.

He followed the cab to the Yeardly Apartments, an unpretentious building sandwiched between two of the outlying business streets, saw his man pay off the cab and go up a flight of stairs.

Zoom switched on the radio and started cruising again. He filed the appearance of the man and the place where he had discharged the cab in a hodge-podge of miscellaneous information which Zoom kept under his hat, and which concerned various and sundry of the night activities of the city.

He had gone a matter of some eight or nine blocks when the sound of the radio, calling car eighty-two again claimed his attention.

"An unconscious man is reported as being in an alley opening off of Fourth Street near McAlpin. Car eighty-two, investigate and report."

Sidney Zoom pushed the throttle of his roadster well down and speeded toward the place described in the radio alarm. There was no stopping for arterial stops, no pausing for speed limits. The roadster rushed through the dark streets, Zoom's gaunt hands gripping the steering wheel.

Once more he found that car eighty-two was ahead of him, but Zoom managed to catch up within the last two hundred feet. The cars swung to the curb together.

There was the form of a man, huddled in the shadows at the mouth of the alley, lying limp and inert. As the officers bent over him, the sound of the clanging gong of an ambulance came to their ears.

Sidney Zoom pushed his way forward.

One of the officers frowned, grunted: "Look who's here!"

The other officer straightened, said: "Hello, Zoom."

The greetings were not particularly cordial, nor were they entirely unfriendly. Lonely men who patrol the night streets, in more or less constant danger, welcome company, even though they do not always agree with the methods used by that company. On two occasions Zoom had been of considerable assistance to the patrol cars. On one evening he had saved the life of an officer who was trapped between the fire of two desperate bandits.

"Dead?" asked Zoom.

"Don't think so. Got a sock on the head. Turn him over, Frank, and let's see if there's any blood."

The men tugged at the inert body.

One of the officers straightened with a whistle, a low note of whistling surprise. His flashlight, illuminating a circle of white brilliance in the darkness of the alley, disclosed something that sent the beam glittering back in scintillating reflections of cold fire.

The second officer lunged toward it, clamped his hands on it.

"Diamond bracelet," he said.

"Genuine?"

"Looks like it."

The ambulance clanged its way to the curb, turned, backed into position.

"Better take a look and see if we can find any more. That looks funny."

They pawed through the man's pockets.

"Here's another one. Guess that's set in platinum, eh, Bill?"

"Looks like it. Take a look through this wallet and see if there's any cards."

The stretcher bearers from the ambulance came up, set down the stretcher. A young man bent over the prostrate form.

"Dead, Doc?"

"Nope. Case of concussion. Think he's coming around. Find out what hit him?"

"Think it was a sock on the bean. Looks as though he'd been robbed, or had been doing some robbery. Here's his wallet, stripped of dough. There's a card, automobile driver's license. Name's Harry Dupree, 1641 Dinsmore Drive. Here's a letter. It's old. Telephone numbers scribbled on the back of the envelope. A bunch of keys. Here, this card mentions that he's a jewelry salesman for Huntley & Cobb. Bet he had some samples and got stuck up."

The ambulance man said:

"Well, he's coming around. He can tell us for himself what happened."

One of the officers said: "You better telephone in a report, Frank. I'll stick around and listen to the radio and see if anything breaks."

The inert figure shivered, stretched, turned and was gripped with nausea. "Okay," said the ambulance man, "let him alone for a minute. Okay. Now give him this. Here, brother, swallow. No, no, swallow!"

The man gulped, retched, sat up, supported by the stretcher men. He stared about him with wide, bloodshot eyes and groaned. "We're officers," said the man from the radio patrol car. "Tell us what happened."

"I was robbed," groaned the man.

"See who did it?"

"Somebody who was hiding in the alley ... I walked past ... He socked me."

"What'd he get?"

"I don't know ... Had some money ... Not much, about eighteen bucks."

"It's gone," said the officer. "Your name's Dupree?"

"Yeah ... Oh my head!"

"That's okay, Buddy. You'll be all right in a little while. How about the jewelry?"

"What jewelry?"

"Didn't you have some gems, some samples or somethin'?"

The man started to shake his head, then gave a deep groan with the pain. One of the stretcher men said: "Don't shake your head, Buddy. Don't move any more than you have to. Think you can walk to the ambulance?"

The groaning man leaned far to one side and retched again. The officer who had gone to telephone came back and said: "Report's just come in of a robbery at Huntley & Cobb's place. Guy had keys and got in, laid in wait for the watchman, socked him and tied him up. When he didn't turn in his box they sent out to investigate. Found the watchman tied up and the safe looted."

"How come?" asked the other officer.

"That's all I know. They gave me the dope on the telephone. Car fifty-seven's out there now. I reported this bird as being employed there. We better check up. They said to hold him and follow the ambulance in. Looks like he had something to do with it."

There was a moment of silence, then the officer who had telephoned crouched down so that his eyes were on a level with those of the man who was propped up by the stretcher men.

"Look here, Dupree, had you been to Huntley & Cobb's tonight?"

"No."

"Sure?"

"Of course."

"Have any samples on you?"

"No."

The officer produced the articles of jewelry he had found near the unconscious man. He held them cupped in his hand, flashed the beam of the light on them and said: "How about these? Ever see 'em before."

Once more the man tried to shake his head, and once more the effort brought on nausea.

The officers exchanged glances.

"Okay, Buddy," said Frank. "You better take a nice ride to the hospital. They'll shoot you some dope there that'll make that head of yours feel better."

He motioned to the stretcher men.

"Better boost him, boys. He's wanted for questioning. We'll follow you in. Them's orders. There's something phony here."

The men lifted the half limp figure. He struggled to rise.

"There, there, lie back."

He stretched out on the canvas. They raised him and slid him into the ambulance. The door clicked shut. The ambulance motor whirred into speed. The officers climbed in their car and drove away. The radio was whirring its demand for attention as they rounded the corner.

Sidney Zoom got in his roadster and turned it toward the place where Huntley & Cobb had their jewelry store and warehouse. He was scowling and he kept the throttle well depressed.

GEORGE DIKE enjoyed the notoriety. He had a welt over his left eye, and there was a thin bit of dried blood which had stained a dark red stream from the corner of his left nostril, down his chin.

The police had finished with him, temporarily, but Dike was relating to any one who was curious enough to ask, or, for that matter to listen, exactly how it had all happened.

"I thought there was sumpin' behind that bale of stuff, and I turned to get the flashlight on it then I seen him jump up. I seen he had sumpin' in his hand, and I made a swing. I don't even know whether I connected or not. I can't remember that far. It seemed like somebody'd set off a firecracker inside my dome, and the next thing I knew the cops were bendin' over me.

"I can just remember seein' sumpin' red. I think it was his necktie. It musta been his necktie. I bet I'd know the guy if I seen him again, though. There was a way he had of throwin' his shoulders when he raised his arm, that I won't forget. An' he had a funny sort of neck, kind of short and thick like.

"I guess I musta got an awful sock, because it was just like the fourth o' July. Sock, an' I got it! A whale of a lam. Lookit the ridge it made. But it didn't bust the skin. A regular slung-shot."

There was a little knot of spectators in front of the place. A uniformed officer prevented them from crowding too close. Every once in a while he muttered a mechanical: "Move on, move on! Don't be blockin' the sidewalk!"

Some of the men who had drifted to the door of the robbed company remained. For the most part, however, the crowd was formed of straggling units who drifted up to the place, paused to listen to Dike's story, saw the welt over his eye, and then drifted away into the night. They were couples for the most part, young men with attractive young women who remained only long enough to find out what it was all about. Then the night claimed them.

Sidney Zoom heard the story of the watchman.

He saw the chauffeur pilot the big limousine to the curb, saw the very portly gentleman with the white face and flabby lips get laboriously from the car and plunge into the entrance of the storeroom.

He paused only long enough to give a name to the uniformed officer who guarded the place, and those who were near enough to hear that name sent the whispered gossip to the outskirts of the little group of spectators.

"Frank Huntley, the senior partner. Just got the call."

There was another interval of silence. Then a whispered rumor sprang up from nowhere like a breath of wind in the desert, and seeped through the crowd, passing from man to man.

"They've inventoried the loss. It's more than twenty thousand dollars. They've got the man that did it. They're bringing him out here. Going to confront him with the watchman and the scene of the crime. He had the combination of the safe. They say he worked here. He had an accomplice, and the accomplice got away with all the loot. Tough when a guy has to stick a place up and then gets stuck up himself."

Sidney Zoom heard that rumor, also. He waited, standing there gaunt and grim, six feet odd of unsmiling efficiency, staring with eyes that took in every single detail.

A police car came shrieking from the boulevard. It skidded to the curb. Men jumped out. A white-faced young man with slumped shoulders was in the car. His wrists were handcuffed. They pulled him to the pavement and hustled him into the store. The crowd surged and swayed as its members sought to obtain a glimpse of the man.

A taxicab honked its horn persistently, crawled through the tangle of vehicles, discharged a lone passenger.

She was white-haired. Her eyes were blue. Her face gave indications of serene age. The lips smiled placidly. But the depths of the blue eyes contained a trace of panic. She spoke in a throaty voice.

"Has my boy come yet? Have they brought Harry? They said they were bringing the boy here."

No one answered her. They stared with heartless, expressionless curiosity. Sidney Zoom inched his way toward her and lifted his hat.

"You mean Harry Dupree?" he asked. "Yes, they have taken him inside."

She sighed. "I'm his mother. I wonder if they'd let me in?"

Sidney Zoom saw that those nearest him were taking in the conversation. He took the woman by the arm.

"Perhaps," he said, "it would be wise to talk matters over first. They might make things a little disagreeable for you."

"But it's all a mistake. He didn't do it. He couldn't have done it. They wouldn't have charged him with it if it hadn't been that they didn't understand!"

Zoom soothed her, led her to his car, sat her in the cushioned seat beside him.

"Do you know how your son happened to be out tonight?" he asked.

"He had a date," she said. "I don't inquire too closely into his dates. I don't think mothers should pry into their sons' affairs. He's a good boy. Some day he'll marry and leave me. I don't know who he was going to see tonight. It was a girl. I heard her voice over the telephone. I heard him say he was to wait for her somewhere."

Sidney Zoom nodded thoughtfully.

"Would you mind waiting here?" he asked.

"You're going to see Harry?"

"I don't know. I want to talk with the officers for a moment. If you'll just wait here, I may be able to get you some good news. Do you drive a car?"

"I can," she said.

Zoom nodded, said crisply: "Then wait right here. I won't be long."

He left the car and strode toward the store. With the advent of the gray-haired woman upon the scene, his manner had undergone a change. He was no longer the bystander, but an aggressive individual, moving purposefully.

The uniformed officer barred his path. Zoom spoke briefly and to the point. "I've got to see Huntley," he said. "If I see him I may be able to help in solving this case. If I don't, the police may lose a clew."

The officer beckoned to one of the detectives.

"This guy wants to see Huntley," he said.

The detective glared at Sidney Zoom.

"About what?" he asked.

"Important business," said Sidney Zoom.

The detective stared again, grunted: "Okay. C'mon in. I'll see if he wants to see you. What'd you want to see him about?"

Sidney Zoom strode into the store. He passed a knot of detectives chatting, smoking, came to a huge safe where a fingerprint man was dusting white powder over the black steel surface. Then he saw Huntley, slumped down in a chair.

He walked to the jeweler.

"Can you sell me a diamond bracelet with your price mark still on it?" he asked.

Huntley looked at him, moistened his flabby lips and said, vacantly, "Huh?"

The officer tugged at Zoom's arm.

"That ain't what you said you wanted to see him about," he complained.

"Because," said Zoom, "if you will, I think I can clear this case up."

Huntley got to his feet.

"What's that?" he asked. "How can you clear it up? What are you talking about?"

Zoom shrugged his shoulders, took out a well filled wallet.

"I am only asking," he said, "that you sell me a bracelet or some rather expensive bit of jewelry that has your price mark on it."

Huntley growled.

"The store ain't open."

Zoom said: "I think I can get you your property back if you give me some coöperation."

The detective stared at him. Huntley moved toward the safe. "Gimme that tray," he said. "The one with the bracelets on it." He selected a bracelet at random and said: "Four fifty."

Sidney Zoom passed over the money.

He took the bracelet, started for the door. One of the detectives gripped his arm. Zoom shook him free. He walked out of the store. The detective hesitated, started to follow, then turned back. Zoom went out of the door, to his car. The detective went back into the store.

Zoom started the motor. He was smiling, but it was the grim smile of a fighter who is about to encounter some welcome conflict. The white-haired woman watched him speculatively.

"Are you a friend of Harry's?" she asked.

He nodded. "Yes. The name is Zoom."

She frowned and said: "I don't believe he's ever spoken of you. Are you a close friend?"

Zoom said: "I'm a friend now that he's in need. That makes me a friend indeed."

She smiled at him, a warm, maternal smile.

"Do you know," she said, "I believe you are going to get Harry out of this trouble. I have a hunch. Do you believe in hunches?"

"Certainly," said Zoom.

She nodded and settled back.

"You can look very stern when you want to," she remarked, "but I think you've got a kind heart. Go right ahead, young man. If I can help you, let me know."

Sidney Zoom piloted the car to the apartment house where he had seen the man with the red necktie go on up the stairs.

"I'm going," he said, "to run a bluff, and a big one. It may work. It may not. If it works everything will be fine. If it doesn't you may have to take this car and call the police. Tell them I went into that apartment house with my dog. Give me fifteen minutes. If I'm not out then, give the alarm to the police."

He left the car, motioned to the dog.

"I've got a hunch it'll be all right," said the woman, as Zoom strode up the steps of the apartment house.

The manager was a woman, not young, not good looking, and not good natured. She pulled a scanty robe about her ample figure and glowered at Sidney Zoom. In the end she gave him the information that he was after. The man who answered the description of the one Zoom had picked up on the street had the apartment on the top floor, well to the back. The number was fifteen.

Zoom went up, and the dog went at his side, tail waving proudly.

Zoom indicated the door of the apartment to the dog. Then he placed the article of jewelry he had purchased from Huntley in the dog's mouth. He bent forward and made a gesture with his hand, as though scratching on the door.

The dog watched him with ears cocked rigidly upright. Zoom made another motion with his hand. "Bark," he whispered. The dog barked. The bracelet fell to the floor. Zoom motioned toward it and the dog picked it up. Zoom scratched on the door. He repeated this operation until he heard some one stirring on the inside of the room.

When he heard bare feet hit the floor, Zoom whispered a word of command to the dog, ran down the hall. The dog, obedient to that whispered command, remained at the door. As the bolt clicked back and the door opened, Sidney Zoom came running up the steps, as though he had been exerting himself to the limit of his endurance. He was puffing and blowing, and the sound of his breathing filled the hall.

The man, who was attired in pajamas, stared at the spectacle of the dog on his threshold, and the man who was puffing his way down the corridor. The light which came from the apartment glittered from the bracelet that the dog held in his teeth.

Sidney Zoom raced down the carpeted corridor. The man looked from the dog to the master, then recognition dawned on his face. It was a recognition that was uncordial, gave way to downright concern. Sidney Zoom, on the other hand, let his face break into smiles.

"Well, well, so that's the explanation," he said. "The dog managed to trail you after all!"

The man gruffed a hostile question.

"What're you talkin' about?" he demanded.

Zoom grinned, the grin of a man who has done a favor for which he will be rewarded.

"When you got out of the car," he said, "you dropped this. I called to you, but you'd gone out of sight in the hotel. It took me a minute to get the car parked, and get into the hotel. I didn't have your name, but I described you to the clerk. He said you weren't registered there. He remembered having seen you come in, he said, but knew you weren't registered.

"I had something of an argument about it with him, and then remembered that the dog was trained to return lost property. I gave the bracelet to him, told him to find you. He remembered your odor, of course. They've got wonderful noses, these dogs.

"I thought he'd go to the elevators, but he didn't. He went to the side door and barked. I gave him his head. He led me here, but it was a long chase."

The man gasped.

"That's impossible!" he said. "The dog couldn't have followed me. I was in a cab."

Sidney Zoom's smile was patronizing.

"That doesn't make any difference. Here you are, and the dog found you. I thought maybe I was going to have to consult the store that had sold you the bracelet, for your address, though. You see it's Huntley & Cobb. They're big jewelers. I figured you'd bought the bracelet there today and they'd have your address."

The man's eyes narrowed ominously. He stared at the bracelet.

"It's got their name on it?" he asked.

"Yes," said Zoom, "on the tag."

"I never saw it before," said the man in pajamas.

Zoom laughed as though the matter were a fine joke. "That's a good one," he said, "when I saw you drop it. That's rich! A man dropping a five hundred dollar trinket and then saying he had never seen it before!"

After a moment the man in pajamas joined in the laugh. He laughed heavily and mirthlessly.

"Come in," he said.

Sidney Zoom walked into the room. The dog followed, caught a motion from Sidney Zoom's signalling hand, and flopped down in a corner. The apartment was a one room and a kitchenette affair. The bed pulled out from the wall and let down. There was a bathroom which opened off the bedroom, and the bottom of the door joined the threshold loosely enough so that a ribbon of light came through from under the door.

Sidney Zoom noticed that there were twin blotches of shadow in this ribbon of light, that these blotches moved slightly. He noticed, also, that there were two pillows on the bed, pillows which lay side by side, and each pillow contained the impression of a head.

The man sat down on the edge of the bed, took the bracelet.

"You want a reward," he said, as though making a statement rather than asking a question.

Zoom shook his head.

"Not at all. It was a relief to find the owner. I was going to get in touch with the jewelry company."

The man nodded his head.

"Well, it's mighty nice of you. I'm Rogers, an exporter of gems, and an importer. I buy and sell and deal all sorts of ways. The reason that bracelet has the price mark on it is that it was a sample that was offered me in connection with rather a large order."

Zoom stretched his arms, yawned, laughed.

"How about the others you have?" he asked.

"What others?"

"Don't try to fool me. That lie chained you up with the robbery. You lured Harry Dupree into a position where you could make it seem the job was done by him. I presume the reason you did that is that you're connected with the firm in some way, and you knew it'd be tagged as an inside job right from the jump. So you figured you'd get some one for a fall guy."

The man got from the edge of the bed. His eyes were narrowed to mere slits.

"Are you accusing me?" he asked.

"Who in hell did you think I was accusing?" asked Sidney Zoom easily. "You planted some evidence on Dupree, left him where he'd be found and promptly suspected. You lifted the loot."

The man laughed, a laugh of cold scorn.

"Prove it," he said.

Sidney Zoom chuckled.

"That's a nice way to express a challenge. And I rather think I shall prove it! You know I'm something of an opportunist in the field of crime detection. When I walked into this room I hadn't the slightest idea of how I was going about the proof of this particular crime. I wanted to make certain of your identity by seeing if you'd identify the bracelet as something that belonged to you. As soon as you did that, you branded yourself as the crook. You stole so much stuff that you naturally couldn't remember the various items. As soon as you saw the tag price of Huntley & Cobb on this bracelet you were willing to accept my statement that you'd dropped it, at its face value.

"But, do you know, now I've got an idea of a very fine way in which I can pin the crime on you and recover the stolen property."

Sidney Zoom reached for his pocket.

The man exploded into swift action. His hand jerked out from behind his back. He held a gun which he had slid into his hand as he sat on the edge of the bed, worming it out from under the pillow.

"Is that so?" he snarled. "Get your hands up, you damned dick!"

Sidney Zoom stared into the gun.

"Get 'em up, I say!"

Zoom elevated his hands. As he raised them, he said:

"All right, Rip."

The police dog went from the floor into a long spring. His lips were back from the glistening fangs. The tawny eyes glittered with menace. A throaty growl emerged from his throat.

The man with the gun whirled the weapon. Sidney Zoom snapped his hands down and lunged forward. Zoom, the police dog and the man with the gun all tangled in one simultaneous merger of motion which swept the man back on the bed, thudded the gun to the floor.

Zoom slipped handcuffs from his pocket, snapped them on the man's wrist. And he snapped the other handcuff around the steam pipe on the radiator.

The man snarled at him: "You still haven't proved anything!"

Zoom laughed. "Come, come, not with this murderous attack of yours? And then there's the matter of the gun. You've been using that gun somewhere. Probably in some other stick-up, or perhaps a killing somewhere. My dog detected the odor of powder in the barrel. These dogs have keen powers of smell, but, even so, I would say the gun had been fired within forty-eight hours, and had not been cleaned afterwards. The police will probably be interested in that gun, and in your possession of it."

The man, chained to the radiator, moved uneasily, and the handcuff rasped up and down the steam pipe as he moved. Sidney Zoom stole a glance at the bathroom door. The ribbon of light still showed under the door, and the two blobs which were made by the feet of a person standing inside the bathroom, just against the door, had moved their position somewhat, but were still visible.

"You haven't found the stuff that was taken from the jewelry store, and you can't find it!" said the man. "Until you find it you can't convict me of anything."

Zoom shrugged his shoulders.

"That's a problem for the police. I have no doubt you concealed it rather cleverly. I'll get the police here and they can figure that angle of it out for themselves. I've just made certain, my friend, that you'll be here when the police arrive, that's all."

And he beckoned to the dog, strode to the door of the apartment.

"Ain't you going to search here?" asked the man, obviously disappointed.

"No," said Zoom. "That's a job for the police."

Chuckling, he strode out of the apartment and pulled the door shut behind him. The lock clicked into place. Sidney Zoom strode rapidly down the corridor, down the stairs, out into the night. The white-haired woman looked at him anxiously.

"Did you get anything?" she asked.

Zoom got into the roadster, started the motor, ran half a block to an alley, backed into the alley and turned off his headlights.

"I can't tell just yet. I think I did. I'm gambling on my judgment of character and on a guess as to what happened. I think that we'll see some action pretty soon."

He waited for less than two minutes. Then the door of the apartment house opened. A trimly formed feminine figure stepped out into the night. She carried a little handbag in her hand, and she walked rapidly, with swiftly nervous steps that sent her heels click-clacking against the cement of the sidewalk.

She walked in the direction of Zoom's car, and Sidney Zoom watched her curiously as a street light illuminated her features. She was pretty, yet the prettiness was a bold, brazen type of beauty which would soon dissolve under the unkind hand of ruthless time into a coarseness of feature and a hardness of eye.

In the meantime she was something which would cause masculine eyes to turn and follow her in appraisal and approval. Her clothes were cut so as to accentuate the feminine lines of her form. The dress was very short and the legs were encased in black silk stockings. The legs were slender at the ankles, well molded. She wore a hat which was pulled down on her head, a brimless little hat that served as a bit of color for the blond hair which tendrilled out on the sides. The hat was a vivid red. The eyes were dark and large, the nose straight, the lips thick.

That much Sidney Zoom saw of her, and then she walked past the circle of illumination, past the alley where his car was parked.

Sidney Zoom waited a moment and started the motor. He didn't turn on the lights. The car slid softly and smoothly out of the dark alley into the street. The form of the woman, walking rapidly, was visible some half block ahead.

The dog, crouched on the back seat, sensing the object of the chase, whined softly. The white-haired woman asked a question. It went unheeded. She settled back on the cushions of the seat.

The girl paused in her rapid walk. Sidney Zoom promptly slid the car to a stop. The girl looked back, then peered about her. She was standing in front of a brick wall which surrounded a private dwelling. She moved her hand, as though counting bricks. Then she moved her shoulder, leaned against the brick wall.

Sidney Zoom pushed his car into sudden speed.

He snapped on the headlights. They showed the young woman standing before the brick wall from which a loose brick had been pulled. There was a dark cavity back of this loose brick, and she was sweeping the contents of that cavity into the little handbag that she carried.

"All right, Rip," said Sidney Zoom. "Catch her. Hold her!"

The dog's claws rattled on the polished fender as he scrambled into a position from which he could leap. As he sailed through the air, Sidney Zoom stopped the car, flung open the door and stepped to the sidewalk. There was a police whistle in his lips. He blew it loudly.

The girl started to run.

The dog, dashing along, belly close to the sidewalk, overtook her, got in front of her, crouched, growled, snapped up his head and caught her skirt in his teeth.

Coming along behind her, Sidney Zoom said, quite courteously: "Really, there's nothing you can do. You can't escape. You'd better be nice about it."

She whirled to stare at him from black, sullen eyes. Her thick lips opened and rasped forth a curse. Somewhere in the night, a block or so away, sounded an answering police whistle. Sidney Zoom blew his own whistle once more.

The girl moved toward him, smiling seductively.

"Listen, big boy," she smirked, moving so that her body was close to that of Sidney Zoom. "You and me can reach an understanding ..."

Sidney Zoom turned away. The girl rasped another expletive and sent her hand flashing to the front of her dress. The dog growled ominously.

Sidney Zoom said, casually, speaking over his shoulder: "I wouldn't. He'll leave teeth marks on your arm if you pull a gun. He might even break the skin, and that wouldn't be so good. There'd be an infection, perhaps."

A figure rounded the corner, running heavily but purposefully.

The street light glinted on a badge and brass buttons.

Sidney Zoom raised his voice and called: "This way, officer." The white-haired woman got out of the car and stammered questions. The officer came running up. The young woman drew herself up scornfully.

"Go ahead," she said. "I'll beat the rap. I always have so far, and I will this one." Zoom shrugged his shoulders.

"What is it?" asked the officer.

Zoom opened the handbag. The street light showed a glittering array of jewelry of the finest quality. Sidney Zoom said: "She was the lure who kidded Harry Dupree into being at the mouth of an alley where her accomplice could crack down on him with a black-jack. They planted some stuff on him to make it seem he had robbed Huntley & Cobb.

"This girl, and the man you'll find in apartment fifteen at the apartment house a block or so down the road, robbed Huntley & Cobb of around twenty thousand dollars' worth of jewels. They gave every one the slip and hid them in a place they'd arranged for in advance.

"I figured out who the man was and called on him. From his manner I knew the jewels weren't concealed in the apartment. I knew there must have been a female lure to have trapped Dupree. I saw that two people had been in the apartment and that some one was hiding in the bathroom, listening to my conversation. So I handcuffed the man in a position where he was helpless and walked out, telling him I was sending the police to pick him up.

"I figured that the woman, having betrayed one man to his ruin, would be just the type of rat who would run out on that man if she thought she could get away with it. I counted on her figuring that the man was held helpless in the apartment, and coming down here to feather her own nest with the swag and walk out.

"You take the credit for the arrest. I don't want to figure in it."

The officer stared at Zoom, at the white-haired woman who stood open mouthed, wide eyed.

"Who's she?" he asked.

"The mother of an innocent young man," said Zoom, "who was about to be railroaded to jail by the pair of crooks."

The woman clutched at his arm.

"A grateful mother," she said, and started to sob her happiness.

The officer frowned.

"Well," he said, "we gotta telephone to headquarters and get this thing straightened out."

Sidney Zoom yawned.

"That's okay. Only you take the credit of cleaning up the case. Say that I just happened along. It'll mean a feather in your cap. It won't mean anything to me."

SIDNEY ZOOM was at the wheel of his yacht. The bar was choppy. A fresh breeze was ripping off the tops of the chops and sending spray drops as large as buckshot rattling against the windows of the cabin. The yeasty water, churned into an agitated mass of tumbled foam, hissed past the sides of the rocking craft. The yacht rose lightly on tumbled wave crests, only to be smashed by disordered cross swells.

It was weather such as Sidney Zoom liked, a stiff breeze, a sea that pounded his yacht, plenty of freedom and elbow room.

Vera Thurmond, his secretary, was straightening out the report of the radio calls that had gone over the police broadcasting system the night before.

"This robbery of Huntley & Cobb's place was cleaned up," she said. "The police got a confession."

Sidney Zoom's hawk-like eyes remained fixed upon the roaring waters.

"Yes?" he asked, shifting the wheel a bit so that he would quarter up a big roller.

"Yes. One of the men from the wholesale department did it. He framed things so it would seem another employee was guilty. A patrolman caught the woman accomplice taking the loot from a brick wall. There was something like twenty thousand dollars' worth. He's going to get a promotion out of it. They found the man and he confessed and blamed the woman. She was the one who lured Dupree, the man they first suspected."

Sidney Zoom yawned.

"Well," he said, "if it's a closed case, tear up the records. It's dead, as far as I'm concerned, when the case is solved."

She regarded him curiously.

"You were out getting the radio reports last night. I wonder that you didn't get in on that. Weren't you interested?"

"Oh, yes," said Zoom, "I looked the ground over."

He reached in his pocket and pulled out a bracelet, studded with small diamonds and rubies.

"By the way," he said, "you might like that."

He tossed it over to her.

She rose to her feet, braced herself against the roll of the yacht, let her breath come in a gasp as she saw the exquisite workmanship of the bracelet.

"For me?" she asked.

He nodded. "Yes, a present from Huntley. He tried to give it to me, and I laughed at him, told him I didn't wear bracelets. So he asked me if I didn't have some secretary who might like it. I told him yes. Better drop Huntley a note of thanks."

The girl was staring at the bracelet, fitting it around her wrist.

"Why," she exclaimed, "it's worth hundreds of dollars! Why in the world would Huntley have given you such a bracelet?"

Sidney Zoom shrugged his shoulders.

"Oh, I don't know. I just happened to be in the place when the stolen jewelry was recovered. He was feeling generous, I guess."

She said, sharply: "You were there when the stolen jewelry was brought back?"

"Yes."

She laughed.

"No wonder another patrolman gets a promotion!" she said.

"Well," explained Sidney Zoom, sheepishly, "he had a family, and he ran as though his feet were about to give out pounding pavements."

"I see," said the girl, and her eyes, watching the lines of Sidney Zoom's grim back, were soft with a tenderness that was purely feminine, yet held no trace of being maternal.

But Sidney Zoom's unwinking hawk-eyes were fastened upon the confused waters over the bar. His hands caressed the spokes of the wheel tenderly, and the yacht throbbed her way out into the storm.

LIFTED BAIT

CHAPTER I

Two Tickets to Midvale

THE HAWK eyes of Sidney Zoom peered into the lighted window of the telegraph office.

Sidney Zoom, tall, dynamic, sardonic, paced the midnight streets of the city, accompanied by his police dog, taking the part of the oppressed, and making war upon the oppressors. Experience had taught him the haunts of those bits of human flotsam who were spewed out to one side by the ruthless tide of the great city.

There were those who said that Sidney Zoom fought for the underdog because of a vast human sympathy beneath the sardonic exterior. There were others who claimed that Sidney Zoom was merely a born fighter, and that he cultivated the unfortunate because he wished some cause for combat.

Be that as it may, Sidney Zoom frequented the midnight streets. He knew the haunts of those unfortunates who were about to commit suicide. He knew the cheap restaurants where human derelicts came drifting at night, dispirited, discouraged and all but impoverished.

And he knew that the foundation for many grim tragedies has been laid in the lighted interiors of the telegraph offices during those hours after the theatre crowds have ceased to surge along the pavements, and when human vitality is at its lowest ebb.

The young woman who caught the eyes of Sidney Zoom was twisting a handkerchief about her fingers as she stood at the counter of the office.

Sidney Zoom pushed his way through the swinging door. His well trained police dog dropped to the sidewalk, flattened against the side of the building, ears cocked forward, delicately attuned to the steps of his master.

Sidney Zoom approached the telegraph counter and stood beside the young woman.

She did not so much as glance up. Her eyes were fixed upon the lone attendant who was shuffling through a sheaf of telegrams.

The clerk turned and approached the counter, empty-handed.

As the eyes of the girl saw the empty hands, she gave a quivering, sobbing gasp.

"No, Miss Allison," said the clerk, "There's nothing for you."

"But," she said, "I sent her a wire this evening, about nine o'clock. It certainly should have been delivered."

The clerk looked inquiringly at Sidney Zoom.

"I'll wait," said Zoom.

The clerk turned to face the white despair of the girl's features.

"Did you want me," he asked, "to look up the telegram and see if it was delivered?"

She nodded. "It was sent to Evelyn Bostwick, and my name is Ruby Allison. The address was 2932 Cutter Avenue, Chicago."

"Just a moment," said the clerk.

He opened a filing drawer, thumbed rapidly through a list of cards, took out one, and brought it to the young woman.

"Apparently," he said, "she was not at her apartment, but was expected later. The telegram is reported undelivered."

The girl gasped, clutched the edge of the counter, then turned wordlessly and walked toward the nearest chair. She sat down as though her knees had collapsed.

Abruptly, she became conscious of the gaze of the two men, and flashed them a resentful look. She turned to the oak desk in front of which she was seated, pulled down a pad of telegraph blanks, picked up a pencil and started to scribble a message.

The clerk looked inquiringly at Sidney Zoom.

"Have you," asked Sidney Zoom, "any message for Zoom? Sidney Zoom."

"Just a moment, Mr. Zoom," said the clerk.

He once more consulted the sheaf of telegrams, then shook his head.

"Nothing, Mr. Zoom."

Sidney Zoom walked to one of the other desks, sat in front of it, and pulled toward him a pad of blanks, while he started to scribble a message which was but a meaningless jumble of words. From time to time he hesitated, as though seeking exactly the proper word, or crossed out some word which he had written. Upon those occasions, his eyes surreptitiously surveyed the young woman.

She finished writing her telegram, read it, hesitated, bit her lip, looked at the clock, tore the telegram in half and dropped it into the wastebasket. She pushed back her chair, walked with firm, determined steps to the counter and caught the eyes of the clerk.

"I'll come back again in about an hour," she said. "They certainly should be able to deliver that telegram, and there'll be an answer for me."

The clerk nodded.

"Very well," he said. "We're open all night. I'll try and get another report for you, Miss Allison."

She nodded, turned and walked swiftly through the door, out into the night.

Sidney Zoom waited a moment, then moved over to the desk where the girl had been sitting. Once more, he took a telegraph blank and scribbled aimless words upon it. Then he made a gesture of frowning annoyance, crumpled up the blank and dropped it into the wastebasket.

A moment later he leaned forward, as though to retrieve the crumpled telegram. The clerk had ceased to pay any attention to Sidney Zoom.

Zoom's fingers picked up the torn fragments of the telegram which the girl had written. He placed these torn fragments together upon the desk and studied the message.

The telegram was addressed to Mr. George Grace, 912 West 25th Street, and read: *Require hundred dollars immediately save me from jail Wired Evelyn but have had no answer Can you spare money Send me care Western Union here.*

Sidney Zoom regarded the message for several minutes, then dropped the torn pieces into his pocket, arose and strode from the lighted room, into the street.

The police dog rose from the shadows near the door. Gravely, sedately, he padded along by the side of his master.

Sidney Zoom went to the place where he had parked his roadster. A wave of his wrist, and the dog, catching the signal, leapt up from the pavement in a long arch of graceful motion, and dropped into the rumble seat.

Sidney Zoom started the motor and drove rapidly and purposefully, going to a branch telegraph station that he knew was open.

He parked the car, entered the small room, and said to the operator in charge: "Here is a hundred dollars. I want it wired to Ruby Allison, care of the telegraph company here. You may waive identification."

The clerk frowned heavily at Sidney Zoom.

"You want to send it to some person care of the company in *this* city?" he asked.

"Yes," said Sidney Zoom. "So that it will go to your main office for delivery."

The clerk looked dubious for a moment, then handed Sidney Zoom a blank.

"Very well," he said, "fill it in."

Sidney Zoom took one hundred dollars from his pocket, placed the bills on the counter, asked for the amount of the charges, and paid those.

The clerk looked down at the signature Sidney Zoom had affixed to the blank.

"You've simply signed 'A. Friend.' "

"Certainly," said Sidney Zoom.

"But we can't accept money signed like that. You can sign a telegram any way you want to, but ..."

Sidney Zoom smiled.

"It happens," he said, "that that is my name—Anson W. Friend, and I always sign it 'A. Friend.' "

"Very well," said the clerk, and took the money.

Sidney Zoom turned on his heel, strode once more out into the night. Now he was chuckling to himself, scenting adventure.

He drove back to the main office of the telegraph company, parked his car in an advantageous position, settled back against the cushions, and smoked a cigarette.

He had been there approximately twenty minutes, when he heard the click of heels on the pavement, and the young woman walked past his parked automobile and into the office, her steps quick, short and nervous, her face drawn and set.

Sidney Zoom watched her through the glass as she went to the counter, saw the clerk's reassuring smile, saw him come to her with papers to be signed, and then saw the one hundred dollars which the clerk counted out and passed over to her.

The clerk said something, and the young woman frowned. There were several moments of animated discussion, and Sidney Zoom surmised that she was learning, for the first time, the mysterious name which had been used by the donor of the money.

However, the young woman finally shrugged her shoulders—a shrug which indicated very plainly that she had other matters to concern her—flashed the clerk a smile and a word of thanks, turned and walked rapidly from the telegraph office.

Sidney Zoom had rather expected she would go to some apartment, but she did not. Instead, she walked to a corner where an all-night bus line ran to the Union Station. She waited some ten minutes, caught a bus to the station, presented a check at the parcel checking counter, and received a suitcase and a hat box.

She lugged these to a ticket window and engaged in conversation with the clerk, pausing to look at the clock frowningly.

Sidney Zoom had parked his roadster after he had followed her to the depot. He had entered the foyer of the big depot, and gradually moved up to where he could hear the conversation between the young woman and the agent.

"... not until two o'clock?" she asked.

"That's right."

"And this train for the South leaves in fifteen minutes?"

"That's right."

"Very well," she said, "give me a ticket on that."

"Where to?" he asked.

She hesitated a moment, then pushed fifteen dollars through the barred grille.

"As far as that will take me," she said.

He looked at her curiously, then consulted a schedule of rates.

"I can sell you a ticket to Midvale for fifteen dollars and twenty-five cents," he said.

Wordlessly, she opened her purse, and pushed twenty-five cents across the marble slab. The clerk stamped a ticket and handed it to her.

"Pullman?" he asked.

"No," she said. "How soon can I get on the train?"

"Right away," he told her. "It leaves in exactly thirteen minutes."

She picked up the suitcase and hat box and started for the train gates. Sidney Zoom moved up to the window.

"Midvale—single," he said.

202 Erle Stanley Gardner

CHAPTER II

The Flight from Crime

THE TRAIN gradually gathered momentum as it rumbled through the dark outskirts of the city. The young woman, her face still drawn and tense, her eyes dark with terror that amounted to panic, flashed a surreptitious glance at the tall, mysterious man who sat at ease in the seat across from her. His fingers toyed with a ticket and held it in such a position that the young woman could see the destination printed upon the ticket was that of Midvale.

Abruptly, she held her eyes upon his.

"You live in Midvale?" she asked.

Sidney Zoom shook his head.

"Can you tell me what sort of a place it is?" she asked.

Sidney Zoom leaned toward her. His hawk-like eyes stared at her steadily; circles of cold ice, in the center of which were twin pinpoints of inky mystery.

"It is a place," said Sidney Zoom in low, solemn tones, "where one who is hiding from the police could readily be found."

For a second or two the full import of his words did not dawn upon her consciousness. She sat staring at him with an expression of stupefied terror upon her countenance. Then she gave a quivering gasp.

"Perhaps," said Sidney Zoom in a kindly tone, "you would care to tell me about it."

"Tell you about what?" she asked.

"About the reason you're going to Midvale," said Sidney Zoom.

"I'm going there," she said, defiantly, "to visit a sick aunt. I don't know what you're talking about, and I don't care to have any further conversation with you."

"Evidently," said Sidney Zoom, "you were overtaken by some emergency which demanded immediate flight. You packed your suitcase, took it down to the depot and checked it. Then you tried to get sufficient money to get out of town. You sent telegrams until you finally secured one hundred dollars. You came down to the station and took the first train leaving town. Now, perhaps, you would care to tell me why. I might help you."

Her stare was that of icy scorn.

"I presume," she said, "that this is just another trick of a fresh masher. I shouldn't have spoken to you in the first place, but you looked like a gentleman. However, just to show you how wrong you are, it happens that my Aunt Agnes is quite ill, and she wired for me to come and nurse her. She also wired me the money for transportation, if you want to know. Come to think of it, it seems to me that I did see you watching me in the telegraph office. I don't know just what your game is, but I shall certainly call the conductor and make a complaint if you speak to me again."

Sidney Zoom sighed.

"Somehow," he moaned, "I always *do* make the wrong approach."

"Well, you've certainly done it this time," she said icily.

Without another word, he reached into his pocket, took out the torn pieces of the telegram he had picked up from the wastebasket, and fitted them together in front of her astonished eyes. Then, from his wallet he took the receipt which the telegraph company had given him for the money he had telegraphed to her.

"I am the one who sent you the money."

"You?" she gasped.

He nodded.

She reached swiftly forward, scooped up the torn pieces of the telegram, crumpled them into a ball.

"You can't leave that around," she said, "where people can see it!"

Her voice was a terrified whisper.

Sidney Zoom nodded.

"Now," he pleaded, "won't you please understand that I want to help you? I wanted to find out what it was all about before I spoke to you. I didn't know whether you were really running away, or whether that expression you used in the telegram, about being saved from jail, was just a stall to get the money."

"No," she said, in a low voice, "I needed it to pay my expenses in running away. I didn't have a cent when it happened."

"What was it that happened?"

"A murder," she said.

There was an interval during which the pair stared at each other; the eyes of Sidney Zoom hawk-like in their cold appraisal; the eyes of the young woman pathetically helpless. The train rumbled on through the night, gathering speed.

Sidney Zoom leaned toward her, so that there was no chance of her words being overheard by other passengers.

"Tell me," he said.

"That's all there is to tell," she told him, speaking excitedly, "just that."

"Did you commit the murder?" asked Sidney Zoom.

"No," she said, "of course not."

"Why are you running away then?"

"Because it happened in my apartment."

"Do you know who killed him?"

"I have suspicions, that's all."

"How did it happen?"

"I never liked him," she said. "But he kept trying to force his attentions on me."

"Who?" Zoom inquired.

"Frank Venard," she said.

"All right, go on."

She told him the facts in low, throaty tones.

"Venard came to my apartment. He knocked on the door and said it was a telegram for me. I opened the door a little ways. I wasn't dressed. He pushed the door open and came in. He had been drinking, and he was nasty. I started to fight. We struggled around the apartment for awhile. It was horrible—just one of those things that a girl has to put up with once in awhile. Finally I told him I was going to scream. He laughed and told me he'd choke me if I did. Then I heard the pistol shot."

"In your apartment?" asked Sidney Zoom.

"No," she said, "I don't think so. I think it was from the fire escape outside of the apartment—just the one shot. And I felt him jerk as the bullet hit him … Oh! It was horrible!"

"Well," he said, "go on from there."

She shook her head dubiously.

"That's all," she said. "He was stone dead. I tried to get him to a bed, but I couldn't lift him. I got blood all over my clothes. The shot struck him in the side and must have gone through the heart. He died instantly."

"Why didn't you notify the authorities?"

"Because I was framed."

"How do you mean?" he asked.

"Remember," she said, "I wasn't dressed and there was blood on my clothes. I didn't want to notify the authorities, and get a lot of publicity in the papers. I ran in the bedroom closet and put on some more clothes. When I came out, there was a gun lying by the body."

"Well?"

"And," she said, "my fingerprints were on that gun—I knew they were."

"How did you know?"

"Because," she said, "Paul Stapleton got me to handle the gun. I should have suspected something at the time. He's one of those fellows who is always giving someone the double-cross."

"Who," he asked, "is Stapleton?"

"He's the man I work for."

"What do you do?"

"I'm his stenographer and secretary."

"And he got you to handle the gun?" asked Sidney Zoom.

"Yes," she said, "I came into the office and found the gun on my desk. It was greasy. I picked it up and carried it in to him and asked him what it was doing there. He said that he had been cleaning it and had left it on my desk. I didn't think anything more of it at the time, but I knew that Frank Venard and Paul Stapleton had been having trouble. Venard knew that Stapleton had been taking some bribes. There was some marked money that was given."

"What was Stapleton being bribed for?" Zoom asked.

"He's got something to do with the narcotic business," she told him. "He has charge of searching certain incoming vessels. Frank Venard was a private detective who had been employed by someone, I don't know just whom. Venard would never tell me. He was trying to get something on Mr. Stapleton, and finally he did it. There was a large sum in marked money given as a bribe. I don't know who it was that gave him the bribe. Somebody was back of it; I couldn't find out who."

"Did Mr. Stapleton know that Venard knew about the bribe?" Zoom asked.

"Yes," she said in a low voice, "he knew that he'd been trapped."

"But what became of the money?"

"It was concealed somewhere in his house. He didn't dare to bank it and he didn't dare to carry it with him. They had searched the house, but they couldn't find it."

"Suppose," said Sidney Zoom, "you tell me more about that."

"Well," she said, "there was some man who came to the house. I think he was a big Chinese merchant. He gave Mr. Stapleton a bribe. Anyway, that's what Venard told me. That's all I know about it. The Chinese merchant was a plant, but he gave Mr. Stapleton ten thousand dollars in marked money. Then he came out and signaled the men who were watching the place that he had given the bribe to Stapleton. The men rushed in with a search warrant. They searched the house and they searched Stapleton, but they never found the money."

"Perhaps," said Sidney Zoom, "the Chinese was wily, and pocketed the money himself, but gave the signal to the men just the same."

"No," she said, "Venard was guarding against that. He searched the Chinese, too."

They sat in silence for a moment, the train swaying and lurching as it roared through the night.

"All right," Zoom said, "go on from there. What happened next?"

"That was all," she said. "Venard swore that sooner or later that marked money would show up. He was waiting for it. He had some other evidence; I don't know just what it was, but he was getting some evidence that was going to make things pretty hot for Mr. Stapleton."

"How did it happen," Zoom asked, "that you became friendly with Venard, if he was working against your employer?"

"I didn't," she said. "Venard became friendly with me. He tried to force his attentions on me at first, so he could get a point of contact with Mr. Stapleton and what was going on in the office. Then, when he found he couldn't do that, he kept right on. He was objectionable to me, but he seemed madly infatuated. I had had some trouble with him before.

"That was why I just couldn't stand and face the music. When I realized that Frank Venard had been shot in my apartment, and that the gun which had done the shooting lay on the floor by the body, with my fingerprints on it, I knew that I was trapped. You see, I'd threatened to shoot him if he didn't leave me alone."

Zoom stared at her thoughtfully.

"You should have notified the police," he said. "Even if you had shot him, you would have been acquitted."

"I know," she said, "but think of the publicity and the scandal that would be attached to it. They'd hold me up in the newspapers for the public to stare at."

Zoom regarded her steadily.

"That's not it," he said. "There's some other reason. What is it?"

She lowered her eyes and sat staring at her clasped hands.

"I can't tell you that," she said.

"I can't help you," Sidney Zoom told her, "unless you do."

"If I should tell you," she asked, "could you help me?"

"Perhaps."

"Well," she said, slowly, "I didn't dare to let them take my fingerprints. As soon as they took my fingerprints, they'd have known who I was."

"And who," he asked, "are you?"

"I ran away once before," she told him.

"From what?"

"I ran away," she said, "from an investigation. I did it to shield a man who was unfortunate—a man that I loved. He had been guilty of embezzlement; that is, I guess he had, looking back on it now. But at the time I didn't believe he had. He told me that things went bad for him. He was in a tough place and they were going to send him to the penitentiary, so I took the blame for the embezzlement, and ran away. That shielded him. He was to join me afterwards, and we were to be married. But ..."

"But he didn't join you?" asked Sidney Zoom.

"Yes," she said, in a low voice.

"And Stapleton knew this?"

"I think," she said, slowly, "that he did."

"How did he find it out?"

"He used to question me about my past," she said slowly.

"Some things I told him too much about, and some things not enough. He started checking back on me and I think he found out."

"And you think Stapleton is the one who killed Venard?"

"Yes, I think so."

"Have you any proof whatever?"

"None."

"The gun," said Sidney Zoom, "must have been tossed into the room after you went into the closet."

"Yes, of course."

"Then the window was open?"

"Yes."

"The fire escape runs just outside of your window?"

"No, it runs down from the hallway, but it comes close to the room."

"In other words," said Sidney Zoom, "you believe that Stapleton intended to murder Venard? He managed to get Venard drunk and inflamed with the idea of going to your apartment. Then Stapleton tricked you into leaving your fingerprints on a gun, sat out on the fire escape, killed Venard, and, when you had gone into the closet, tossed the gun into your apartment."

"That's right."

"And he thought that you'd run away."

"He knew," she said slowly, "that I'd have to. Otherwise, it would mean prison on the other charge, even if I weren't convicted of murder."

"Perhaps," said Zoom, "Stapleton left some of *his* fingerprints on that gun."

"No, he's too smart for that. He'd use gloves."

"Where," asked Zoom, "is your apartment?"

"In the Richmore Apartments—35B."

"Give me your key to the apartment," Zoom said.

She hesitated a moment, then took a key from her purse and handed it to Sidney Zoom.

"Would it do any good," said Sidney Zoom, slowly, "if I should tell you that I am inclined to believe your story?"

She shook her head.

"Not a bit," she said. "I was a little fool. I let myself get talked into becoming a fugitive from justice. I'm all right as long as they don't take my fingerprints. Whenever they take my fingerprints I'm finished. Then I made the mistake of letting Stapleton know about it. You don't understand that man. He's a fiend incarnate; one of those shrewd, scheming individuals who is so smart he's always one jump ahead."

"Do you think that he got the marked money that was given as a bribe?" Zoom asked.

"I'm certain of it."

"Do you know where he hid it?"

"No, he concealed it some place in the house; some place where no one would ever think of looking."

"They searched the house?"

"Yes, they had a warrant and they searched the house."

"What did Stapleton do while they were searching the house?"

"He stood by and laughed at them; told them Venard had framed up something on the whole outfit; that if they had trusted Venard with ten thousand dollars, they were simply fools."

"Did you," asked Sidney Zoom, "search Venard's pockets before you left?"

"No, of course not. I got in a panic and ran out of the door without thinking. I threw some things in a suitcase and went down to the depot. I intended to get out of town. Then I suddenly remembered that I was virtually broke. It's two days to payday and I had spent all of my money."

"You didn't have any savings?" he asked.

"I had some," she said. "They were in one of the banks that closed and didn't open."

The locomotive gave a long, shrill blast on the whistle. The coaches started to rumble as the brakes were applied, and the train slowed. Sidney Zoom placed his face against the cold glass of the window and peered out into the darkness. Then he got to his feet and nodded to the girl.

"Leave all of your baggage here," he said. "Come with me."

"What are we going to do?" she asked.

"We're going back," he told her.

"No," she said, "I can't face it—that's all! They'll put a murder charge against me and then they'll hold me on that old embezzlement charge."

"Can you prove what happened in that case?" he asked.

"No," she said. "I was just impulsive and foolish and I let them make me the goat."

Sidney Zoom took her arm and piloted her down the length of the swaying car.

"Well," he said, "they'd arrest you before nine o'clock tomorrow morning if you tried to get away the way you're doing now. You're leaving too broad a back trail. The ticket fellow will remember you, and so will the man at the telegraph office. The first thing the police will do will be to check up on the persons who took the night trains out of town."

"What are you going to do?"

"We're going back by automobile and we're going to see Stapleton."

"See Stapleton?" she gasped.

Zoom nodded grimly.

CHAPTER III

Zoom Accuses

SIDNEY ZOOM fitted the key to the spring lock of the apartment, pushed the door open, stepped inside and found the lights blazing down upon that which lay on the floor.

Hastily he kicked the door shut and stood staring about him at the apartment; at the sprawled shape which lay near the window, on the floor.

Slowly, bit by bit, he started reconstructing the crime. There could be no question that there had been a struggle. Chairs were overturned and a small vase had been broken. The window was open.

Carefully, Sidney Zoom stepped across the body of the man, to peer out of the window. He could see the fire escape running up the side of the building, like some dark serpent.

He stepped into the closet and looked over the clothes which hung from the hangers; looked also at the pile of soiled clothes in the corner. Then he returned to the room and stood, as nearly as he could determine, in the position which the man must have occupied when the shot was fired.

Looking at the angle which the bullet must have traversed, he realized that it would have been impossible for a man to have stood upon the fire escape and fired the shot which had plowed in the dead man's heart. He stood by the body and looked down at the gun which lay on the floor. Then he peered out of the window once more.

Finally, he crossed the apartment, switched out the lights, opened the corridor door, walked to the corner of the corridor, around the turn, down four doors, and knocked gently on the door of an apartment.

There was no answer.

He knocked again, and when there was still no answer, took some passkeys from his pocket and inserted them carefully in the lock, trying them one at a time. The fourth key clicked back the lock. Sidney Zoom opened the door and stepped into the apartment.

It was furnished, but apparently untenanted. He switched on the lights, looked the place over and saw that it had not been lived in for some time. The swinging wall bed had a cobweb hanging in such a position that had the bed been pulled out, the cobweb would have been broken. The kitchenette held a musty smell of stale odors which combined into a rancid assault upon the nostrils.

Zoom walked toward the window of the apartment, knelt down in front of it, and saw that he had a good view of the apartment which had been occupied by Ruby Allison. A chair was drawn up in front of the window, and Sidney Zoom dropped into the chair. As he did so, he let his eyes drift about the floor near the chair, and noticed several little piles of white ash. A wastebasket yielded the stubs of four cigarettes. The cigarettes were all of the same brand—Marlboroughs with cork tips.

Abruptly, Sidney Zoom straightened, set his jaw in a line of grim determination and strode purposefully toward the door. He pulled it open, clicked the lights out and let the spring latch snap into place as the door closed. He paused in the hallway long enough to consult the address book in which he had jotted down the place where Paul Stapleton resided. Then he left the apartment, got in his roadster, and drove through the deserted streets.

HE found the house that he wanted, brought his car to a stop, muttered a command to the dog to stay in the car, and walked up the narrow strip of cement which led from the sidewalk to the porch, his feet awakening muffled echoes.

His long, gaunt forefinger pushed steadily against the bell by the side of the front door, holding it with steady insistence.

From the interior of the house came the sound of the jangling bell; after a while, the noise of voices and the sound of feet coming down a flight of stairs.

Sidney Zoom ceased ringing the bell and stepped slightly to one side.

A bolt clicked back. The door came open a mere two inches, where it was held in position by a brass guard chain. A man's voice said, "Who is it, and what do you want?"

"The name is Zoom. And I want to see Mr. Stapleton upon a matter of importance."

"Mr. Stapleton has retired," said the voice.

"Get him up then," said Zoom. "I want to see him. It's important."

"It will have to wait until morning."

"It won't wait until morning. I want to see him now."

A man's voice from the back of the corridor said irritably, "What is it, James?"

"A man who wants to see you, sir."

There was the rustle of motion, then a form in pajamas pushed itself up against the narrow crack in the door.

"What do you want?" said the man.

"I want," said Sidney Zoom, "to see you at once."

"What about?"

"About a murder," said Sidney Zoom, his cold, hawk-like eyes piercing the darkness.

"Can you be more explicit?" asked Stapleton. There was a slight catch in his voice.

"Certainly," Sidney Zoom told him, "but not here, and not now."

Fingers fumbled with the chain on the door, and then the door opened.

"Come in," said the man in pajamas.

Sidney Zoom stepped into the corridor, conscious of the startled, perplexed eyes of a servant. He followed the slippered feet of the man in white pajamas, crossed the corridor, entered a room and went through the room into an adjoining room. Light switches clicked, and Sidney Zoom found himself in a library, with the walls panelled with books, huge chairs grouped invitingly near reading lamps that cast mellow rays in a glowing circle. He looked into the face of a man of about fifty years of age; a man whose eyes were wide and brown, whose shoulders were held squarely back, whose chin was thrust forward, and whose lips twitched with the ghost of a smile.

"You wanted to see me," he asked, "about a murder?"

Sidney Zoom stared steadily at him.

"Do you," he asked, "know a gentleman by the name of Frank Venard?"

"No," said Stapleton.

"You mean to say you don't know him?"

Stapleton's scowl was cold and mocking.

"I know him," he said. "He's not a gentleman; he's a private detective who has been guilty of subornation of perjury and of planting evidence."

"Very well," said Sidney Zoom. "He's dead."

"Do you expect me to express regrets?" asked Stapleton.

"I was simply making the statement to you."

"How did he die?" asked Stapleton.

"He was murdered."

"Indeed," said Stapleton. "I had rather expected that one of these days his activities would bring him to an untimely end. However, that is neither here nor there. The man is dead, and we will let it go at that. What was it you wanted to see me about?"

"The thing that I wanted to discuss with you," said Sidney Zoom, "was the identity of the murderer."

"I'm sure I couldn't help you," said Stapleton.

"I think perhaps you could."

"In what way, Mr. Zoom?"

"You have a young woman working for you named Ruby Allison?"

"Yes, a very gifted secretary."

"She has an apartment in the Richmore Apartments?"

"I'm sure I couldn't tell you where she lives, without looking up the card index that I have in my office. I have an index which gives the addresses of my employees."

"Well," said Sidney Zoom, "she lives in the Richmore Apartments. Frank Venard was killed in her apartment some time this evening. He was killed by a .38 caliber Colt revolver."

Stapleton raised his eyebrows.

"In *her* apartment?" he said. "Impossible!"

"Nevertheless, that is a fact."

"And does she know who killed him?"

"Yes."

"Who?"

Sidney Zoom pointed a long, level forefinger.

"You!" he said, and the word cracked like a whiplash.

Stapleton stood for a moment staring at Sidney Zoom, then he smiled, and the smile became a chuckle.

"Zoom," he said, "I like your dramatic and forceful manner. Doubtless you're a detective of some sort. I don't know what your game is. If I am to believe what you tell me, Frank Venard is dead. I will not profess any friendship for the man. He was a man that I detested. He was a private detective who attempted to discredit me by using perjured evidence. However, that is neither here nor there. It is this accusation of murder which causes me some amusement, and perhaps a little concern. I don't know what you're trying to do, but you're going to walk out of this house and if you so much as intimate that I have been guilty of murder or have been concerned in any way with the death of Frank Venard, I will see that you are arrested and charged with criminal slander. Do you understand that?"

Sidney Zoom pulled his hat down low on his forehead, turned toward the door.

"I understand," he said.

Stapleton watched him curiously as Zoom walked across the room to the front door. The servant held the front door open, and Sidney Zoom strode out into the night.

"Just a moment," called Stapleton, unable to restrain himself longer, as Zoom made his wordless exit. "I don't want you to misunderstand me, Mr. Zoom ..."

Sidney Zoom whirled to face him.

"I don't misunderstand you," he said. "Either you are guilty of murder, or I have been misled. I just want to tell you that *if* you are guilty of murder, all that suave cunning which has heretofore served you will not stand between you and your punishment. Do you understand that?"

Stapleton's face did not change expression. There was still the same mocking glint in his eyes; the same sardonic smile twisting his lips.

"Yes," he said, "I understand what you say, but your words mean nothing to me."

"You have," said Sidney Zoom, "always outwitted the persons with whom you came in contact. That has been your strong point; the thing that has hitherto enabled you to laugh at justice. Now I am telling you that there is something higher than the ordinary technical man-made justice that you have been mocking; something that is more infallible than the laws of man filled with technicalities that you have taken advantage of, and I have the honor, sir, to wish you a very good evening."

Zoom waited for no further words, but strode across the porch, down the steps, then along the walk to his automobile. He slammed the door and drove off into the night.

Behind him, Paul Stapleton stood in the doorway, staring along the road after the gleaming ruby which marked the tail light of Zoom's automobile.

The expression of mocking, sardonic humor was no longer on Stapleton's face. His eyes were slitted in thought, and his face had set into grim lines.

"James," he said, without turning his head.

"Yes, sir," said the servant.

"If that man ever comes near this house again, see that he doesn't get in."

"Yes, sir."

"If you catch him prowling around, act on the theory that he is a burglar, and shoot him."

"Yes, sir."

"And shoot to kill."

"Yes, sir."

Paul Stapleton stepped back into the house and slammed the door. The servant slipped the safety chain into position.

CHAPTER IV

Mad Dog

ONCE MORE, Sidney Zoom entered the chamber of death. He entered for a particular purpose, and moved with swift efficiency. The lights clicked on. Zoom walked across the room, stooped to the murder gun, picked it up and started polishing its greasy surface with a handkerchief. He polished the gun until the steel fairly shone; polished it until all of the oil and grease had been removed from the blued steel surface. Then he breathed upon it and polished again, taking care all of the time not to touch it with the tips of his fingers, holding it only with the cloth touching the steel.

When he had carefully and completely obliterated all fingerprints from the gun, he looked around the apartment until he found a small bottle of oil. He placed a thin coat of oil over the steel of the gun, rubbing it with the corner of his handkerchief so that it was evenly distributed. Then, holding the gun in the folds of the handkerchief, he once more left the apartment.

Sidney Zoom moved with a swift purpose, as though his actions had been carefully rehearsed. He went down the corridor, turned the corner, stepped to the door of the vacant apartment.

He knew now exactly which skeleton key delivered results, and it was but a moment until he had clicked back the bolt and opened the door.

Once in the apartment, he walked directly to the window, then paused for a moment, thinking. Finally he nodded to himself and slipped his hand to his coat pocket. He took out several .38 blank cartridges which he had carried up from his automobile, which was a veritable storehouse of various weapons and munitions.

Taking care not to leave any fingerprints on the weapon, he swung open the cylinder and dropped blank cartridges into the chambers, slipping the one empty cartridge and the five loaded ones into his pocket.

Lifted Bait

It was but a matter of seconds until he had fixed the gun to his liking, leaving it on the floor by the chair, and had once more stepped into the corridor, pulling the door shut behind him.

He went at once to his automobile, drove five blocks to an all night drugstore, looked up the telephone number of Paul Stapleton, and dialed the number on the telephone.

He knew at once from Stapleton's voice that the man had not been asleep. He had, instead, been near the telephone, perhaps waiting for a call. His voice when he answered was calm and cautious.

"Hello," he said, "who is it?"

Sidney Zoom lowered his voice to a deep, rumbling bass.

"Do you know a guy by the name of Sidney Zoom?" he asked.

"What about it?" asked Stapleton.

"Never mind what about it," said Zoom, still using his deep bass voice. "I happen to be trailing Zoom around because I'm trying to get something on him. He came out to your house an hour or so ago, and busted on in. I want to know if he gave you his right name and what he talked to you about."

"I'm afraid," said Stapleton, "that I can't help you."

"Well, get a load of this," said Zoom in the same rumbling monotone. "I don't know whether it makes any difference to you or not. But after Zoom left your place, he went to the Richmore Apartments and went into apartment 35B. He's got a key that fits it. He came out of that apartment carrying a gun, and tiptoed around the corner of the corridor to apartment 38E, and when he came out, he didn't have the gun with him.

"Now, I don't know what happened, but that fellow's a smooth worker, and I have an idea that perhaps when he was out at your place he might have picked up something that belonged to you. See? And maybe he planted that stuff in that apartment—38E—together with the gun. Now, I don't know what's up or what he's doing, but anything he's trying to do, I want to block.

"Personally I think he's a crook. He's always messing around and pulling some fast stuff and gets by because nobody has called him on it. But I'm calling him on it, and I just thought perhaps you'd like to know what he was doing. I thought perhaps the information might interest you."

Zoom ceased speaking.

There was a moment of silence, broken only by the buzzing of the telephone connection, then Paul Stapleton's voice, calmly, suave and courteous.

"I'm sure," he said, "I haven't the faintest idea what you're talking about. It is true that a man named Zoom called upon me, but I wasn't interested in the proposition he had to offer, and he left at once. I'm certainly not interested in any of Mr. Zoom's subsequent activities."

And the receiver at the other end of the line clicked onto the hook.

SIDNEY ZOOM strode to his automobile, drove to a point half a block from the apartment house, where he could leave the automobile in the shadows of the driveway, then sat on the running board and watched the entrance to the Richmore Apartments.

He sat smoking calmly and contentedly, apparently without the slightest trace of nervous tension. Everything about the man seemed relaxed, save his eyes, which were keen and hawk-like. Those eyes stared in a concentration of scrutiny that was cold and unwinking.

Sidney Zoom was half way through his third cigarette when there was the sound of a roaring motor. Tires skidded on the pavement as a machine lurched around the corner. The machine came to a stop, and a tall, well knit individual stepped from the machine and looked about him.

Apparently the entire street was deserted, and the man, having assured himself of that fact, moved toward the entrance of the apartment house with calm assurance.

Zoom gave the man a head start of approximately five seconds, and then beckoned to the police dog.

Master and dog moved with swift, silent strides, gliding along the pavement like shadows of the night.

Zoom didn't wait for the elevator, but took the stairs, two at a time, running up with light, springy steps, the police dog padding along at his side.

Zoom went at once down the corridor to the door of apartment 38E.

He could hear the sounds of surreptitious motion behind the closed door.

Sidney Zoom indicated the door to the police dog.

"Watch, Rip," he said. "Let no one out."

The dog dropped to his stomach, pointing his sensitive nostrils toward the door, his eyes staring in fixed concentration.

Zoom turned back down the corridor, raced down the steps, and was half way to the lobby when he heard the sound of a pistol shot booming from the upper corridor. A moment later there was another shot.

Zoom sprinted down the street, jumped in his car, stepped on the starter and threw in the clutch. He pressed his hand on the horn button and roared through the quiet apartment district.

Three blocks from the apartment house he found a uniformed officer. Zoom pulled into the curb.

"Passing along the street here," he said, "and I heard shots."

"Where?" asked the officer.

"Back at an apartment house. The Richmore, I think, was the name."

The officer loosened his service revolver in its holster, climbed to the running board of the car.

"Let's go," he said.

Zoom whipped the car into an abrupt turn and stepped on the throttle. As he approached the apartment house, he drew into the curb and slowed.

"This is the place," he said.

The officer jumped to the sidewalk.

"Better wait here," he said.

Lights were on in the apartments. As the officer pushed his way into the lobby, a woman screamed.

Sidney Zoom waited.

Three minutes later a police radio car swung around the corner at high speed and pulled into the curb.

An officer pushed his way into the apartment house.

Another officer debouched from the car and strode over to Sidney Zoom.

"What is it?" he asked.

"I don't know," said Zoom. "I heard shots when I was going past here, and I picked up an officer three or four blocks up the street. He came back with me and told me to wait here."

The officer nodded and then pushed his way into the apartment house.

Sidney Zoom placed his fingers to his lips and gave a shrill, penetrating whistle.

Ten seconds later there was a tawny streak which flashed through the lobby of the apartment house. Rip jumped to the sidewalk, gathered himself, and hit the back of the roadster in a long arc of graceful motion. Sidney Zoom stepped to the back of the car, pushed the back of the rumble seat forward.

"Down, Rip," he said, "and stay there."

The back of the car latched into place. Sidney Zoom got back into the car.

An officer came puffing down the stairs and stood in the doorway of the apartment looking up and down the street. Then he crossed to Sidney Zoom.

"See anything of a police dog that came out here?" he asked.

"Yes," said Zoom, "a big one. He busted out of the place and swung around the corner. What's the matter, officer?"

"You're the man that brought Mike here?" asked the policeman.

"I guess so. I'm the man who picked up the uniformed officer on the beat and brought him here."

The officer nodded, then looked back at the apartment house.

"Funny thing," he said.

"What is?"

"A man who gave his name as Richard Horton was trapped in an apartment by a mad dog. The man fired six shots at the dog, but none of them took effect. The dog dodged every time he pointed the revolver."

"Did he bite the man?" asked Zoom.

"Bit him on the wrists a couple of times, but seemed to be trying to make him stay in the room. The door was open into the corridor, and the shots were heard in some of the other apartments. The tenants put in a call for the police. We picked it up in the radio car and came out here."

"The man live in the apartment?" asked Zoom.

"No," said the officer, "nobody lives there. We're holding the man for questioning. Documents in his pockets indicate that his name is Paul Stapleton. He can't give a satisfactory account of what he's doing there."

"Perhaps," said Sidney Zoom, smiling, "he has a secretary who lives in the building, or something."

"Well, he's been visiting somewhere," said the officer, "and he's going to tell the truth before he gets out."

"Going to put a charge against him?"

"We'll want to find out a little more about how he happened to have the gun and what he's doing in the apartment," answered the officer.

"And the dog ran away?" asked Zoom.

"Yes," the officer said. "We didn't think he was mad. He seemed to be all right, but he just wouldn't let the man out of the apartment. We figured that he was a trained police dog, and had detected an apartment house thief. Naturally, we supposed he belonged to the manager of the apartment. It wasn't until just a minute ago we thought he was mad. The dog seemed all right in every way, until all of a sudden he jumped to his feet and went down the corridor like a streak of greased lightning. We heard him banging down the stairs, and that's the last we've seen of him."

"He went around the corner like a streak of lightning," said Zoom. "I guess there's no need for me to wait for that officer."

"No, there's nothing he'll need you for, and thanks for going out of your way to report the shooting and bring him here."

Sidney Zoom bowed his head.

"Not at all," he said. "It was a pleasure."

The roadster purred into motion and slipped out into the middle of the street. The officer from the radio car looked up and down the street once more, then shrugged his shoulders and turned to the apartment house.

CHAPTER V

Zoom Goes Fishing

SIDNEY ZOOM'S powerful sea-going yacht, the *Alberta F.*, creaked against the mooring float with wind and tide.

In the main cabin, Sidney Zoom paced back and forth, irritably, impatiently.

At a table, Vera Thurmond, his secretary, regarded him with eyes that were warm and maternal, despite the fact that she was some five years his junior.

Seated beside Vera Thurmond, her eyes filled with gratitude, was Ruby Allison.

"I really can't let you do this for me," she said. "I know enough about law to know that you are likely to get in serious trouble over this."

Zoom shook his head with a single swift gesture of impatience, and continued pacing the floor.

At the forward end of the cabin, a radio with loudspeaker made little sputtering noises of static.

"Why the devil don't they discover the body?" said Sidney Zoom.

There was no answer. The two young women stared at him in silence. Something in the very impatient savagery of the man made them keep a watchful silence.

Abruptly, there was the whirring noise of a siren whistle over the radio. Then a masculine voice said:

"Calling all cars for a further report on the shooting at the Richmore Apartments."

Sidney Zoom breathed a sigh of relief.

"Here it comes," he said.

The masculine voice droned through facts in a weary monotone. "The man who fired the shots and who gave the name of Richard Horton, and who claimed to be a tenant in the building, has been identified positively as Paul Stapleton, in charge of narcotic investigations relating to incoming ocean liners. A check-up on the tenants of the Richmore Apartments showed that a Ruby Allison had apartment 35B, and was employed by Paul Stapleton in the capacity of stenographer and secretary.

"When she failed to answer her door, detectives effected an entrance and found the dead body of Frank Venard, a private detective, lying sprawled on the floor. Venard had evidently been shot, but there was no weapon found within the apartment.

"The ballistic department is making a series of experiments with the gun found in the possession of Paul Stapleton, to determine if the bullet was fired from that gun.

"In the meantime, all cars are warned to be on the lookout for Ruby Allison, a young woman, age twenty-three, height five feet four and a half inches, weight one hundred and seventeen pounds, hair dark, eyes dark. When last seen, wearing a tweed coat. She has been traced to the Union Depot, and positively identified as having purchased a ticket for Midvale; but a search of the train discloses that she did not remain on the train, but evidently left it en route. She is wanted for questioning in connection with the murder of Frank Venard.

"We will repeat the description of the girl: Ruby Allison ..."

Sidney Zoom strode to the instrument and snapped over the switch which cut it off.

"That," he said, "is that."

The two women stared at him in silence.

"Now," said Sidney Zoom, "it remains to collect from Stapleton."

"How do you mean?" asked Vera Thurmond.

"I mean," he said, "that I am convinced the story told me by Miss Allison is correct, and that it is true in every particular. It remains, therefore, for me to assess some contribution against Paul Stapleton—a contribution which will compensate this young woman in some measure for the publicity, the humiliation, and the expense which will doubtless become necessary in connection with securing legal representation."

He turned and strode purposefully toward the door.

Rip, the police dog, who had been lying by the radio, raised his head and cocked his ears inquiringly.

Sidney Zoom shook his head.

"No, Rip," he said, "you are going to stay there. This is one time when I must resort to subterfuge and disguise."

"You're not going to do anything dangerous?" asked Vera Thurmond anxiously.

Sidney Zoom smiled grimly at her.

"Everything that one does is dangerous," he said. "And perhaps the most certain way to court danger is to try to avoid it. The man who allows his style to be cramped because he fears consequences, is one who never gets any place."

Sidney Zoom pushed his way out into the early dawn, and if he was conscious of the warm tenderness in the eyes of Vera Thurmond, he did not show it, but strode grimly forth as a warrior going into battle, his mind concentrated only upon a plan of attack.

THE sun was not yet up, but there was sufficient light to show something of color. The East was blazing into a golden hue. Birds were commencing to flit restlessly about from house top to tree top. The air was fresh, buoyant and life-giving.

Sidney Zoom strode entirely around the house of Paul Stapleton, paused before the side door of the house, and gave the lock some careful attention. A moment later he inserted a skeleton key, and twisted the bolt back. He stepped into the house and listened. There was no sound.

Zoom knew that there was at least one servant in the house. He also knew that the servant would have no hesitancy about shooting first and asking questions afterwards. Therefore, Sidney Zoom made no attempt at being quiet.

He adjusted a mask over his features, slipped a revolver into his right hand, and stepped into a closet which opened from the library. He saw that there was ample room for concealment in this closet, then boldly walked out into the center of the library, and toppled over a bookcase.

The books fell to the floor with a terrific crash of breaking glass, splintering wood and thudding volumes.

Zoom stepped back and waited.

He had not long to wait. There was the sound of hurried steps running down the stairs, and then the figure of the man who had stood at the elbow of Paul Stapleton the night before entered the room. The man was attired in pajamas and slippers, and carried a heavy caliber revolver in his right hand.

Zoom, hiding in the closet, his eyes glued to a crack between the partially open door and the casement, saw the man enter the room; saw the expression of puzzled bewilderment on his face; then saw the expression of bewilderment gradually change to one of annoyance. The gun was slightly lowered as the man stepped forward to inspect the damage.

He looked around the room, then bent over the wreckage of the bookcase and the scattered books. Sidney Zoom pushed the door of the closet open and noiselessly stepped out. The first intimation that the man had of Zoom's presence was when the muzzle of Zoom's gun made a cold pressure against the back of the bare neck.

"Stick 'em up!" said Zoom.

The man grew rigid. For a moment he hesitated, then slowly his hands moved up in the air.

"Drop the gun," Zoom told him.

The gun dropped, struck a book, glanced and skidded along the floor.

"Put your hands behind your back with your wrists together," Zoom said.

When his command had been obeyed, Zoom took handcuffs from his hip pocket, fitted them over the wrists and clicked them shut.

"Now," said Zoom, "you can tell me where Stapleton had the marked money concealed."

The man turned a curious head over his shoulder, saw the tall form, with the mask covering the features.

"There wasn't any marked money," he said.

Sidney Zoom laughed, and the laugh was grim.

"Do you know?" he asked.

"Of course I don't know. I tell you there wasn't any."

Sidney Zoom spoke after the manner of one who thinks out loud.

"Not the usual servant," he said. "Either an intimate of your master or one of the conspirators who works with him."

The man grunted a comment that caused Zoom to prod his pistol into the tender short ribs.

"That'll do," he said. "Shut up if you can't speak decently."

The man winced, and Zoom's hawk-like eyes looked swiftly around the room.

"Were you here," he asked, "when the search was made?"

The man muttered a grudging assent.

"Did they, perhaps," asked Sidney Zoom, "look through the books in the library?"

"They looked everywhere," he said. "They searched this house from top to bottom. They spilled books all over the floor, tore up carpets, pounded walls, pulled out the casements from the windows and examined the window weights. They looked everywhere."

Zoom laughed grimly.

"That," he said, "makes it nice. It only remains for me to conduct a very limited search."

Curiosity mastered the handcuffed man.

"How do you mean?" he asked.

"Simply," said Sidney Zoom, "that they have looked in all of the *likely* hiding places. It only remains for me to look in the *unlikely* hiding places."

The man's laugh was sarcastic.

"They looked everywhere," he said.

"Well," said Sidney Zoom, "we might as well look the house over a little bit. Come on and march around. Remember that I'm behind you with a gun. If you make any funny moves, I'm going to smack the barrel of this gun down on the top of your head, unless I should think the situation calls for sterner reprisals."

"Where do you want to go?" asked the other.

"Oh, just lead the way around the house," said Sidney Zoom.

The man started walking, his slippered feet shuffling along the floor. Behind him came Sidney Zoom, gun held ready, hawk-like eyes sweeping the premises in glittering appraisal. Sidney Zoom, however, said nothing. His every faculty was concentrated upon looking over the house, inspecting the various rooms through which they passed.

It was when they entered a room on the third floor that Sidney Zoom suddenly showed interest.

"What's this room?" he asked.

"The master's bedroom."

"Why does he sleep on the third floor?"

"I don't know—because he wants to, I guess."

Zoom looked the room over.

He glanced about him for a moment. Then he started talking, and his voice was the expressionless monotone of one who is thinking aloud.

"As I size up your master," he said, "he's a man who would want to have the money near him at all times. He's a man who would be very much inclined to hide any valued possession close to his sleeping quarters."

His answer was a sarcastic laugh.

Zoom paid no attention to the laugh, but stood in the center of the room, looking around it.

"Obviously," he said, still speaking in the same monotone of one who is thinking aloud, "the obvious and likely places have been searched. Therefore, it remains to look for some place that would have naturally escaped search."

"They took this room to pieces," said the man, and there was a trace of bitterness in his voice.

"And found nothing?"

"And found nothing."

Sidney Zoom stepped to the window, looked out into the well kept yard. The sun had gilded the roof and tree tops. Birds were fluttering about, chirping and singing.

Abruptly, Zoom stiffened to attention.

The room was in a tower which looked out upon the lower portions of the roof. Some ten feet away was a rigid mast, some eight or ten feet in height, and on the top of this mast was a little platform decorated by a bird house.

"Who put that up?" he asked.

"Mr. Stapleton," said the man.

Sidney Zoom stared steadily at the bird house.

"Now Stapleton," he mused, "is the type of man who ordinarily wouldn't be interested in birds. His temperament is cruel, cold, supercilious and mocking. He's the type of man who is intensely cold-blooded and self-centered. Yet he's very intelligent. Therefore, I wonder ..."

Sidney Zoom's voice trailed away into silence. He looked about him, staring once more at the bedroom itself.

The eyes of the handcuffed man were fastened upon Sidney Zoom with intense interest.

Abruptly, Sidney Zoom pointed to a long bamboo pole which was suspended on pegs along the side of the room.

"What's that?" he asked.

"A fishing pole," said the man. "Can't you see?"

Sidney Zoom nodded, but his nod was preoccupied. He strode to the pole and inspected it.

There was a reel on the pole. The line was heavy. The guides for the line were placed closely together, and were of the best material. The thing which was most noticeable, however, was the fact that the pole did not come to a tapering tip, as is usually the case, but had been cut off where the rod was still quite thick.

"That's not a casting rod," said Sidney Zoom.

The handcuffed man said nothing.

Sidney Zoom took the rod from its pegs and balanced it in his hand.

"Too stiff," he said, "for fishing with bait. Not built right for a casting rod. I wonder ..."

He took the hook on the end of the line between his thumb and forefinger, and inspected it.

"A hook," he said, "that's heavy enough to land a shark."

He walked to the window, peered out once more and abruptly chuckled.

"My dear James," he said, "do you, by any chance, happen to notice the ring in the top of the bird house?"

The handcuffed man forgot his hostility in order to peer in sudden curiosity.

"I think," said Sidney Zoom, "that I will show you a little high class fishing."

He pushed the end of the fishing pole out of the window, shortened the line on the reel until the hook hung down but a few inches below the tip of the pole. It took but a moment to drop the hook inside of the ring on the bird house.

Sidney Zoom held the reel with the fingers of his right hand. With his left hand he lifted the pole. The pole bent slightly. Then the entire bird house lifted from the wooden platform. Thus he brought it into the room, disengaged the ring from the hook, and set the bird house on the table.

He inspected the miniature structure for a moment, then manipulated two clasps, and the entire roof lifted clear. It was entirely filled with sheafed currency.

The handcuffed man lurched forward, his breath coming in a hissing exclamation.

Zoom whirled and the gun jabbed into the man's stomach.

"Careful," he warned. "Get back there!"

The man stared at the treasure in the bird house with bulging eyes and a sagging jaw.

"Cripes!" he said. "And I put in three days searching every place in the house I could think of, to try and find it."

Zoom nodded.

"Quite so," he said. "I figured you for that kind."

Almost casually he pocketed the bank notes. When he had finished, he fitted the fish hook into the ring, put the bird house back into position, shook the hook free, pulled the fishing pole back, and placed it once more on the pegs.

"When you see your master," he said, "you might tell him that his cache was robbed. However, I don't think that you'll do it, because as soon as you do, your master is going to think that you were the guilty party. Moreover, I think it's going to be some time before you see your master. I fancy he's going to be detained by the police on a murder charge. However, if you *should* see him, and if you *should* tell him, I rather fancy he'll choose to remain silent about the entire matter.

"*If*," said Zoom, "Paul Stapleton should complain that he had been robbed, and *if* he should, by any chance, divulge the identity of the robber, and *if* the police should obtain any proofs of my complicity, they would at the same time secure the proof of bribery and corruption on the part of Stapleton that they have been searching for.

"You might call those matters to Mr. Stapleton's attention, in the event you should advise him of his misfortune, although, as I've said before, I don't think you will, because Stapleton would immediately jump at the conclusion you had been the one to rob him."

Zoom bowed affably to the enraged individual.

"As I go out the front door," he said, "I will drop the key to the handcuffs on the hall carpet. You can find it and eventually free yourself. It will take a bit of patient manipulation to get the key into the lock. I would suggest that you hold it in your teeth and try turning it, by twisting the arms.

"In the meantime, I have the honor to wish you a very good morning, my dear James."

SIDNEY ZOOM sat in his stateroom on the yacht.

Across the table from him, Ruby Allison stared at the pile of bank notes with bulging eyes.

"But," she said, "it wouldn't be right."

Sidney Zoom laughed sarcastically.

"You know that it's right," he said. "What you mean is that you're afraid of man-made laws. As a matter of fact, you are the one who is entitled to this money. You admit that it's bribe money. It could never be returned to the persons who had put it up. Obviously, Paul Stapleton shouldn't be allowed to keep it. Moreover, Stapleton has done you a great wrong. He has, as it happens, walked into his own trap, but that was due to the fact he fell for the bait which I held out to him. If it hadn't been for that, you would have been a fugitive from justice right now, charged with murder.

"Law is but a man-made attempt to secure justice. In many instances, laws fall down because it is impossible to anticipate all of the complexities of human conduct. Those are the cases in which I interest myself. I endeavor to do substantial justice, without regard to laws."

He pushed the currency toward her.

"But how about you?" she asked.

Sidney Zoom smiled patiently.

"I," he said, "have had a very interesting night's adventure, and now, if you'll pardon, I'll retire."

He arose from his chair, moved swiftly to the door of the stateroom, turned to smile at the young woman, nod at Vera Thurmond, then jerked the door open, stepped out of the stateroom and slammed the door behind him.

Ruby Allison looked in stupefied wonder at Vera Thurmond.

"But," she said, "I don't understand the man."

Vera Thurmond's laugh was wistful.

"You could," she said, "be with him for years, without doing that. You could respect and admire him, but you'd never understand him."

Her eyes were bright.

STOLEN THUNDER

CHAPTER I

Samson's Strange Job

SIDNEY ZOOM hated routine with a bitter hatred.

Night after night, his police dog at his side, he prowled through those sections of the city where human misery came crawling forth with the hours of darkness. His eyes, which could be cold and savage at times, were filled with ready sympathy as he peered into the dark shadows of the city where human flotsam was deposited by the tide of economic struggle.

The park was lighted by blazing incandescents which attracted the first moths of spring and glittered in shining reflections from the green foliage of the trees.

But the lights cast shadows over some of the benches, and on these benches young couples sat in close proximity, conversing in low voices.

Sidney Zoom wasted no time upon such couples. His peering eyes sought out those dark shadows where lone derelicts sat in black despair.

Here was a man whose pasty features and twitching nerves told of dope; another was sodden with cheap alcohol; a third was a drifter, one of those men who refuse to accept opportunity when it is offered; a fourth was a young man whose gaunt face and haggard eyes showed the pallor of malnutrition as he sat hunched forward, his elbows on his knees, his chin on his hands.

Sidney Zoom paused in his walk.

"A nice evening," he said.

The man apparently did not hear him. It was only when Zoom repeated the comment that the man stared upward with strained, incredulous eyes.

"Yes," he said at length in a thin voice, then added, after a pause: "A nice dog you have."

Sidney Zoom nodded.

"Getting the air," he asked, "after a hard day's work?"

The man's laugh was mocking.

"A hard day's work is right," he said. "I had a hard day's work two weeks ago. It's the last I've been able to get."

Sidney Zoom stared steadily at him.

The man spat contemptuously.

"Go on," he said, "I'll take care of myself."

Sidney Zoom turned and walked away, the police dog padding at his side.

The foot and ankle of a woman caught his eyes. He had seen it half an hour before when he had first entered the park. The woman was reclining on one of the park seats. Her head and torso were in the deep shadows. Her left foot and ankle caught a shaft of light which filtered through the trees.

Presently, the officer on the beat would awaken her. Sleeping upon the the park benches was prohibited, but of late the rule had been relaxed so that many of the city's homeless found a certain inadequate resting place on the hard, cold benches. These unfortunates, by some unwritten understanding with the police, did not descend upon the benches until after midnight.

Sidney Zoom moved to the side of the young woman, touched her shoulder.

He could see that she was well formed, that she was in her early twenties, that she was sleeping in an uncomfortable position and that she was sleeping soundly.

He touched her again.

The dog at his side gave a low whimper.

Sidney Zoom took the woman's shoulders and shook her. A small glass bottle dropped from the limp fingers of her right hand, but she made no motion.

Sidney Zoom picked up the bottle. A skull and cross-bones caught his eyes. He held the label to the light, then dropped the bottle to his pocket, knelt and smelled of the young woman's lips. Abruptly, he turned and retraced his steps to where the young man sat hunched upon the park bench.

"My friend," he asked, "would you like temporary employment?"

The man didn't look up.

"Take your sympathy," he said bitterly, "and go to hell with it."

Sidney Zoom's voice was patient.

"My friend," he said, "this is not sympathy. Every night I make it a rule to find some worthy individual who is out of employment and give him work. The work is not orthodox, nor are my methods, but the employment certainly is not charity. If you want the job, say so; if you don't want it, there are probably others who do."

The haggard features raised to his. There was the glint of dawning hope in the eyes.

"You mean it?" the man asked.

"Your name?" asked Sidney Zoom.

"Burt Samson," he said.

Zoom nodded.

"The wages," he said, "will be adequate. They will be on a basis of profit-sharing. The work will be probably within the law."

The man's laugh was rasping.

"I didn't ask any of that," he said.

"Come with me," Zoom told him.

They approached the bench where the young woman lay.

"I want," said Sidney Zoom, "to get her to a taxicab."

Samson flashed Zoom one swiftly searching look.

"How long have you known she was here?"

"I just found her," Zoom said.

"Do you know who she is?"

"No."

"Why do you want to get her to a taxicab?"

Zoom stared at him with steady, uncordial eyes.

"My friend," he said, "if you are going to work for me, you are going to follow instructions without a lot of questions. No matter what a job is, there's only room for one boss."

Samson stooped wordlessly, placed his hands under the girl's shoulders. Sidney Zoom caught one of her arms. They lifted her to her feet. She was motionless, inert, lifeless.

"A drug?" asked Samson.

Zoom made no comment.

"A taxicab," he said after a moment.

They supported her between them, cut across the grass of the park, keeping to the shadows.

"I'll hold her," said Zoom. "Get a cab. Say that the woman passed out after a couple of drinks. Don't offer too many explanations."

The young man nodded, stepped out from the shadows of the park shrubbery to the lighted sidewalk, hailed a passing cab. The driver gave him a searching look, slowed, then speeded on. A second cab answered his hail and stopped. Samson talked for a moment with the cabbie, who opened the door and stared suspiciously toward the park.

Sidney Zoom waited for an auspicious moment, then he strode across the sidewalk, the woman in his arms. He deposited her on the cushions of the cab, nodded to the police dog. The dog leapt into the cab, crouched on the floor. Samson climbed in, hesitated for a moment, then pillowed the young woman's head on his shoulder. Sidney Zoom fastened the insolent eyes of the cab driver with a steady stare.

"Drive down this street to the waterfront," Zoom said. "Turn to the left. I'll tell you when to go out on the docks. I want to get aboard the *Alberta F.*"

"You mean that millionaire's yacht that's moored ..."

"Exactly," said Sidney Zoom, climbed into the cab and slammed the door shut.

CHAPTER II

The Girl Who Wanted to Die

VERA THURMOND was a most efficient nurse. Years of experience with the strange character whom she served in the dual capacity of assistant and secretary, had fitted her to cope with all sorts of people and conditions.

She moved back and forth from the dining salon, in which Zoom and Samson sat waiting, to the room where the young woman moaned and retched.

A pot bubbled on an electric stove, and the smell of coffee filled the air.

"She'll be all right now," Vera Thurmond said, "the emetic has done its work, and I'm going to get some coffee down her. You'd better help me."

Sidney Zoom strode into the bedroom, looked at the features of the young woman, features that were now white with misery. Her eyes were red-rimmed from the nausea which had been induced by the emetic. Her lips were pale and bloodless.

She stared at Sidney Zoom with wide blue eyes, looking at him as though he had been a creature from another world.

"So you took laudanum?" said Sidney Zoom.

She moved her lips but there was no sound. Her eyes filmed over with drowsiness even as he looked at her.

Vera Thurmond appeared with coffee steaming in a cup, coffee that was black and bitter.

"We've got to get this down her," she said, "and make her keep it down. Then you've got to walk her around the deck where she can get the fresh night air."

Together they got two cups of coffee down the young woman's throat. Samson and Zoom got her to the deck, started walking her along the moist planks—planks that were kept spotlessly clean and on which the night dew had left a thin film of moisture.

"Let me alone," she said thickly, "I want to lie down."

Zoom paid no attention to her, but kept pushing her along. By degrees, the fresh air of the night and the coffee got in its work.

"I think we can take her down below now," Zoom said.

"Oh, I'm all right now," she told him in a voice that was bitter. "Why didn't you leave me alone? Now I've got to do it all over again."

Zoom made no comment but assisted her down the companionway to the dining salon.

Samson turned to Zoom.

"I wonder," he said, "if ..."

"Well," said Zoom, "go ahead. What is it?"

"If," said Samson in a voice that quavered, "I could have some of that coffee? I haven't eaten for three days."

He moved toward a chair, stumbled, and pitched forward on his face.

Zoom bent over him, but it was the young woman who reached him first.

"You poor boy," she said.

Zoom raised Samson from the floor and into a chair. His eyelids fluttered as Vera Thurmond brought him a steaming cup of coffee. Samson drank the coffee, turned on them savagely.

"Keep your damned sympathy," he said, "I don't want it."

There had been a few drops of brandy in the coffee and after it had taken effect, Zoom fixed an egg-nog.

"Take this," he said, "and then we'll try something solid and substantial."

He turned to the girl.

"What," he asked, "is your name?"

"Say," she said staring around curiously. "What kind of a place is this?"

"A yacht," said Zoom.

"Who owns it?"

"I do."

"What do you do with it?"

"Sail it occasionally."

"What's the idea of getting this fellow and me aboard?"

"I thought," said Zoom, "I could help you, and at the same time help myself."

"You could have left me alone and helped me a lot more," she said.

Zoom stared at her steadily.

"When I have heard your story," he said, "I can give employment to this man."

"How?" she inquired, curiosity getting the better of her.

"I don't know," he said, "but there will be a way. Things are never hopeless. People who brood over their problems, lose sight of obvious solutions. People who kill themselves because they can't find a way out are like the persons who get lost every year and lie down to die within a few hundred yards of a habitation; like the wanderer in the desert who perishes of thirst within a mile of water."

She looked at Burt Samson.

"Where does he come in?" she asked.

"I am going," said Sidney Zoom, "to give him a job helping to untangle your affairs."

"Who's going to pay him?"

"I'm not," Zoom said. "We're going to collect from some other person."

The young woman stared at him incredulously.

Vera Thurmond nodded her head.

"He always does," she said.

The young woman took a deep breath.

"Okay," she said, "I can stand it if you can. My name's Nell Benton. Did you ever hear of Finley Carter?"

"Rather an eccentric millionaire," asked Zoom, "whose hobby is the collection of paintings and the playing of chess?"

"That's the one," she said.

"I've heard of him," Zoom said.

"Do you know him personally?"

"No. I've never met him."

"I acted as his secretary," she said. "I was discharged."

"Why?" asked Zoom.

"Because of dishonesty," she said.

She stared at Sidney Zoom as though seeking to probe his thoughts.

"You don't seem particularly shocked," she said after a moment, her voice showing the bitterness of her feelings. "Why don't you get a smirking look of self-righteousness on your face?"

Sidney Zoom's voice was patient. "I don't get shocked," he said, "and I am not self-righteous. As far as the law is concerned, it is an excellent system for the majority of cases; it falls far short in certain individual cases. Under those circumstances, I have no hesitancy about stepping outside the law myself."

The blue eyes widened.

"Go on," Sidney Zoom said, "give me the details."

"It was so simple," she said bitterly, "that it sounds absurd. Someone made very fair copies of a couple of rare paintings, and substituted them for the originals."

Sidney Zoom's face showed quick interest.

"One of the originals," she said, "was found in my room, another one was found in a pawn shop. The pawnbroker said that a young woman had left it with him. He had no conception of the value of it, and had given her but five dollars on it. The description he gave of the woman fitted me exactly.

"Mr. Carter," she said bitterly, "was most generous! He simply discharged me and kept the money that was due me. He said that he wouldn't send me to jail, inasmuch as he had recovered the paintings. I tried to get other employment; there was no use. I had been with Finley Carter for five years. It's hard enough to get a job anyway, there aren't many vacancies. Once or twice I got people interested in me. They rang up Carter. He told them that he had discharged me for dishonesty."

Sidney Zoom jack-knifed his lean length into a swivel chair at the head of the dining table. His eyes glowed with a fierce interest.

"This," he said, "is one of the most interesting situations I have ever encountered in my life."

She stared at him, her eyes flashing.

"Are you," she asked, "trying to make fun of me?"

"On the contrary," said Sidney Zoom, "the obvious, outstanding facts not only show your innocence, but convince me that there is some remarkably sinister plot afoot."

"What do you mean?" she asked.

"In the first place," said Zoom, "the fact that the paintings were copied indicates that there is an artist who is in on the conspiracy."

"Naturally," she said scornfully.

"The artist," went on Sidney Zoom, "is a friend of someone in the house. He must have had unlimited opportunity to make copies of the pictures that were stolen. That means that he must have access to the house."

"Yes," she said sarcastically, "even the master mind of Mr. Finley Carter reasoned that far. The fact that the artist had his opportunity to work undisturbed, showed that I was his accomplice."

Zoom shook his head from side to side in silent negation.

"If," he said, "you had been with Finley Carter for five years you would have known the value of the paintings. If you had gone to the trouble and risk of having them copied, you wouldn't have disposed of one of them for five dollars. Moreover, if you had an artist as your accomplice, the artist would have known of channels through which the pictures could have been disposed of to advantage. Therefore, it is perfectly obvious that the object of the scheme was to discredit you."

"But why?" she asked, her face showing interest.

"That," said Sidney Zoom, "is one of the things we will find out. What were your duties?"

"I handled his correspondence."

"Did you have access to any funds?"

"None ... That is, there was an account of five hundred dollars that I handled."

"What account was that?"

"Housekeeping money."

"It was fixed at five hundred dollars?"

"Yes. I made out checks on it. Mr. Carter signed the checks. Usually he signed them in advance. He figured that he could trust me to the extent of five hundred dollars."

"Was it a separate account?" asked Zoom.

"Yes."

"How did he keep it separate from his other accounts?"

"By keeping it in an entirely different bank. It was a branch bank located in the neighborhood—the Second National Affiliate. His regular account was in the Mechanics National."

"How many servants?" asked Sidney Zoom.

"There was James Stearne, chauffeur; Harry Exter, butler and valet; and Mrs. Ethel Clint, housekeeper. There was no one else other than myself. Finley Carter is a crusty old bachelor."

Sidney Zoom glanced at the portholes; they showed the grayish light of coming day. He looked at the haggard, drawn features of Burt Samson, then nodded to Vera Thurmond.

"Get the cook up, Vera," he said. "We'll have breakfast. Put Samson to bed. Send his clothes up to the best ready-to-wear store you can find, and get a new suit of blue serge. Duplicate the other as nearly as you can."

He nodded his head to the pair.

"Vera Thurmond," he said, "will show you your staterooms. You'll get some sleep."

"Say," said Samson getting to his feet, "what kind of a nut factory is this?"

"Shut up," Sidney Zoom said without raising his voice. "You wanted work—you're going to get it, and it's going to be hard work. You're going to get some grub on your stomach; you're going to get some sleep, and then you're going to have a job."

"A job," said Samson sneeringly, "who's going to pay me?"

Sidney Zoom's voice was as final as the tolling of a bell.

"Finley Carter," he said, "is going to pay."

Sidney Zoom turned to Nell Benton.

"During the time," he said, "that you worked for Carter, I take it you became rather familiar with his signature?"

She nodded.

"And can you tell me," asked Sidney Zoom, "where I can find a specimen of his signature?"

"In my purse," she said bitterly. "I asked him for a reference. He gave me a letter stating that it was impossible for him to give me a reference. That I had been discharged because of dishonesty."

Zoom nodded thoughtfully.

"I should like that letter," he said.

"What," she inquired, "do you want to use it for?"

"As a sample," Sidney Zoom said.

"A sample?"

"Yes," he said. "I desire to forge the signature of Finley Carter."

CHAPTER III

Zoom's Plan

SIDNEY ZOOM had considerable aptitude with a pen, and he practiced the signature of Finley Carter until he was able to dash it off with that smooth speed which makes for artistic forgeries.

He presented his forged credentials to the cashier of the Second National Affiliate, and it would have taken an expert some time to have detected the fact that the signature of Finley Carter was, in fact, a forgery.

Perhaps had the signature been on a check, the matter would not have gone through quite so expeditiously, but being on a letter to the effect that the bearer was making an audit of Carter's books in order to secure some information in connection with a refund from the income tax department, the signature was accepted without question.

Within a matter of minutes, Sidney Zoom found himself ensconced in a little cubby-hole office, with the statements and vouchers pertaining to the account of Finley Carter before him.

The account, as Zoom noticed, had been used just as Nell Benton had claimed— for the payment of housekeeping expenses. The account seldom went below three hundred dollars, and seldom above five. Checking over the date and amount of deposits, Zoom was able to ascertain that the millionaire lived unpretentiously and that his existence was governed by a methodic regularity.

It was within the past few days that the account had suddenly broken from its conservative deposits and withdrawals. There were deposits which ran into the thousands, and two withdrawals had been made that had virtually cleaned out the account.

Sidney Zoom armed himself with this information and then waited upon the cashier.

"Can you tell me," he said, "why it is that the account which ran around five hundred dollars for months has suddenly become very active in large amounts?"

The cashier smiled.

"Mr. Carter," he said, "used this bank merely as a housekeeping convenience until quite recently. Then he had some trouble with the bank which handles his main business. There was a misunderstanding over something—I don't know the exact nature of it, but Mr. Carter decided to give us more of his business."

"Would it," asked Sidney Zoom, "be possible for you to tell me how you received this information?"

"Over the telephone," said the cashier.

"And with whom were you talking?"

"With Finley Carter himself."

"You're certain?"

"Quite certain," said the cashier. "I know his voice fully as well as I know his signature."

"The withdrawals," Zoom pointed out, "are quite large and are virtually in the form of cash."

The cashier stared at him curiously.

"Those also," he said, "are okayed by telephone instructions from Mr. Carter."

Zoom bowed gravely.

"Thank you," he said. "I have completed my investigations here."

The cashier was overly polite.

"You understand," he said, "that we want to do everything we can to accommodate Mr. Carter. We consider his account a valuable one, and he can rest assured we will give him the very best of service."

"When I see Mr. Carter," said Sidney Zoom, "I shall tell him that your coöperation with me has left nothing to be desired."

The clerk thanked him, and Sidney Zoom left the bank and entered his automobile. His forehead was furrowed in frowning concentration as he drove rapidly to the float where his yacht was moored.

NELL BENTON, looking rather white, her eyes dark with mingled emotions, wore some lounging pajamas which Vera Thurmond had found for her and surveyed Sidney Zoom with puzzled eyes. Burt Samson, attired in his new suit, seemed somehow to be more certain of himself, to have taken on a certain added vitality which radiated from him in an atmosphere of positive assurance.

Zoom nodded to Vera Thurmond.

"I want you," he said, "to ring the residence of Finley Carter. Tell whoever answers the phone that you're one of the bookkeepers at the Second National Affiliate, that you desire to ask him a question about his account. Ask him if a check for twenty-two thousand dollars, issued to the Wheeling Construction Company, is regular. And I want you, Miss Benton, to listen on an extension telephone. I want you to listen carefully to the sound of Finley Carter's voice. I want you to tell me if it sounds natural."

Nell Benton stared at him with eyes that grew wider.

"Why, he couldn't issue a check for twenty-two thousand dollars on that account," she said. "He doesn't keep anything in it except enough money for housekeeping."

"He's keeping plenty in it now," Sidney Zoom said grimly, "and apparently is keeping in constant communication with the bank over the telephone."

Vera Thurmond put through the call. The yacht had a private switchboard which was connected with a telephone cable at a private connection Zoom had arranged at the mooring float, and Zoom was able to listen on one extension while Nell Benton listened on the other. Vera Thurmond followed his instructions to the letter, making an inquiry about the validity of the check.

Sidney Zoom, listening, could find no faintest trace of tension, no lack of spontaneity. The voice seemed edged with impatience as it announced that the validity of the check had already been confirmed in a telephone communication to the cashier.

"I will," said the voice with petulant impatience, "be forced to transfer my account if these telephone calls continue. Certainly the check is good. Checks that come in over my signature should be honored."

"Yes," said Vera Thurmond in a patient voice, "but you see, the amount was rather large and the Wheeling Construction Company secured what was virtually a cash payment …"

"What the devil do I care what they did with it?" rasped the voice. "The check was given to them for a consideration. I received the benefit of it. They're entitled to the cash. That's what the check is for. Any time you people feel that you can't cash my checks, all you've got to do is to say so."

"It's not that," Vera Thurmond said sweetly, "but the fact that the check was rather large in its amount. We simply wanted to protect you and your account, Mr. Carter."

"The amount isn't large," said the voice, "that is, it's not unusually large. My account is an active account and a large account."

"Thank you," said Vera Thurmond, and hung up.

Sidney Zoom glanced inquiringly at Nell Benton.

"It's his voice all right," she said, "but I can't understand it. I don't think it's like him to talk that way, and yet there can be no mistaking his voice."

"Did he sound as though he might be under a strain, or as though he were being threatened?" asked Sidney Zoom.

She shook her head slowly.

"No," she said, "he sounded exactly natural—that is, his voice did—but I don't think he would have adopted that attitude toward a check for that amount. There's something funny about it."

Sidney Zoom nodded.

"Just who of the servants," he asked, "comes into personal contact with Finley Carter?"

"The chauffeur," she said, "doesn't unless he's called. Exter is in constant contact with him. The housekeeper comes when she's summoned, otherwise she does the cooking and has charge of the house. A woman comes in to do the cleaning."

Zoom turned to Burt Samson.

"Samson," he said, "you will take this letter. The signature is forged. It purports to be a letter from Finley Carter, written to you some two weeks ago, asking you to be sure and drop in and see him when you arrive in the city. The dictation marks show that it was dictated to Nell Benton. No one else will know about it."

Samson stared curiously.

"Carter will know about it, won't he?"

Zoom nodded.

"Carter will know about it," he said. "If Carter makes any trouble about it, you are to get in touch with me at once on the telephone. I will stand back of you. But I don't think Carter is going to make any trouble about it. I don't think you're going to see Carter."

Samson nodded slowly.

"What I want," said Zoom, "is to find out just who it is that keeps you from seeing Carter."

Samson took the letter, slipped it in the inside pocket of his coat.

"Okay," he said, and moved purposefully toward the companionway. Food and clothes had made a big difference in him.

When he had gone, Nell Benton said slowly, "What do you think has happened, Mr. Zoom?"

Sidney Zoom's voice was as crisp as the cracking of a lash.

"There's no question about what's happened," he said. "In some way, Exter planned to get complete control of Finley Carter. He knew that there were checks signed in advance and drawn on the housekeeping account that you supervised. Naturally, he wanted to get rid of you. He did that by seeing that you were accused of crime, and knew that Carter would discharge you. What I can't understand is how he has been able to get Carter to talk over the telephone, unless he has an accomplice who is a very finished actor and who is able to mimic Carter's tones over the telephone. That is the probable solution. We've got to get Burt Samson's report in order to find out."

"But," she pointed out, "Samson doesn't know Finley Carter. They might have someone posing as Finley Carter and let Samson go in to see him."

"That," said Sidney Zoom, "is why I phrased the forged letter so it would appear that Samson was quite intimately acquainted with Carter."

She frowned thoughtfully.

"They wouldn't try withdrawals from the bank where Carter regularly keeps his large deposits," Zoom said slowly. "They started building up deposits in the Second National Affiliate, which probably has been very anxious to get Carter's account."

She nodded slowly.

"Should we," she asked, "notify the police?"

Zoom shook his head.

"Not yet," he said. "In the first place, we have nothing to go on except suspicions; in the second place, I am not entirely certain that Finley Carter has a generous disposition."

"What do you mean?" she asked.

"I am not entirely certain," he said, "that he would make proper restitution to you."

"He wouldn't," she said. "He's obstinate, and he's tight."

"He pays plenty for his original paintings, doesn't he?" Zoom asked.

"Yes," she said bitterly, "but that's all he does pay out for. He never paid me a decent salary all the time I worked for him. I'd have gone to some other position if it hadn't been that jobs were so scarce."

"Yet," said Zoom slowly, "if we save Carter from exploitation at the hands of a bunch of crooks, we are entitled to a reward, and the fact remains that Carter, himself, will not care to pay that reward. Therefore, it remains for us to do it for him."

"You're talking in enigmas," she said.

Zoom smiled at her.

"Don't worry about methods," he said, "simply leave the entire thing to me."

CHAPTER IV

An Interview

SIDNEY ZOOM prided himself upon his ability to fight the devil with fire so adroitly as to leave no backtrack.

Following Samson's report that he had been curtly denied admission to the Finley Carter residence, despite the letter which he had produced, a letter which assertedly was signed by Carter himself, Sidney Zoom, attired in a neat-fitting, well-pressed business suit, presented himself at the door of the residence.

"I," he said, "am from the Second National Affiliate. I desire to discuss a matter with Mr. Carter personally."

The butler in the doorway eyed Sidney Zoom with cold suspicion.

"Do you," he asked, "know Mr. Carter personally?"

Zoom appeared to notice nothing unusual in the question.

"I am familiar with his signature," he said. "I have heard his voice over the telephone. I have never met the gentleman."

The grim-faced hostility of the butler relaxed slightly.

"And what did you wish to see Mr. Carter about?"

"I merely wished to get his okay concerning certain withdrawals."

"I beg your pardon, sir," said the butler with ponderous servility, "but I think that matter has been discussed with Mr. Carter over the telephone. He might become very much displeased if you took the matter up with him again."

"That," said Zoom gravely, "is a chance I will have to take on behalf of the bank. Please tell him that Mr. George Coleridge, from the bank, is here to interview him."

Sidney Zoom gravely extracted a leather wallet from his pocket, took from it an embossed card, handed it, with something of a flourish, to the butler.

The butler examined the card.

"I see," he said slowly. "George Coleridge, special investigator for the Second National Affiliate."

"Exactly," said Sidney Zoom. "And will you please tell Mr. Carter that if he refuses a personal interview, his refusal may lead to banking complications."

Sidney Zoom's smile was reassuring, but his eyes were steady.

"Please step in and be seated," said the butler. "I will take the matter up with Mr. Carter."

Zoom was ushered into a reception hallway, given a seat. The butler climbed a flight of stairs. Somewhere from the upper corridor, Zoom heard the deep-throated barking of a big dog, the slamming of a door. There followed an interval of silence, and then the thud of the butler's returning feet became audible.

"If you'll be so kind as to step this way, sir," he said, "Mr. Carter will be glad to give you a few moments. He is not feeling well and wishes you to make your visit as brief as possible."

Sidney Zoom surrounded himself with a cloak of banker-like dignity as he followed the butler up the stairs.

A big police dog lay in front of a closed door. As he saw Sidney Zoom, he twisted his lips back from his fangs and gave a deep-throated growl, but made no motion to leave the door.

The butler opened a door across the corridor.

"Mr. Carter," he said, with something of a flourish.

A man, attired in bathrobe and pajamas, sat up in bed. Pillows were bolstered behind him. Both hands were concealed beneath the covers of the bed. His eyes were deep-set and glittered irascibly. When he spoke, his voice had the distinctive rasping harshness that Zoom had heard over the telephone.

"You're Coleridge," he said, "from the Second National Affiliate?"

Sidney Zoom bowed.

"What I want to know," said the man, "is what the devil you folks mean by making so much commotion about a few ordinary withdrawals. I gave you an account some time ago. You thought it wasn't large enough and kept asking me to give you more of my accounts. Recently I decided to do it. You've made so much commotion about it that one would think a check for more than one hundred dollars never went through your bank oftener than once a year."

Zoom's smile was reassuring.

"Hardly that, Mr. Carter," he said, "but, you understand we're a branch bank. The parent bank desired a report. I'm from the parent bank."

"I don't give a damn who you're from," the other said. "You're making a confounded nuisance out of yourself. I'm putting money in your bank. I have a right to draw it out whenever I wish. I'm putting in some rather large deposits. I want to withdraw them whenever I want to."

"The deposits are made only with a rubber stamp endorsement," Sidney Zoom pointed out.

"That's the way deposits are made in any active account," Carter said. "That's the way nine-tenths of your commercial houses make their deposits. The withdrawals are all made by checks that bear my personal signature."

"I have here a list of withdrawals," said Sidney Zoom. "Would you mind okaying them?"

The man sighed with annoyance.

"Very well," he said, "but I'm playing a correspondence chess game, and you're making me so mad I can't concentrate on it the way I want to."

He indicated a chess board on the table beside the bed, a chess board on which men had been arranged. A pawn or two had been moved. Aside from that, the men were arrayed in two rows on opposite sides of the board.

Sidney Zoom stared thoughtfully at the board.

"Rather a peculiar opening," he said.

"It's the opening I like to play," the other told him.

Zoom handed over the list. The long, thin fingers of the other man checked off the withdrawals.

"All correct," he said, "and all in order."

"Would you sign it?" asked Sidney Zoom.

"No," snarled the other, "I won't sign it. I've given you enough of my time. You've had my okay over the telephone. You've got my signed checks. I've gone over this and okayed it. If you don't like it, I'll take my account out of your bank and put it somewhere where it's appreciated."

Sidney Zoom bowed.

"Very well," he said, "and thank you."

Turning, he walked toward the door with rigid dignity.

The rasping voice of the man on the bed called to him as he reached the door.

"Don't think I don't appreciate your interest, Coleridge," he said, "I do. I know you're just safeguarding my money, but I want the privilege of withdrawing checks from my own account in my own way."

Sidney Zoom's bow was grave.

"Thank you," he said.

CHAPTER V

A Trap Is Baited

SIDNEY ZOOM was never happier than when he was concentrating upon some mental problem.

He raised his long, thin legs to place his feet on the table in the dining salon. His eyes glittered with concentration. His fingers were interlaced across his thin stomach.

"An impostor," he said, "a rank impostor. I find that there have been very few pictures of Finley Carter taken."

"Yes," Nell Benton said, "he was suspicious of cameras."

"But I nevertheless located one," Zoom said. "This man looks something like him, but he isn't Carter. Moreover, Carter is a chess expert. The man who has engineered this crime knows nothing about chess. Knowing that Carter was a chess player, the man sought to impress me by having a chess atmosphere about the room. A chess board sat at the side of the table. Some men had been moved, but they weren't in the position in which players would have moved them. Moreover, the white queen had been placed on the black square instead of the white."

"Then," said Nell Benton, "we must go to the police."

Sidney Zoom shook his head.

"No," he said, "Finley Carter deserves to be punished. He discharged you, when, if he had used his brains, he would have known you were the victim of a conspiracy which was soon to involve him. Moreover, there is compensation which you must receive. Carter has never been generous. The salary that he paid you shows you that he hasn't even been fair. No, there's another way of handling this. Let me think."

He stared with a fixed, unwinking scrutiny, his eyes fastened upon distance.

At length he spoke; there was an accentless quality to his voice, as though he had been talking in his sleep.

"How many checks were signed when you left, Miss Benton?"

"I don't know, half a dozen perhaps. Why?"

"These men aren't forgers," he said, "or else they know that they can't forge Finley Carter's signature well enough to fool a bank … Did Mr. Carter keep a police dog?"

"No. He's afraid of dogs. He wouldn't have them in the house."

Zoom nodded slowly.

"We could," said Samson, "go to the police and get a detective into the house as a building inspector or something."

Zoom shook his head.

"There's the matter of payment," he said, "and there's one other matter. I'm satisfied that they'll kill Carter before they'd let him talk. He's under guard, probably somewhere in the house."

Suddenly he chuckled.

"I think," he said, "I have it."

He turned to Samson.

"You," he said, "have got to act a part. You've got to keep your head. If anything goes wrong, you've got to be able to show that you were doing what you were doing for the purpose of exposing the guilt of these people."

"What," asked Samson, "am I supposed to do?"

Zoom made no reply, but picked up a telephone and dialed the number of Finley Carter's residence.

"Will you," he said, "please tell Mr. Finley Carter that I am Mr. Coleridge of the Second National Affiliate, and that I desire to talk with him over the telephone for a few moments."

There was a moment of silence, then the receiver made a metallic noise, and Sidney Zoom said affably, "Our bank regrets causing you inconvenience in connection with your account, Mr. Carter, but we feel called upon to take determined steps to protect your interests. In order that there may be no possible misunderstanding, would you mind telling us what checks you have outstanding against your account? That is, checks that have not been cashed, but which may be presented within the next twenty-four hours."

The metallic diaphragm of the receiver registered a squawking protest which sounded like static, then Sidney Zoom said, "I understand all that, Mr. Carter. I can only repeat that this is for your own protection."

The receiver made more violent noises and Sidney Zoom's voice lost its purring pleasantry.

"Very well," he said, "if you want to take that course, you may do so. I was only trying to protect your interests ... When may we expect this check to come in? ... Very well, thank you."

He slammed the receiver back into place and nodded to the little circle of his attentive listeners.

"Well," he said, "I've done it."

"Done what?"

"Led them to believe that the chase is so hot they've got to dust out. They were looking for an excuse."

"What do you mean?" Nell Benton asked.

"They planned," he said, "to make as large deposits as they possibly could in the account of the Second National Affiliate. They planned to withdraw those deposits by checks which had previously been signed by Mr. Carter, checks that were signed in blank because he knew that they couldn't be raised. The fact that the account was limited to five hundred dollars kept him reasonably safe. What Carter overlooked, was the fact that it's easy to make deposits where the money goes into a regular bank account, so the crooks simply took over Carter's affairs, collected whatever sums came in through the mail, or whatever they could collect otherwise, and made huge deposits. Then they made large withdrawals in the form of what amounted virtually to cash."

"Well?" asked Nell Benton.

"Now," said Sidney Zoom, "the man who poses as Finley Carter, convinced that the game is about at an end, and thinking that he was talking to the bank, has advised me that he is sending down a check closing out the entire account. The balance, as I happen to know from my investigation, is ten thousand two hundred and ninety-one dollars and fifteen cents."

Sidney Zoom opened a drawer in the table, from it he took a pad of blank checks drawn on the Second National Affiliate. Working with the skill of a practiced penman, he filled out a check in an angular handwriting. The check was payable to cash. The amount was ten thousand two hundred and ninety-one dollars and fifteen cents, and Sidney Zoom signed the name of Finley Carter to that check—signed it so perfectly that Nell Benton gave an exclamation.

"But," she said, "it's a perfect imitation of his signature."

Zoom nodded.

"Therefore," she said, "a forgery."

Zoom nodded once more.

"And," he said with pride in his voice, "a very good one."

"But," she said, "it's against the law, you'd be sent to prison."

Sidney Zoom smiled.

"After all," he said, "my methods are irregular, I've warned you of that."

"But," she told him, "you mustn't do that. It's not right. It's not the way to handle it."

Sidney Zoom smiled at her.

"If," he said, "I should tell you that by using this check I would save Mr. Carter ten thousand two hundred and ninety-one dollars and fifteen cents which he would otherwise lose, would you think that it was right?"

"Yes," she said slowly, "if that's the case."

"That," said Zoom, "is the case."

He beckoned to Burt Samson.

IT was a few minutes before closing time at the bank when Sidney Zoom presented himself at the cashier's window.

"You will remember me," he said, "I was checking up on Mr. Carter's account."

The clerk nodded.

"I have been given a check," said Sidney Zoom, "by a man who claimed to represent Mr. Carter, stating that he desires to close out his account. The amount of the check is for ten thousand two hundred and ninety-one dollars and fifteen cents, which is, I believe, the exact amount Mr. Carter has on deposit."

The cashier frowned.

"We don't want him to draw out his account," he said. "There must be some misunderstanding."

Sidney Zoom said slowly, "I don't think there is any misunderstanding, I think the check is a forgery."

"You think it's a forgery?" said the cashier.

Sidney Zoom nodded and produced the check.

"I have every reason," he said, "to believe that check is a forgery."

"Well," the cashier said, "we'll settle that in short order. I'll get Mr. Carter on the telephone right now."

He took the check and stepped to a telephone booth. Sidney Zoom could see the man through the glass of the booth. Could see his face darken with anger. Saw him try to talk, only to be interrupted.

A moment later the door banged shut and the cashier stepped back to the cage. His face was wrathful.

"The man," he said, "is positively insulting. He told me that I could either pay this check or he would sue the bank for damages."

"But it looks like a forgery," Zoom said.

"It can't be a forgery," the cashier said, "he says that he talked with one of the representatives from our main bank and told him that he was going to clean out the account, that he issued the check to clean out the entire balance and that if we don't cash it, he's going to sue us for damages … Who gave you the check?"

"A man," said Sidney Zoom, "whom I do not know, who asked me to present it for him. He claimed to be working for Mr. Carter. I believe he said he was a butler or something. The whole circumstances seem strange and suspicious to me. Moreover, the signature looks to me like a forgery."

"Well," said the cashier, "the check isn't a forgery. I'm quite familiar with Mr. Carter's voice over the telephone. He told me unmistakably that I should cash that check."

"Don't you think," said Sidney Zoom, "it would be a good plan to compare the signature with the signatures on some of the other checks?"

The cashier stared suspiciously at Sidney Zoom.

"What were you supposed to do with this money when you got it?" he said. "Were you to give it to the man who handed you the check?"

"No," said Sidney Zoom, "I was to deposit it to the account of Nell Benton."

Relief flooded the face of the cashier.

"Oh," he said, "that's all right then. Nell Benton was his secretary. I'm familiar with her, and familiar with her signature. Where were you to make the deposit?"

"In this bank," said Sidney Zoom.

"She has an account here now," said the cashier, taking the check and banging a rubber stamp down on it. "It's quite all right. I'll simply add this to her account."

"Well," said Sidney Zoom, "you can do as you want to, but it looks like a forgery to me. However, I've washed my hands of the transaction."

"Mr. Carter," said the cashier, speaking with frigid dignity, "was a most unsatisfactory customer. His language over the telephone was abusive."

Zoom shrugged his shoulders and turned away from the cashier's window.

"Well," he said, "you'll remember that I did my duty."

"Yes," said the cashier, "you did your duty."

Sidney Zoom left the bank. At the corner he climbed into the car which Burt Samson had parked at the curb.

"Well?" asked Samson.

"Now," said Sidney Zoom, "we wait until we see Harry Exter, the butler, drive up to the bank."

They waited for some five minutes and then a shining automobile slid smoothly into the curb, a liveried chauffeur at the wheel. A man got out of the car and entered the bank with quick, rapid steps.

"That," said Sidney Zoom, "is Exter, the butler. Now step on it and see if we can break a few speed laws getting to Carter's residence."

Samson's voice was dubious.

"I guess," he said, "that you know what you're doing. I hope you do."

Sidney Zoom chuckled.

CHAPTER VI

Unmasked

AT TIMES, Sidney Zoom could be smilingly suave, his manner radiating an urbane dignity.

Now, as he stood before the residence of Finley Carter, his long forefinger pressing the bell button, his lips were twisted in a smile. He motioned his police dog over to a corner back of the door, where it was not readily visible. Burt Samson stood slightly to one side.

There was an interval of silence following the jangling of the bell, and then a thick-necked individual with broad shoulders jerked the door open.

"What do you want?" he asked.

"There has," said Sidney Zoom, "been some mistake made in connection with Mr. Carter's account at the Second National Affiliate. I was here previously to see him in regard to that account. The name is Coleridge. He'll remember me."

"He won't remember you," said the man, "because he won't see you."

Listening, Zoom could hear the sounds of feet moving about, could hear noises that seemed to come from people who were moving about in surreptitious haste.

A telephone bell rang somewhere in the interior of the house.

"There has been a mistake made somewhere," said Sidney Zoom. "Two checks have been presented to the bank, both checks closing out Mr. Carter's account."

"Well," said the man, "he's got a right to close it out if he wants to, hasn't he?"

"But," said Sidney Zoom, "there were *two* closing checks. One of them must be a forgery."

The eyes stared in hostile appraisal at Sidney Zoom. The telephone continued to ring.

"I've got to answer the telephone," said the man. "You stay here."

The door was slammed shut in Sidney Zoom's face.

"That's as far as we'll get," said Samson.

Zoom shook his head in smiling negation.

"Stick around," he invited.

There was an interval of some two or three minutes, and then the door opened. The thick-necked individual had changed his manner. There was no longer surly hostility in his demeanor, but, instead, a puzzled bewilderment.

"Come on in," he said. "Mr. Carter wants to see you."

He held the door open, and Sidney Zoom courteously stood to one side to let Burt Samson enter ahead of him.

"Who's this man?" asked the thick-necked one.

"My assistant," said Sidney Zoom.

The men filed in through the door. Zoom turned.

"All right, Rip," he said, "you may come in."

The dog slipped through the door like a tawny streak of light.

"Hey, wait a minute!" said the man who had opened the door. "That dog can't come in here!"

"Oh, yes," said Sidney Zoom, brushing the matter aside as though it were of no moment, "he has to come in. You see, he's very valuable and I wouldn't dare to leave him outside. He might be stolen."

As Zoom talked, he headed toward the stairs.

"Wait a minute," said the thick-necked individual.

"Quite all right," said Sidney Zoom. "It's quite all right, my good man. I know the way. You don't need to show me."

Sidney Zoom went up the stairs two at a time, his long legs carrying him upward with but little apparent effort. A stair or two behind, Burt Samson was straining every effort to keep up. The thick-necked individual who had been left well behind in the race, was pounding awkwardly up the stairs at a dead run, protesting as he climbed.

"Listen, what are you guys trying to pull? You can't come busting in here that way. I said Mr. Carter would see you. That doesn't mean he's going to see the whole bank, and you can't get that dog ..."

Zoom reached the upper corridor. The police dog that had been guarding the door of the room at the end of the hall was still on duty. He rose to his feet, hair bristling. Zoom's police dog, padding at the side of his master, gave a throaty growl.

The thick-necked man, dashing up the stairs, suddenly tugged at his hip pocket.

"Say, you guys!" he yelled. "Stop right there!"

Samson whirled, faced the thick-necked individual.

"Get your hand away from that gun," he said.

The police dog at the end of the corridor charged.

Sidney Zoom spoke quietly to the four-footed companion of his midnight prowls.

"All right, Rip," he said.

The two dogs came together in a flash of swift motion, raising their front quarters up from the ground, teeth gleaming, flashing and snapping like the jaws of steel traps.

A door burst open and the man who had posed as Finley Carter stepped into the corridor, an automatic glistening in his right hand.

"Listen, you guys," he said, "stand back."

His voice was deadly with menace.

Sidney Zoom strode forward, passed the fighting dogs.

"Drop that gun," he said.

There was the sound of a struggle behind him as Samson flung himself on the bull-necked individual. The gun in front of Sidney Zoom blazed once.

Zoom flung himself to one side with the agility of a fencing master. The bullet struck a glancing course along the side of the hallway, ripping off plaster, thudding into a lath, glancing to one side and down.

A gun boomed at the end of the corridor. There was the sound of a thudding blow.

Sidney Zoom's long arm shot out. His fingers closed about the wrist that held the blued-steel. He gave a swift jerk.

The gun roared once more.

A tawny flash of four-footed motion sprinted along the hallway, then leapt into the air, bloodied muzzle pointed at the throat of the man who had posed as Finley Carter.

The man saw the dog coming in time to fling his left arm in front of his throat.

Then the hurtling dog struck with an impact that smashed the man backwards to the floor. Zoom held the gun in his hand as the man went backward.

"Watch him, Rip!" he shouted.

Zoom turned toward the place where Samson was battling with the bull-necked individual. That man was clubbing his gun, striking Samson indiscriminately about the head and shoulders.

Zoom jumped over the inert police dog that lay with torn throat and glazed eyes in the center of the corridor, flung up his gun.

"Hands up!" he shouted.

The heavy shoulders swung about. The gun snapped up.

"Damn you!" gritted the heavy-set man.

Samson swung his fist from the vicinity of his hip pocket, giving it every ounce of force he had. The blow crashed to the big man's jaw, rocked him back to his heels. Samson's left swung to the belt buckle. He steadied himself and crashed home another right.

The gun dropped from the limp fingers as the man swayed, then toppled backwards.

Samson wiped blood from his forehead, grinned at Sidney Zoom through cracked lips.

"Why the devil didn't you use that gun I gave you?" Zoom demanded.

Samson's grin stretched wider, to show a bleeding cavity where a tooth had been knocked from the front of his face.

"You never did ask much about me," he said, "but I lost my job for okaying a forged check. I was a department manager in a hardware store. This is the guy that gave me the bum check."

"He weighs fifty pounds more than you do," Zoom remonstrated, "and you haven't been eating regularly for a month or two. You should have used the gun."

"He could have weighed a hundred pounds more than I did, and I'd still have taken him to pieces," Samson retorted.

Zoom turned back to where Rip was standing over the prostrate form of the man who had posed as Finley Carter.

"Bust open that door, Samson," he said, "I think we'll find the real Finley Carter held in there as a prisoner."

Samson tried the door. It was locked.

Zoom nodded a signal. The men crashed their shoulders against the door, which splintered free of the lock, shivered on its hinges.

A man with his legs tied to a heavy chair waved his arms and snarled irascibly.

"It certainly is time you rescued me. A hell of a fine bunch of police you are! Or, I suppose you call yourselves detectives, since you don't wear uniforms, but I'm a taxpayer and a big taxpayer. I'm entitled to better protection than this. I've been a prisoner for days and you are just now getting here ..."

Sidney Zoom's grin was malicious.

"You're wrong," he interrupted. "We're not just getting here, we're just leaving."

With a nod to Samson, he slammed the door shut in the face of the expostulating prisoner.

CHAPTER VII

Curious Accounting

SIDNEY ZOOM sprawled at long-legged ease on the deck of his yacht, watched the sun glint on the sparkling waves, felt the swing of the craft as it rolled to the long, lazy swells.

Seated opposite him, his lips chewing nervously at a cigar, was a hatchet-faced individual from whose spectacles dangled a long black ribbon which from time to time was swung gently by the warm breeze.

"As your attorney," he said, "I would say that you had not violated the law. A forgery is not a criminal act unless it is perpetrated with the intention to deceive, and the fact that you advised the bank at the time you presented the check to be cashed that it was forged probably constitutes a defense.

"It is, moreover, apparent that you did not profit in any way by any of the forgeries. You used them to detect crime, instead of to perpetrate crime."

Zoom smiled, elevated his long legs and placed his feet on the rail of the yacht.

"On the other hand," said the attorney, "the police are making a widespread inquiry for the purpose of ascertaining the identity of the tall individual who entered into the case. They have a very good description of you."

"Description," said Sidney Zoom, "don't mean anything. I'm on the point of taking a month's cruise to tropical waters, anyway."

The attorney nodded his head slowly.

"As between Finley Carter and the bank, however," he said, "there is a very peculiar legal problem. Carter received most of the money that had been withdrawn from his account when the police nabbed Harry Exter and his confederates. The man who posed as Finley Carter was an actor who had spent some time studying Carter's voice until he could mimic it perfectly. Of course, Exter got the idea when he learned that Carter was in the habit of signing blank checks drawn on his housekeeping account, and leaving them in the hands of his secretary. Carter, of course, thought he was protected by the fact that he never kept over five hundred dollars in that bank. He didn't realize what would happen if some crooks got possession of all of his mail and made deposits in the account. It only required a rubber stamp to deposit the money to Carter's account.

"On the other hand, the checks that made the withdrawals were genuine checks, with the exception of the forged check which cleaned out the account. But, as I have stated, the bank was advised at the time that check was presented that it was probably a forgery. Nevertheless, the check was cashed and the money deposited to the account of Nell Benton."

Sidney Zoom stretched his arms above his head, took a deep inhalation of the fresh ocean air.

"Well," he said, "that was what I wanted to see you about particularly. I don't know just how repentant Carter will be for the wrong that he did Nell Benton, or just how grateful he will be to Burt Samson for the part Samson played in rescuing him from the crooks. I want you, therefore, to represent the interests of Miss Benton."

"You mean in asking a reward?" the lawyer inquired.

"No," said Sidney Zoom, "in tactfully explaining to Mr. Finley Carter that she has a very good cause of action against him for defamation of character.

"You might further explain to all parties concerned that there is quite a question as to the legality of the deposit in Miss Benton's name, inasmuch as the legal questions seem somewhat confused. In other words, what I want you to do is to add confusion to the legal question."

"To what end?" inquired the attorney.

"To the end," said Sidney Zoom, "of securing a very good cash settlement from Mr. Finley Carter—a settlement which will take care of Burt Samson, as well as Nell Benton."

"You had some figure in mind?" inquired the attorney cautiously.

"Yes," said Sidney Zoom, "I thought that after the legal questions had been properly confused, a settlement might be made for ten thousand dollars. That could be effected by having Nell Benton execute a complete release and make a check in favor of Finley Carter for two hundred and ninety-one dollars and fifteen cents, because, you see, the ten thousand has already been deposited to her account."

The attorney blinked his eyes at Sidney Zoom.

"Well, by heaven," he said, "you're the coolest customer I ever had to deal with! Some day I'm going to see you on your road to jail."

"In the meantime," said Sidney Zoom, "I will have derived a lot of amusement from life, and have, perhaps, done some good."

"You've got all the money you want," the attorney rasped. "You've got nothing to do except cruise around and enjoy life. Why the devil do you mess around the big cities, mixing into crime?"

"For the same reason," said Sidney Zoom, "that I am going into tropical waters and fish for swordfish with light tackle—because I like it. When it gets dark I'll swing in close to the shore, put you in a launch and see that you're landed—just like the rum-runners used to land their cargo. And, of course, you'll add to my bill fair compensation for whatever inconvenience is caused you."

The lawyer sighed.

"Well," he said, "I guess it's all right. You saved Carter's life. They probably would have killed him when they got ready to take it 'on the lam,' as the crooks express it. But you certainly skated on thin ice yourself. You stole some of the crooks' thunder."

Zoom lit a cigarette.

"Yes," he said, as he sent twin streamers of smoke through his satisfied nostrils, "I stole some of the crooks' thunder, and, all in all, it was a very satisfactory job of larceny."

THE CASES OF SIDNEY ZOOM

"The Higher Court." *Detective Fiction Weekly*, March 8, 1930.

"Willie the Weeper." *Detective Fiction Weekly*, March 8, 1930. Collected in *The Casebook of Sidney Zoom*.

" 'My Name Is Zoom'." *Detective Fiction Weekly*, April 12, 1930. Collected in *The Casebook of Sidney Zoom*.

"Time in for Tucker." *Detective Fiction Weekly*, September 13, 1930.

"Stranger's Silk." *Detective Fiction Weekly*, January 3, 1931.

"The Death Penalty." *Detective Fiction Weekly*, January 17, 1931.

"Borrowed Bullets." *Detective Fiction Weekly*, March 21, 1931. Collected in *The Casebook of Sidney Zoom*.

"The Vanishing Corpse." *Detective Fiction Weekly*, August 15, 1931.

"Higher Up." *Detective Fiction Weekly*, September 19, 1931. Collected in *The Casebook of Sidney Zoom*.

"The First Stone." *Detective Fiction Weekly*, October 24, 1931. Collected in *The Casebook of Sidney Zoom*.

"It Takes a Crook." *Detective Fiction Weekly*, October 24, 1931.

"The Green Door." *Detective Fiction Weekly*, August 20, 1932. Collected in *The Casebook of Sidney Zoom*.

"Cheating the Chair." *Detective Fiction Weekly*, September 17, 1932. Collected in *The Casebook of Sidney Zoom*.

"Inside Job." *Detective Fiction Weekly*, January 7, 1933. Collected in *The Casebook of Sidney Zoom*.

"Lifted Bait." *Detective Fiction Weekly*, October 21, 1933. Collected in *The Casebook of Sidney Zoom*.

"Stolen Thunder." *Detective Fiction Weekly*, March 19, 1934. Collected in *The Casebook of Sidney Zoom*.

THE CASES OF SIDNEY ZOOM

The Casebook of Sidney Zoom by Erle Stanley Gardner, edited by Bill Pronzini, is set in Garamond and printed on 60 pound Natural acid-free paper. The cover is by Juha Lindroos, and the Lost Classsics design is by Deborah Miller. *The Casebook of Sidney Zoom* was published in January 2006 by Crippen & Landru Publishers, Norfolk, Virginia.

CRIPPEN & LANDRU, PUBLISHERS
P. O. Box 9315, Norfolk, VA 23505
E-mail: info@crippenlandru.com; toll-free 877 622-6656
Web: www.crippenlandru.com

LOST CLASSICS

Crippen & Landru is proud to publish a series of *new* short-story collections by great authors who specialized in traditional mysteries. Each book collects stories from crumbling pages of old pulp, digest, and slick magazines, and most of the stories have been "lost" since their first publication. The following books are in print:

The Newtonian Egg and Other Cases of Rolf le Roux by Peter Godfrey, introduction by Ronald Godfrey. 2002.

Murder, Mystery and Malone by Craig Rice, edited by Jeffrey A. Marks. 2002.

The Sleuth of Baghdad: The Inspector Chafik Stories, by Charles B. Child. 2002.

Hildegarde Withers: Uncollected Riddles by Stuart Palmer, introduction by Mrs. Stuart Palmer. 2002.

The Spotted Cat and Other Mysteries from Inspector Cockrill's Casebook by Christianna Brand, edited by Tony Medawar. 2002.

Marksman and Other Stories by William Campbell Gault, edited by Bill Pronzini; afterword by Shelley Gault. 2003.

Karmesin: The World's Greatest Criminal – Or Most Outrageous Liar by Gerald Kersh, edited by Paul Duncan. 2003.

The Complete Curious Mr. Tarrant by C. Daly King, introduction by Edward D. Hoch. 2003.

The Pleasant Assassin and Other Cases of Dr. Basil Willing by Helen McCloy, introduction by B.A. Pike. 2003.

Murder – All Kinds by William L. DeAndrea, introduction by Jane Haddam. 2003.

The Avenging Chance and Other Mysteries from Roger Sheringham's Casebook by Anthony Berkeley, edited by Tony Medawar and Arthur Robinson. 2004.

Banner Deadlines: The Impossible Files of Senator Brooks U. Banner by Joseph Commings, edited by Robert Adey; memoir by Edward D. Hoch. 2004.

The Danger Zone and Other Stories by Erle Stanley Gardner, edited by Bill Pronzini. 2004.

Dr. Poggioli: Criminologist by T.S. Stribling, edited by Arthur Vidro. 2004.

The Couple Next Door: Collected Short Mysteries by Margaret Millar, edited by Tom Nolan. 2004.

Sleuth's Alchemy: Cases of Mrs. Bradley and Others by Gladys Mitchell, edited by Nicholas Fuller. 2005.

Who Was Guilty? Two Dime Novels by Philip S. Warne/Howard W. Macy, edited by Marlena E. Bremseth. 2005.

Slot-Machine Kelly: The Collected Cases of the One-Armed Bandit by Dennis Lynds writing as Michael Collins, introduction by Robert J. Randisi. 2005.

Rafael Sabatini, *The Evidence of the Sword*, edited by Jesse Knight. 2006.

Julian Symons, *The Detections of Francis Quarles*, edited by John Cooper; afterword by Kathleen Symons. 2006.

Erle Stanley Gardner, *The Casebook of Sidney Zoom*, edited by Bill Pronzini. 2006.

FORTHCOMING LOST CLASSICS

Ellis Peters (Edith Pargeter), *The Trinity Cat and Other Mysteries*, edited by Martin Edwards and Sue Feder.

Lloyd Biggle, Jr., *The Grandfather Rastin Mysteries*, introduction by Kenneth Lloyd Biggle and Donna Biggle Emerson.

Max Brand, *Masquerade: Nine Crime Stories*, edited by William F. Nolan, Jr.

Hugh Pentecost, *The Battles of Jericho*, introduction by S.T. Karnick.

Mignon G. Eberhart, *Dead Yesterday and Other Mysteries*, edited by Rick Cypert and Kirby McCauley.

Victor Canning, *The Minerva Club, The Department of Patterns and Other Stories*, edited by John Higgins.

Elizabeth Ferrars, *The Casebook of Jonas P. Jonas and Others*, edited by John Cooper.

Anthony Boucher and Denis Green, *The Casebook of Gregory Hood*, edited by Joe R. Christopher.

Philip Wylie, *Ten Thousand Blunt Instruments*, edited by Bill Pronzini.

Erle Stanley Gardner, *The Adventures of Señor Lobo*, edited by Bill Pronzini.

SUBSCRIPTIONS

Crippen & Landru offers discounts to individuals and institutions who place Standing Order Subscriptions for its forthcoming publications, either all the Regular Series or all the Lost Classics or (preferably) both. Collectors can thereby guarantee receiving limited editions, and readers won't miss any favorite stories. Standing Order Subscribers receive a specially commissioned story in a deluxe edition as a gift at the end of the year. Please write or e-mail for more details.

Lost Classics